THE SWEETWATER ISLAND FERRY COLLECTION

A HEARTWARMING, FEEL-GOOD TRILOGY

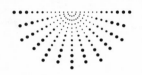

SOPHIE MAYS

Text and Illustration Copyright © 2019 by Sophie Mays

ISBN: 9781795308106
ISBN: 9781074811921 (Large Print)

Publisher
Love Light Faith, LLC
400 NW 7th Avenue, Suite 825
Fort Lauderdale, FL 33302

CONTENTS

FOR LOVE...AND DONUTS

TO LOVE...AND RENOVATE

WITH LOVE...AND REALITY TV

FOR LOVE...AND DONUTS

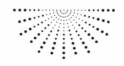

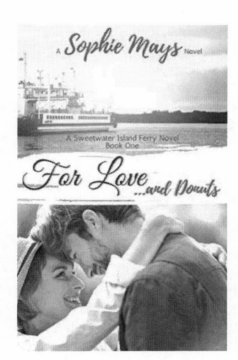

To Julia and Caroline ~

You have each made this story, and this dream, possible in your own unique ways. There are not enough donuts in the world to express how much I appreciate you both.

From the bottom of my heart,

Thank You

CHAPTER ONE

*V*irginia Ellis shoved the last bite of a Maple-glazed Pistachio donut into her mouth. Her eyes were unable to break from the scene in front of her as she chewed. The sight of Jason blatantly flirting with the slim, beautiful brunette sales assistant, his new hire at the TV station, felt like a hand gripping callously around her heart. She reached absently for her sparkling water and sipped. She was being melodramatic, she knew.

She had turned off the car's engine when she'd pulled up, intending to jump out and scamper into Jason's work. Instead, she caught sight of the two fraternizing figures and froze. As she sat in the stagnant car, too hypnotized to turn the AC back on, it ran through her head that this wasn't exactly her best decision ever.

The unseasonal afternoon temperature had soared into the eighties, and she could feel the sweat forming on her brow, as both she and a dwindling half dozen donuts were melting into the car seats. Yet, she still couldn't manage to glance away from where Jason and the girl were standing. The whole scene played out like a romantic comedy, complete with doubled over laughter and animated chatting. The petite brunette was making a huge show of how endlessly funny

Jason was being. Virginia knew Jason all too well, and while he was without a doubt charming, his jokes weren't known to have people rolling on the floor. Yes, this had all the makings of a classic rom-com set up, except...except for the part where his heartbroken girlfriend sat less than twenty feet away feeling absolutely pathetic, frumpy, and dejected, yet again. That part felt way less funny in real life.

Virginia may not have been destined to be a supermodel or even the type of girl who commanded much attention when she walked into a room, but she had always prided herself on being a kind person, an honest one, and someone who genuinely cared about people. She'd always felt comfortable with simply being herself. Unfortunately, her self-esteem was shot these days, and it had been for some time. And now, here she was spying on her boyfriend. Last she checked, that was the ultimate cliché when it came to depicting an insecure girlfriend.

Now, as she watched him joke with his giggly co-worker, lightly touching her arm as they leaned against the wall of the building, obviously on a break, Virginia couldn't help but wonder if trusting him was naive.

Tearing her eyes away from the couple, she glanced to the passenger seat and fished around for another donut. She wished she didn't know what went into them. The creamy European butter and eye-averting amounts of sugar that she poured into each batch of oversized gourmet donuts made them insanely delicious, but wasn't doing much to support her yearly resolution of a whittled waist line. Most days, she happily baked her goods, fueled her tiny side business and partook in little more than a lick of the spatula when she finished the icing. On days like today, however, she found herself dipping heavily into her inventory like the weak, un-savvy drug dealers she always saw on Jason's TV shows. Those guys never fared well, and the comparison wasn't lost on her.

Jason leaned back against a waist-high cement barrier, stretching out his toned torso under a snug fitting white button-down and apparently said something else rip-roaringly witty. Her eyes glazed over, memories of seeing him in high school way before they ever started dating. For as long as she could remember, she had loved Jason. Sure, she'd had crushes on other boys, but from the moment she and Jason had started dating their senior year of in high school, she'd known they would be together forever.

He was everything that a high school art student could have dreamt of: Captain of the baseball team, outgoing and popular, with dark hair, a chiseled jaw and piercing hazel eyes. She had always been slightly awkward in high school: pretty but shy, an honor student interested in the visual arts, books, baking, and little else. The fact that a boy like Jason bothered to look her way at all was a minor miracle as far as she was concerned. And when he kissed her for the first time at the homecoming dance, she knew that there would be no one else. She and Jason would live happily ever after.

And so, they would. This was nothing. Men flirted with women all the time. It didn't mean anything. He always came home to her, in a manner of speaking. Jason had told her a thousand times that he respected her decision not to live together until they were married, even if that came at a cost. I mean, he'd also made it known that he wanted to live together and that he thought it was a little silly and old fashioned not to. He wanted to do all the things that couples do when they live together, but somehow he'd still stayed with her when she just couldn't give in to that.

She was raised as a good Christian girl in a good Christian household. Even though she hadn't been to church in a few months, and hadn't really prayed in weeks, some things still didn't change. And living with a man she wasn't married to was still going to be one of them.

A tiny, horrible voice in her head whispered that maybe, just maybe, that was the reason he was chatting up the pretty young assistant. Maybe, if she gave him all the things modern men expected to get from their girlfriends, Jason wouldn't be looking for it elsewhere.

Virginia popped the end of the next donut in her mouth, huffed and dismissed the voice immediately. He said he was willing to do whatever she thought was best and hadn't given her any reason to think otherwise. Besides, even though this girl was young and thin and beautiful, something that he had alluded to Virginia not being anymore, she couldn't help but notice that she looked quite a lot like Virginia had looked several years before. In fact, whenever she saw Jason flirting, anyone could easily see that the girls resembled her in her younger years. That was a good sign, right?

She had to admit that between working two jobs to help put Jason through graduate school for his Marketing degree, starting the side business catering small-batch donuts, teaching art to school kids, and the long hours she had put in to make it all work, it had taken a bit of a toll on her. It made sense that he flirted with other girls. Over the last few years, too much stress and too little exercise had caused her thin figure to fill out significantly. She wasn't what anyone would call overweight, but no one would stop short of calling her pleasantly chubby, or maybe "soft" on a good day.

Suddenly her phone beeped with a text. "So, what did the will say?"

It was from Jason. "Thought you were going to text me when you were done and stop by." Virginia hesitated, swallowing the lump in her throat. "Yeah, be there soon." She fought back the sinking feeling in her stomach.

Besides, he'd been under stress, too. And stress affected people in different ways. She couldn't blame him for looking. It said a lot about him that he had stayed with her despite all they had been through. She opened the car door, took in a refreshing breath of the late Spring air, and wiped at the rims of her eyes clean. She got out of the car and walked into the building.

"Hey, babe!" Jason exclaimed casually, peering out at her from behind his computer screen, as she approached his section of the sales office. "Did you bring us some donuts?" He threw a smirk to the pretty sales assistant who was seated at the front desk. The girl gave Virginia a demure, almost embarrassed smile as Virginia walked past her, before turning away and pretending to focus on something on her computer screen.

"Um, yeah," she shook her head absentmindedly, "I did bring some, but I forgot them in the car. Sorry. I can go out and get them in a sec."

Jason chuckled, "That's my honors student," he said playfully. "Always on top of things."

Virginia smiled at his easy tone, his flirtation with the sales assistant nearly forgotten.

"Well, I've had a lot on my mind today," she said smiling with a mock defensive tone.

"Oh yeah. What did you find out about the will?" he asked leaning forward in his chair and lowering his voice.

He was talking, of course, about her Aunt Emily's Last Will and Testament. Virginia had gotten a phone call the previous week from her late aunt's attorney saying that she was named in her aunt's will.

To say that Jason was curious about the will was an understatement.

"This could be the answer to those student loans you've been worrying about!" he had said at dinner one night. "And, if it's enough money, who knows? We might even be able to talk about getting married finally." Talk of their wedding was a double-edged sword for Virginia. On one hand, what girl wouldn't want to talk endlessly about the magical day when she would marry her lifelong love. But, Jason had grand plans for their wedding which far outweighed her own, and the finances to fund it had become an insurmountable hurdle that kept pushing it back and back and back. She wouldn't have cared if they got married with just a few close friends at the park down the street. Jason however, had dreams of a show-stopping opulent affair. He went on to tell her about some of the more impressive wedding venues he'd heard about, causing her to choke at the associated price tags he quoted.

Jason was one of those people who just looked like he should have money. He carried himself like a Kennedy, and it was no secret between them that he aspired to live a luxury lifestyle one day. In the meantime, he did all he could to create the pretense to the outside world that he was already well off. But the reality of the situation was that the last few years had been lean.

They had decided some time ago that any money they made should be considered theirs, plural. And the idea had been that it made the most sense for Virginia to support Jason while he was building a solid career foundation, with the thought that it would all be an investment in their combined future. So, she had done all she could for the last few years to make it so he could get ahead by focusing on school and not worrying as much about working.

Thankfully, Jason finally had a job as an Account Executive, which brought in a decent salary, but it wasn't enough to cover the massive student debt he'd built up in addition to his everyday living expenses. So, Virginia had been slowly paying down his school loans every month, not leaving a whole lot of money for other things. And while Jason dreamed of having money, he admittedly wasn't the best at managing it, and always seemed to be living slightly beyond his means. Which was why he was so anxious to hear about the money Virginia was soon to come into. It was also why Virginia was so hesitant to give him the news.

"Well, it's not what we thought it would be," she said with a small sigh. Her heart constricted when Jason's face fell.

"You mean it's less than what we expected?" he asked.

"Not...not exactly," she said. "It's...kind of complicated..."

"Now you're making me nervous," he said with a little smile and a chuckle, clearly attempting to make light of the nerves he felt.

"It's just...it's not money," she said.

"What do you mean?" he asked. "Is it like an antique table or something?"

"Bigger than that," Virginia said. "She left me the old summer cottage on Sweetwater Island."

"A house?" he asked. His eyes squinting in confusion and surprise.

"I haven't been there in a few years. Not since Aunt Emily moved to the city," Virginia admitted, "but it's the same one I used to go to every summer when I was little."

He leaned back in his chair nodding in recognition. Then he bit his lip and furrowed his brow. Virginia knew this look well. It was the one Jason always got when he was thinking seriously about something.

"Is it for you and Samantha to share?"

"No, Sam was given our aunt's jewelry collection. She's been obsessed with it her entire life, and Aunt Emily always told her it would be hers one day," Virginia reported on her sister's inheritance.

Jason paused a minute before asking, "But, you said it's a nice house, right? Like a Victorian sort of place? Any chance we could...you know...sell it?"

Virginia felt her chest clench.

"Sell it?" she asked.

"Yeah," he said, "I mean, we just...we really need the money you know?"

"I know," Virginia said slowly. "I just. I hadn't thought about-"

"Jason?"

The pretty sales assistant swiveled in her chair towards them.

"I could use your help with this sales packet. I mean...if you're not busy," she said, throwing a slightly guilty look at Virginia.

This look brought the scene she'd witnessed outside the building back to the front of Virginia's mind. The shame and anger she'd felt sitting in that car, watching them, came back along with it.

"Look," Virginia said to Jason, a little more harshly than she'd intended. "You're clearly busy. Just...come over for dinner tonight and we'll talk about it. Ok?"

Jason blinked and looked slightly taken aback.

"Ok," he said slowly. "Honey, are you feeling ok?"

Realizing how harsh she'd sounded, Virginia took a deep breath and told herself to calm down.

"Yeah," she said. "I'm fine. I just...I've got a ton of donut orders to fill today. I guess I'm a little stressed."

Jason nodded in understanding.

"Make sure you don't work yourself too hard," he said gently, putting a hand over hers and squeezing it sympathetically.

Virginia smiled at his touch, the anger and shame almost completely gone.

"Same goes for you," she said. "I'll bring those donuts in. Then I'll...see you tonight."

"See you tonight, hun," he said.

She quickly walked out to the car, grabbed the donuts and brought them in to Jason, whose joking mood had returned.

"I see you already sampled a few," he teased within earshot of his co-workers. "You know, that's how the weak drug dealers always get taken out on TV." He raised his hands in a dramatic gesture. "You never do your own drugs! You don't have enough self-control! The drugs will control you...Aughhh..." He cracked up at his reenactment, "I should've been in movies, not selling advertising for them." She forced a light laugh and walked out.

As she took the familiar drive back to the home she shared with her sister Samantha, she tried pointlessly to push the earlier scene she'd witnessed out of her mind. You're being paranoid she repeated to herself. You know he loves you. No matter how often he looks at other girls, he would never cheat on you. That's why he was so excited about the will, wasn't it? He wants to marry you!

Even so, the paranoid, insecure feelings nagging at the back of her mind wouldn't leave her alone. And she knew they wouldn't go away until she let them out. Tonight, when Jason came over for dinner she would have to talk to him about it.

She didn't know how she was going to go about it; confrontation had never been her strong suit. But, she did know that her mind would never settle until she did.

CHAPTER TWO

"Is pretty boy coming over?" Samantha asked offhandedly as she bounced down the steps of the little duplex she and Virginia shared just outside of Seattle.

Virginia rolled her eyes. Her sprightly, flaxen-haired sister, despite being two years Virginia's junior, had always been overprotective of her.

After their parents had passed away, Samantha had insisted on moving in with Virginia. Of course, Virginia understood why and it was an instinct she shared. Both girls had been left enough in a trust fund for each of them to have their own place, even in a market as expensive as Seattle, yet they agreed that they would prefer to live together. They had been raised well, but humbly. The trustee, an old friend of their father who served as his longtime financial manager, sat down with the girls to make a plan for the money in a way that would keep with their parents' wishes to have the girls grow up responsibly. He encouraged them to let him invest the bulk of the money, allowing them to live off the interest and dividends, though they had a standing policy that the girls could ask for a larger amount of money for special things, like the purchase of their duplex.

At this point, the amount they received wasn't significant, which was why Samantha worked a part time job at night and went to college during the day. It was also why Virginia had started her baking business, and also worked part time as a floating art teacher for the nearby school district. Each girl was encouraged to try to build their own self-sufficient wealth above and beyond the trust.

Still, at the end of the day, Virginia knew the other reason Samantha moved in was that she didn't trust her sister in the big, mean city.

Sam had never liked or trusted any of Virginia's boyfriends. And that included Jason, who she still referred to as 'pretty boy.'

"You know Jason always comes over on Wednesday nights," Virginia said.

"I still don't understand why you always have to cook for him," Samantha said. "And I don't understand why you can never go over to his place."

"He only has a little efficiency," Virginia said. "The kitchen's too small there to do any cooking. Besides, you're always at work when he comes over."

Samantha worked the night shift at an upscale 24-hour fitness center. This meant that she was often asleep during the morning when Virginia was baking for her donut business, and she was away at night when Jason would often come over for dinner.

Even so, Samantha looked at her older sister skeptically.

"Come on, Sam," Virginia said with a hint of playful frustration. "You know Jason's not going anywhere. You're going to have to get used to him."

"I am used to him," Sam said. "Doesn't mean I have to like him."

Virginia rolled her eyes as Sam made her way into the kitchen and opened the fridge. She pulled out a cup of yogurt and nothing else.

Now it was Virginia's turn to look at her little sister skeptically.

"You're going to need more than that for an eight-hour shift," Virginia said.

"You know I'm on a diet," Samantha said with an eye roll. This was a point of contention between Virginia and her sister. Samantha, who was short, blonde and incredibly skinny, was always convinced that she needed to lose weight. And Virginia was convinced that, if her sister didn't eat more, Samantha was going to fade away before her eyes.

"Look, just...for my sake. Take a banana with you to work or something."

"Do we have bananas?" Sam asked.

"Just bought some," Virginia answered. Sam smiled at her sister.

"I never thought I'd see the day you would willingly purchase fruit," Sam said.

"It's for a new donut recipe I'm trying out," Virginia answered.

Samantha heaved a playful sigh. "Well, it's a start anyway," she said.

Samantha sat on top of the kitchen counter as Virginia prepared the chicken breast she was making for that evening's dinner. Samantha, meanwhile, entertained her with the amusing late-night antics she encountered at work. While her acting chops probably wouldn't win her an Oscar, Sam's reenactments of the gym clients were always performed with gusto. Whether they were the young, overworked corporate-types stumbling in late at night to try and sleep in the locker rooms before hustling back to their nearby offices, or groups of riled up guys rolling in when the bars close because a bet got out of hand as to who could bench press the most, they always made Virginia laugh.

Though the stories in and of themselves were hilarious, Virginia couldn't help but be glad she had not followed in her sister's footsteps, job-wise.

Just as Virginia was putting the chicken in the oven and Samantha was preparing to leave for work, the lock clicked in the front door.

"That's probably Jason," Virginia said wiping her hands on a dish towel and moving towards the front door. Before she left the kitchen, she turned back to her sister.

"Be nice," she warned Samantha.

Sam pursed her lips and narrowed her eyes.

"I will as long as he doesn't act like a jerk," Samantha said.

Virginia, realizing she wasn't going to get a better promise out of her little sister, walked to the front door which swung open as she approached.

"Hey babe," he said walking in and giving her a kiss. Virginia smiled at Jason as she pulled back and noticed a six pack of beer in his hand.

"Glad you remembered," she said.

Two nights before he'd complained loudly about Virginia not having booze in the house. She'd told him that her sister wouldn't allow it. So, if he wanted beer, he'd have to bring it himself.

"I still don't get why your sister doesn't like alcohol," he said following Virginia into the kitchen.

"It's part of her diet," Virginia said evenly.

"Well, a diet that doesn't make room for beer isn't any diet I'd want to be on," Jason answered with a laugh.

It happened that just at that moment, they rounded the corner to the kitchen where Samantha was waiting, her arms crossed and frowning at Jason.

Virginia cursed inwardly. She could feel the tension coming off her sister before anyone spoke. Apparently, Jason was oblivious to it.

"Oh, hey Sam," he said moving past both Virginia and Samantha and taking a seat at the kitchen table. "Didn't know you were here."

"You don't say," Samantha said through gritted teeth. She turned to him and gave him one more glare which Jason did not seem to have noticed before she turned her gaze back to Virginia.

"I've gotta go. See you tomorrow morning," Samantha said.

"See you then," Virginia said, feeling a faint pang of relief at the thought that her sister and her boyfriend would not be in the same room for long.

With one more sneer at an oblivious Jason, Samantha grabbed the banana Virginia had made her take and stalked towards the front door. Jason waited until it had closed completely before he spoke again.

"She still doesn't like me," he said. Virginia's guilt surged as she realized that Jason apparently wasn't as unaware of Sam's agitation as she'd thought.

"Sam's just protective," Virginia said.

"Yeah, I understood that when we were first dating," Jason said. "But...I mean...you'd think she'd have warmed up by now."

"There are very few people Samantha actually likes," Virginia said. "The fact that she tolerates you should make you feel all warm and fuzzy inside."

Jason let out a full buoyant laugh. Virginia couldn't help but smile fondly at the sound. She'd always loved the sound of his rich, deep, full-throated laugh. It was one of the things that had first made her fall in love with him.

"I guess I should be grateful," he said. "Who knows, one day Sam and I might even have a civil conversation. If I'm really lucky, she may just smile at me."

"It has been known to happen," Virginia said dryly.

"I'll tell you one thing," Jason said grabbing a beer from his six pack and cracking it open. "I won't hold my breath until it does."

He offered a beer to Virginia who declined. She filled a glass with sparkling water instead and sat at the table with Jason.

They talked about safe, simple things. Things like his day at work. The new orders she'd gotten in for her donut catering business. What the traffic had been like for him on the way over to her house.

She knew Jason wouldn't bring up what he really wanted to talk about until dinner was on the table. Just like she wouldn't bring up what she needed to talk about until Jason was full and satisfied.

As per usual, Jason's point of discussion came up first. Virginia had just placed his chicken onto the bed of brown rice on his plate and was doing the same with her own when Jason spoke.

"So, have you thought any more about what you want to do about the house?" he asked.

Virginia pursed her lips as she set the serving in front of him and sat down. She hesitantly took a fork full of food.

"I don't know." Not wanting to elaborate she took a larger bite of her dinner.

"Well, think about it," Jason said. "I mean, we couldn't really do much with a rundown house. I've already got a place. And, you're happy living here, aren't you?"

"Yeah," she answered, though it was slightly non-committal. While she knew how lucky she was to get a duplex in the city, and while she enjoyed her sister's company, she couldn't pretend that she hadn't often thought longingly of the little town where her Aunt's old cottage was.

A small town surrounded by woods and the scent of pine. Shops where her Aunt knew each of the owners. Walking trails brimming with wildlife and flowers. The scent of the sea filling the air when you sat on a rock along the coastline. It was the sort of place she'd always imagined herself living when she grew up. As a child, and even a teenager, it had been her dream home.

Of course, that was before she'd met Jason. Before she'd realized that he was a city boy through and through.

"Besides, it's not like we don't need the money," he said. "We've still got all my student loans to pay off. Not to mention credit card debt. Money from the house could help us take care of all that."

"I know," Virginia said.

And she did. She and Jason had discussed all their economic difficulties in great detail. They considered themselves a team, one that was committed to working toward their future together. Early on, they had decided to invest in Jason's ability to become their main provider when they eventually started a family, and she couldn't pretend that it wouldn't be a relief to get rid of some of that burden.

Still, the idea of just giving the house up was not particularly enticing. It was like giving away a beloved family heirloom or a treasured childhood toy. A piece of her childhood would disappear along with the house. It would be a small piece, but a piece none the less.

"If you know that," Jason said, "then, what's the problem?"

"It's...it's sentimental, I guess," she said. She knew the moment she said it that Jason wouldn't really understand. Both his parents were still alive. He'd never really lost anyone close to him before.

Even so, when she looked at him, he gave her a sympathetic smile and reached over to touch her hand.

"Babe, I know you loved your Aunt," he said. "And your Aunt knew you loved her. That's why she gave you the house. She wanted you to use it in the best way you could."

"But, did she really expect me to...sell it?" Virginia asked.

"She didn't leave any instructions, did she? Nothing that said you had to use it any specific way?" he asked.

"Well...no," Virginia answered honestly. Jason smiled almost triumphantly as he patted Virginia's hand before taking his away.

"There you go!" he said. "If your Aunt knew how much we needed the money, I'm sure she would've understood."

Virginia gave a reluctant nod. Truth be told, Jason had a point. Aunt Emily was always trying to take care of Virginia and her sister, Sam. Her Aunt had no children of her own, and she had sort of adopted her nieces and nephews.

Aunt Emily was forever telling Virginia that if she needed money or a loan not to hesitate to ask. Virginia had always turned down the offers. She felt guilty about asking for money, even though she knew her Aunt Emily could afford to lend it.

Perhaps this was Aunt Emily's way of helping Virginia out financially. Something Virginia couldn't refuse.

"It's...it's going to take some work," Virginia said reluctantly. Putting in her last defense against the sale of her childhood haunt.

"I know it's old," Jason said. "But, I've got a little money saved up. I'm sure you do, too. How much do you think it'll take?"

"I'm not sure, honestly," Virginia said. "I haven't been there in a few years. Not since Aunt Emily moved out."

The cottage had been abandoned since Aunt Emily became sick and moved to an apartment in the city to be near the hospital. She knew even then that there was no point in having someone take care of the house. She knew even then that she would never return.

"Well, then, we should probably make an appointment with that real estate agent. Get down there and check it out," Jason said finishing the last bite of his meat.

Virginia nodded, but a guilty pang filled her stomach once more. Maybe it was the idea of consulting a real estate agent. Even though Virginia already had someone she liked that she and her sister had used to purchase the duplex, the idea of consulting her about her Aunt's cottage just seemed so...official.

"Hey," she heard Jason say gently as she looked up from her plate. "This is the right thing to do. Nobody can blame you for fixing the house up and selling it to someone who'll use it."

"I...I guess I know that," Virginia said.

Jason set his fork down and looked at her thoughtfully.

"How about this?" he said finally. "We won't make any decisions until we actually see the place with the realtor. If we can't get much money for it, even after it's been renovated, we won't sell. Does that sound ok?"

Virginia looked at him, hesitating for a moment.

He reached across the table again, put his hand over hers and gave it a squeeze. She looked into his eyes and the soft, sympathetic smile he gave her made them sparkle.

Her heart melted and the guilty feeling dissipated.

"Yeah. That's fair," she said finally. "Thanks."

With another squeeze of her hand, he stood up from the table. He walked around until he stood at her side and put an arm around her shoulder.

"I know you've had a rough day," he said. "So, why don't you pick the movie tonight? Anything you want. Even one of those silly romantic comedies. I promise I won't complain."

Virginia gave a surprised snicker and looked up at him. He rarely let her pick what they watched after dinner. Try as she might to get into his shows, the truth was that their tastes tended to differ widely.

"You're sure about that?" she asked.

"I think, after what you've been through, the least I can do is stomach some girly tv," he said with a teasing smile.

"Ok," she answered, "but no takebacks."

"No take backs," he said, "I promise."

He leaned down and placed a gentle kiss on her temple. She closed her eyes as his warm lips and the scent of his spicy cologne filled her nostrils. His strong, steady arm curled around her shoulders, and she couldn't help but smile.

A moment later, he pulled away.

"I'll go into the living room and get the TV set up while you clean up in here," he said.

With a quick and charming wink thrown her way, he left the kitchen.

Virginia's smile remained on her face even as she stood to gather the plates and put them in the dishwasher. True, a better offer from Jason would have been to do, or at the very least help with, the mountain of dishes. But, she knew with him, baby steps were to be praised. Plus, giving up precious control of the TV remote was a big baby step.

That's why, as she basked in the memory of his soft kiss on her temple, she forgot all about the discussion she'd wanted to have with him about his assistant...

CHAPTER THREE

*V*irginia's car gently idled as she sat in the line queued up for the ferry which would take them to Sweetwater Island. She flinched in pain as she bit down, realizing that she was absentmindedly chewing on her thumbnail. The plan was for Jason to park in the commuter lot, then hop into her car with her so that they could go over and meet with the real estate agent, Amanda. Jason had to work, so they figured Virginia could get a jump on the car line by going early.

Her phone beeped, and she glanced at her side window to see if she could see Jason walking toward her car. She would be much calmer once he was with her. Knowing that they were in this together made her feel more confident and at ease about the whole thing. A quick daydream of the moment she would finally look into Jason's eyes over a perfect bouquet of creamy white lilies and say "I do" brought a dreamy smile to her face.

Focusing back on reality, she scooped up her phone to check the message. Jason probably couldn't find her car in the lineup.

She scanned across the words, "Sorry, I can't make it. Something came up with work. Tell me what you find out."

Her jaw clenched and she rolled her eyes, cursing him for the fourth time that day.

She knew that wasn't really fair; it was a Wednesday morning, after all. He'd told her he might have trouble getting off work, even though he'd put in for a half day.

Suddenly, Virginia felt even more uncertain about the outing than she had that morning. She was already nervous about seeing the beautiful summer home that had filled her childhood, likely neglected and in ill repair. But, having to do it alone, or nearly alone, was even worse.

Still, she knew there was nothing to be done about it.

She drove onto the ferry's containment area, got out of the car and made her way up to the top deck.

A deep and hollow horn bellowed through the air, and she felt the initial jolt as the boat began to move. Closing her eyes, she could feel the wind blowing across her face. The wisps of her feathery brown hair whipped into her eyes and fluttered across her cheeks. While the sensation was a little annoying, it also reminded her of the first time she had stepped foot on the boat as a child. She'd laughed when her hair had flown into her face back then.

She remembered the thrill of excitement her much younger self had felt riding this same old ferry boat so many years ago. Once her father had made his first million, her parents had started taking summer trips to Europe, just the two of them. Samantha and Virginia had gotten to spend those times vacationing with Aunt Emily on their magical island. She smiled at the memory. Even now, there was something magical about getting on the boat and leaving your cares behind on the mainland. She hadn't spent nearly enough time out here in the last few years.

A squawking gull above the stern reprimanded her for her failure to visit. Virginia smiled up in apology to the hovering bird.

The ferry was one of only two ways in which to get to Sweetwater Island, and it was by far the most efficient. The land road towards the island took over an hour from almost the same spot as the ferry, and if the rickety old bridge that led to the island was out, it could take much longer.

The ferry took only twenty minutes. Virginia was surprised to find herself so disappointed when the boat pulled to a stop. The hollow, nervous feeling which had disappeared almost completely on the ferry ride over, returned as she got back into her car.

She drove down the pothole filled road into the main town of Sweetwater and tried to remember what Jason had said. They didn't have to make any decisions until they'd talked to Amanda. And if the house wasn't worth much of anything, even after renovations, they might not sell it at all.

As Virginia drove past the lovely Victorian cottages at the outskirts of the town, with their pale purple shutters, steepled roofs, and mysterious towers springing up from their sides, she found herself hoping that the house would not be worth anything. That meant that she would have more of an argument to keep it, she reasoned to herself.

Of course, she felt more than a bit guilty when she thought about that. After all, shouldn't she want to get them out of debt? Didn't she want Jason to be able to pay off his student loans? Didn't she want to have enough money to get married?

Besides, Jason was right. What were they going to do with a house so far from the city? They both worked in Seattle, and if they lived on the Island, commuting would be hell. Even with Virginia's inheritance, there was no possible way they could afford to keep a "summer" house.

No, if it were at all possible, the cottage would have to be sold.

Even so, when Virginia pulled into Sweetwater's small downtown, a nostalgic smile crept across her face.

Driving down the main street, she passed the old ice cream parlor. Aunt Emily would take them there on Saturdays when they'd been good all week. To tell the truth, even when they hadn't been as good as they could have been, they would still make the trip to the ice cream shop. Aunt Emily couldn't seem to help spoiling the girls.

Just across from the ice cream parlor was another treat. The second-hand bookshop where they would go on Sunday afternoons after church. That was where Virginia had found an entire set of Nancy Drew mysteries and her little sister had fallen in love with Gossip Girl.

Next to the bookstore was the Supermart. Though it wasn't as exciting as the other places, Virginia and Sam always felt very grown up when Aunt Emily asked them to walk down to the Supermart alone and get her the ingredients for supper, or occasionally, a frozen pizza.

Virginia looked at the shop next to the Supermart and felt a jolt of disappointment when she saw a shiny new electronics store in place of where the old video rental shop used to be. She supposed she should have expected that. Since streaming had come down the pike, everything happened over Wi-Fi now. Even in remote places like this, there were no video stores left.

Still, as everything else had been the same, she naively thought it would be there; an antiquated building frozen in time to remind her of Friday nights with her aunt and sister when they would rent three movies, usually silly comedies, and watch them back to back.

She turned her attention away from the offending electronics store and headed down the main street and up the small hill that led to the cottage. As soon as the last shop was passed, Virginia entered into what looked like desolate woodland. There was nothing on the hill next to the cottage except tall pine trees on either side of a barely drivable dirt road.

Even so, the woods she drove through were every bit as filled with memories as the main street she had left behind. Her eyes quickly found the tree with extra low limbs that she used to climb. Closer to the cottage, she spied the twin rocks facing the town that she and her sister used to sit on.

Then, just beyond the rocks was the house itself.

Virginia nearly gasped when her eyes landed on it. She had expected the house to look exactly as she remembered it. When she was young, the quaint, two-story wooden home looked like something out of a fairytale. The gables of the roof were painted white and the window shutters were pink. There was a high, pointed roof and a light turquoise blue door highlighting white scalloped shingles covering the facade.

Now, the paint on the once beautiful blue door had been peeled so thoroughly that the ugly brown color of the original door showed through. The white gables were so overrun with pollen from the surrounding trees that they now sported a kind of sickly greenish-yellow color. The pristine little window shutters were hanging off their hinges, and the once blushing pink color was molded with dust and grime.

Had it not been for the familiar pointed roof still standing tall amidst the forest of pine trees, Virginia would not have believed this was the same cheery house she came to every summer as a girl.

Trying as best she could to stifle the sinking feeling in her heart at seeing the house in this state, she pulled up to the side of the grassy hill that functioned as the driveway and parked next to a white Chevy Cruiser.

A tall, older woman with plump, rosy cheeks and short, curly, brightly dyed red hair, stood next to the car talking to someone on her cell phone.

Virginia's mood lifted a bit at the sight of the real estate agent. It was nice to know that Amanda Benson was exactly as she remembered her from two years before, even if the house was very different.

"Look, honey, I know your brother took your toy, but you have to learn to share," Virginia heard her saying in a high pitched voice. Amanda turned and gave Virginia an apologetic smile. Virginia waved, in turn, telling her it was all right.

"Ok," Amanda continued to the mysterious child on the phone. "Do you promise you're going to be good? Ok. Remember, you can't break a promise. I love you, too. Bye bye."

With a heavy sigh, Amanda clicked the end button on the phone and turned fully to Virginia.

"Sorry about that," Amanda said. "My daughter's husband was transferred overseas, and she's gone over to find a new house and whatnot. So, the grandkids are staying with me until they get things settled."

"How old are they?" Virginia asked.

"Lilly's four," she said. "That's who I was trying to talk some sense into on the phone. And Mikey is two."

Virginia gave her a sympathetic smile. She knew Amanda was in her late fifties. What's more, her husband had passed away ten years before. It was hard to imagine her taking care of two young kids on her own.

"That can't be easy," Virginia said.

"Well, I've got a lot of help," Amanda answered. "My neighbor has a little girl around Lilly's age. So she takes the kids when I go out to show houses. Luckily I'm not working at the office anymore so...I can make it work."

Though she was attempting to toss the issue aside, Virginia could easily see the worry lines on the woman's face. Those hadn't been there two years ago when Amanda had sold Sam and Virginia the duplex.

"Well," Amanda said blatantly attempting to change the subject. "Shall we take a look at the house?"

"I guess we should," Virginia said reluctantly. "I haven't been here in what feels like forever. I didn't realize how much it had been let go."

"Oh, don't let that get you down," Amanda said in her light and genuinely cheerful voice. "Remember, I've seen a lot of houses that don't look like much at first. Some of them have become my favorite projects. It's amazing what can happen when you put just a little time and a lot of love into a place."

Despite Amanda's reassurance, as they entered through the sad, peeling door, Virginia couldn't help but think that this house needed much more than time and love.

They stepped into the front walkway and Virginia was immediately assaulted by another flood of memories mixed with a heavy layer of dust.

The grime on the outside of the house was nearly as bad on the inside. Even so, the warm wood floor of the front walkway was the same as she remembered it being when she was young.

When she looked to her right, toward the living room, Aunt Emily's old, tufted mauve couch was still there, too. It was moth-eaten now and covered in dust. But, when Virginia caught sight of it, she could vividly remember sitting right beside her aunt as she read to Virginia and her little sister.

Aunt Emily was a great fan of children's literature, and when the girls were small, she would read all of her favorites to them. These included The Wind in the Willows, Alice in Wonderland and nearly every book by Roald Dahl in print.

"The carpet will have to be torn up, of course," Amanda said as they moved into the living room. This brought Virginia's attention to the horribly stained carpeting beneath her feet. It had been white at one point but was now a sort of brownish color.

"Aunt Emily always talked about putting in wood floors anyway," Virginia said. "I think she'd like it if we changed that."

She moved through the old living room, coughing slightly at the dust that came up from the surfaces as she did so. Moving to the window, she stopped when she saw an intricate spider's web hanging from the corner.

"Oh, don't worry about that," Amanda said following her gaze. "There'll be a lot of spider webs in here. Nothing a good dusting won't fix."

Virginia was not worried. In fact, she couldn't help but smile as she watched the light hit the small strands, causing the colors in the web to shift and fold into one another.

Her Aunt Emily had always loved spider webs. When they found one, the girls were never permitted to ruin it if they could help it.

"Spider webs are good luck," she insisted. "If you see one, especially in your house, it means that something really good is about to happen."

Of course, Virginia had no idea where this legend had come from. In fact, she was almost certain that Aunt Emily had made it up. But still to this day, it had instilled in Virginia a sort of respect for both spiders and the webs they spun.

"There's a lot more that'll need changing of course," Amanda said as she led Virginia through a small archway that separated the living room from the family room and connected to the kitchen.

As Amanda continued the tour, Virginia could see that she was right. Her Aunt's antique furniture, most of which was still sitting in the old house, looked in disrepair and would have to be replaced.

Amanda also suggested retiling the kitchen and bathrooms as the flooring had become too dirty to be salvaged.

Virginia didn't mind this so much. She knew before she'd passed away, Aunt Emily had talked about making changes to the house. In fact, she'd been talking about it for years. She just couldn't seem to set aside the time to do it.

Now, Virginia thought, even if they did have to sell it, making the changes her Aunt had always wanted would give her a slight sense of peace. Like a last tribute to Aunt Emily. It wasn't until Amanda took her to see the bedrooms that a bittersweet sadness filled Virginia's chest.

"I definitely think we'll want to update the rooms," Amanda said opening the door to the second largest bedroom to the right of the small hall off the kitchen.

Virginia let out a small gasp when the door opened. This bedroom was the one Virginia had slept in every summer when she came to the cottage. And it was almost perfectly preserved.

Her stuffed animals who had made their home here still sat on the small day bed just next to the window. That day bed was still decorated with an old, stained, purple comforter with a lace frill on the bottom.

To the right of the bed stood her bookshelf. It still housed her, now very dusty, complete collection of Nancy Drew mystery novels.

"I think we could turn this into a nice office or guest room if you-"

"I don't think I'll change much in here," Virginia said in a rush. Amanda turned to look at her surprised. It was the first time Virginia had protested any suggested change.

Realizing how forceful she'd sounded, Virginia felt her face go red and she looked at the floor as she explained herself.

"It's just...this was my old bedroom. I liked it this way and...I think...I mean if we just change a few things...some other kid might like it too."

When she looked up, she was pleased to see that Amanda was giving her a sympathetic smile.

"I understand," she said giving her arm a small pat. "You probably won't want to change it completely. You lose a lot of memories that way."

They continued the tour upstairs through the other bedrooms and bathroom where Amanda suggested similar updates to the draperies and flooring. Finally, they made it to the back deck. Or rather, the entranceway to the back deck.

"The wood rot's too bad for us to risk going out on the deck right now," Amanda said. "That'll be the first thing we'll have to replace when you start working on the house. It's a safety issue."

Virginia nodded, looking out past the rotted back deck. An old tire swing swung in the light summer breeze that she and Samantha had put up their third summer there. It was strange to see it looking so empty. Just as strange as it was to hear the backyard so quiet. Virginia's memories of this yard had always been filled with loud peals of children's laughter.

"Well," Amanda said closing the door and jolting Virginia back to the present. "That's about all I can show you. There's the attic too, of course, but, that's as bad as the back deck. We definitely wouldn't want you falling through the floor up there."

Amanda gave a good-hearted chuckle. Virginia smiled and gave a polite nod, her mind whirling from the tour of her past.

"Just from what I can see now, the foundation of the cottage is actually very good," Amanda said. "As we say in the industry, it has good bones. But, it'll need a lot of work."

"How much do you think we'd have to put in to get it back in shape?" Virginia asked.

"It won't be cheap," Amanda said. "I'd say somewhere in the fifty to one hundred thousand dollar range."

"You're right. That's not cheap!" Virginia said, taken aback. When she remembered all the debt she still had to pay off from Jason's schooling, she wondered how such a huge sum, taken out all at once, was going to affect her bank account.

Maybe it wouldn't be worth it to sell the house with all the money they'd have to put into it. Virginia couldn't help but feel oddly hopeful at the thought.

"But," Amanda continued, "If you do get it fixed up, I could sell it for two or even three times what you put into it, plus what the property itself is worth."

"Really?" Virginia asked. Trying to sound excited even as she felt the disappointment wash over her.

"Oh, yes," Amanda said eagerly. "As I said, this house has a great structure. Not to mention, this market has really taken off. Lots of people are moving from the city out to the islands."

"So, you think we'd be able to make a profit on it?" Virginia asked, once again, trying to keep the disappointment out of her voice.

"I'm positive," Amanda said. "That is if you're willing to put the money for the repairs in?"

Amanda looked at Virginia expectantly, awaiting her answer. Virginia knew what that answer had to be.

She'd told Jason that, if Amanda said they could make a profit on the house, she would put up the money for repairs. Virginia knew she had the money in her trust fund. And while it would take a chunk out of the inheritance she'd gotten from her dad, it wouldn't bankrupt her completely.

"Yeah," Virginia said. "Yeah, we can do that."

"Perfect," Amanda said excitedly as she led the way back to the family room, past the living room and out to the front yard.

"Now, we'll just need to find you a good contractor," Amanda said just before they reached their cars.

She reached into her purse and rooted around for a small card case. Shuffling through it, she pulled out two crisp, clear and very professional looking business cards.

"Now, these two are excellent companies. But, I should warn you, their prices tend to run a little higher than normal. Are you willing to go over one hundred thousand if it comes down to it?" she asked hesitantly handing Virginia the cards.

Virginia bit her lip. She knew that she could just spare the hundred thousand by tapping into her highly guarded savings account, and applied what she could from her meager teaching and baking incomes. If she paid the bare minimum on Jason's loan and was careful with her own spending for the next few months, she could make it work. Anything over that, however, would become a good deal more complicated.

"I...I don't know," she answered.

Amanda looked at her thoughtfully. It was a moment before the older woman began shuffling in her purse again.

"Well, if you want something a little cheaper but still reliable," Amanda said pulling out another card. "You might try this new company."

She handed Virginia a small and plain business card. This one had no colorful logo. Simply the words Solid Rock Contractors printed in large, bold letters. Beneath these was the name Tristan McPherson along with a phone number and email address.

"Strictly speaking, my real estate company hasn't used him before," Amanda said. "But, he goes to my church, and I've hired him for some repairs around my own house. He's very reliable and very affordably priced. Not to mention, he's wonderful with my grandkids. They call him Uncle Tristan now. But, I don't suppose that matters much to you."

Virginia looked up at the woman and smiled.

"I don't know," she said half teasing. "They always say that dogs and little kids have a better sense about people than adults do. If a dog or a young child likes someone, I'm more inclined to trust him."

Amanda's smile widened.

"That's what I've always said," she answered.

They said goodbye and Virginia promised to let Amanda know when she'd settled on a contractor.

As she drove back through the town, Virginia tried her best not to look at the familiar shops, storefronts, and homes. The guilty feeling she had at deciding to sell the place that she'd loved so much as a child was still stubbornly beating in her chest.

At least, she reasoned, as she made it back to the dock for the ferry, I can fix up the house first. Which means I'm sure I'll get to come up and see it again a few times before it's sold.

36

Yes, she told herself, a proper goodbye was all she needed. She felt increasingly certain that, with time, she would feel ready to say goodbye.

CHAPTER FOUR

"*A*bsolutely not!" Jason said. His voice was so loud that Virginia had to move the cell phone away from her ear.

She'd just called both of the first places Amanda had recommended. When she'd talked to Jason about their options the night before, he wanted to go with one of the first two companies, mostly because the real estate company had used them for home renovations before. Plus, they looked more professional than the third, admittedly newer option.

Virginia had warned Jason that the quotes might be a little high. He said he still wanted her to check them out first. Now that she'd gotten the quotes, one of which was just at one hundred thousand and one of which was a good amount over, Jason was audibly unhappy.

"You didn't see the place, Jason," Virginia said. "It needs a lot of work."

"The realtor said the work is just aesthetic, right?" Jason asked. "I mean, they don't need to fix the plumbing or anything. How much overhead could there be putting in a hardwood floor and a few tiles?"

"Amanda said they might be a little pricey," Virginia countered.

"Well, she was right about that," Jason huffed. "I don't want to see you lose another chunk of your trust fund to a bunch of highway robbers."

"Well," Virginia said, "we do have that third option."

"The church guy?" Jason asked a slightly derisive note in his voice.

"Yeah, Amanda said he would probably be more affordable."

"But will he be as good?" Jason asked.

"Amanda's used him on her own house," she answered. "She says he does good work and he's really reliable."

She didn't feel the need to mention that he was good with kids. She knew Jason wouldn't exactly appreciate the significance of that. Men never seemed to. There was a pause over the phone during which Virginia was sure she could hear Jason thinking.

"Ok," he said finally. "Go ahead and give him a call."

They said their goodbyes and I love you's before Virginia hung up. She fished the third card out of her purse and stared at it for a good few minutes.

At first glance, she could see why Jason had been reluctant to try this company. Besides the fact that the card was very plain, the email address was Gmail rather than a company server. The phone number was doubtlessly a personal cell phone as well.

But, Virginia knew from her dad that sometimes, small businesses did the best work. And those small businesses could often grow beyond even the founder's wildest dreams.

With that in mind, she sat on her couch and dialed the number on the card. The phone rang twice before a voice on the other end answered.

"Solid Rock Contracting, this is Tristan."

The musical, tenor voice implied a much younger man than Virginia had been expecting. The way Amanda had described him, reliable, good with the grandkids, she had expected a kindly older gentleman.

"Hi," she said a little timidly. "I was hoping to get a quote for some work I need done on a house?"

"Oh, you must be Virginia," the man said cheerfully. "Amanda said you might be calling."

"Yeah," Virginia said, feeling some relief. She was happy that she wouldn't have to explain the whole situation to Tristan. "Did she tell you about the work that needed to be done on the house?"

"Most of it," he said. "I just need to be filled in on a couple of the details."

They discussed the work Virginia and Amanda had talked about wanting to do. Amanda had already told Tristan about the outer deck and the attic. Virginia filled him in on the new wood floors she wanted to have put in and the new tiles she wanted in the bathroom.

"I know you'll probably need new furniture to show the house, too," Tristan said. "I've got a furniture guy I work with. Would you like me to put a call in to him?"

"Oh, don't worry about that," Virginia said hastily. "I can take care of the decorating and stuff on my own."

Truth be told, that was the one aspect of this job Virginia was looking forward to. It had been a long while since she had put any of her artistic sense to use outside of her teaching job and it would be fun to have something other than baking to keep her busy during the summer.

"Ok," Tristan said. "If you change your mind about that, let me know." Virginia thought he sounded skeptical but reminded herself that this was to be expected. Guys who made their living working on houses always had their doubts about amateurs doing a professional's job.

In the end, Tristan gave her a quote for the entire project that was a good deal lower than what both of the other contractors had offered.

"I'll have to talk to my boyfriend," Virginia said. "But, it sounds like we'll probably go with you."

"Great," Tristan said sounding much more excited than either of the guys from the larger company. She wondered if, perhaps, this was the largest job his small company had ever gotten.

"Ok. I'll send you an email tonight with confirmation and sometimes when we could go and check out the house. You can let me know which of them will work for you."

"Sounds perfect," he said. "Can't wait to get started."

As soon as she and Tristan said their goodbyes, Virginia ended the call and immediately sent a text to Jason. She knew his break would be over by now and texting was the only way she was likely to get a hold of him.

She texted him the quote Tristan had given her. It was only a few minutes before her phone buzzed with a text in reply.

"Ok. Let's go with him."

As soon as she read the text, a wave of relief flowed through her. Virginia shot off the promised confirmation email to Tristan with several suggestions of meeting times within the next week.

As she put her phone away and moved from the living room back into the kitchen where a cooled batch of donuts awaited icing, she realized that the sense of dread she felt about the house had gone away completely. In fact, after talking to Tristan, she felt lighter than she had in weeks.

Perhaps that was why it did not surprise her at all to see a shining spider web in the corner of her kitchen window, even though she swore it had not been there when she'd left the kitchen less than two hours before.

She simply smiled at the little design, wondering if it was a sign of Aunt Emily's blessing.

With a happy sigh, she decided that it was just that.

CHAPTER FIVE

*T*he second ferry ride in a week was just as fraught with the mixture of anxiety, excitement, and disappointment as the first had been.

She felt an exhilarating burst of energy at going back to Sweetwater again. The town's charm had not been lost on her the last time she came out. And this time, she'd planned to spend some time perusing around the little shops. Maybe even get an ice cream from the shop where she and her sister used to go.

As she exited the ferry and drove back down the single road towards the town, her brain shot into overdrive. She couldn't help but stress about the money she was spending on the renovations for the cottage. Even though Amanda had assured her that she could sell the house for twice as much if not more, nothing was certain and it was a substantial amount for anyone, most particularly someone with an income like hers.

After all, the sale price depended on what the market was like, whether luck was on their side and, perhaps most of all, on how good this contractor was.

This would be Virginia's first meeting with Tristan McPherson, and she supposed Jason's doubts about this newer and less tested company had rubbed off on her. Even though Jason had agreed to hire Tristan's company, he still wasn't one hundred percent sold on them.

"I mean, sure he's cheap," Jason said only one day after he had agreed to Tristan's quote, "but that might come with a cost all its own."

Of course, when Virginia reminded Jason that he'd agreed to hire Tristan's company, Jason had defended himself by saying that he was just 'playing devil's advocate.' Trying to make sure they were ready for every possible scenario.

Though she knew Jason meant well, his form of 'disaster preparation' had put her on edge.

Of course, some of Jason's fears might have been put to rest if he'd been able to come out with her today and meet Tristan for himself.

That was where Virginia's disappointment came into play. She'd once again invited him to come out to the island with her, and once again, he'd backed out at the last minute. Another pressing matter had come up at work.

Though Virginia knew she shouldn't complain, she still wished he would double-check things at work before agreeing to come with her in the first place. Although knowing that she would have to go alone three days ago when she'd made the appointment would still have been a little disappointing, it would have been nothing compared to the hurt she felt when, the morning of, he texted her to tell her 'Sorry. Can't make it after all.'

Trying to take Jason off her mind, she glanced out the window as she drove through town once more. This time, she noticed the small shop that sold antique furniture. She made a mental note to spend some time in there after the meeting. She could find some nice pieces to put in the house once it was finished.

44

She passed the rest of the trip up the hill pleasantly painting a picture in her mind of what she wanted each room in the little cottage to look like when she had finished with it.

The anxiety didn't come back until the car crawled to a stop at the top of the hill just outside the front door of the house. She saw an unfamiliar blue pick-up truck parked outside that wasn't the gleaming, logo-encrusted company vehicle she had imagined that the other guys probably drove.

Its bed was piled with wood, lumber and what looked like several other tools. Obviously, the contractor was already here, but there was no sign of him near the truck.

She got out of her car and moved curiously from her parking spot around to one side of the house.

"Hello?" she called out. No answer.

She padded around the side garden, now overgrown with weeds, hoping to see any sign of human life. She didn't find any.

Virginia wondered, suddenly, if the contractor had gotten tired of waiting for her and somehow left. But she dismissed this almost immediately. She was only five minutes late. Plus, between the state of his truck and his easy voice over the phone, she surmised that Mr. Tristan McPherson was not particularly finicky about time constraints.

She moved through the tall grass shaded by the high pine trees to the back of the house. That was where she found him.

A slim male figure bent over a piece of old wood on the weathered back deck. Even though his back was turned to her, she could sense an air of deep concentration emanating from him. From out of his red flannel shirt, Virginia saw a sun-stained hand move out and touch the dark, ruined wood with an odd sense of reverence.

The action was so charged with feeling that Virginia did not feel quite right about interrupting it. Still, she knew she had to. She hadn't planned on the tour taking too long since she still wanted time to look at furniture in the town shops.

Feeling slightly guilty, she cleared her throat.

She was surprised when this elicited no response. The man simply turned to the side, his eyes still focused on the wood in front of him. Now that she could see his face more clearly, Virginia was forced to admit that he was much better looking than she'd expected him to be.

When she thought about handymen who owned small businesses, an image of large, usually bearded men with leathery skin and slight beer bellies came to mind.

This man was not particularly brawny or burly or bearded. He was lean and strong, but had an almost boyish air about him. His light brown hair was tousled and his chin was completely clean shaven, not to mention very defined. The hand he still ran across the splintered wood was not at all aged or leathery. It was fair, with a light tan from the gentle Washington sun and looked very smooth.

He was now moving his feet along with the motion of his hand. Moving along the edge of the deck as though trying to memorize it.

She would have to try again to get his attention.

"Tristan?" she asked, making her voice as loud as she dared. The young man whirled around to face her. His bright blue eyes startled. When they finally took stock of her, a pink blush rose up in his light cheeks. She thought she could make out some very light freckles scattered across them too. It made him look quite cute, all things considered.

"You must be Virginia," he said sounding the tiniest bit self-conscious. "Sorry, I was just-"

"Don't apologize," Virginia said with what she hoped was an encouraging smile. "I was the one who was late."

He gave her a sheepish smile in return and moved forward to shake her hand.

"Nice to meet you," he said in the same light tenor voice she had heard on the phone. She put her hand out to shake his and thought to herself that his hand was just as smooth and warm as it had looked when he'd been examining the wood.

"You too," she said with a blush of her own. She released her hand from his as quickly as she could and brought her attention back to the deck.

"I see you've started looking at the deck. Hope it didn't scare you off."

"Not at all!" Tristan said. "To tell the truth, I've wanted to work on one of these old, Victorian cottages since I started my business. Before this, all I got were small jobs on modern suburban houses. Not nearly as much fun."

"Probably not as much effort either," Virginia countered.

Tristan gave a vague nod in her direction before moving back to the deck. Once more he put his hand out to touch a piece of rotting pine.

"You don't see a lot of places with the original wood still in place," he said. His voice was impressed, almost awestruck. "It's amazing that it's still here at all."

"Judging by the rot, there's probably a reason most people don't keep the original," she replied.

"Oh, that part can be replaced easily enough," he said with a dismissive wave of his hand and moving back over to the deck. He took a rolling measurement tape out of his back pocket and put it up to the front steps of the deck.

"I'd still like to use local wood if you wouldn't mind," he said. "It would be nice to keep as true to the original look and feel of the place as possible."

"I wouldn't mind at all," she said feeling genuinely impressed as she watched him carefully measure the step. He stood up and pulled a small notebook from his side pocket. She had a sudden feeling that, once again, he hadn't heard her.

"In fact, I'd like to keep the original look of the house as much as possible," she said slightly louder hoping that would get his attention. It did; he turned around and looked at her blinking once more in surprise.

"Really?" he asked. "No modernizing? No bringin' it into the twenty-first century?'"

His look of surprise had turned to slight skepticism as he looked her up and down. Virginia realized that she was wearing her "business" clothes today. She had a meeting with one of the clients she catered donuts for after this, and she always made a point to dress well when she went to those.

However, she realized that when Tristan looked at her in her pencil skirt, gauzy navy and white blouse and wedge heels, he saw something that didn't sit well with him. And what's more, his prejudice didn't sit well with her.

"You sound surprised," she said. "Did you think I'd want to change everything?"

"Most people do these days," he said unashamedly. "Especially interior designers. Amateur or otherwise."

Now, she recognized the tone he'd used with her on the phone when she'd told him that she would take care of the interior decorating.

"Well, I guess I'm not most people," she said, frowning at him for the first time. "And I'm definitely not just some amateur interior designer.

This house is special to me. I spent every summer here from the time I was six to the time I was sixteen. Is it so amazing that I'd want to keep it the way I remember it?"

He blinked, and she was slightly satisfied when she saw another light pink blush come into his cheeks.

"I'm sorry. I didn't mean...I mean, I shouldn't have...it's just, I thought..."

He mumbled as he looked down at his feet. His shamed face and half-finished apologies were enough to make Virginia feel sorry she had spoken to him so harshly.

"Don't worry about it," she offered up, giving him a small smile. "Honest mistake. Now, would you like to see the rest of the house? Or is the deck enough for you to go on?"

He looked up and gave a small smile at her joke.

"No, I'd love to see the rest of it," he said. "If the deck's anything to go by, I'm going to love this project."

That was also surprising, Virginia thought, as she led him around the side and back to the front door. This contractor was perhaps the first person she'd ever met who could get excited about a deck filled with rotting wood. Original or not.

She was even more surprised that his enthusiasm continued as they moved through the rest of the house. He didn't seem to be able to help gushing over the unpainted woodwork on the walls.

"Your Aunt was smart not to paint this over," he said. "Most people do. But, really, the wood is meant to show through. It looks so much better this way."

He was equally thrilled about the fireplace and the window panes. "She even kept the original fireplace tile! That'll be perfect."

He did have ideas and suggestions for changes. Both he and Virginia agreed that they wanted to open up the kitchen a bit and, of course that the bathrooms would need to be re-tiled and spruced up.

Overall though, he seemed determined to remain true to the original character of the house. He seemed to bounce around from room to room, measuring and openly admiring the craftsmanship and woodwork. The way most guys got about football or video games, Tristan, apparently, got about old houses.

As they finished the tour, Virginia found all her doubts about Tristan's lack of experience had melted away. He clearly appreciated this house as much as she did. That was enough to let her know that she was leaving it in good hands.

"So, do you think you'll be able to have it ready by September?" Virginia asked. "I know Amanda said that having it ready to show by fall would be best."

"Oh, no problem," Tristan said eagerly. "I've got most of the materials I'll need already. The rest I can get pretty easily. I'll bring my assistant out here to get started tomorrow morning."

"That soon?" Virginia asked, once again surprised.

"The sooner, the better," Tristan said. "Especially if we want to get it finished by fall. Though, truthfully, it's mostly 'cause I can't wait to get started here." He grinned as he threw her a quick side glance.

"Glad to hear it," Virginia said. "I'll be over sometimes to see how things are going."

"That's fine," Tristan said, though she noted some skepticism had returned slightly to his voice, as though he were an artist who did not like the idea of an outsider intruding on his work. "Just be sure to call me first. I don't want there to be any accidents if you were walking around looking for us and didn't know where to watch your step. That can sometimes happen when outsiders visit a site."

Once again, the way he said 'outsiders' didn't quite sit well with Virginia. It was as though he saw her as an "other." Someone who didn't really appreciate what he was going to do with the house.

"Trust me," Virginia said, her tone a tad defensive. "I know my way around construction sites. And, I'll be sure to call."

"Ok then," Tristan said. This time he didn't seem to feel the need or desire to apologize for unintentionally offending her. He simply stared back at her, his wide blue eyes meeting her green ones with a small smirk on his lips as though she'd said something funny.

Virginia didn't say anything more, but gave him a quizzical look as she led the way back out the front door and down the steps to their cars.

"Here's the key," she said fishing the large, antique key out of her purse. It was the one her aunt had given her when she was young. It had an ornate heart fashioned into the handle and Virginia loved it.

Even though she had decided that she trusted Tristan with the house, she still felt a pang of reluctance at handing the key over.

He must have seen the hesitance on her face when he reached for the key because his expression changed when he took hold of it. He regarded her deeply as though he was trying to read what was written on her face.

As he eased the key out of her hand, a knowing expression came over him. It was as though he finally understood why she was so hesitant.

"I'll take good care of it," he said earnestly, "I promise."

"Please do," she said. "This place is...very special to me."

He gave her a wide, empathetic smile which she couldn't help but return.

"I can see why," he said. "It's in good hands."

"Thank you," she answered. Virginia felt a silent sigh release in her chest. She was relieved that, at last, someone understood her reluctance to part with this magical place.

They said their goodbyes and Virginia watched as Tristan got into his truck and headed down the hill. The feeling of relief remained as she got into her own car, and in fact, it followed her all the way into town as she browsed for furniture.

As she looked at antique wooden wardrobes and bed frames, she found herself wondering if Tristan would approve of these pieces. Would they be 'original' or 'authentic' enough for him?

She didn't quite know the answer. But, the questions made her smile.

CHAPTER SIX

"Are you baking for pretty boy again?" Samantha asked, wandering into the kitchen, yawning with her school books under her arm. It was almost eleven thirty in the morning, and Sam had just woken up from her too-short seven-to-eleven nap before going to her afternoon class.

"If you mean Jason," Virginia answered wearily. "No, I'm not. He's gone on a business trip down to Portland for a couple of days."

"Is he taking that hot sales assistant with him?" Samantha asked wryly. Virginia, unable to keep entirely quiet about the dalliance she had witnessed outside the television station had mentioned it to her sister. Something she was now beginning to regret. It had given Samantha even more reason to hate Jason.

"Sales assistants don't go on business trips, so that you know," Virginia said tossing her second batch of donuts in the oven and grabbing the icing for the first. "And really, you need to lay off Jason about that," she continued, her back turned towards her sister. "It was probably nothing."

Samantha gave a snort of disbelief but, thankfully, said nothing more. Virginia heard Sam move to the refrigerator as she focused on filling a pastry with the new banana cream she'd promised herself she would try.

"So, if you're not baking for your boyfriend, who are those for?" Sam asked from behind Virginia. She turned to see Samantha setting down her books on the kitchen island while coffee brewed on the counter behind her.

"Well, the second batch will be for an order I need to ship out by tomorrow," Virginia said. "This first batch is kind of experimental. I've been playing with some new flavors."

"I hope you don't expect to test them out on me!" Sam said vehemently. Virginia rolled her eyes at her sister.

"I know that trying to get you to eat a donut would be a waste of time," Virginia said. "I thought I'd take them up to the renovation team working on the house. I should check on their progress anyway."

Samantha stared at her sister with an oddly pointed look. Virginia turned back around to the donuts, a sense of guilt washing over her. Though she wasn't sure just why.

"You know, I still can't believe you're selling it," Samantha said.

"I asked you about it," Virginia said. "You told me you didn't really care, remember?"

"That's true," Sam said. "I don't particularly. I mean, I loved going there when I was a kid but, that's really not the sort of place I'd like going now. I'd rather just keep the memories. But...you're not like that."

"Not like what?" Virginia asked hoping her voice sounded light enough that it didn't make her sister suspicious.

She heard Samantha heave a sigh.

"You know what I mean," Samantha said. "You love quaint little island towns and antique shops and old Victorian houses. I mean, you're happier when we go out to the country camping than I've ever seen you in the city. Getting rid of what should be your dream house just isn't...like you!"

Virginia recognized the tone in her sister's voice and knew she would have to give her some kind of explanation. She turned to look at Samantha with a sigh of her own.

"Look, Sam, you know money's kind of tight right now," Virginia said. "Besides, Jason and I really want to get married, and we can't do that until we get some extra income."

Sam's skeptical look didn't go away. She stared Virginia down as though trying to see through her. Virginia, unsure what else to do, stared right back. Finally, with a shrug of her shoulders, Sam turned back towards the coffee, grabbed hold of the carafe and poured herself a cup.

"Whatever you say," Sam said in a resigned tone. "I know getting you to give up on pretty boy is like you trying to get me to eat donuts."

Virginia gave a half-hearted laugh and continued decorating the rest of the batch.

Sam and Virginia ended up leaving the house at the same time. Sam set off for class at the university only two blocks away while Virginia, donuts in hand, got in her car and made her way to the ferry.

When she arrived at the loading dock, she looked at the long line of cars waiting to drive onto the boat. The lunch rush, she supposed. Early morning, noon and around five o'clock in the evening were the worst times for taking the ferry out to the island. She cursed herself for not remembering that.

Just looking at the huge line of cars made her feel a restless urge to get out of her driver's seat and move. Glancing sideways at the nearly empty parking lot beside the loading dock, she made a snap decision.

Turning her steering wheel right, she moved away from the car line and towards the parking lot. She would go on the ferry as a foot passenger. It wasn't a long walk from the bay to the cottage, and no one could argue that she didn't need the exercise.

Grabbing the box of donuts beside her, she got out of the car and joined the much shorter line of foot passengers onto the boat.

The ferry ride seemed much shorter this time around than it had in the past. In no time, she had set her feet on the island and was moving up the hill the back way to the cottage.

The little walking trail didn't go through the small downtown of Sweetwater. Instead, it wound through the tall pines and oaks taking her along the picturesque hillsides where she had a view of the sparkling blue ocean.

She, Aunt Emily, and her sister had walked this path to the ferry many times in the past. Virginia remembered coming back from shopping trips in Seattle with bags of clothes or toys in hand. She and her sister happily racing one another to abstract markers like the tree with the weirdly shaped trunk or the huge boulder at the top of the hill.

Every whiff of pine and blow of the ocean breeze seemed to take Virginia back there. To that much simpler time when she did not have to think about how much money was left in her bank accounts, or whether or not her boyfriend would really propose once they had the cash from the house.

Finally, she reached the cottage and could see Tristan's truck parked in the expected spot just beside the front door. As she moved closer, she could hear the sound of pounding as well as a raised voice swearing oaths at a particular wall in the house.

She knocked on the door though she was sure it couldn't be heard over both the hammering and one-sided argument. She tried the doorknob, and to her surprise, it opened immediately.

"Hello?" she asked hesitantly. "Tristan?"

"Oh! Come on you stupid wall!" he exclaimed from the kitchen. She moved cautiously through the front hallway which was now littered with tools and a hefty layer of sawdust. Finally, she entered the kitchen where Tristan was facing a wall, large hammer in hand, with no sign of an assistant anywhere.

"Hello?" she asked again.

He gave a small start and turned around. His eyes widened when he caught sight of her. His flannel shirt and jeans were covered in the same heavy layer of dust as the hallway outside, and sweat was dripping down his brow.

"Virginia!" he said. "I...I didn't know you were coming by today."

His cheeks colored in what she had to admit was a very cute shade of pink. Clearly, he was embarrassed to be seen in such a state, though Virginia couldn't think why. It was no more than she'd expected.

"I thought I'd surprise you," she answered looking around. "I brought donuts for you and Ross. Where is he?"

Virginia moved further into the kitchen wondering if she might find Tristan's assistant hiding behind one of the appliances.

"He broke his leg while we were working in the attic yesterday," Tristan said. "Went to the emergency room. The doctor says he won't be able to work for another few weeks. So...I'm on my own here until I can find someone else."

Virginia turned back to face him. For the first time, she realized just how tired he looked. There were shadows beneath his eyes, his light brown hair was rumpled, and his face looked distinctly worried.

"But, you will find someone, right?" She asked feeling a mixture of pity for Tristan and concern for the project. After all, this was much more than a one-man job. Tristan would surely need help.

"I've been calling all night and this morning, every guy I know," he said. "They're all either busy on other projects, on summer vacation or out with injuries. So, it looks like, for now at least, I'm on my own. Though truthfully, I'm not sure how long I'll be able to keep it up once I get to the bigger stuff."

He moved over to the counter where Virginia had set down the donuts and leaned against it. He stared at the box but didn't seem to have strength left to even lift it open.

Virginia looked at him and felt an old tug in her heart. She'd felt it before, many times when she saw someone else in crisis. Her aunt told her it was her own special gift.

"God gave you a soft heart for other people," Aunt Emily use to say. "That's a strength, not a weakness. When God tugs on your heart and asks you to help someone, you should always listen to him."

Maybe it was the memory of her aunt's voice in her head that made her do what she did next. Maybe she was simply bored with Jason being gone on his business trip and Samantha away at school all day and at work every night lately. Either way, she didn't think too long before saying to Tristan:

"Maybe I could help."

Tristan stopped staring at the unopened box and turned to look at Virginia, his eyes even wider than they had been when she'd stepped into the kitchen one moment before. She could see his mind racing between his initial instinct to say no, mixed with his absolute desperation for a solution to the situation.

"Virginia," he said hesitantly. "It'll be a lot of work, and I wouldn't feel right taking up too much of your time."

Virginia gave him a smile and rolled her eyes.

"Tristan, if I've got time to take surprise trips up here with homemade bakery items in hand, then I've clearly got time to help with the house renovations."

Tristan looked at her thoughtfully. His eyes traveled her body up and down as though trying to decide what type of work she would physically be able to do. Now, it was Virginia's turn to blush.

""Are you sure you want to do this?" Tristan asked.

"Absolutely," she answered confidently. "What do we need to do first?"

With one last skeptical glance, Tristan finally shrugged his shoulders and relented. "Well, what I really need is to tear down this wall right here. It takes two people."

"I take it that's why you were swearing at it when I came in," Virginia said with a grin. Tristan smiled as his cheeks turned flush once more.

"Well," she said, rolling up her sleeves and moving past him to face the stubborn wall "Let's do it."

Tristan gave her a large hammer which she was surprised to find she could swing quite well after a couple of tries. Once they started, it was clear why Tristan had been cursing the kitchen wall. It was particularly stubborn. But, the longer she hammered at it, the easier it became. In fact, once she found a rhythm, it became easier and easier. Eventually, she realized she was enjoying herself. As she tore the wall down she felt a release, she felt strong, capable, she felt amazing! When they were done, she turned to Tristan and exclaimed, "What can we tear down next?!"

"Whoa, slow down there tiger," he laughed. "Next we've gotta move out to the deck." He walked over to the counter where the unopened donut box still lay and flickered her a boyish, hopeful glance. "But I was wondering if maybe we could have a tiny snack break first...? I don't know what's in there, but the smell is so good, I think I'm addicted to it already." Virginia laughed and popped open the cardboard top. Tristan's mouth fell agape at the impressive looking pastries.

"Those look incredible. Where'd you get them?" he gushed, lifting a cream-colored donut with chocolate glaze and a peanut butter crumble to his mouth.

"I make them," Virginia said feeling warmly proud. "Be warned, I'm trying out a new recipe on you."

Tristan nodded excessively while he gave her an emphatic thumbs up and chewed, rolling his eyes in obvious approval. Virginia had to laugh as she took a small bite out of her own. Two and a half donuts later, Tristan's vitality looked restored.

"I have no words for how amazing those are, but I'm pretty sure I could live on them if that gives you an idea." He grabbed up his hammer and gave a little yelp of enthusiasm. "Ready to get to it?" he exclaimed.

"Lead the way," Virginia chorused. She followed Tristan out to the deck with the kind of energy she hadn't felt in years. It seemed strange but, even though she could feel her muscles aching and the sweat running down her brow from the effort it had taken to knock down those walls, she didn't feel tired at all. In fact, she felt invigorated.

"We'll have to remove the rotted wood on the deck," Tristan said. "That means most of the railing will have to go. We'll start with that. Probably get to the lower boards tomorrow."

It turned out that taking the railing of the deck out was much more time consuming and not nearly as fun as tearing down walls. It was tedious work that required pulling the rusty nails from the boards up and out, before setting the rotting planks aside.

Luckily, as they worked, Tristan regaled her with amusing stories from some of the houses he had worked on before this one.

"I learned a lot from my dad," Tristan said. "He worked for a construction company, and he used to do little projects around our house. The first time I broke my arm as a kid was when we were building a fort in the back yard."

"The first time?" Virginia asked pulling a nail up from a board.

"Definitely wasn't the last," Tristan answered. "After my third trip to the emergency room, my mom wanted to put an end to our weekend construction projects, but my dad wouldn't hear of it. 'If we keep the boy from falling down he'll never learn how to get back up.' That's what he always said."

"Can't say I blame your mom," Virginia said imagining what it would be like to take her own hypothetical child to the emergency room every other week. "It can't have been easy on her."

"Yeah, I realize that now," Tristan said. "Still, I'm glad my dad kept me working. If he didn't, I wouldn't be doing what I'm doing now."

"You do seem to enjoy it," Virginia said. He turned and grinned at her, blue eyes glinting through a face full of sweat. Virginia had to admit that it looked good on him. The hard work, sweat, and sheer physical effort. It was made more appealing by the fact that he truly did seem to enjoy it.

Even in the relatively hot afternoon sun, he never complained. In fact, the warmer and more difficult the work got, the more excited he became.

"I was thinking of replacing the wood out here with some local pine," he said eagerly surveying the outer edge of the now rail-less deck. "It would look better with the surroundings than the oak that's here now."

Virginia, who was not quite finished with the rails on her side gave a grunt of approval as she ripped a particularly stubborn nail from the oak finish. She was standing at an odd angle trying with all her might to budge the things, and when it finally came out, she felt herself falling forward. With a little scream, she landed face first on the forest floor beneath the deck; her forehead hit against something small but very hard. Something that felt like it was made of metal.

"Virginia!" she heard Tristan call out. His footsteps sounded on the deck rushing over to her. "Virginia, are you ok?"

She pushed herself up from the ground and was about to answer when the piece of metal that had hit her forehead, gleaming in the sun, caught her eye. She reached down slowly and, wiping the dirt off of it, picked it up.

"Virgina? Are you-"

"My key," she said in surprise, barely hearing Tristan's voice on the deck above her.

"Your...your what?" he asked.

She grasped the little bronze key with an ornate handle similar to the house key, in the palm of her hand and pushed herself up.

"I buried it years ago," Virginia said turning to Tristan, "So my sister wouldn't find it."

He reached down and offered her a hand up, still looking perplexed. She grasped his hand and allowed him to pull her up to the porch, the other hand still clutching the cool bronze.

"Is it a key to the house?" Tristan asked. "Why wouldn't you want your sister to find that?"

"No," Virginia said with a little chuckle as she opened her palm and showed the key to him. It was much, much smaller than a house key. Smaller even than a mail key. "It was the key to my diary."

"You had a key for your diary?" Tristan asked. He still looked confused, but amused at the same time, as though he thought it might be some kind of joke.

"Lots of girls have locks for their diaries," Virginia said. "That way no one can see what we write about."

"And what kind of stuff did you write about?" Tristan asked. She looked him in the eye, and he immediately shifted his gaze away from her, his cheeks turning that embarrassed pink color. "I mean, I'm just curious. I didn't have any sisters or anything so, I don't really know about that kind of stuff."

He looked so adorably awkward that she just had to laugh before answering.

"That's ok," she said. "It's not a big secret or anything. Mostly I just wrote about things that were going on in my life. Really, if anyone had read it, they would have been bored to tears. Though, I guess I did write about boys sometimes."

"Boys?" Tristan asked.

"Of course," Virginia said. "I was twelve. Almost thirteen. That's what girls that age start to think about. Isn't that true for boys too?"

Tristan shrugged, obviously more intrigued now than embarrassed.

"I guess," he said, "but we certainly didn't write about it in diaries."

"No," Virginia said with a teasing smile. "You probably just kept it all bottled up inside until it exploded in a fit of unexpected rage."

"What can I say?" Tristan said jokingly. "That's the manly way."

There was only a bit more work left to do on the deck. Once they were finished, the sun was starting to hang low in the sky. Virginia knew that the last ferry of the day would be making its way towards the dock any minute.

"I'd better start heading out," she said. "I don't want to miss the last boat."

"I'll drive you," Tristan said, gathering his tools. "The dock's on the way to my apartment anyway."

"Thanks," Virginia said. As they climbed into Tristan's small blue truck, she began to realize just how little she actually knew about him.

Despite the stories he'd told her about his dad as they worked, he offered no specifics. He didn't tell her where the house with the tree fort was located. She didn't know if he'd grown up in Sweetwater or in Seattle or even in the state of Washington. And, now, as she watched him drive through the small downtown and make his way to the ferry, she couldn't help but feel an intense curiosity about this man beside her.

"So," she began as they passed the old ice cream parlor, feeling a bit awkward. "I guess you grew up on the island."

"No, actually," he answered. "I grew up in Northern California. A little town called Thousand Oaks."

"Oh," she answered turning to him now more than curious. She'd assumed that he was a local boy. "How did you find yourself here then?"

His face suddenly fell, and she saw his lips purse closed. There seemed a longer than normal pause before he answered.

"I...um...well, I graduated high school, and a buddy of mine was planning to move to Seattle. Asked if I wanted to join him. I said yes," he answered.

"So, that's how you got to Washington," she said, "but what made you move all the way out to the island?"

Now his cheeks turned red, but it wasn't with the kind of adorable embarrassment she'd seen earlier. This looked a lot more like shame.

"I just...I guess I just wanted a change," he said.

She knew immediately that it wasn't the full story. Still, she also knew that it was best not to press. After all, she was his employer. Plenty of employers didn't know their employee's life stories. And that was fine.

In fact, it was often better that way. They drove in silence for several more minutes until they arrived at the dock just as the last ferry was pulling up, packed with rush-hour passengers commuting home to the island from the city.

"Thanks for helping out today," he said. "I really appreciate it."

"No problem. It was fun," she answered genuinely. "Will you need someone to help out tomorrow?"

He looked at her, his eyebrow cocking slightly.

"You...want to help out tomorrow too?" he questioned.

"Yeah," she answered. "I haven't got anything else to do. Besides, like you said. It's a two-man job."

"Oh. Ok," he said slowly as though still trying to process what she was saying. "Could...could you be here by nine?"

"Absolutely," Virginia said.

"Ok then," he answered with an impressed smile. "I'll see you tomorrow."

They said goodbye and Virginia made her way onto the ferry, walking much more quickly than she had getting off.

She hadn't felt this good about her day in years. Maybe it was that she spent the entire day being productive. Maybe she just needed more exercise like the kind she got when she worked on the house.

No matter the reason, as she stood on the deck watching the sun sink lower in the sky over the bay, Virginia couldn't help the consuming smile that crept across her face.

CHAPTER SEVEN

*V*irginia ended up going out to Sweetwater almost every weekday she could for the next several months. Each time, she found herself parking her car at the bay and taking the ferry over as a foot passenger.

She found that she enjoyed the walk through the woods and up to the cottage much more than she did the drive. Even if the drive did take her through the quaint downtown, the woods gave her space and time to think. It made her concede that her sister was right about Virginia's preference for country over city life.

She was starting to realize that she felt more at home among the hills and pine trees of Sweetwater than she did amidst the concrete, traffic, and noise of Seattle. Beyond that, her appearance had even begun to show improvement.

Three weeks after she'd started working on the renovations with Tristan, she noticed that she'd lost a bit of weight. The sun had given her pale skin a tan and put the healthy glow that she'd had when she was younger back into her cheeks.

Even Jason had noticed a difference.

"I see you've finally started on that diet," he'd quipped one night at dinner, "It's paying off."

"Thanks," Virginia said, "but I've been eating normally. Just been walking a lot. And working on the house has really helped."

He'd paused at that and looked down at his plate. For a moment, Virginia thought that she'd said something wrong, or that he wasn't all that pleased to hear her mention her work on the island.

A moment later, however, he looked back at her with that same charming smile that was so familiar.

"I've always said you should exercise more," he said. "I mean, that's how I've stayed in such good shape."

He set down his fork and pulled up the sleeve of his shirt. Virginia had to stop herself from rolling her eyes. She had seem this move before.

Sure enough, with a chuckle, he flexed his still very firm bicep.

"See? Just look at that," he said.

"I know," Virginia answered with a smile, trying to hide her weariness. "Solid as a rock."

"Solid as a rock," she repeated. They didn't mention the island or the house the rest of the night.

Yet Jason's indifference, for a reason Virginia could not explain, seemed to spur on her trips to Sweetwater. She almost felt as though she were doing something rebellious by going to help Tristan every day. Which, of course, she wasn't. She and Tristan didn't do anything other than work on the house while she was there. Of course, he did occasionally drive her back to the ferry. And now that many of the primary renovations were nearly completed, they had gone into town together to look at furniture a few times. But that was only because there was no one else to furniture shop with. Sam had no desire to visit the island and Jason always claimed he was much too busy with work to come with her. This was something that even Tristan took note of as they walked through the antique shop looking at several wooden wardrobes that might fit into the master suite.

"You know," he said. "I just realized I've yet to meet this famous boyfriend of yours."

"Jason's an account executive for a television station," Virginia answered running her hand down the front of a handsome set of drawers made of chestnut. "They keep him pretty busy there."

"Hmm," Tristan said. Though, Virginia was certain there was something behind his vocalization. She turned from the chestnut set of drawers to her companion.

"What does that mean?" she asked, noticing too late how defensive her voice sounded.

"Nothing," Tristan said though he didn't look at her. Instead, he turned his gaze to a nice pine wood desk beside an old bookshelf.

"Just...if my girlfriend was working on a house that meant this much to her...I don't know. I'd at least want to come and see it once or twice."

Virginia, not sure at all how to answer that, turned back to her wardrobe.

They didn't speak for several moments, both pretending to examine their own individual artifacts. Though Virginia had a feeling that Tristan was about as focused on his desk as she was on the wardrobe in front of her.

"You know, I've been wondering," Tristan said finally turning to her. "Whatever happened to the diary? You know, the one the key belonged to?"

"Oh, I think I threw it away," Virginia said. Glad that the subject of Jason had apparently been dropped. "See, after I buried the key, I forgot where I put it. And, a diary without a lock is pretty useless. So, I stopped using it. Eventually, I think I must have gotten rid of it."

"You just...got rid of your innermost thoughts?" Tristan said turning from his desk to look at her as though she were insane. "Do most girls do that with their diaries?"

"I don't know, to tell you the truth," Virginia said. "Some keep them, I guess. But, like I said, my teenage thoughts were not exactly noteworthy. Mostly it was stuff about the weather, crushes, which were probably on TV characters, some early sketches."

"Sketches?" he asked interestedly. "Like drawings?"

"Yeah," she answered. "I've always liked painting and drawing. I even got my major in art history in school. I really started sketching up here during the summers."

"So, you're an artist," he said. "And here I thought you were just a trust fund kid with a penchant for baking."

With a laugh, she reached over and swatted him playfully on the arm. He side stepped away from it with a chuckle of his own.

"You know I teach art at the elementary schools," she said.

"Well, yeah," he said. "But, anybody could do that. I didn't know that you really drew stuff."

Virginia rolled her eyes at him. The idea that anybody could teach art, even to young children, was an idea she'd been fighting against since she took up her career.

"Why'd you stop?" Tristan asked.

"Who says I stopped?" Virginia said, not looking at him. She felt heat race through her features when she realized that Tristan had come closer to the truth than even she realized.

"You never talk about painting," he said. "Or drawing. You talk about baking, about your boyfriend, about your aunt and your sister. But, you never talk about art."

She went silent for a moment as she found herself fiddling with the handle of the wardrobe. Not for any particular reason, just to give her hands something to do while she tried her best to think of a way to answer him.

"Well, I...I mean...I did think about going to graduate school," she said. "Getting a master's degree. I even wanted to teach college at one point, but then Jason decided to go to graduate school, and I had to get a job to help him out."

"But, he's got a job now, doesn't he?" Tristan asked. "Have you thought about going back to school now?"

Virginia, still unsure what to say, simply shrugged.

"I don't know," she answered as honestly as she could. "Maybe when the house is finished. Then at least I'll have some time to think about it."

There was a moment of silence. Eventually, Virginia dared to look from the wardrobe handle back up to Tristan. He was staring at her, blue eyes narrowed and focused. It reminded her vaguely of the way Samantha looked at her when she knew Virginia was hiding something. Maybe it was the sudden resemblance between them that made Virginia slightly unsettled.

Finally, the look disappeared from Tristan's face, and he smiled at her.

"Well, I'm happy to keep you busy until then," he said.

"I'm happy to be busy," Virginia answered. "There are only so many donuts I can bake, after all."

They decided that they would buy the chestnut wardrobe for the master suite. Virginia also bought a few odds and ends that she would put in the bedroom. It was mostly antique doll furniture, the kind she'd loved when she was a little girl. The kind her aunt definitely would have approved of being in her home.

Tristan arranged for the wardrobe to be delivered to the house the next day, and Virginia took her purchases with her in two bags.

"Do you want me to keep that stuff in the truck?" Tristan asked. They would be driving right from the antique store to the ferry at the dock. While the packages were not particularly heavy, they were awkwardly wrapped.

"No," Virginia answered feeling determined. "I want my sister to see the doll furniture set I got. I know she'll love it. It's just like the one we used to have when we were little."

"As long as you're sure it'll be ok," Tristan said looking skeptically as she tried to maneuver the packages into the truck cab in a way that would leave room for her to sit. No matter how she tried, the unwieldy bags did not seem to want to make room for her.

Finally, she gave up and agreed to put them in the bed of the truck. Tristan popped that tailgate down and gave Virginia a hand as she climbed into the back of the pickup. He handed her up the bags, then stood back and watched. Virginia took the two bungee cords Tristan had and crisscrossed them over the packages, securing them to the truck tie down hooks. Tristan stood with his arms crossed, watching with an inner amusement as she scurried back and forth, locking her goods in place. When she was satisfied that they wouldn't blow away once they started driving, Virginia stood up, proudly placed her hands on her hips and proclaimed, "We are good to go."

She made her way to the back of the cab, but before Tristan could move to help her down, she hopped off the back of the tailgate and down to the ground. As Virginia's feet landed on the loose, rocky asphalt, her shoe caught on the gravel and sent her flying forward. Tristan barely had time to open his arms to catch her.

Luckily, he was quick enough and grabbed her just before she hit the ground. His arms flung around and secured her tightly. Virginia quickly scrambled to regain her footing, gripping Tristan's strong shoulders to pull herself up. She tried to hide her embarrassment as she stood to thank him. As soon as she was upright, her breath caught immediately in her chest. He was much closer than she'd anticipated and his eyes were once again, giving her that penetrating, searching look. Only this time, they didn't remind her of her sister's at all. Virginia blinked, then forced a chuckle.

"Thanks," she said slowly while straightening up and moving slightly away from him.

Tristan re-opened her car door and helped her in. She tried to busy herself so as not to watch him walk around to get in on the other side. They didn't speak on the short drive back up to the ferry, but the entire way there Virginia felt that tug in her chest. She knew this was the same one her Aunt Emily had told her to listen to.

She didn't know what it was saying, exactly. And even if she did guess, she thought, she wasn't sure that she should listen to it this time.

As she said goodbye to Tristan, took her packages and made her way onto the ferry, the tug in her chest grew stronger. And strangely, so did the memory of Tristan's secure arms wrapped around her.

CHAPTER EIGHT

"You're coming on the camping trip, right? None of your bags look packed yet."

Virginia turned from the skillet where the tofu stir-fry for dinner was cooking to look at her sister. Samantha was leaning against the kitchen counter, purse in hand, ready to head out the front door as soon as Jason showed up.

"I don't know," Virginia said turning back to the stovetop. "Tristan might need me on the island. We've still got a decent amount of work to do on the house to finish it up."

"Turning down the annual cousins camping trip to do manual labor?" Samantha said a teasing note of surprise in her voice. "Either you really like this contractor guy, or you're thinking about going into the construction business."

Virginia turned to Samantha over her shoulder and gave her sister a half-hearted glare. Sam had been teasing Virginia about Tristan for the past week, ever since Virginia had shown her the doll furniture and told her how Tristan had helped to pick it out.

"You know I've always liked interior decorating," Virginia said. "And, who knows, maybe I will start up another side business."

"I'd have thought you were too busy for that," Sam said. "Between baking and your job during the school year."

"I'm free during the summer, though," Virginia said. "And I have a pretty reliable schedule for my donut business. Most of my clients have regular, standing orders. So it's not like I've got to be constantly baking."

She turned back to peer at her sister just in time to hear Samantha let out a scoff.

"Still," Sam said. "You never miss the camping trip. Not even when you do have donut orders to fill. You can try to hide it all you want, but there's something different going on at that house."

Virginia couldn't help but smile when she thought about that and she realized she didn't have any argument against it. It was true that being back at her Aunt's house, working so hard on it, seemed to have sparked something in her. She was much more cheerful now that she was busy arranging the rooms for showing and helping Tristan fix up the attic.

"It is coming along nicely," Virginia said. "In fact, now that we've got some of the furniture in, it looks better than it did when Aunt Emily was living there."

"Well, Aunt Emily had it cluttered with little doilies and stuffed animals," Samantha said. "I'm sure you've got a better eye than that."

Virginia rolled her eyes to herself again. It was true that Aunt Emily had a tendency to collect what most people would call clutter. And it was true that Virginia, while keeping the original aesthetic, had done away with some of the frills and Victorian dolls that her Aunt had been fond of. But she still liked Aunt Emily's taste. She'd always been more fond of it than her sister.

"And, I'm sure your contractor friend is helping a lot too," Samantha said slyly. Virginia felt another blush come into her cheeks. This was the most annoying thing about Samantha's teasing. Her sly implications about Virginia and Tristan.

What was worse, Virginia was never quite sure how to answer them. Of course she'd told Samantha they were just good friends, which was the absolute truth, but every time Virginia made the assertion, it sounded fake. Hollow even to her own ears. She and Tristan had truly bonded as friends, as really good friends.

Finally, Virginia settled on an answer that might put both Samantha's teasing as well as her own strange fears to rest.

"You should come by one weekend and check the house out," Virginia said. "It's been awhile since you've been to the island. It's also been awhile since you've had a date. And Tristan is cute. Not to mention single."

Sam scoffed as Virginia took the stir fry off the heat and allowed it to cool.

"Have you ever known me to be attracted to the handyman type?" Sam asked. Virginia had to admit that Samantha had a point about that. Despite her derision of Jason as "pretty boy," Samantha had always been attracted to men of Jason's type. Clean cut city boys who had rarely if ever done any actual work with their hands.

"Besides, I wouldn't want to take him away from my big sister," Sam said with another teasing smile. Virginia cursed herself silently when she felt her cheeks begin to grow warm again. She took a breath and made a vain attempt to laugh it off.

"That's not a great thing to joke about with a girl who's about to get engaged," Virginia said.

Sam rolled her eyes.

"Has pretty boy put a ring on your finger yet?" She asked.

"Not yet," Virginia admitted. "But, when the house is sold he-"

"Do you know that? For sure?" Sam asked. She was giving Virginia that pointed look. The one where she narrowed her eyes and tried to look through her.

Virginia tried to think of some argument, a definitive come back she could make, but realized that she had none. The truth was, she couldn't be absolutely sure that Jason would propose once the house was sold. They'd talked about it as if it were a fact for the last few years, but, nothing seemed definite.

Still, Virginia knew she had to come up with some answer. She opened her mouth, hoping that something would come to her. Luckily, at that moment, the doorbell rang.

Silently thanking Jason's timing, she moved to the front door while her sister followed, purse in hand, ready for work.

"Hey babe," Jason said when she opened the door. She was slightly embarrassed, but not shocked to see that he had, once again brought his own six-pack.

"Hi Jason," Virginia said pulling him inside and giving him a quick peck on the lips.

"Hey Sam," Jason said pulling away from Virginia at seeing her sister behind her. "What's up?"

Samantha didn't answer. She simply glared at him for a moment before pushing past him to the front door.

"Let me know if you're coming on the camping trip," Samantha said to Virginia over her shoulder as she made her way down the driveway.

"That's right," Jason said as Virginia closed the door behind her sister. "That camping trip with your cousins is this weekend, right?"

"Yeah," Virginia answered, leading Jason to the kitchen. Every year she, Samantha and two of their cousins from her dad's side got together at a state park for a girls camping trip. These were always a lot of fun, and Virginia had never missed one before, which was why she felt slightly guilty about the desire to skip this year.

"It's good timing," Jason said sitting down at the table and waiting to be served. "I'm going on another business trip to Portland."

"I thought you just went there a couple weeks ago," Virginia said surprised.

"Yeah," Jason said, "but the client wanted more time to think about the deal. So, a group of us have to go back this weekend. But if you're on that girls camping trip, I won't feel too guilty about leaving you alone again."

Virginia turned and offered him a weak smile as she moved to the table with both their plates in hand. She thought about not telling him her plans to go to the cottage instead. After all, if he was going to be gone, he wouldn't really care where she was. And there was no chance of Samantha telling him. She never gave Jason the time of day anyway.

Her conscience grappled over the idea for a minute, then decided that felt too much like a kind of betrayal. She'd always prided herself on being completely honest with Jason, and she was determined that wouldn't stop now.

Taking a deep breath as she sat down to her dinner, she told him the truth.

"Actually," Virginia said. "I'm not sure if I'm going to go on the camping trip this weekend."

"What do you mean?" Jason asked, taking a bite of tofu. "You go every year."

"Well...yeah," Virginia said, "but we've still got some work to do on the house. I'm doing the interior decorating now, and I don't want to leave Tristan there all weekend with a whole bunch of work still to do."

The casual smile on his face faded at the mention of Tristan. His expression seemed to darken as he put his fork down on his plate.

"You've been spending a lot of time up there already, haven't you?" he asked.

"Well, as I've said, since Ross, Tristan's assistant got hurt, I've kind of stepped up to fill in," she said. "We've done a good job all things considered. We should have it done within the next couple weeks or so."

"And you really think spending the weekend there is going to speed things up?" he asked skeptically. Virginia looked across the table and gave him a reassuring smile.

"I won't be spending the weekend there," Virginia said. "Just Saturday during the day. I'd be back here on the last ferry."

His skeptical expression didn't change. His hazel eyes met hers, and they were darker than Virginia had ever seen them. For the first time, they didn't dance or pierce her heart, there was something sulky and almost jealous in them.

"I was actually going to ask you to come up and see it this weekend," Virginia said hurriedly. It was true, she had thought about asking Jason to come up with her to look at the house. He hadn't seen it at all since they'd started doing renovations.

"But I didn't realize you had a work trip," Virginia said.

"I can't get out of it," Jason snapped, a peevish note in his voice.

"I know that," Virginia said, "I didn't ask you to. You can come up some other weekend maybe. Or once we're finished."

With slight hesitation, she glanced back up at him. That dark expression was still there. For some reason, it made Virginia shiver unpleasantly.

"I still think he's making you do too much work," Jason said finally pulling his eyes back to his plate. "You're paying him, remember? Not the other way around."

"I like doing it," Virginia said, though she noticed her voice was smaller than she'd meant for it to be. "Besides, like I said, we're almost done."

"Well I'm glad of that," Jason said. He didn't look at her, but stabbed his food a little more forcefully than was necessary.

Virginia watched her boyfriend the rest of the night, noting what a strange mood talk of the house had seemed to put him in. If she didn't know better, she would have guessed that Jason was jealous. Jealous of the time she was spending with the house, and with Tristan.

That was surprising, to say the least. Jason had always been self-assured, brimming with confidence. This new side of him was surly and possessive, and she wasn't at all sure that she liked it.

Even though they didn't mention the house or the island again, she felt that same surly attitude from him the rest of the evening. No matter what she did or said, she couldn't seem to shake him from it.

When he went home that night, for the first time since they'd been together, she was glad to see him go.

CHAPTER NINE

*O*n Friday night, Virginia told her sister that she wouldn't be coming on the camping trip. Samantha, to Virginia's surprise, was not at all upset by her sister's announcement.

"Say hi to your friend for me," Sam said with a wink as she left the house on Saturday morning. Virginia rolled her eyes as her sister closed the door, but felt her cheeks grow warm.

As soon as Sam left, she packed up another batch of donuts she'd baked to share with Tristan for breakfast and headed to the ferry.

It was only a little past nine in the morning when she arrived on the island. The normally warm August sun was still fairly low in the sky, its power not as strong as it would be in the afternoon. This, combined with the light mist that still hung along the wooded path to the cottage, made the walk quite pleasant. Virginia stopped several times to watch a hare cross the path in front of her as quickly as it could. She remembered naming the furry brown creatures when she was younger. She and her sister even developed ways to tell them apart, then named them accordingly.

When she arrived at the cottage, she moved quickly past the familiar sight of Tristan's truck parked out front and hurried inside.

Looking around the hallway, she couldn't help but smile at their handy work. The newly restored floor gleamed as the light from the front windows shined down onto it. The smell of sawdust had almost completely disappeared from the rooms around her. The walls in the family room had been expanded, and the antique accent pieces gave the entire house a cozy feel.

This feeling was complimented by the dark, rich scent of coffee wafting from the kitchen. Virginia lifted her head and followed the scent, feeling a bit like a character in a cartoon led on to some mischief by the smell of apple pie.

When she moved into the kitchen, she found Tristan fiddling with an old-fashioned coffee maker on the counter.

"I hope you made enough for everyone," she quipped. As usual, he jumped when she spoke before turning around and giving her a wide smile.

"Are those donuts?" he asked immediately.

"Well, they're not Brussels sprouts," she said moving to set the box on the kitchen counter. His smile widened, and she nearly laughed as he rushed to the box.

"Virginia, you are a lifesaver," he said opening the box eagerly and immediately stuffing a glazed donut into his mouth.

This time, Virginia let out a full laugh.

"You'd think you hadn't eaten in a week," Virginia said.

"I feel like I haven't," Tristan answered. "Spent most of last night working in the attic. I had to replace most of the wood before I could put in the insulation. Didn't get home until almost nine o'clock."

When she looked into his face, she could tell immediately that this was the truth. Though his smile was just as bright as normal, it was a bit weary and, once again, he looked slightly worse for wear.

"Did you get it finished?" Virginia asked.

"Not quite," he said. "Honestly, I wouldn't mind some help in there this morning."

Virginia, who had learned early on not to be picky about the tasks she was handed in this project, none the less, put on a teasing skeptical smirk.

"Is this the same attic where your last assistant broke his leg?" she asked.

"That depends," he said swallowing a bit of donut and leaning towards her across the counter. "Are you scared to go up there?"

Virginia looked into his eyes and felt another little tug in her heart. They were not close together. Definitely not as close as they had been the night he'd kept her from falling on her face in his truck. Even so, that same tug was there. It made her feel strange and more than a little uncomfortable.

Finally, she gave a nervous laugh and backed away from him.

"I've been up there plenty of times," Virginia said. "Nothing about this house scares me anymore. But, if I do break my leg, it's coming out of your check."

Tristan let out a laugh as well, and Virginia thought it sounded almost as nervous as her own.

"Fair enough," he said.

After two cups of coffee and several donuts; they headed up to the attic. She couldn't help but marvel at the thought that Tristan had eaten almost half the box by himself. As it turned out, Tristan had done a good bit of the insulation the night before. The rest took the two of them no more than a couple of hours. By lunch time, they were back in the kitchen eating two corned beef sandwiches that Tristan had packed.

"So, what needs doing after lunch?" Virginia asked.

"Well," Tristan said taking a sip from his bottle of water which he'd also brought in his lunch sack. "The only thing we've really got left to do are the two small bedrooms. And that's not going to require any real manual work. It's just going through the old stuff in there, deciding what you want to keep, and what needs to be boxed up."

"Sounds right up my alley," Virginia said. Feeling a tiny thrill of excitement. Ever since they started this project, she'd been waiting to go back into her old bedroom. She couldn't help but feel curious about how many of her old childhood treasures Aunt Emily had decided to keep.

She soon discovered that there was more in her old bedroom than she ever could have imagined. Almost everything she remembered from her childhood was stacked in boxes inside the closet whose door was falling off its hinges.

"I'll fix the closet if you promise to sort through the boxes," Tristan said. Virginia was more than happy to agree.

This task took a lot longer than either of them had expected. Each box brought on a flood of new memories. Virginia would come to a sudden stop and exclaim excitedly each time she came across another little treasure.

"Oh! My jewelry box!" she said pulling out a handsome brown chestnut box that had been a present from her Aunt Emily when she was only eight years old. "My old bracelets are still in here."

She happily moved through a pile of clunky costume bracelets. Most of them in lavishly bright colors. Suddenly, she had an idea.

"You know, I think I finally know where that key's going to go," she said fishing the small diary key that she'd taken to keeping in her pocket.

"You're going to put the key in the jewelry box even though the diary's been thrown away?" Tristan asked with a small chuckle.

"It's a memory," Virginia said with a shrug. "And, since I can't read my diary anymore, this is all I've got left of it. I might as well keep it."

"The last memory of all your innermost thoughts as a teenage girl?" Tristan asked as he watched Virginia set the key amidst her bracelets and close the jewelry box lid.

"Something like that," she said.

"You're lucky, you know," he said. "My parents threw all this kind of stuff out when I moved away."

"Why would they do that?" Virginia asked curiously. She knew that both her aunt and her mother had held on fervently to Virginia and Samantha's childhood toys. They didn't go in the trash bin until Sam and Virginia said they should.

When she looked at Tristan, his face sunk slightly.

"Well, it was my dad, mostly," he said. "See...he and I didn't part on great terms. He wanted me to stay and go into his business. I wanted to work on my own. He still hasn't really forgiven me, I don't think."

Virginia saw Tristan's lips purse closed and his eyes dart to the side. It was apparent that this was a subject he wasn't particularly keen on. Virginia couldn't blame him, she knew fighting with your parents was always painful.

Instead of answering, she grabbed hold of another box.

"Oh my gosh! I'd forgotten about this," she said when she saw what was written in black sharpie on the side of the brown cardboard.

"What is it?" Tristan asked, thankful for a change in subject.

"Virginia Ellis Originals," she read from the side of the box. "It's what my aunt called my paintings. She said they were going to be worth a lot of money one day."

Carefully, she opened the box, and another altogether different tug pulled at her heart when she saw the painting beneath the lid.

It was a landscape, detailing the view of the woods from the deck, there was even a hint of greenish blue, indicating the ocean beyond the trees. Virginia remembered sitting out on the deck for weeks one summer, carefully working on detailing the leaves of the trees, the color of the sky. She could even see the original, bright wood of the deck, just as it was in its prime.

"Can I see?" Tristan asked. Virginia looked up at him startled. She'd been so lost in the memory that she had nearly forgotten anyone else was in the room. Shaking herself awake, she passed the framed picture over to Tristan.

He took it gently and looked down at it. His eyes broadened, and he tilted his head curiously. He took his hand and moved it over the frame as though he was trying to memorize it.

"This is...this is really good!" he said surprised.

"Thanks," Virginia said. "It's one of my first paintings. Not perfect, but I loved doing it."

"You can tell," he said. "The care definitely comes through."

He continued to look at it thoughtfully as though making some kind of decision.

"I think we should hang it in here," he said finally.

"What?" Virginia asked stunned.

"Why not?" Tristan asked. "We were going to need to buy some paintings for this room anyway. Why not hang one that's personal. That means something to the house."

Her first instinct was to say 'no.' She'd always been very cautious about who she showed her work to.

Then she remembered Aunt Emily. Her aunt had proudly displayed her nieces work not only in the bedrooms but also in the family and living rooms. Often despite Virginia's protests. If she wanted this house to be a tribute to her Aunt's memory, she had to admit that this was part of it. Besides, it was only for show. The pictures would come down when the new owners moved in.

"I...I guess we could," she said. "It'll save us money on art anyway."

They spent the rest of the afternoon hanging pictures. Tristan, like her aunt, insisted that Virginia's prints be hung not only in the bedrooms, but several other rooms as well. In the end, Virginia had to admit they added some personality to the place. Plus, they were specific to Sweetwater and the time she spent here; they meant something.

Tristan and Virginia worked hanging the pictures and sorting through boxes well into the late afternoon. By the time the last box was packed away in the newly insulated attic, Virginia had completely lost track of time. It took Tristan, or rather Tristan's appetite, to remind her.

"We should probably get something for dinner soon," he said. "There's a Chinese take-out place not far away."

The mention of dinner made Virginia pause as she walked down the stairs from the attic.

"Dinner? What time is it?" she asked.

"It's almost six," Tristan said.

Virginia's eyes widened, and her heart began to pound. The ferry. She'd missed the ferry.

"I...I didn't plan on staying that long!" She said. "The ferry..."

"What?" Tristan asked. "The last one doesn't leave until seven, right?"

"On weekdays," Virginia reminded him. "The last one is at five thirty on Saturdays."

His face fell as he realized her predicament.

"Well...I mean I know it's a ways but...I've got the truck. I could drive you back."

Virginia shook her head.

"They're doing construction on the bridge tonight," she said. "I saw the notice this morning on the ferry coming over."

Tristan furrowed his brow in thought, even as Virginia began to panic. As she ran through her list of options, the reality set in that there was no way she was getting off the island tonight.

Apparently, Tristan agreed with her internal assessment.

"How about this?" Tristan said thoughtfully. "I've got a buddy who runs a bed and breakfast in town. I'll call him and see if he can get you a room for tonight."

"Are you sure?" Virginia asked. "I...I wouldn't want to put anybody out."

"Don't worry about it," he said. "With that bridge, stuff like this happens all the time. Do you want me to give him a call?"

Though Virginia knew she didn't have much choice, she still hesitated. It was true that Jason was gone for the weekend, and so was her sister. There was no real reason to go home, but she'd told Jason that she wasn't going to spend the night on the island.

No matter what else she did, she had always said that she would never break a promise, even an implied one, to her boyfriend. Still, now, there didn't seem to be any way to avoid it.

"Sure," Virginia answered in a slightly defeated tone.

She slumped down on the comfortable, worn in couch she had purchased for the living room, while she listened to Tristan talk to his buddy on the phone. It wasn't long before they appeared to have reached an agreement.

"Great, thanks man," Tristan said before coming back into the room.

"Good news," he said. "My friend says he had someone cancel on him just this morning so, they've got a room open! They said you can head down to check in any time before eight o'clock."

"Well then," she said, rallying her mood. "Sounds like there's time to order Chinese after all."

They ordered takeout and Virginia set up her iPad on the coffee table so that they could watch a movie on her Netflix account. As there was no Wi-Fi set up at the cottage, she had to use her data but, she found she didn't care.

She picked a goofy comedy. The same kind that she used to watch with her aunt and sister during summers at the cottage. In fact, as she laughed out loud with Tristan on the couch, she couldn't help but think that, if they were eating frozen pizza instead of Chinese, she might as well have been back in her aunt's old living room watching VHS tapes on the little television screen.

The sun had begun to sink deep down in the sky by the time the movie finished.

"You'd better start heading down the hill if you're going to make it to the bed and breakfast by eight," Tristan said. "I can drive you if you like."

"No thanks," Virginia answered feeling much more energetic than she'd felt that morning. "I think I'm in the mood to walk."

"In that case," Tristan said after a beat, "I'll walk with you."

"You don't have to do that," Virginia said with a small chuckle.

"I know I don't have to," Tristan answered. "But, I don't like the thought of you stranded in Sweetwater on your own. Besides, I could use a good walk."

Seeing no need and feeling no desire to argue anymore against his offer, Virginia accepted, and the two of them headed down the hill towards town.

"Not many people out tonight," Virginia noted. "Saturday night, you'd think there'd be more activity. Even in a small town like this."

"It's actually more active on Friday night than Saturday," Tristan said. "A lot of people go to church on Sunday mornings here."

"I take it you do too," Virginia asked. "That's why you never work on Sundays I was assuming."

"I try to go pretty faithfully," Tristan said. "I thought Amanda may have mentioned it to you. She goes to the same church I do."

"She did say something about it," Virginia said. They walked along in silence for a good while. For some reason, the talk of church had sparked a guilty little twitch in her heart. It reminded her of the church her aunt used to take them to on Sunday mornings on the Island. It also reminded her of how infrequently she went to church anymore. She had one that she visited occasionally, maybe once every couple of months. It was nice, small and very traditional. When she went, she always felt as though she was the youngest person in the congregation. The fact that neither her sister nor her boyfriend was ever willing to go with her made the motivation to attend more difficult.

It suddenly struck her that while she was on the island working on her aunt's house, she had a feeling she owed it to Aunt Emily to go to a church service, for old time sake, if nothing else.

"So...what church do you go to?" Virginia asked. "Amanda never told me."

89

"Morning Star Bible," Tristan said. "It's a really small church. We actually meet in the old movie theater just two blocks from the bed and breakfast."

"Church in a movie theater?" she asked raising an eyebrow. Tristan shrugged.

"The pastor didn't have enough money to build a new place, and no one was using the theater," he said. "Besides, it seems to work well for us."

Virginia nodded and stared straight ahead as they walked. She felt strangely hesitant to ask Tristan what she knew she wanted to.

"So...what time does the service start tomorrow?" she asked finally.

He turned to her and even in the dying light of the sun she saw his eyebrow one raise slightly.

"Do you...want to come?" he asked.

"Sure," Virginia answered. "I haven't been to church in a while and it's always in the back of my head that I want to go. It would be a pretty good silver lining to getting stuck, right? That is...if it would be ok."

Tristan looked down, the corner of his lips twitching slightly in thought. He seemed just as hesitant to accept her offer to attend the church with him as she was to ask him if she could. Finally, she saw some kind of decision come into his eyes as he looked back over at her.

"Why not?" he said. "Service starts at ten. I'll come pick you up around nine thirty. We can walk over together."

"Sounds good," she said.

They reached the bed and breakfast which was tucked into a little house between two shops on the main street. An older, thin gentleman with gray hair greeted them.

"Frankly dear, I'm happy to have another guest," he said as Virginia signed in for her key. "If you hadn't come along it would be the third night in a row that room's gone unused."

As the owner left the front desk to get Virginia's key from a hook in the back, she turned to Tristan.

"So, I guess I'll see you in the morning," she said. Even though she tried her best to make the farewell sound light and friendly, she couldn't help an odd shaking sound in her voice. She wasn't quite sure where it had come from.

"Yeah, see you then," Tristan said. For some odd reason, the shaking sound had come into his voice, too. He didn't move, but stood in the doorway looking at her oddly, as though he wanted to say something else, but wasn't sure if he should.

Finally, he seemed to decide against it. Instead of saying anything more, he simply gave her a tight-lipped smile and a nod before moving out the door.

Without thinking about it, Virginia moved to the window in the front lobby of the bed and breakfast and watched Tristan move down the street and back up the hill. The setting sun casting a long, dark golden shadow behind him as he moved.

CHAPTER TEN

*A*s promised, Tristan met Virginia at the front of the bed and breakfast at nine thirty, and they headed up the street together.

"I didn't have anything very nice," Virginia said reluctantly. "They let me use their washer and dryer last night for my jeans and t-shirt. But, I know it's not exactly church appropriate."

To her surprise, Tristan laughed.

"Trust me," he said. "It's perfectly appropriate for this church."

When they reached the building, Virginia could see what he meant. Everyone there seemed to be in blue jeans and t-shirts. Some women were in dresses or skirts but, these were very much the minority.

People milled around the lobby of the movie theater talking and laughing as they sipped on free coffee from Styrofoam cups or nibbled small donut holes. Everywhere Virginia looked, people seemed to be smiling and joking. It didn't remind her at all of the Baptist church she'd been going to recently. It wasn't even like the old church her Aunt Emily used to take them to on Sundays.

In both the other places, church was a much more serious affair. Everyone dressed in their finest clothes and talked to each other in hushed tones as though laughter or loud speech might somehow offend God. There seemed to be no worry of that here.

"Uncle Tristan!" a small voice shouted from the other side of the lobby. Virginia turned to see a little girl in a pink shirt with a Disney princess on the front rushing towards Tristan with a determined look on her face.

Tristan let out a boisterous 'Hey!' as the little girl reached him. He leaned down, opened his arms and picked her up swinging her around once.

"Lilly!" he said. "It's so good to see you!"

"Lilly! There you are!" a voice very familiar to Virginia said. Sure enough, she turned to see Amanda striding towards them. A little boy no older than two years old on her hip.

"I'm sorry Tristan," she said. "But, Lilly's been wanting to see you for weeks. We haven't been able to get out to church for a while."

"Understandable," Tristan said. "I know it's a bit of a drive for you."

"Speaking of a bit of a drive," Amanda said turning to Virginia with a surprised, but pleased smile. "I'm amazed to see you here, Virginia. Especially this early."

"It's a long story," Virginia said wearily. "Suffice it to say, I ended up staying at a bed and breakfast here last night."

"She came to help with the house yesterday, and we lost track of time," Tristan explained. Amanda laughed as the little boy on her hip began to poke at her cheek.

"Well, I can't say that hasn't happened to me," Amanda said. "Those ferry schedules can be chaotic."

Virginia was about to voice her agreement when a small voice at Tristan's feet stopped her.

"Why haven't you come to visit us?" Lilly asked looking up at Tristan with accusation lining her voice.

"I've wanted to," he said, "but I've been working on another house. It's really old, so it needs a lot of love."

"Doesn't our house need love too?" Lilly asked, unwilling to let the subject drop.

"I think your house has all the love it needs already," he said leaning down with a smile. "Remember, you've got to spread love around if you want it to do any good. And my friend Virginia's house needs just as much love as your house did."

Virginia smiled down at Lilly who looked skeptically up at this new competitor for her Uncle Tristan's time and attention.

It seemed whatever Tristan said about needing to spread his house-love-work time around, Lilly wasn't entirely buying it.

A moment later, they were all called into the theater for the service.

The service, like the lobby, was unlike anything Virginia had ever seen at a church. Before anything else happened, a band got up on the stage, which had an acoustic guitar and drum set already set up. Immediately, they began to play an upbeat tune that talked about how they could 'sing unending songs because of God's great love.'

All around her, people were clapping and singing. A few kids only a little older than Lilly even ran out into the aisles and started dancing, complete with well-practiced hand motions.

The mood was infectious. Soon Virginia found herself smiling and clapping along to the music. By the second song, she'd started to sing using the words projected onto the huge film screen behind the band.

When things slowed down on the third or fourth song, she realized that she was singing with her eyes closed and her hands raised. That tug in her heart was back, and it was stronger than it had ever been before. Almost as firm as it had been the day in her Aunt's little church when Virginia had walked up the aisle and asked to be baptized.

It seemed as though the band stopped playing much too soon for Virginia's liking. She sat down in a seat next to Tristan as a man with a polo shirt, glasses and neatly cropped brown hair walked onto the stage. This, according to Tristan who leaned over and whispered in her ear, was the pastor.

The theme of the sermon, which was projected brightly behind the man on the big screen, was Change.

"Change is scary," the man affirmed. "God knows that. God knows a lot of times we don't want to change. He knows how comfortable we are in our own routine, our own lives. Even if our lives aren't perfect. Even if they're miserable, he knows that we won't want to change. Take, for example, the Israelites. They were slaves in Egypt. Forced into unpaid labor. Poor housing, little food, no freedom. But, when God takes them out of captivity, when God sets them free, are they happy?" he paused here, and Virginia shifted uncomfortably in her seat. She shifted uncomfortably because she thought she knew the answer to that question. And, what's more, she thought she knew how it might apply to her.

"They were happy for a while," he said. "But as soon as things got a little bit difficult, what did they want to do? They wanted to go back. They wanted to go back to the way things were. Back to the world they knew. Back where, even if they weren't happy, they were comfortable." Virginia's discomfort grew as the pulsation in her heart began again. This time, Virginia knew, it would continue to grow much stronger than she'd ever felt it before.

"It would be easy for us to judge them, wouldn't it?" The pastor said. "It would be easy if we weren't exactly the same way. Think about it. Don't we all do the same thing? I know I do. Even when I know something's not good for me. Something doesn't make me happy. Something is pulling me away from my relationship with God or my family, I still don't want to give it up. Sometimes it's a pastime that's taken over. Sometimes it's spending too much time at work, hoping to earn that extra buck. Sometimes it's a relationship with someone, and you just know is toxic. It's hurting both you and them but, you just don't want to let go of it. It's too comfortable."

Just as Virginia had predicted, the tug in her heart grew much more forceful. She thought about Jason, and the urge to run from the pastor's words began to collide with that tug in her heart that insisted she stay and listen.

'When you feel that tug in your heart,' Aunt Emily's voice whispered in her memory. "That's God talking to you. The best thing you can do is listen to him."

So, she stayed.

"I'm here to tell you today, that as hard as it may be to give up whatever it is you're clinging to, as hard as it may be to change, you have to let go," the pastor insisted. "You have to trust God, close your eyes and take that leap. Because I promise, he wants to lead you to something a thousand times better than anything you have right now. He wants to lead you to a land flowing with milk and honey. But, he can only do that, if you'll let go of your comfort. Let go of whatever it is that's holding you back and agree to follow him."

The pastor spoke longer, but Virginia's mind stayed fixed on that one last line. 'Let go of whatever it is that's holding you back and agree to follow him.' Deep down, she had a feeling that God was speaking directly to her. And, what's more, she knew he was trying to tell her about Jason. She knew her relationship with her boyfriend was far from perfect. She always thought if they just had a little more money, enough for him to get her a ring, to propose, then they would be fine. But she was beginning to realize now that a diamond ring wouldn't fix her problems any more than a little more money would.

The fact was, she and Jason were two very different people. She knew that having differences was something that in and of itself wasn't a bad thing. But, when those differences were so fundamental, like his refusal to go to church with her, and the ease with which she knew he sometimes lied to her, deep-down she felt that he didn't truly respect the person she was. She just didn't know if those things could be fixed by sheer love and determination.

By the time the service had ended, she'd made something of a decision. She would have to sit down and have a serious talk with Jason. Perhaps the first really honest talk they'd had in several years.

She was still contemplating how best to go about this when little Lilly's voice once again burst into her thoughts.

"Grandma, can Uncle Tristan come to the park with us?" Lilly asked eagerly as Amanda, her little brother Mikey, Tristan and Virginia made their way through the doors of the church.

"Honey, I'm sure Tristan already has lunch plans," Amanda said.

"We don't actually, do we Virginia?" he asked, looking over at her.

"Uh...no, I guess not," Virginia answered a bit at a loss as to what was going on.

"Would it be ok if Virginia came too?" Tristan asked Lilly. The little girl's smile faded a little bit as she looked from Tristan to Virginia. Lilly's wide brown eyes were still skeptical as she sized up Virginia, however after a moment, she gave a silent nod of assent.

"Ok!" Tristan said happily. "Let's go then!"

"Race me!" Lilly said as the group turned towards the park on the other side of the movie theater.

"Not too fast," Amanda reminded as Tristan moved up where Lilly was.

"Ok," he said. "Ready, set, go!"

Tristan and Lilly both took off running, though Virginia noticed that Tristan moved deliberately slow. She knew he was doing this to give his little-legged opponent a fighting chance to make it to the park first.

"Sorry about that," Amanda said moving Mikey from one hip to the other. "I know a picnic in the park probably wasn't your first idea for lunch."

"Actually, it sounds nice," Virginia said. "I haven't had a picnic in years. In fact, I think the last one I had was on the island."

"Well, this'll just be sandwiches," Amanda said, "but the kids seem to like it. And we've got plenty for you and Tristan."

As it turned out, there were egg salad, peanut butter and jelly, as well as roast beef sandwiches. Apparently, Amanda didn't mess around when it came to packing lunch. These were complimented by several bags of chips. Virginia had to admit that the sandwiches Amanda made were far superior to Tristan's, but she still gave him an A for effort.

After lunch, Lilly insisted that Tristan push her on the swing, a task that Tristan readily agreed to. Virginia spent the afternoon talking about the house with Amanda and occasionally accepting blades of grass as gifts from little Mikey who seemed intent on pulling up every bit of lawn in the park.

"Oh, thank you," Virginia said as Mikey put another long blade of grass in her hand. The two-year-old smiled at her before running off to get more treats.

"So, the house is coming along well?" Amanda said.

"Yeah," Virginia answered. "Really well. We've even got some artwork on the walls to show it. The whole thing should be ready in another week or two."

"Perfect," Amanda said. "I've already got a few clients lined up to see it."

Virginia felt a dull thud in her chest when Amanda reaffirmed the interest other people had in the house. This one, she knew was a feeling of sadness and loss mixed with guilt. After everything she'd done with the house, all the work she'd put into it, she wasn't sure that she wanted it to go to some stranger. Someone who wouldn't truly appreciate what it meant.

After several more swings, Amanda told the kids that it was time to say goodbye. Despite several protests from Lilly who nearly insisted that Uncle Tristan come back to their house for dinner, Amanda and the kids parted ways with Tristan and Virginia at the front of the park.

"Do you need to check out of the bed and breakfast or anything?" Tristan asked. "You could do that, then I'll come pick you up to take you back to the ferry in about an hour."

"I checked out this morning," Virginia said. "Besides, I don't really feel like being alone at the moment. After that church service and a picnic, I think I'm ready for another adventure."

She said this in a light tone with a smile. That's why she was surprised when Tristan's face fell, and he looked away from her, down at the ground the way he always did when he was embarrassed.

"It's just...it's just I've got to do something this afternoon. It...it won't take long but, you probably wouldn't want to come."

"Try me," Virginia said. As though unable to help himself, a small smile crept across his face.

"Ok," he answered reluctantly.

He led the way back up the hill to where his truck was parked and opened the door for Virginia to get in. They were completely silent as they drove, a strange kind of tension filling the air. The truck made its way through downtown, past the movie theater, the park, down a ways toward the opposite side of the island and finally turned into a small neighborhood.

The houses along this street were quaint, and most were nicely kept. A few had peeling paint or ill-kept lawns, which were the only things that told Virginia this was not a wealthy neighborhood.

They stopped and parked across the street from a small house that was painted yellow with white gables, similar to the ones on her aunt's cottage.

Tristan kept his eyes fixed on the little house, his shoulders tense as though he was waiting for something. Virginia had the urge several times to ask him what it was. But his tension was so high that, in the end, she didn't dare. Instead, she turned to the house and watched it expectantly with him.

Finally, a small family came out. First to emerge was a boy around twelve or thirteen, followed by a girl who was nine or ten. A woman with prematurely graying brown hair and a knee-length red dress followed them. All three of them got into the van parked in their driveway and drove off down the street.

Tristan kept his eyes on it until it disappeared in the distance.

"Wait here," Tristan said. The sound of his voice made her jump. She realized that he hadn't spoken since they'd stepped into the truck.

She didn't answer but gave a nod of her head as she watched him close the door and walk across the street to the house.

He marched purposefully up to the mailbox, slipped something small and white inside of it before closing it again and making his way back to the truck.

"What was-"

"Nothing," he said. "Don't worry about it."

They started the truck again and made their way back down the little house-lined street. Virginia kept glancing at Tristan on their journey back towards the ferry. They were just as silent now as they had been on their trip to the mysterious house. Tristan's face was still set, his jaw still tense.

Virginia had never seen him look that way. Tristan was usually so casual and down to earth. He laughed and smiled easily and never took himself too seriously. But now, he looked as though he might just break.

She had to know why, even if he didn't want to tell her. If she didn't find out, the tension might just break her, too.

They stopped at the parking lot that led to the ferry entrance. It was still another forty-five minutes before the ferry arrived. When he stopped the car but didn't move to get out, she figured it was her best chance to get what she needed out of him.

"So, are you going to tell me what that was all about?" she asked.

"I told you not to worry about it," Tristan said. "It's a long story."

Virginia rolled her eyes and pointed to the clock on his dash.

"We're early," she said. "There's plenty of time for a long story."

He turned to her and looked her right in the eye. He searched her face, and she could see a deep pain beneath it for the first time.

"You really want to know?" he asked.

"I really do."

Tristan looked at her with blue eyes narrowed. Finally, he let out a long sigh and looked straight ahead at the water in the bay.

"It started about eight years ago," he said. "I'd just graduated from high school. Just moved to Seattle. And I...had some problems then."

"What sort of problems?" Virginia asked.

"Drinking problems," Tristan said darkly, still looking determinedly out at the water.

"Anyway, some buddies of mine invited me out to this bar a little ways from the city. It wasn't on Sweetwater, but the island just next to it. I drove because I knew I'd be out late."

He paused, and she saw his jaw clenching tightly. "It was the worst mistake I've ever made." When she looked down at the steering wheel of the truck, she could see his hands clutching it so hard that his knuckles nearly turned white.

"Anyway, I had a bunch of drinks with my friends, and by the time I was ready to drive home, I was pretty hammered. My memory of it is pretty hazy, but I didn't want to drive, so my buddy took my keys and convinced me to sleep in the back of the car. But then at some point, he decided to drive us back to the city. It was really early in the morning," he went on. "Amazingly, he didn't run into a tree or a rock or anything, until we got to the bridge. And then..."

His voice began to waver.

"...I don't remember what happened. I just remember seeing some headlights coming towards us. Then everything went black. Next thing I knew, I woke up in the hospital with some cuts, some broken bones, and a bad headache. Police were there. They said...they said I was under arrest for vehicular homicide."

He pried one hand off the steering wheel and ran it over his face which had gone from ashen to red.

"They...they said that we'd swerved into the wrong lane and the car we ran into...it was pushed off the bridge and she...she died. She was on her way to pick up her two grandkids for the weekend from their mother who lived on the island. A boy and a little girl."

This one point brought Virginia's mind back to what had just happened in that neighborhood. What she'd seen Tristan do.

"Was...were those....those kids..." she began, unsure how exactly to ask the question.

He nodded. Now, she could see tears running down his cheeks as he brought his other hand up from the steering wheel and furiously whipped them away.

"Do you mind if we walk for a little bit?" he asked without looking at her.

"Of course not," she said as lightly as she could and pushed open her car door. She couldn't believe what she had just heard. So many thoughts swirled through her mind as they made their way down to the rocky coastline.

They had shared so many stories over the course of their new friendship, but she had noticed a certain avoidance when it came to why he'd moved to the island, why he hadn't seemed to really date much, and a few other topics that he always managed to skirt. She realized now that this was a person who was consumed with a deep guilt and it was probably something that guided much of what he did. She was amazed that he allowed himself to do work that made him as happy as it did because as she listened to him, she got the distinct feeling that he didn't believe he deserved to have true happiness.

Tristan walked with his hands shoved deep in his pockets, stooping into the whirling wind coming off the bay. Virginia followed behind him, navigating the rocky terrain. Finally, Tristan came to a large, flat rock and sat down, still keeping his gaze focused far, far away from reality. Virginia settled into a smooth dip in the rock where she was partially sheltered from the wind by Tristan's body next to hers.

"My friend and I had both been thrown from the car. Nobody could remember anything. They put John into an induced coma because of brain swelling. None of our other friends that we were with us that night had seen us leave, and everyone was looking to me for answers. I hadn't thought I was driving, but honestly, I couldn't remember. We had been so out of it, that when they questioned me, it just felt like anything was possible. And the fact that it was my car, the police assumed that I had been the driver. After a couple of days in the hospital, they had me on so many painkillers, and I was being questioned constantly, I didn't know what to think. I became convinced that I'd done it."

She saw his eyes clench shut, and his face tense as he fought back the pain of the memory.

"When John woke up, there was a lot more confusion, and they held us both until an investigation could be launched. I sat there, day in and day out realizing what we'd done. It didn't matter who was driving, another person had lost their life. And for what? So that we could forget our stupid worries for a few extra hours? So we could be home in time to sleep off our hangovers the next day? There was nothing that could have justified her dying and me living." He swallowed hard, resolute in his statement. "And it's so hard to drive out the what-ifs. If I hadn't gone out that night, if I hadn't been so young and naive, so stupid to take my car, so many small variations, better choices...she'd still be here."

Virginia sat silently beside him, listening and watching him.

"Eventually the police investigation obtained some video from a street camera that showed John driving and me laying down in the back. I was released, and he was arrested. It was awful, every part of it was completely awful. Her family..." he trailed off.

"So, I put an envelope with money in their mailbox every month," he said thickly. "I've...I've never met them. I thought about it. Initially, it was why I moved to the island, in fact. Afterward, they had moved here and, I, I just didn't know where else to go. For whatever reason, no matter how much I argued with myself, it was the only thing that made sense to me. I thought...maybe I could see them. Ask forgiveness. But, every time I've tried, I just...something stops me and I can't..."

His voice broke off, and Virginia knew he wouldn't be able to say anymore. She looked at him for a few moments almost unable to process everything he'd said. Tristan, her strong, funny and often wise friend was now staring vacantly at the rocks a few feet in front of him, looking broken.

She realized then that her problems seemed very small compared to his. Her issues with Jason, her guilt over the house, weddings and days when she felt sorry for herself, all paled in comparison to the pain and guilt this man next to her was feeling.

Instinctively, before she could stop herself, she reached over and threw her arms around him in a fierce hug. He paused a moment, as though unsure of what was happening. Then, slowly, she felt his arms move around her. Before long, he was sobbing against her shoulder, and she placed her hand on his head, the way she remembered her mother doing when she was upset. It always made her feel safe, to be held tightly like that.

She didn't know how long it was before he pulled back, taking deep shuddering breaths. She pulled back too. Though her instincts told her that she shouldn't.

"Thanks," he said. His voice still thick as he was wiped his eyes and was regaining his composure.

"You know, I...I usually don't tell people that, I mean, I never tell anyone," he said. "Last time I did was at an AA meeting. You were a lot nicer to me than they were."

He offered her a small watery smile.

"I'm sure that's not true," she said.

"Well, they didn't boo or hiss," he said. "But, I didn't get hugged or have my head stroked either."

"You can thank my mom for that," Virginia said with an equally awkward smile. "That's what she always did for me when I was upset."

"Well, she was a wise lady; it works," he said.

They sat quietly for a moment. The air around them was still tense, but it was a different kind than it had been before. The sound of the rolling waves became more present than it had been.

"You are forgiven, you know?" she said. She didn't know exactly where the words came from, but she knew they were true.

"God's forgiven you," she continued when he looked at her slightly disbelieving. "You don't have to prove anything to him. You know that, right?"

He stared at her for a moment before nodding slightly.

"Yeah," he said. "Yeah, I know."

He gave a small smile that told her, no matter what he said, he couldn't quite believe her. She was about to say something else to him, something consoling or fervent but, before she could, she heard the familiar call of the ferry horn.

"You'd better get going," he said with another weak smile. "Don't want to miss this one."

"Yeah," Virginia answered with a smile of her own. He stood up and dusted off his pants, then lowered his hand to help Virginia up. Still holding his hand for balance, she tiptoed up the rocky incline until she regained her footing.

When they got back to the ferry area, she turned to him. "See you tomorrow?"

"Sure," he said, apparently appreciative and a little amazed that she would want to see him again after what he'd told her.

With a last smile and a nod, she reluctantly made her way down the ramp to the ferry.

Virginia got up onto the deck and stared out at Tristan's little blue truck sitting on the shore. Even when the ferry began to move, she kept her eyes on the car until it disappeared from sight.

The wind blew through her smooth brown hair as she stared at the bright, sparkling water beneath her. It was hard to believe that she'd ridden this same ferry only yesterday morning.

It seemed like a lifetime ago that she'd made this crossing. So much had changed since then and yet, when she looked around her at the water, the birds, the little green islands dotting their way, everything looked exactly the same.

The things around her hadn't changed. No. She'd changed. Something inside her had changed. Something was prompting her, more fully than ever to listen to the feeling in her heart. The tugging that told her she couldn't be comfortable anymore. The tugging that told her, after this weekend, she couldn't go back to life as it was. Life was too short, too precious to waste time being half-happy.

She knew the tugging came from God. And, what's more, she knew that she had to follow her aunt's advice. She had to listen to it. She had to let go and follow where God led.

It had taken a car accident to make Tristan listen to the prompting in his heart. And she knew that if she didn't follow God now, it might take something equally drastic to change her. Well, she wouldn't wait for that to happen.

As the ferry pulled back into the dock where her car was waiting, she knew what she had to do. Things in her life had to change. Things between her and Jason had to change. She wanted them to change. Yet, the looming fear hovered over her that if he weren't willing to make that change with her, she'd have to make it alone.

CHAPTER ELEVEN

*I*t was late afternoon when Virginia made her way back home on Sunday. She had spent the entire car ride from the dock parking lot back to her duplex rehearsing in her head what she was going to say to Jason.

She couldn't ignore her heart anymore. The pastor had been right. If she was ever going to be happy, truly happy with Jason, then things in their relationship needed to change. She couldn't keep cooking for him, cleaning up after him, laughing off his jabs about her weight or watching him flirt with other women.

If this relationship was going to last, he was going to have to make a commitment. A real commitment to her. And that meant he was going to have to start doing some of the work.

As she pulled into her driveway, she had decided exactly what she needed to say. A surge of pride came over her as she walked up to the front door and unlocked it.

The feeling disappeared entirely when she saw what was inside her house.

It was a complete mess.

Empty beer bottles stood on nearly every empty surface. Two empty and crust-scattered pizza boxes lay next to each other in the living room.

As she walked from the hallway into the family room adjoining the kitchen, Virginia felt a tremor of fear pass over her. Maybe someone had broken in while she was gone. Maybe they'd been robbed.

However, when she glanced at the television in the living room, she noted that it was still there. So was all their stereo equipment, as well as Samantha's laptop computer which she always kept downstairs.

Virginia was confused for only a moment before she saw the pile of dirty clothes on the family room couch. She knew at a glance who they belonged to. As she moved towards them, she noticed the little note written in Jason's handwriting placed on the coffee table that confirmed her suspicions.

GOT HOME EARLY *from the business trip, so I invited a few friends to hang out at your place and watch the game. I knew you wouldn't mind. Hope you had fun on your girl's camping trip! If you get a chance, could you wash the clothes on the couch? The washing machine in my apartment's out again.*

Thanks,

Jason

VIRGINIA READ the letter several times over trying to comprehend the new low to which her boyfriend had sunk. She knew he could be a little inconsiderate. She knew that he sometimes said or wrote things without thinking, but this, coming over when he knew she wouldn't be there. Not bothering to ask whether or not she was alright with it.

Inviting other people to her house and then leaving it a mess for her to clean up...this was a new low even for him.

Cursing Jason in her mind, cursing herself for letting him get away with this type of thing, she crumpled the note and threw it in the trash. She knew now that she would seriously have to amend the talk she was going to have with him. It was no longer going to be a talk to try and fix their relationship. No, it was going to be a talk about ending their relationship.

She moved back to the couch and began to pick up the beer bottles on the coffee table. As she did, something lying between one of the cushions of the couch caught her eye. Trying to be sure of what she was seeing, she moved in closer to inspect it.

Sure enough, there, contrasted against the red fabric of her couch was a lacy black thong. What's more, without question, the skimpy little piece of underwear certainly hadn't come from Virginia's closet. And she knew her sister's wardrobe well enough to know that it hadn't come from Sam's either.

There, staring at a foreign piece of woman's clothing, Virginia finally admitted what she'd refused to see for years. Jason had cheated on her.

Maybe with the pretty little sales assistant, maybe with someone else. Maybe it had happened once, maybe it was an ongoing thing. But there was no denying it now. Not with the evidence right here in front of her, clear as day.

She stood looking at the skimpy piece of fabric for several moments, feeling the anger and betrayal and rage well up inside of her. Then, marching to the pantry on the other side of the kitchen, she grabbed an empty cardboard box.

Taking it into the family room, she threw all of Jason's clothes, along with the thong and all the beer bottles she could fit into the empty box. She had to get another box for the rest of the beer bottles, paper, and pizza boxes.

By the end of the night, she'd stormed through the house making sure that nothing of his remained. All of the books he'd left at her home, his movies, and various sales papers were stuffed unceremoniously into the same boxes as his dirty clothes and garbage.

The next day, she woke up early and packed each box into her car. Once that was done, she scribbled a handwritten note of her own.

Jason, it's over. Here is everything you left at my place including your black thong. Don't come over again. Don't call me. Don't try to see me at all.

-Virginia

Taking the note in hand, she made her way to his television station. Placing the note inside the top box, she marched inside just as the doors opened.

Her smaller than average frame was fully covered by the boxes and from the corner of her eye, she could see people staring and pointing at her. She didn't care. In fact, she was surprised to find that she liked the attention she was getting from this little stunt.

She reached the station's sales desk and plopped the boxes down in front of the sales assistant whose eyes widened at the sight of both her and the boxes.

"Are...are you here to see Jason?" the girl asked timidly.

"No," Virginia answered. "I don't want to see him. Just let him know that I dropped these boxes off for him. And, if he has questions, tell him to read the note."

Without another word, Virginia turned on her heel and made her way determinedly back out of the sales office. People in the hallways still occasionally stared at her and whispered behind their hands, but she paid them no mind.

Instead, she focused on marching to the front of the building and straight out the door. It was only when she got back into her car that the shaking started. She didn't know if it was brought on by rage or happiness or freedom or fear. But, it was there.

She took her hands off the wheel, sat back and tried her best to process what had just happened.

Virginia couldn't believe she'd actually done it. She left him. Her chest heaved and felt tight, but also free in a way she had never felt before. It felt as if the weight of the world had been lifted off of her. She was sad and freaked out, but also, dare she say it, excited.

An entirely new world was open to her now. There was no one left to tell her what she could and could not do. She wasn't attached to anyone else's dreams or plans anymore. Now, she could do exactly what she needed to do for herself.

It was still terrifying. She hadn't been on her own since high school. Along with the exciting possibilities came a crushing sense of responsibility. There were a million things she would have to do now. Decisions she would have to make for herself that she had never made before.

That was not to mention the deep hurt she felt everywhere inside when she thought about Jason. They had been together for so many years. He had cried with her when her mom died. He'd helped her with Aunt Emily as well. And now...all that was over. The chapter of her life where she'd had a strong, capable boyfriend, the kind she'd dreamed about her entire life, was gone.

This unfamiliar mix of sorrow, excitement, and fear left her paralyzed for several minutes. She sat in her car staring down at the wheel as though not quite sure what to do with it. Finally, she felt that tug in her heart again. And, this time, she knew exactly where it was leading her.

CHAPTER TWELVE

*W*hen she arrived at the island, she was surprised to see two cars waiting for her at the cottage. One was the familiar sight of Tristan's little blue truck and the other was Amanda's sedan.

Curious, Virginia put her car in park and moved towards the house.

"Of course, we'll still need to put some new door knobs on before we show it," Amanda was saying to Tristan. "But, overall, it looks amazing. Virginia's going to be really happy."

"What am I going to be happy with?" Virginia asked walking up the steps to the front door. Both Amanda and Tristan jumped slightly and turned around.

"Oh, Virginia! There you are." Amanda said moving down to greet her. "Tristan called me and said the house was just about finished. I thought I'd come up and take a look."

Virginia glanced over Amanda's shoulder at Tristan who was smiling apologetically at her.

"I know you still wanted to do some finishing touches," he said. "But, after you left on Sunday I came up and worked on the rest of main punch list. So, that's all finished."

"Oh," Virginia said. She wanted to feel happy and proud of what they had done, and she did. Still, she'd expected to be there when they decided the house was ready for Amanda to see. She supposed she'd imagined that, after all the work she and Tristan had done on the house together, there would be a special moment between just the two of them where they took it all in.

Apparently, that wasn't what Tristan had in mind.

"I'm...I'm glad you like it," Virginia said trying to keep her voice light.

If Amanda noticed anything amiss, she gave no sign of it. Virginia did notice when she passed Tristan, he was giving her that narrow-eyed appraising look that he got when he thought she wasn't exactly telling him the truth. She looked up at him and smiled, hoping to relieve his worry. He smiled only tentatively back at her and stepped aside to usher her into the house.

They toured the entire cottage top to bottom. As they went through each room, Virginia tried to listen to the gushing praise that Amanda was giving to the woodwork and the furniture. -"Oh, that pine looks absolutely stunning on the deck!...I'm so glad you were able to move that wall out...The whole kitchen looks so much bigger". But she found that her mind couldn't focus.

Instead, as she moved through the house, she found herself bombarded once again with memories. Unlike the first time she'd come to the house, these memories weren't just of her aunt and her sister and her childhood. They were fresh from the past few months. When they walked through the kitchen, she smiled as she remembered the first time she'd torn down a wall with Tristan. As they moved through the family room, she remembered sitting next to Tristan on the couch just two nights before, laughing at a stupid silly movie. When they walked through the deck, she remembered

Tristan's stories about building tree houses with his dad. When they moved to the yard, she looked at the spot where she'd found the old key to her diary. The one that was now in a jewelry box up in the attic.

She wondered if she should have kept the key. Then she wondered what on earth she would have done with it.

Finally, they made their way out of the house and back to the front where Amanda's car was parked.

"Well, I'm sure we'll be able to get a really good offer on this place," Amanda said. "It's so charming and cozy! In fact, it looks better than it did years ago! And I love the artwork on the walls. Where did you find it?"

"You've got Virginia to thank for that," Tristan said. "We found some of her earliest paintings in her aunt's old boxes. So, we thought we'd hang them."

"You did those?" Amanda asked, looking at her in surprise.

"Yeah," Virginia said looking down at the ground and feeling her cheeks grow warm. "I just...well...we didn't want to have to spend more money for art to hang around the house so, we used those."

"Well they're very nice," Amanda said. "Would you mind if I sold a few of them along with the house? I know a couple of my clients would love to have those prints hanging up. Gives the whole place an authentic feel. I'd pass the money on to you, of course."

Virginia blinked at Amanda trying to decide if the agent was being sarcastic or kind. Amanda looked back at her, apparently very serious about the prospect. Even so, it was a few moments before Virginia was able to answer.

"Um...yeah. Yeah. Of course," she said.

Tristan and Virginia said their goodbyes to Amanda and watched in silence as the sedan made its way back down the hill. As soon as the car disappeared, tension began to fill the air between them.

"Ok. What's wrong?" Tristan asked turning to Virginia.

"What makes you think anything's wrong?" Virginia asked. Though, she knew that the way she was looking down at the ground and fidgeting with the sleeve of her shirt told him that she was lying.

"I thought you'd be happy about Amanda coming to see the place," Tristan said. "But, you didn't seem excited at all."

She looked up at him, and his eyes were searching. There was no use trying to lie to him anymore. No point in trying to pretend to be happy about selling the house.

"I just...I just wish you'd called me or something to tell me she was coming," Virginia said weakly.

"I'm sorry," Tristan said. "I kind of wanted to surprise you. I worked all night Sunday to get everything finished I..."

He trailed off and looked away, averting the slightly rejected look on his face.

"...I thought you'd be happy. That's all."

The way he now turned his eyes to the ground and looked sideways caused a guilty knot to form in her stomach. After all, he'd tried to do something nice for her by finishing the house before she came out this morning. Which really was a very sweet gesture. She would have been thrilled if it were not for Jason and all the rest of it.

"I'm not unhappy with it, Tristan," she said gently. "This was really nice. And you did a great job. I'm just...I'm a little upset with other stuff going on right now."

"What other stuff?" he asked looking up at her concerned.

She looked at him and knew she should tell him. After all, he'd been so open with her about his past yesterday. And it would be good to have someone to talk everything out with. But, when she looked into his bright blue eyes and saw his lips formed into a slight frown, the wind blowing in his curly hair, she wasn't sure how she could talk to him about Jason. Truth be told, she wasn't sure how exactly to talk to Tristan about another man at all.

"It's...it's a long story," she said. To her surprise, he smiled and rolled his eyes at her.

"I tried that with you just the other day as I recall," he said. "You wouldn't let me get away with it. Now, I'm not letting you get away with it either."

She smiled weakly and looked down once more at her hands.

"I just...I don't really know where to start," she said.

"Let's go inside and start with tea," he said holding his hand out to her. "My mom always said, no matter what the problem is, tea can make it better."

Though she wasn't quite sure if she believed his mother's old adage, she smiled anyway and took his hand, strong and warm in hers, and allowed him to lead her through the house to the kitchen.

It turned out that the tea helped. As they sat there sipping on what Tristan called 'Lady Grey Tea,' which was a kind of sharp black tea with notes of orange in it, Virginia found herself telling Tristan the whole story.

She began with thinking about his pastor's sermon on the ferry ride home, rehearsing a conversation to have with Jason. Then, she told him about finding the mess when she arrived back at her house.

When she told him about the thong, she was surprised to feel tears begin to prick her eyes. That hadn't happened before. Even when she first found the underwear. She was upset, of course, angry even, she felt betrayed, but she hadn't cried. Now, however, she found tears pouring down her cheeks even as she tried to wipe them away.

Finally, she managed to finish that part of the story. Then she told him about the boxes and the note she'd written and put inside one of them.

He laughed at the image of her marching through a TV station piled with boxes of garbage and dirty clothes. To her surprise, she laughed too.

"So, what happens now?" he asked gently.

"Now, I ...I don't know," she said. "I haven't been alone in a long time. It's kind of scary. But, I was thinking...I was thinking about not selling the house after all."

"Really?" he asked leaning over towards her from his chair beside hers at the kitchen table. He seemed eager. Almost as though he was trying to force down his excitement.

"Maybe," she said reluctantly. "I don't know. Everything seems just really up in the air right now."

"I can see that," he said. She looked up at him, and he gave her a fortifying smile that she couldn't help but return. As she looked at him, she thought about everything he'd done for her so far. Not just finishing the house, but listening to her problems so non-judgmentally, letting her come up to help even though he probably could have done the job more quickly without her, shopping with her, taking her to church... And, she'd never thanked him for it. Not properly anyway.

"You're...you've been a really good friend Tristan," she said. "Through all of this...everything, I mean. With the house and me and...I don't know how I would have gotten through the past few months without you."

That adorable pink tinge came into his cheeks, and he gave her another infectious smile.

"For what it's worth, the feeling's mutual," he said.

"I don't know how much I did, to help," Virginia said, feeling blood rush into her cheeks now as well. "I mean, you probably could've done it a little quicker without me."

Tristan smiled and rolled his eyes at her.

"Come on now," he said. "We both know that's not true. You turned out to be the best wall smasher in Washington. Possibly in the country."

They both laughed at the memory. When the laughter subsided, he moved his hand over hers resting on the table. Her heart beat began to speed up when she felt its warmth on top of her skin.

"But, it's more than just the house," he said. "I've...I'm really, really glad I got to know you."

Virginia tried to say that she was glad she got to know him, too. Yet when she opened her mouth to say it, the words wouldn't come. She and Tristan had leaned close to each other at the table. So close that she could feel the warmth of his breath on her cheeks.

Her pulse jumped into her ears as her mind told her that this was a bad idea. Whatever she was about to do. She'd just broken up with Jason. She needed time. She pushed the voice aside as she moved closer to Tristan and closed her eyes.

She felt his lips touch hers. It was a brief kiss. No more than a moment. After that, she heard his chair scrape back from the table, and he stood up.

"Sorry," he said quickly moving to the kitchen door and looking away from her. "I...I shouldn't have done that."

Virginia felt her heart fall in her chest as she looked away from him as well.

"We both did it, Tristan," she said. "It wasn't just you."

"Yeah, but I...I've been..." he couldn't seem to finish the sentence. She wanted to ask him what he'd done, what he'd been thinking about her. About them. But, with Jason still swimming around in her thoughts, she couldn't quite bring herself to ask him that.

So instead she let the silence rush over them. They both stayed in the kitchen, him standing by the window, her seated at the round wooden table, neither looking at one another. The two cups of tea sat mostly finished in front of their seats. Virginia felt as though she should pick them up and put them in the sink. If only to have something to do with her hands.

In the end, she couldn't move even that much. After what seemed like hours but was probably only minutes, Tristan spoke.

"You should call your boyfriend," he said.

Virginia finally turned to look at him in shock. Of all the things she'd expected him to say after what had just happened, this was the very last.

"You mean my ex-boyfriend?" she asked.

"He's not your ex until you've talked things out," he said. "I mean, you haven't heard his side of the story. Maybe there's an explanation. Maybe he's sorry."

"I don't care if he's sorry," Virginia said angrily. Though she wasn't sure anymore whether that anger was directed at Jason or Tristan. This time she thought it was both. "I never want to see him again."

"But, see? That's the problem." Tristan said finally turning towards her. "You can't just end a long relationship like that with a note and an angry whim. You've got to talk it out. At least get closure, if nothing else."

A tiny part in the back of her mind knew that he was right. The rest of her was so angered by what he was saying to her that she couldn't admit it. She glared at him, still in her seat arms folded across her chest.

"So, you think I made a mistake dumping my cheating ex-boyfriend?" she asked.

"I...I don't know," Tristan said. "Maybe."

He looked down at his feet, and a blush returned to his cheeks. It was the first time since she'd seen it that she didn't find it at all cute. In fact, she wanted to smack his cheeks so hard that they turned red instead of pink.

"I see," Virginia said gritting her teeth in anger as she stood up from her seat. "So, you've got this little boy's code, and you want to make sure you're not taking another man's property, is that it?"

"What?" Tristan said looking up at her shocked. "No, that's not-"

"Well, I'm not property," Virginia said. "I can make my own decisions and to tell you the truth, I'm getting pretty sick of men in my life trying to make them for me!"

She grabbed her purse and, for the second time that day, turned on her heel and walked purposefully toward the building's exit.

"Virginia! Wait!" Tristan said following her outside. "I didn't mean-"

"I'll come back sometime next week to get the keys from you," she said ignoring his protests. "Your check will be in the mail."

With that, she headed off down the path towards the dock. She heard him call after her several times but didn't dare turn back. Half of her expected him to follow her down the path to the ferry. In fact, half of her wanted him to. But, the further away she got from the house, the more she realized that he hadn't followed her. He'd given up.

For the second time that day, tears began to fill her eyes. This time, she made no attempt to wipe them away.

CHAPTER THIRTEEN

"*P*ackages have been coming for you all day," Samantha said as soon as Virginia opened the door.

After she left Tristan on the island, she'd spend the rest of the morning and most of the afternoon driving around aimlessly. She didn't know where she wanted to go or what she wanted to do. The only thing she did know was that she didn't want to see either of the men who had caused her this much pain.

"I've got a kitchen filled with flowers, two boxes of chocolates, and something wrapped in a box with little hearts. Don't tell me you've got a rich guy on the side you've been keeping secret."

Samantha, smiling, raised her eyebrows slyly at her sister as she led Virginia into the kitchen where there was indeed a table filled with a dozen red roses which Sam had put in a vase, two boxes of heart shaped chocolates and a thin package that had a note attached.

"Did any of these come with a note?" Virginia asked.

"The package did," Sam said. "I didn't look at it."

Her heart quickened as she lifted the note on the wrapped parcel. She found herself hoping against hope that it would be from Tristan. Even though she knew that was impossible. Not only were big gestures like this not his style, but she'd only left him that afternoon. He wouldn't have time to put all this together.

She knew that in terms of time, Jason was a much more likely candidate. However, she'd never gotten anything like this from him before. She'd never gotten even more than a single rose and a bag of Hershey's kisses from him for Valentine's Day.

Sure enough, when she lifted the covering note on the package, Jason's handwriting stared back at her.

"MY DEAREST VIRGINIA," it began.

I know you said you didn't want to hear from me. And, just like you asked, I didn't come over, and I haven't called. But I had to find some way to tell you how incredibly sorry I am. I know I've been a jerk and I know after what I did this weekend, I don't deserve for you to take me back. But I've done a lot of thinking today. And the one thing I know is that I can't lose you. I really want to see you so we can talk this out. More than that, I'd like to cook you dinner for once. You don't have to say yes or no. If you don't want to see me, I understand. But, if you would like to talk about everything, I'll have dinner for two ready at my apartment tomorrow night at seven o'clock. I hope I'll see you there.

All my love,

Jason.

VIRGINIA STARED at the note in her hands. It was different, so very different from the last note he had left her that she had trouble believing they were written by the same person.

Here he was open and vulnerable, almost pleading. Here, he apologized. She didn't think she'd ever heard Jason say he was sorry before. Not, at least, without qualifying it. But, here, he genuinely seemed to mean it.

Carefully, she set down the note and opened the package. Inside was a blank sketchbook along with a set of pencils and charcoal she'd pointed out to him at an art supply store months before. She'd told him that seeing it made her want to get back into drawing.

He'd scoffed at her then. Said that drawing would take her time away from the things that actually made money, baking and teaching. But, now, here it was. He'd bought her something that he thought was impractical. Just because she'd wanted it. And even more than that, he'd remembered.

It seemed as though every issue, everything she'd wanted to talk to him about, everything she'd wanted to make him realize was either written in the note or set before her in the sketchbook and pencils.

As she stared between the note and her table filled with presents, she felt the hot anger that had spurred her on early that morning begin to melt away. She remembered all the times Jason had made her laugh, the times he'd seen her cry and held her, the times he'd helped her through the most difficult parts of her life.

These memories seemed to merge with the memory of that little black thong, and years of cooking for him and doing his laundry and paying for his graduate school. The two started to become so tangled in her mind that she didn't know how to untie them. She simply stood, sketchbook in hand, staring down at it blankly.

"So? Who's it from?" Sam asked. Virginia started at her sister's voice and seemed to wake from her stupor.

"Oh, they're from Jason," Virginia said. "We...we kind of had a fight."

She hadn't told her sister about the mess she'd found when she came back home Sunday. The boxes with Jason's garbage were packed before Sam came back from the camping trip. Virginia knew even right after it happened, that if she told Sam that she thought Jason had cheated on her, Samantha would fly into a rage. She'd probably have marched right down to Jason's apartment and punched him until he bled.

No matter how angry Virginia had been at Jason, she didn't think he exactly deserved her sister's wrath. Even by simply mentioning the fight, Virginia could see her sister look up eagerly.

"Did you break up with him?" Samantha asked, unable to disguise the hope in her voice.

"I...sort of did," Virginia said. "I just...I just needed some time away. To think."

"And this is his way of trying to get you back?" Sam said giving an undignified snort to the gifts laid out on the table.

"I guess it is," Virginia said.

"So, are you going to?" Sam asked. "Take him back, I mean."

Virginia turned to Sam and saw her sister's pointed look. Sam's arms were crossed over her chest and her eyes were squinted at Virginia in an almost threatening way. She knew what Sam wanted her to say. She wanted her to say that Hades would have to freeze over before she would ever take Jason back. Samantha wanted Virginia to tell her that she was done with pretty boy forever.

But Virginia knew that she couldn't tell her sister that. Even though a part of her wanted to. The truth was, given the note Jason had sent, not to mention what had happened with Tristan on the island, she had no idea what she wanted at all.

All she did know was that she was going to have to figure it all out for herself. She couldn't let anyone, including her little sister, make her choices for her anymore.

"I don't know," Virginia said honestly. "I'm...I'm going to take a walk. Think about it a little bit."

Without turning back, Virginia took hold of the sketchbook, pencils, and charcoal and moved out the door. Once outside, she wasn't one hundred percent sure where to go.

There was a little park with a swing set down the street, and she walked absently until finally, she decided that she would go there.

It was nearly deserted by the time she arrived. The sun was setting in the distance, and she could see it sinking down over the distant waters of the bay. Even with the little wooden swing set in the way, the view was quite lovely.

Without thinking, Virginia took a pencil, opened her sketchbook and began to draw.

As her hand moved across the paper, she remembered something her Aunt Emily had told her about her drawings.

"God speaks to all of us in different ways," she said. "We feel closest to him when we're doing the things that we love to do. I think you feel closest to Him when you draw. I can see your prayer in your paintings."

Aunt Emily had been right about that. Virginia remembered many an afternoon sitting on the back deck of the little cottage, looking out into the woods and talking to God. They weren't the traditional types of prayers. Not the kind that started with Dear God and ended with Amen. No, she simply talked to God as though he were there beside her. As though talking to him was the same as talking to her mother or her sister.

It had been years since she'd prayed, really prayed to God that way. Now, as her hand moved gently across the paper, she found herself talking to God exactly the way she used to.

"God," she said silently. "I don't know what to do. I'm so torn. I don't know who to trust or where to go. I only know...or...I think I know that you've got a better way for me. You've got a plan for me beyond the life I've been living. You want me to use my talents for you and not to please my boyfriend or my sister or anyone else. I just wish I knew how to do that. Please, please show me."

She repeated similar words over and over in her mind as she carefully sketched the swing set and the view beyond it. The sun had almost set now, and the sky had turned from bright orange to deep pinks and purples. The last rays moved slowly down over the water.

Looking out at that water, she couldn't help but think of Sweetwater. And, of course, thinking about Sweetwater made her think about Tristan. Now that hours had passed since the argument she'd had with him, now that her anger had subsided, she could see why he'd pulled away from her. She could see why he'd told her to talk to Jason.

He didn't want to be someone she turned to only because she was upset. Someone she could use to get back at her boyfriend. And, truth be told, that was what she had been doing.

When she kissed him, she was upset and vulnerable and thinking with her anger more than any other part of her mind. Now, the wisdom in Tristan's suggestion seemed to come through.

He was right. She needed to talk to Jason. Maybe she wouldn't take him back, maybe she would tell Jason that it was over for good. Maybe they would be able to work through things together. But, no matter what happened, she had to see him.

As the last ray of light moved down beyond the Pacific, a little tug in her heart told her that she was on the right path.

So, as she made her way home, she pulled out her phone and typed "Dinner with Jason @ 7 pm" into her calendar for the next day.

CHAPTER FOURTEEN

*V*irginia pulled up to Jason's apartment building still dreading what she would find on the other side of the door.

Half of her still protested the idea of seeing him at all. Indeed the part of her that hated confrontation insisted that she run away and speak to Jason only via email or text. But another part, the bravest part of her, told her that she needed to do this. Not for Jason, but for herself.

So, with a steadying breath, she walked out of her car, walked up to his apartment and knocked on the door.

"Virginia," he said opening the door. The widest and most heart-melting smile she had ever seen on him greeted her. He looked both surprised and ecstatic that she had actually accepted his invitation.

His hair had been combed, he'd shaved that five o'clock shadow and he was wearing his best suit. He'd clearly gone to a big effort, and it was all she could do not to smile back at him.

"Come in," he said opening the door wider for her.

She entered the apartment without saying a word and without smiling.

His place really was tiny. It was a one-bedroom efficiency about the size of most college dorm rooms. There was one small space between the television and sofa that made up the living area and the kitchen. This was where he'd set up a table and chairs complete with tablecloth and candles. Virginia also noticed her favorite jazz record was playing.

"Miles Davis?" Virginia asked in surprise.

"I know you think I don't remember this stuff," he said gallantly pulling out a chair for her. "But, I do. Believe me."

He allowed her to sit before moving to the kitchen to get the plates and what smelled like fettuccine Alfredo. Her favorite pasta dish.

As he came back to the table, she told herself that she had to applaud his effort. He poured her a glass of good red wine, and they ate the first few bites of their dinner in silence.

Jason kept glancing up at her as though waiting patiently for her to start the conversation. Finally, she decided that she should indulge him.

"Jason," she started hesitantly. "My coming here...it doesn't necessarily mean that we're going to get back together."

"I know that," he said, "but I figured, after everything I've put you through, I at least owe you a decent meal and a little pampering."

He gave her a charming smile, and this time, she returned it weakly.

"This is really nice, Jason," she said. "So was the sketchbook you sent me and the flowers and chocolates. But...it doesn't make up for what you did."

"I know that too," he said. "And, for what it's worth, there's an explanation about that thong. But, I know you don't want to hear excuses from me. I know you don't want me to tell you how a bunch of this wasn't my fault. I know the truth is a lot of it was my fault. I've done a lot of things that I shouldn't have. I just wanted the chance to say I'm sorry."

He looked across the table at her, those hazel eyes that she had loved since she was sixteen years old, wide and pleading. He reached across the table and put his warm, strong hand on the top of hers.

"And I wanted to ask...do you think you could give us another shot?"

"Jason, I...I don't know," she said. "After so many years I just..."

"I know it'll take work," he said. The pressure from his hand, once soft and gentle became harder on hers. "I'm willing to put the work in, though. I've even gotten in touch with a couples counselor. She says she's got an opening on Friday if you'd like to go."

His hand was still hard on hers, his eyes were pleading and now desperate. It was like his life hung on her answer.

Virginia looked into his eyes and thought. On the one hand, this was exactly what she'd wanted from him. She'd wanted him to put effort into the relationship, to work not just for himself but for her, and more importantly, for them. Now, he said he was willing to do that. She looked in his eyes to find some hint of insincerity, some telltale sign that he wasn't serious. That he would break her heart again. She didn't see any.

So, with another steadying breath, she nodded.

"Ok," she said. "I'm...I'm finished with the house now so, I can make it on Friday."

With a relieved breath, Jason sighed, let go of her hand and leaned back in his seat.

"Good," he said. "Ok. I'll call her tomorrow and tell her."

Virginia gave him another weak smile and looked down at her fettuccine Alfredo, praying she'd just done the right thing.

"So, you're finished with the house?" Jason asked. "How is it looking?"

"Really good," Virginia said. "In fact, better than it did when I was a kid."

"Great," he said. "Does Amanda think she'll be able to get a good price from it?"

Virginia's heart sunk in her chest. This one question reminded her so much of the Jason she used to know. The Jason she'd just broken up with. The one who was more worried about his bank account than anything Virginia wanted.

She knew that telling him she was thinking about keeping the house would put him on edge. And, what's more, if she and Jason were to get back together, if, eventually, they were to get married, she knew she would have to sell it anyway.

So, fighting against the horrible sinking feeling in her chest, she gave him a closed lipped smile.

"She saw it yesterday," Virginia said. "She thinks she'll be able to get more for it than she originally thought."

"Awesome!" Jason said. He flashed the cocky smile Virginia had come to know across the table at her. With some effort, she smiled back at him. They talked about some simpler things through the rest of dinner. Jason let her pick the show that they watched afterward.

When Virginia got into her car that night and made her way home, she knew she should feel less conflicted than she had been before going. After all, she'd done what Tristan had told her to do. She'd talked with Jason, and they were going to try and work it out.

It had been Tristan, after all, who told her that it might have been a mistake dumping her boyfriend so hastily. Tristan who had pushed her to go back to Jason even though she'd fought against him. He had to have known that, if she did go back to Jason, she would sell the house.

Now, she realized, there was nothing left to resolve. She'd followed Tristan's advice and gone back to Jason. Everyone should be happy.

Even so, she still felt a tiny ebb of her heart pulling her in a direction different than the one she was taking. It pulled at her as she drove into her driveway and headed up the stairs to her bedroom.

In an attempt to ease her mind and, perhaps, silence the persistent, nagging feeling that she was making some kind of mistake, she got out her laptop and began an email to Tristan. She'd always liked emailing and texting better than calling. Less chance for a confrontation that way.

"TRISTAN," she started.

I've thought it over, and I think I'm going to sell the house after all. Don't ask why, it's just something I've got to do. Thanks for all your help these past many months and I'm sorry about the way I left things the other day. I was upset and emotional. Just know that it had nothing to do with you. I'll be back to the island to pick up the key to the cottage sometime this week, and I promise to put your payment in the mail tomorrow. You don't have to be there when I come to get the key. You can just leave it under the front mat.

Thanks again, for everything,

Virginia

SHE STARED at the message for several minutes, reading it over and over again, making sure it was exactly what she wanted to say. Her brain felt fried. She thought about telling Tristan about her and Jason; that he'd been right and they were going to work things out. But, in the end, it didn't seem to fit.

Finally, realizing she'd said all she needed to say, she hit send on the email.

She was still up in bed two hours later when the response came back.

It read:

VIRGINIA,

I guess I should say I'm sorry too. I'm sorry about the way I acted. You were right, I had no right to tell you what you should or shouldn't do about your boyfriend. But I have to tell you, I'm not sorry for kissing you. Truthfully, I wasn't even sorry when it happened, even though I said I was. Because, once it happened, I realized that I've been wanting to kiss you from the moment I met you. I know you probably don't feel the same way, but since we're being honest about so many things, I thought I should be honest about that, too.

I never set out to be anything other than a friend to you, but over these last six months, so many things have changed. I've changed. And it even seems like you've changed; sometimes I think you glow when you show up at the cottage in the morning. I know that sounds ridiculous, but it's true. Maybe this project happened in order to help us both grow, I don't know. God's greater plan? Who's to say? But I think I would trust you with my life at this point. You are truly one of the best people I know. And not only at demolishing walls...

I really don't want to have to say goodbye to you via email. But, I also don't want to make the mistake of telling you what to do (again). So, I'll be at the cottage every day this week, from nine in the morning until five in the evening. If you'd like to see me, come and drop the payment off then. If not, at the end of the week I'll leave the key under the mat. I really do want you to be happy, no matter what you do. Also, (one last bit of honesty), this isn't exactly how I planned to tell you this, but no matter what happens I want you to know, I am very much in love with you and always will be.

Love,

Tristan.

HER HAND FLEW to her mouth. Virginia stared at the last two lines for what felt like hours. Her heart raced, and for a minute she thought she might be having a panic attack until she noticed that her cheeks kept creeping up into a crazy, disbelieving smile.

He loved her. Tristan loved her. The thought made her feel flush and excited and scared and numb all at once.

Then the reality of everything that had happened recently came crashing down on her and her thoughts started darting around wildly. Finally, because she didn't know what else to do, she closed the laptop, turned out the light in her room and laid back on her bed. Even so, she couldn't sleep. Tristan's words spun around in her head, interspersed with thoughts of Jason and all the recent events that had turned her world upside-down. In a desperate attempt at peace, she closed her eyes and fell into a fitful sleep feeling far more conflicted than she had been in as long as she could remember.

CHAPTER FIFTEEN

*F*riday finally came, and Virginia grabbed the box of donuts she'd made along with her purse. When she turned to leave, she saw her sister standing in front of the door with her arms folded over her chest as though she was going to keep Virginia from leaving the house.

"Are you really sure about this Virginia?" Sam asked.

"I really am, Sam," Virginia said.

Samantha looked down at the floor and shook her head.

"I still don't get it," she told Virginia.

"I know you don't, Samantha," Virginia said. "And that's what I love about you."

With a smile, she reached across the tiled floor and pulled her little sister into a hug. The box of donuts got a little squashed by her side but, Virginia discovered that she didn't care.

"I'll see you, later on tonight," Virginia said as Sam stepped aside to let her leave.

"Call me and let me know what happens," Sam called out to Virginia's retreating back. Virginia waved in response before getting into her car.

Setting the donuts on the passenger seat, she gripped the wheel, breathed deeply, looked herself in the eye and gave herself a pep talk. Then, she closed her eyes and prayed.

With only slight reluctance, she backed out of the driveway and headed down the road. For eight-thirty on a Friday morning there was considerably less traffic than she'd expected, especially considering that with the arrival of fall, many of the schools were back in session. As soon as the car made its way out of her neighborhood, Virginia's phone vibrated. Spying her favorite coffee drive-through, she pulled into the line and let the car idle while she checked the message. It was from Jason.

"Something came up at work, so I'm not going to be able to make the counseling thing today," it read. "You can go without me. I'll catch up at the next session."

Virginia blinked at the phone in disbelief. She read the message twice more. Though really, she should have known better, she thought. No matter how hard Jason tried to show her another side of himself, no matter how often he said he couldn't lose her, he would always slip back into his old habits. He would always be Jason and, with a sigh, Virginia realized there was nothing she could do about that.

The car line inched forward. Maybe she should go to the counseling session alone. The changes she'd seen both in herself and with the cottage since she started the renovation, were proof that a lot could be accomplished when you gave something proper attention. And she could now admit that before all this happened, Virginia had been the queen of putting everyone's needs before her own. She placed her order, noting that the Pumpkin Spice Lattes had finally arrived for the season. Veering from her normal tradition, she ordered a hot

Maple Latte, another favorite of hers, but one that she usually forgot to order until it was too late and the season had passed.

Her mind kept playing through scenarios. Perhaps if she truly wanted to fix her relationship with Jason, she needed to not only keep working on herself, but incite the help of a professional. After all, no one is born knowing how to be in a relationship. She'd heard that somewhere recently. She supposed there was some truth in it. And people were constantly bemoaning how hard relationships were. Virginia had always felt like relationships shouldn't have to be as hard as people made them out to be. But maybe that was why she over-compensated in her relationship with Jason, she was trying to force it to be easy. The only problem was that she was the one it was taking the toll on. And admittedly it never felt as easy as she wished it did.

She pulled up to the window and got her drink. She smiled at the window attendant, finding appreciation that the simple things in life that could sometimes bring you peace. She dropped the change in the tip box and pulled out. She sipped her drink, the warm, frothy flavor instantly bringing her into the change of season. It reminded her of everything good, of being with her sister and bundling up to play in the leaves, of her parents, of her aunt, of walking to the cottage along the water and feeling strong, like she could do anything for the first time in so long. It was amazing, she thought, how something so simple as a smell or a flavor, could stir up so much.

Though she felt a little shell-shocked by Jason's text, she realized that she really didn't care at this moment. She felt a strange sense of contentment. Her body just wanted to drive, to sip her drink, to take in the beautiful mountains off in the distance, to breathe in the autumn air. She rolled down her windows and drove on autopilot. She passed the bay and glanced out the window to see people getting on the ferry for the islands. She continued on out of the city, taking the most scenic roads she could. The change of season was transitioning the leaves along the roadway from green to differing shades of brown and orange. When she had traveled this particular road as a child, she'd only ever driven it during the summer. But now, with the warm, comforting colors enveloping everything, it was even more beautiful than she remembered.

She drove for a long time, thinking that all that was ever asked of her was to follow her heart. Everything that she needed to know was being told to her. It was just a matter of whether she was open enough to listen to it. And she now knew that without a doubt, regardless of the outcome, she was ready to listen. That was all God asked of her. She was no longer afraid, and she trusted that wherever it led, was exactly where she was supposed to be.

She crossed over a rickety wooden bridge that looked as though it was patched and welded within an inch of its life. The water glittered just below it. Virginia mused that sometimes something phenomenal was just beyond something tattered and ruined. She smiled. She was feeling quite poetic today.

Tracing along the less familiar route, she made her way past the misty colored houses, with their endless charm and shingled roofs. Finally, her car pulled to a stop at the top of the hill.

She nearly laughed out loud when she saw Tristan's truck parked in its normal spot.

Smiling broadly, she grabbed the box of donuts and rushed inside. There was no sign of Tristan in the kitchen or family room. But, she thought she knew where he might be.

She moved down the still slightly dark hallway towards the bedroom. The one she'd slept in when she was young. Sure enough, there he was. His back was turned towards her as he fit the new bronze knob onto her door.

"Going to work before breakfast?" she asked slyly. "That's not like you."

He paused in his work and stood up slowly. He turned around.

When he saw her, his eyes lit up brighter than she had ever seen them. His entire face seemed to glow at the sight, and she couldn't help but return his beaming smile a hundred times over.

"Virginia!" he said. "I...I take it you got my message?"

"Given the donuts that would be a safe assumption," she said still smiling at him. That adorable shade of pink came back into his cheeks but, this time, he didn't look at his feet. His eyes remained steadily fixed on her.

Neither of them spoke for several minutes, though her heart thumped so hard she was afraid he could hear it.

"Would you like to come into the kitchen?" Tristan asked. "I've got a pot of coffee brewing."

"Coffee and donuts," she said. "Sounds perfect."

They moved into the kitchen, a box of donuts in Virginia's hand. She set them down on the counter and sat at the pinewood table while Tristan went to fill two cups of coffee. As she sat there, she couldn't help but look around at the house.

Taking in the furniture she'd bought, the beautiful shimmering new floors that Tristan had laid and best of all, her artwork on the walls. She couldn't help but feel that it was just what Aunt Emily always wanted.

Of course, it didn't look quite the way it did when Virginia was young. Not quite the way it did when Aunt Emily was alive. But everything looked like it fit here. It looked as though it was the same old house, ready for a new chapter of its life. And, Virginia thought, she was ready for a new chapter too.

"I've...um...I've got the key in here," he said as he brought a coffee mug and set it down in front of her. "I guess you'll need to give to Amanda if she's going to be bringing buyers in to see it."

He was looking determinedly away from her as though he'd prepared himself for this. For her to say goodbye forever. For her to give up the house and everything they'd worked on together.

She reached out to him and, without hesitation, touched his hand. He looked up at her, his eyes shining with surprise.

"Actually," Virginia said. "I'm going to keep the house for a while."

"Really?" he asked, his face brightening again. She felt his hand turn from the table top and grip hers gently. "What made you change your mind?"

"Will it sound silly if I say you did?" she asked sheepishly. "When I got your email, I realized that when you said you wanted me to be happy...I was happiest when I was here. In this house. To tell the honest truth...I was happiest when I was with you."

His eyebrows shot up at the realization of what she had just said. Then slowly, he gave her that narrow-eyed intense look that he got when he wanted to know the truth. He studied her for a moment, then, still silent, his other hand came up from the side of his chair and covered her hand as well.

He smiled up at her as he took his right hand back off of hers. He began fishing for something in the pocket of his jeans.

"I hoped you'd come back at least one last time," he said. "Because I made this."

He straightened up and held something small out to Virginia. Curious, she took it in her hand. Once she did, she realized what it was. A beautiful bronze ring with a tiny, shimmering jewel placed at the top.

"I know a lot has happened, and this isn't much. But I couldn't let another bit of your heart get thrown away like your diary. That key is special to you...just like you are to me."

She looked down and saw the remnant of the tiny bronze key that had once unlocked her diary. The same one she'd put into the jewelry box and stuffed up into the attic. Somehow, he had worked the metal and fashioned it into an amazing ring like nothing she had ever seen before.

As she ran her fingers along the edges, staring in disbelief, he continued. "I know you might need to go live life and see what's out there, so I wholeheartedly want you to do whatever's right for you, and take as much time as you need. And I know we don't know each other well in the grand scheme of things, but...I want you to have this promise ring to know that I will be here waiting for you," he paused and shifted his weight. Then he looked her straight in the eyes. "And when you are ready...and if you will take me...I would be privileged to spend the rest of my life with you."

Virginia wasn't breathing by this point, and when her eyes met his, she felt another deep tug at her heart. But this time she knew for certain that this one wasn't pulling her in any different direction.

"I mean, you don't have to take it now," he said looking back down and into his coffee cup, the pink coming back into his cheeks. "And, if you'd rather, I could just-"

She stopped him from saying another word by reaching across the table, putting both hands firmly on his warm cheeks and meeting his lips with hers.

This kiss lasted much longer than their first one had. Though, somehow, it seemed just as simple and every bit as sweet.

She didn't know who pulled back first. But when they did, they were both smiling.

"Is that a yes?" he asked.

"Yes, yes," she said chuckling. "Absolutely yes!"

With a chuckle of his own, he pulled Virginia back in to meet his lips again. And this time, when Virginia felt the little tug in her heart, she knew exactly what God was telling her.

She had taken a leap of true faith and was now, finally, on the path that was meant for her.

EPILOGUE

*V*irginia was floating on air when she shared the news with Samantha. Virginia loved her sister so much and had hated not telling her everything that had been going on. At the same time, she was thankful she had been able to make the decisions that she had on her own.

The girls invited Tristan over to dinner in the city, and to Virginia's disbelief, he and Sam hit it off famously. They had a natural give-and-take with their humor and just had a really easy way with one another. The three of them ate dinner, played board games and laughed late into the evening. Virginia especially noted when all three of them worked together in the kitchen to clean up from dinner. Sam even gave Tristan a hug when he left. Life, Virginia thought, was definitely changing.

Sam was finally able to come out to see the house for the first time since the renovation. The girls spent the entire day running around, reliving memories in every nook and cranny of the cottage. Sam couldn't believe what a transformation the house had gone through. "It's almost enough to make me want to live out on the island!" she had exclaimed. Later that day Sam told her sister, "Don't take this the wrong way. I love seeing you every single day, ridiculously so. But I have no doubt in my heart that this is where you belong right now. I'm really glad you did this."

Watching the sunset just like they used to do when they were growing up, Sam punctuated her thought with, "Aunt Emily was a smart woman. This place is perfect, and I'm glad she knew that it was perfect for you." Virginia agreed, which prompted the girls to start shouting into the cool, amber-hued night, "We love you, Aunt Emily! We miss you, Aunt Emily! Thank you for everything Aunt Emily! I miss your corn bread Aunt Emily!"

Virginia slowly started bringing personal belongings over to the cottage whenever she had a free day. She had decided to leave the downstairs room that had been hers as it was, and began spending more time setting up the large master bedroom. It almost felt like a right of passage, as if something had changed in her. She had grown out of the weaknesses of her youth, and moving into the upstairs room was a clean slate for the newer, wiser version of herself. It felt like the move Aunt Emily had in mind. She was now the lady of the house, and Virginia had to agree that it suited her.

In just a few short weeks, she and Tristan fell into a regular pattern where Virginia would arrive on the first ferry of the morning and would be met at the dock by Tristan, who came armed with two ceramic travel mugs of coffee. They would walk as slowly as the morning dictated back to the cottage, talking about everything and anything that they felt like. The most recent discussions were about the future. These conversations were becoming so enlivened, that one day they sat on the back deck, where they usually ended up at the end of their walk, and made a decision. They decided that Virginia deserved to have proper closure on the last, very long chapter of her life. They wanted to be 100% certain that nothing they were doing was out of overly built up emotion from having an intense experience together...though they both secretly felt in their hearts that things were unraveling exactly as they were supposed to.

~

SAMANTHA AND VIRGINIA decided to plan an impromptu sister's retreat, just the two of them, so they could catch up on everything. They agreed that it was long overdue and it would provide the perfect chance for Virginia to have a little space to heal before moving on. They were lucky enough to take advantage of the last blip of good weather when they road tripped up to Vancouver, BC. They even made their way over to Vancouver Island, where they camped near the water and just focused on getting back to basics.

One day while sitting out overlooking the rolling tide, a lightness rose around Virginia. She looked out and watched the seagulls commune along the sandy beach. She realized that the heavy burden that had lorded over her for so long had been swept away by a large Pacific gust. She felt so free being out from under Jason's oppressive personality and debts. Virginia looked out over the water and saw freedom, possibility, and hope ahead. After grilling some local salmon over an outdoor fire one evening, the girls sat at the little wooden table and discussed it.

"What would you think if I just took a little time not teaching art and just figuring out what I want to do next," Virginia asked her sister. Sam looked at her skeptically, and Virginia felt a bit disheartened. After a few minutes of staring at her sister, Sam leaned in and gave Virginia a look like she was an idiot. "Well duh! That's exactly what you should be doing," Sam chided. "Virginia, you are so much more talented and amazing than you give yourself credit for. What you do, or have been doing, is the bare minimum. You have so much more to offer the world, and if you don't move out to the cottage and spend some time getting to know yourself again, and figuring out what you want to do next, I'll change the locks on the duplex and force you out...Or at the very least, I'll be super annoyed with you for at least two weeks." she looked up mischievously and threw her sister a wry wink.

They both fell into giggles, raised their white wine and clinked glasses. It did feel like a special occasion after all, a chance for them to celebrate new beginnings, sisterhood, and all the things that they had to be thankful for.

VIRGINIA AND TRISTAN had decided to try not to email or text during the time she was gone, which was really only made possible because there was zero signal where they were staying. They told each other that if they really felt the need to communicate, then they could write each other letters old-fashioned style, and they would exchange them when she was back. It had been a cute idea, and even Sam had to admit, a pretty romantic compromise. Now, Virginia found herself writing to Tristan almost every night. Not the long letters she had envisioned, but instead short, almost journal-like entries. She told him about her childhood and her family growing up, about her losses, her regrets, and even more so, she told him the dreams that she had been carrying around for so long.

The longer Virginia was away, the stronger her clarity grew about Tristan and the house and the need for a new direction in her life. At the end of the trip, she bound her journal-letters into a homemade book for Tristan. It didn't seem like life-changing information, but she was glad that she'd written it, as much for herself as to share with him.

The girls sang and talked the entire drive home. They made a game of stopping at every restaurant or rest stop that deemed itself "famous" on its roadside sign. By the time they re-entered the state of Washington, they had already ingested more crab, poutine, coffee, and fried dough than any one human should in a day. Samantha griped loudly about the hours she would have to clock in at the gym to undo all the damage they were inflicting, but then she would career right back off the road as soon as she saw the next "world famous" sign.

When they finally arrived back home, Virginia found four letters hand-addressed to her mixed in among the bills and junk mail. That night she fell into bed, a cup of chamomile tea sat next to her reading lamp, and read. She felt like a giddy pre-teen with her first enormous crush. She couldn't remember the last time she had received a handwritten letter from someone, let alone four. Each one relayed some cute scenario that had happened to Tristan while she was gone. Something funny at church, the chaos that arose from materials for a job being on back order, his poor assistant Ross's girl problems. It allowed Virginia to feel like she had been there the entire time, and she found herself giggling and reacting along as she read. The last one was her favorite, though. She traced her finger over the words as she read:

"While you've been gone, I thought about my entire life. Everyone I've known, everyone I've dated, all the situations I've found myself in, and I realized something. I feel weird saying this and don't know how to go about it without seeming too over-the-top or too...too much? Too soon? Just "too" everything. But sometimes you just have to blaze ahead regardless of embarrassment or potential disaster, so I'm going to say it (here on the safety of a piece of paper). I feel like, without question, without a doubt, that you are the person I want to spend the rest of my life with. I have never been so certain about anything in my life. And I don't care if we don't have money or we don't have direction, but I know if we're together miracles will happen. So, like I said before, take all the time in the world to heal, but know that I will be here waiting for you always. And I promise that I will always support you, lift you up when you're down & no matter what, I promise I will always be your friend."

When Virginia read that last line, her eyes welled. He had written so many cute, funny and loving things, but the idea that he loved her as a friend beyond anything else, struck her deeply in a way that she hadn't been prepared for. Somehow his saying that meant more to her than any grand gesture he could have done. Best of all, she absolutely believed him...and felt the exact same way.

VIRGINIA ARRIVED at the dock with a white box tied tightly with red twine. Making her way down the floating platform to solid ground, she quickly spotted Tristan over in the little grassy park with two paper coffee cups in hand. Once she got within 15 feet of him, impulse overtook her, and she placed her box down on a nearby bench and ran at him full speed. He set down the tall paper coffee cups he was carrying just in time to catch her as she flung herself into his arms. They kissed for so long that Virginia started cracking up. Then she kissed him a little more for good measure.

They walked through town so that Virginia could see the early efforts that were being made of putting up holiday lights. She had brought cinnamon buns from a popular bakery in Vancouver, and he had decided to surprise her with Maple Lattes for a change. They walked arm in arm through the little town that was now starting to feel very much like home.

When they stopped at a crosswalk, Tristan pulled her in close and kissed her temple. The warmth of his skin against hers, mixed with the smell of his shampoo filled her with a warm comfort. When the intersection was clear, they began to walk again. The telltale tugging in her heart now felt more like tiny explosions. It was intense and amazing, and she hoped she would feel it for a very long time to come. She looked up to the crisp blue sky with its stretches of perforated white clouds, and with all the appreciation in her heart, mouthed, "thank you."

ACKNOWLEDGMENTS

I have so much love and appreciation in my heart for my amazing family and friends. I could not imagine life without each and every one of you!

To my mother-in-law Julia: Thank you for being the initial inspiration for this part of my journey. You are the original muse, and I hope you know how loved you are. Your support, brainstorming sessions and late nights reading add light to my life and make this process so much more rewarding.

To my BFF Caroline: I could not, would not, be able to do this without you. You are the rocket fuel to my very talkative rocket ship, and my life is better because you are in it. To making our dreams come true!

To the illustrious Rachel: Your creativity and inspiration have been tantamount to this project! Thank you for all that you do! Like Virginia's tugging heart, I just knew instinctively that you were meant to be part of this team. You are endlessly appreciated!

To the love of my life Drake: I love you so much, even though you are the wackiest, most complex man I know. Thank you for tolerating my antics, helping to add a man's perspective to things, and for always doing the dishes.

To my parents: I love you more than words can say. Nothing I have ever done would be possible without you. You have supported me, loved me, guided me and rolled your eyes at my goofy nature. No girl on Earth is as lucky as I am. Thank you, from the bottom of my very full heart.

TO LOVE...AND RENOVATE

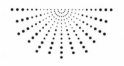

This book is a reminder that sometimes we have a plan that we think is right, so we plow head first toward our goal (whatever that may be at the time). At some point we find that the meticulously thought out schedule, the grand ideas, aren't working out quite the way we planned. We've gotten derailed somehow, or life seems to be hinting that we should be moving in a different direction. It's something that can be so hard to grapple with because we work so hard and we want to see our ideas succeed. But then, if we take the time to be silent, to listen to the tiny voice within, to trust what we know our heart is telling us, we just may find that an even better path has opened up and is waiting for us to run to it with open arms.

I hope we each find ourselves on the right path, in life, love, and all pursuits. However many twists and turns it takes, listen to that tiny voice within, and have faith that the best is still yet to come.

CONTENTS

CHAPTER ONE

*V*irginia Ellis looked down at her left hand and smiled.

Even after almost a year, she still couldn't help but stare at the delicate handcrafted ring glinting up at her. It was strange to think about how far she had come.

A little over a year ago, she'd been more miserable than she cared to admit. Her beloved Aunt Emily had passed away and she was completely blinded and unsatisfied in a relationship with a man who would never fully commit to her. Though at the time, she was in it way too deep to see that fact clearly.

Now, almost exactly twelve months later, here she was, living in her aunt's old cottage on a perfect little island just off the Seattle coast, planning her wedding to a man who was more than capable of commitment, and basking in a daily happiness that she'd long ago assumed didn't exist for real people.

When she thought about the two versions of her life, they seemed more different than she could have possibly imagined. It was as if they were lived by two completely separate people.

"Oh come on, you stupid bow." The words came from the striking blonde who struggled to affix a small ribbon around a delicate, but wily floral bouquet.

Then again, Virginia thought, not everything had changed. She glanced over at her sister who was seated next to her on the wood floor of the cottage, talking, once again about the trials and tribulations of her job at an upscale Seattle gym.

"I mean, I took this job because I thought it would be nice and easy and I could do my school work there," Samantha said angrily grasping for another baby blue ribbon to tie around the bouquets of winter flowers they were arranging.

"But guys like that make it almost impossible to focus on anything else," Samantha finished.

"Sam, it's customer service. What did you expect?" Virginia asked reasonably, her green eyes focused on the arrangement of the lavender and white flowers in her hand.

"I know it's not always quiet and civilized," Sam said. "I mean, I've dealt with muscle heads coming in at night and doing stupid stuff before. But this guy is...I don't know. He just makes it impossible to concentrate!"

"Impossible to concentrate on your school work, or on the job they're paying you to do?" Virginia asked throwing a cheeky glance at her sister.

"Very funny," Sam said with an eye roll at Virginia. "And it's both, if you must know. Every time I pull out a school book, he looks over my shoulder and tells me what I should underline. Or he offers to tutor me. And work stuff is no better. Every time I pull up the schedule he tells me that there's an easier way to do it or something. He doesn't shut up; he's a nightmare!"

Despite her sister's apparent distress, Virginia couldn't help but smile. She knew Sam wasn't really half as annoyed with this guy as she pretended to be. If she were, she would have told her boss about him and gotten the whole thing taken care of. The fact that she'd been moaning about this young man, who'd taken to coming into the gym every night Samantha worked for the past month, told Virginia that there was a lot more to Samantha's feelings than annoyance.

"You said he was good looking, right?" Virginia asked as tactfully as she could. Sure enough, she saw a slight pink flush appear on Samantha's cheeks.

"Most of the guys who come into the gym late at night are at least decent looking," Sam said with emphasis. "Doesn't mean they're not arrogant jerks. Besides, why do you care? You never go for the muscle head type."

"As we're putting bouquets together for my wedding, you should take that as a hint that I'm not asking for me," Virginia said, turning to her sister with her eyebrows raised playfully. Samantha rolled her eyes again, the pink blush still on her cheeks.

"Don't start on that 'my sister needs a date' stuff again," Samantha said. "Besides, if you knew how annoying this guy really was, you wouldn't want him to date any woman. Least of all me."

"If you knew how annoying you could be sometimes, you might eat those words," Virginia countered, trying to refrain from laughing.

Samantha put on an expression of fake outrage and threw a ribbon at Virginia, who grabbed it stealthily mid-air. Sisterly love; they both knew they were lucky to have it.

"Speaking of annoying," Sam said. "I don't get why you've got to do all these bouquets by hand. Aren't there people you can pay to do this kind of stuff?"

"That costs money," Virginia said. "And we're trying to save as much of that as possible right now."

"You could've waited, you know," Samantha said with a sideways glance at Virginia. "At least until you'd saved up enough. You could still have a winter wedding next year."

"We didn't want to wait," Virginia said simply. "Besides, neither of us really wanted a huge, fancy wedding anyway."

Samantha shrugged her shoulders as if to say 'to each her own' but Virginia didn't miss the skeptical glances her little sister kept throwing her way.

Virginia did her best to ignore it, knowing that Sam was simply overprotective of her big sister. Samantha was a jaw-dropping beauty which had led to a lifetime of being hit on by men, and Virginia's little sister had grown nothing if not wary of romance because of it.

It wasn't that Samantha didn't like Tristan. In fact, Tristan was the only one of Virginia's boyfriends her little sister had ever actually approved of. In fact, Virginia was still surprised when Sam didn't object to Tristan joining them for dinner or lunch, even though he'd done it several times since proposing. In fact, they were scheduled to do it again this evening as soon as he got off his latest renovation project.

Despite that, Sam had never been an out-and-out romantic and just wanted to make sure her sister wasn't rushing into things.

Virginia, however, had never felt less rushed or more at ease. Despite the mountains of things she still had to prepare for the ceremony and reception, she couldn't help but feel both calm and ridiculously happy.

At the end of the day, it didn't matter whether the bouquets were all exactly arranged alike or if the caterer came through for the reception. As long as she found herself facing Tristan at the end of the aisle, the man she knew she loved and felt she was meant to be with, then that was all that mattered to her.

Besides, after waiting years for her ex-boyfriend, Jason, to propose, she was sick of putting off this major milestone.

"That's the last of them, I think," Virginia said as she handed the perfectly arranged bouquet over to Samantha so that her sister could tie a lacy ribbon around it.

"Thank God for that," Samantha said. "I don't care if I never see a fresh flower again in my life."

"I hope it doesn't take you too long to get over that," Virginia said. "You'll be holding plenty of them at the wedding."

Samantha heaved a dramatic sigh. "I guess that's a sacrifice I can make for my big sister."

"You know I'd do the same for you," Virginia winked.

Samantha's smile turned into a small frown as she wrapped the ribbon around the last of the bouquets.

"I don't know if you'll ever get the chance," Sam said matter of factly. "It seems the only guys who are interested in me are the meatheads at the gym. Not exactly marriage material."

Samantha looked up as though she were making a joke, but Virginia recognized all too well the worry behind her words. She'd felt it herself a million times with Jason. While she pretended that years of waiting for a ring from him was all part of his plan to propose perfectly, she knew, deep down, it wasn't. There was always something real behind it.

And she could tell that there was something just as real behind Samantha's jovially sad expression. What's more, Virginia thought she knew how to fix it.

"Tristan wanted me to ask you out to lunch with us on Friday," Virginia said. "His best man will be there. He thought you two should meet before the wedding."

Samantha set the bouquet down and gave her sister a knowing glare. "This isn't another one of your matchmaking schemes, is it?"

"It's not my scheme," Virginia said defensively. "It's Tristan's. But while we're on the subject, his friend is single. And much nicer than those guys at the gym."

Samantha still looked at her sister skeptically, but finally, she heaved a sigh and seemed to relent.

"Ok, I'll go," she said, "but only because I think it'd be good to meet the guy I'm walking down the aisle with before the wedding."

"That's all I ask," Virginia said.

Even though Samantha rolled her eyes wordlessly, Virginia could see a small smile creep across her sister's face as she placed the last bouquet in line with the others.

Virginia knew that, despite Samantha's protests to the contrary, her little sister was just as excited about the prospect of a good date as any other woman she knew.

As soon as Sam and Virginia set all the fully arranged and tied bouquets in the small box set aside for them a knock sounded at the door.

With a huge grin, Virginia rushed down the hall to the front door and pulled it open.

Her heart still thudded when she saw the tall man with tousled brown hair, a smooth complexion, and bright blue eyes smiling back at her.

"Hey, you," Tristan said with a smile just as bright as hers.

"Hey yourself," she answered.

When Tristan entered Virginia couldn't help but allow the attraction to show on her face. He was tall and slim, with a naturally lean and muscular body from doing the physical work of his job. He had all of the earmark signs of possessing a youthful Irish charm, but when he walked into a room there was no question that he was a man. She often thought of him as the heartthrob in a Hallmark movie. Not the leading man from an action flick that was overtly in your face, but that guy who came in with his boyish smirk and charming, understated personality and slowly won a girl's heart.

She loved the way his textured hair was always a little bit disheveled, yet somehow perfectly well-maintained, and his eyes were always slightly crinkled in the corner from the small smile that danced on his lips.

She put her arms around his shoulders and stood on her tiptoes for a kiss. Being a bit shorter than average, Virginia usually stood on tiptoe to hug men. It used to annoy her, but with Tristan even this made her feel special somehow.

It wasn't until she pulled away, that she saw the small bag of groceries in his hand.

"Are you planning on staying?" she asked nodding to the bag. "Or is this just a quick hello before you head home to put your groceries away?"

"No such luck, you're still stuck with me for a while tonight," he said. "I thought I'd bring dinner over. With all the work you've been doing for the wedding, I figured you wouldn't have time to get to the store."

"Well, you were right about that," Virginia said leading him into the house and closing the door behind him. "At least we've finally got the bouquets done, but they took most of the afternoon."

"Please tell me that's dinner," Samantha called from the living room as Virginia and Tristan walked into the hall.

"Ask and you shall receive," Tristan replied. "Courtesy of the corner grocery store."

Virginia saw Sam wince slightly at this. While the local store in Sweetwater was very quaint and provided all of your basic needs, some even gourmet, nothing there was particularly healthy. Despite her thin physique and long blonde hair, health and weight-loss were big watchwords for Samantha.

"I take it that it's not salad then," Samantha said sounding slightly wary.

"It's pasta," Tristan said faltering slightly. "I didn't even think to get salad."

He threw a slightly nervous glance to Virginia. After several months of getting on Samantha's good side, Tristan was still slightly afraid of Virginia's sister. He knew how close the two girls were and he was also very aware of the fact that Sam rarely approved of Virginia's romantic partners, so at times like these he merely kept quiet.

"Honestly, Sam," Virginia said. "I think you can stand to eat carbs for one night. Your diet can survive one meal."

At Virginia's stern look, Sam relaxed back into her seat and heaved a sigh. "Well, at least we won't have to cook," she relented. "After putting all those floral arrangements together I don't want to do anything else tonight."

"I thought you might feel that way," Tristan said. "That's why I got pasta. It's the one foolproof dish I know I can make without burning anything down."

"That's not quite true," Virginia pointed out. "I taught you to make that roast chicken dish and you didn't manage to catch the chicken or the house on fire."

"True," Tristan answered. "However I still don't trust myself to do it without you hovering over my shoulder. Or at least standing nearby with a fire extinguisher."

Tristan insisted that the girls sit on the couch and turn the TV on while he set up in the kitchen. As he moved out of the room, a ringing came from his pocket. Shifting the bag of groceries to his left hand, he took out his phone.

Virginia saw his face fall when he read the name displayed. He stared down at the phone for a strangely long time, seemingly contemplating what to do, before hastily clicking the end call button.

"Who was that?" Virginia asked.

"No one," Tristan said unconvincingly fumbling to put his phone back into his pocket. "Wrong number."

He looked over at her and gave her a small smile that looked more like a grimace before hurrying off into the kitchen.

"What was that about?" Sam asked, a suspicious note in her voice.

"I don't know," Virginia admitted. "Probably nothing."

She didn't know if she was trying to convince herself or her sister when she said it. Immediately, she knew that she hadn't been successful on either front.

Samantha threw her a skeptical look but said nothing as she grabbed the remote and began flipping through the channels before landing on a silly looking reality TV show.

As much as Virginia tried to pay attention to the TV, she found she wasn't able to. Her thoughts kept drifting to the 'wrong number' Tristan had hastily ignored before scampering away to make dinner.

He'd gotten a lot of 'wrong numbers' the past couple of days. Each one was greeted with that same white-faced look of familiarity and discomfort. No matter what he told her, Virginia knew that none of them were 'nothing'.

She'd tried to tell herself that she was just paranoid. After years spent with Jason, who had happily flirted with other girls and very likely cheated on her several times, it was only natural that she would be cautious in her new relationship.

Even though she knew, or at least she thought she knew, that Tristan would never cheat on her, she couldn't help that niggling little fear from eating away at the back of her mind.

After all, Tristan had promised to never keep any secrets from her, and never to lie to her.

And even if these phone calls weren't from other girls, they certainly were not 'wrong numbers'. Tristan telling her they were, was the first lie he had ever told her, and the realization of it unnerved her.

CHAPTER TWO

*B*y morning, Virginia had completely put the mysterious phone calls Tristan had been ignoring out of her head. She had told herself that, despite Samantha's assertion that she and Tristan had only known each other for a relatively short time, it felt like much longer. She truly felt in her heart that she knew Tristan. She was convinced, in fact, she knew Tristan much better than she'd ever known Jason.

No matter what Tristan's reasons were for keeping the phone calls from her, she was certain he would never, knowingly, do anything to hurt her. By the time she finally fell asleep the night before, she'd managed to convince herself that whatever secret Tristan was holding, was his own to bear, and she was sure he would tell her about it when the time was right. Plus, she had wedding prep to do and there was only so much headspace she could spare at the moment.

As firmly convinced of his innocence as she could possibly be, Virginia packed up half a dozen donuts and headed out to Tristan's apartment on the outskirts of downtown.

The newly fallen December snow had recently made driving on the small island roads a bit more perilous than usual. In light of this, Virginia decided to walk. In a town as small as Sweetwater, you could even walk to 'the other side of town' if you weren't in a rush. Today was perfect for a nice brisk winter walk, with the sun glimmering off the crystalline snow and the air as refreshingly nippy as ever. Being able to walk was one of Virginia's favorite things about living on the island, especially when her path took her through the middle of the picture-perfect downtown.

All the lights lining the main street had been strung with thick, cheerful green garlands tied ceremoniously with red bows. The small shop windows proudly displayed an array of holly wreaths, miniature Santa Clauses, reindeers and nativity scenes.

This, combined with the still white snow, gave Sweetwater a very Norman Rockwell feel, as if it were straight out of one of his quintessential small town paintings. Virginia was convinced that the whole place should be memorialized on the front of a Christmas postcard.

That was one thing she hadn't really experienced as a child. When she was young, she was here almost every summer but was rarely on the island for Christmas. Now, with Christmas just two weeks away and her wedding three weeks out, everything seemed that much more magical.

The scene brought her such warm, giddy feelings that she was almost sad to leave the bright lights and cheery shop windows of Main Street behind as she turned the corner towards Tristan's small apartment complex.

The Cedar Avenue Apartments where Tristan lived, boasted small balconies and few amenities. It was a rare building on the island that didn't sport much personality outside of the requisite seaside charm that simply resulted from being located here. While it wasn't the worst place in the world, when Virginia first visited Tristan there she had used as much tact as she could to offer him help in finding a better place to live.

"The location is perfect and I'm out on jobs most of the time that I don't spend much time at home," he'd said. "Besides, with this place I can actually afford to stockpile money into my savings while living here. That alone is good enough for me."

After the wedding, the plan was for him to move into the cottage with her; the house that they had literally re-built together.

That thought made her smile as she lifted her hand and rapped on the door. A moment later, her smile widened when Tristan's gleaming blue eyes appeared, his hair still slightly mussed with sleep, his slight five o'clock shadow more prominent than usual.

"You look like you could use a little morning pick me up," she said, lifting the box of homemade donuts.

"Uh, you're a savior!" he said groggily, opening the door and ushering her inside.

"I thought I'd come over a little early for the counseling appointment. That way we could eat breakfast without feeling rushed."

With a quick kiss, they moved into the kitchen where Virginia could already smell the coffee brewing, though, from the look of the pot, Tristan had just started it.

"You're starting the brew a little late this morning aren't you?" she asked.

"Is it still considered late if that's my second pot?"

Virginia turned to him and raised an eyebrow as she set the donuts down on the counter.

"You drank a whole pot of coffee by yourself?" she asked. "And you still need more?"

"It's been a rough night," he said.

SOPHIE MAYS

As Virginia readied breakfast, he told her that he'd spent most of the night going over plans for the job he and his assistant Ross were supposed to go out to that afternoon.

"It was supposed to be a quick and easy job," he said, "but it turns out the client is impossible. She's made 'adjustments' to two sets of approved plans already. And it wasn't until I got up this morning that I saw she had finally okayed the latest ones."

"She's cutting it down to the wire, isn't she?" Virginia asked while filling his cup from the fresh pot and arranging the donuts on a plate.

"That's what we both told her."

He took the cup with a nod of thanks as they moved into the living room attached to the kitchen and sat down on the surprisingly comfortable couch.

"But she's old and pretty demanding," he said. "I just hope she won't interfere too much once we actually get started."

"Which'll still be this afternoon?" Virginia asked not trying to hide the hint of trepidation in her voice as she picked up a caramelized banana brulee donut and bit into it. To tell the truth, she'd secretly been hoping that this particular job which was located on a neighboring island would be postponed yet again.

Renovating the guest room and bath for a wealthy widow would certainly bring in money that they needed for the wedding, but it also meant that Tristan would have to be away a lot during the week and would end up working late nights with the added commute. That was certainly not something Virginia was looking forward to.

"Actually," he said setting down his coffee mug and turning to look at her apologetically. "Ross and I'll probably have to leave as soon as we're done at the church."

"I thought you wouldn't have to leave until after lunch?" Virginia said feeling her stomach sink with disappointment.

172

"I'm sorry, V. Would it help if I promised to bring you breakfast tomorrow to make up for it?"

He took her hand and she looked over at him. His eyes were every bit as earnest as they always were. Slowly, she relented with a playful eye roll and nodded.

"No donuts though," she countered. "I don't want you buying from my competition."

"Fair enough," he answered, and put his arm around her shoulder. "I'll get breakfast sandwiches from the cafe downtown."

Virginia smiled and felt her body relax. "That sounds good to me."

With that, she turned her face towards him and he bent down kissing her full on the mouth.

It was a sweet, gentle kiss, the kind they usually shared when they said either hello or goodbye to one another. Soon, however, Tristan's fingers laced into her soft brown hair and Virginia could feel their bodies fall back against the pillows of the couch.

The kiss deepened and before she knew it, her arms were wrapped tightly around Tristan's body. She told herself it wouldn't go too far, it would only be for a few minutes, but deep down she knew that her attempts at rationalizing their procrastination were easier than admitting the truth. It was becoming more and more difficult for both of them to keep their hands off each other.

This became apparent when Tristan moved over her on the couch, his hand running up the side of her body. Virginia knew she should put a stop to this, pull away, sit up, but, the truth was, she didn't want to.

Luckily, or unluckily, depending on the point of view, it was at that moment that Virginia's cell phone perched on the coffee table rang. Tristan stopped and he pulled away with an adorably apologetic expression.

He moved from over the top of her and she sat up taking the cell phone in hand. She looked down at the name on the screen. It was Amanda.

Out of the corner of her eye, she saw Tristan adjusting his jeans on the couch as she pressed the button to accept the call.

"Hey, Amanda," Virginia said, with a glance toward Tristan to let him know who was calling. He grinned in recognition.

Amanda was the real estate agent who had originally put them in contact when Virginia first needed renovations done to her then newly-inherited cottage where she now lived.

"Hello, Virginia," Amanda said. "I hope I didn't catch you at a bad time."

The older woman's voice sounded hurried on the other end of the phone, something Virginia had come to expect. Amanda had been caring for her two young grandchildren since their parents had moved overseas. Amanda had agreed to look out for them until her daughter and her husband got their house ready, but job uncertainties and housing setbacks had made it so the grandkids hadn't yet gone to join their parents permanently. Though as hectic as it made Amanda's life, Virginia knew that she was thankful to be able to provide the love and stability the kids needed.

"Not at all," Virginia answered. "What's up?"

"Well, I have a sort of favor to ask," she said sounding a bit reluctant. "It's a favor of you and Tristan really. But I thought I'd call you first."

"What kind of favor?" Virginia asked. She always happy to help Amanda if she could. She looked over to Tristan as she asked the question, indicating that he was involved in this as well. He seemed to get the message and moved to sit on the edge of the couch, watching Virginia's conversation with interest.

"The owners of the bed and breakfast in town have decided to sell," Amanda relayed. "However it needs some renovating to bring it up to date before I can get a decent price for it. They don't have a lot of money to spend, but they are just the sweetest people, as you know. And the place has so much character and potential. I was hoping you and Tristan would be willing to take a look at it."

Amanda's voice sounded both hopeful and tired. Virginia knew she didn't have it in her to refuse the older woman. After all, it was Amanda who had sold her and her sister the townhome in Seattle where Sam still lived, she was the one who introduced her to her future husband, and on top of both of those things, those bonds had begun to develop into a friendship.

Amanda went on to say, "I mean, I know that you don't work together as an official team per se, but with your design vision and his architectural eye, it just makes sense. Particularly on a project like this. The cottage came out gorgeous, and I know you've been lending your hand to his projects over the last year, and I don't know, it just works. I just can't get it out of my head that the two of you are the perfect people to do this."

Virginia felt herself blush at the compliment. She did love working alongside Tristan and she adored dreaming up ways to infuse renewed personality into the old properties in the area. Regardless of her soft spot for Amanda and old properties, with the wedding and Virginia's painting and the donut business all vying for her attention, she wasn't sure there was any extra time.

"Listen," Amanda said. "I know it's not a great time for you with the wedding and everything, but if you could just come by the property and take a look, I'd really appreciate it."

As though to emphasize the difficult spot Amanda was in, Virginia heard Amanda's granddaughter Lily screaming while Lily's little brother Mikey began to cry in the background. Amanda certainly was under a lot of stress. Surely it wouldn't hurt to just take a peek.

"Tristan's got a project he's working on right now," Virginia said reluctantly, "but I could come and take a look at it. When would you like me to stop by?"

"Oh, any time today or tomorrow would be great," Amanda exhaled, relief evident in her voice. "In fact, I'm headed over there right now. Thanks, Virginia, you're a lifesaver."

"No problem," Virginia replied. "I'll probably see you a little later today."

"Bye, Aunt Virginia," Virginia heard little Lily's voice call through the phone and she couldn't help but laugh.

"Sorry about that," Amanda said.

"Don't be," Virginia answered. "Tell Lily I said goodbye to her, too."

"Will do," Amanda answered.

With that, Virginia hung up the phone and turned back to Tristan.

"I hope you didn't commit us to another project," Tristan said, brow furrowed in mock distress. Although the undertone of his voice gave him away because she knew full well that he didn't have the heart to turn down Amanda any more than she did.

"I didn't commit to anything," Virginia answered. "I just said I'd go by and take a look. It's the old bed and breakfast. Apparently, Roger and Kathy are selling."

Tristan's brow furrowed for real as his gaze drifted down in somber contemplation. Virginia thought she knew why. Roger had always been a friend of his.

"I'd heard they were thinking about it," Tristan recalled. "Apparently it hasn't been doing well the past few years, and I know that they'd like to spend more time traveling while they're still able-bodied enough to do so."

"Amanda said it'll need some renovations," Virginia continued. "She wants us to take a look and see what we think we could do with it."

Tristan sat back on the couch, a pensive look on his face.

"I would like to help Roger out, to tell the truth," Tristan said. "I mean, he's done a lot for me over the years."

He looked over at Virginia, a question forming. "Do you think we could take on a project? I mean, with the wedding and everything."

"I don't know," Virginia admitted. "It couldn't hurt to go down and just take a look at it, could it?"

Tristan looked down for a moment then back up at her, a small smile crossing his face. "No," he said. "I guess it couldn't."

She smiled back at him and gave a little nod.

"Good," she said leaning back into the sofa and nuzzling under his arm. "I'll probably go over sometime today or tomorrow."

"Ok," he answered. His soft blue eyes looked right into her cheerful, loving green ones and she could tell he was only half a moment from picking up where they had left off before Amanda's call had interrupted them.

Suddenly, he broke the connection, cleared his throat and moved his arm away from the back of the couch. Virginia felt her body register the disappointment.

With an animated expression he glanced over to her brightly. "Speaking of things that couldn't hurt," he said. "I suppose it wouldn't hurt to head over to the church a little early. In fact, it would probably help us stay away from the temptation of the couch."

Before she could answer, he stood and offered her a hand up. She took it half gratefully and half regretfully. She knew he was right. Sitting on the couch like that had become way too tempting lately.

177

Then again, as the date for the wedding got closer, a lot of things had become tempting.

"I'll clean up a bit, then we can start walking over," she told him.

"Good plan."

Before she could turn to pick up their coffee mugs, he grabbed her hand and pulled her in for a kiss.

This one was quick but searing. Tristan moved his lips to her ear, and Virginia almost gasped when she felt his warm breath on her skin.

"If it were up to me I'd marry you tomorrow," he whispered, then after a long moment, he kissed her on her temple. A second later, he pulled back with that sweet, half sinister smile and said, "I'll wait outside."

Before she could say anything, he walked to the front door of his apartment, opened it, and disappeared down the stone steps, leaving Virginia gaping after him in the living room, her heart pounding. She let out a huge exhale before she forced herself to finish clearing the breakfast dishes. She couldn't help but agree with Tristan on at least one point, that couch could definitely not be trusted.

CHAPTER THREE

*T*he church Virginia and Tristan attended in downtown Sweetwater was housed in the old, abandoned movie theater. When Virginia walked into the lobby, she swore she could still smell the intense aroma of popcorn and butter permeating the air. She had always loved going to the movie theater and there wasn't anything she didn't love about popcorn, so adding those two things to an incredible church community, and Virginia was in heaven every time she walked through the heavy gilded doors.

The red carpeting was still there, stained with permanent soda markings from the spills of years past. From what Virginia had come to learn, the church had been talking about moving into a new building for years. The money for it, however, was very hard to come by for everyone it seemed, and while the building was a little cramped, it was large enough to hold the Sunday crowd. For now, their ever-optimistic pastor, Phil Sherman, said that was enough.

Virginia and Tristan walked hand-in-hand down a narrow hallway off the main lobby that led to the pastor's office. It was uncharacteristically locked when they arrived.

"That's what we get for showing up early," Virginia said reluctantly sliding against the wall, a to-go cup of coffee in hand. They'd stopped at the local cafe for two latte's hoping it would kill some time before their appointment.

"Well, it's not that early now," Tristan said pulling out his phone and checking the time. "In fact, Phil should have been here about two minutes ago."

"Not everyone is always on time like you are, Mr. Punctual," Virginia teased, lightly nudging his arm.

"I've never heard any complaints from you," Tristan retorted with a smirk.

She was about to give a teasingly snarky retort when quick footsteps sounded from down the hall.

"Sorry I'm late," Phil Sherman said shifting a stack of papers from one hand to the other. "Got a call from a client who wanted to do a breakfast meeting. It ended up running later than I'd expected."

Phil had recently taken on some part-time work for an online company. It gave him the flexibility to attend to all of his church duties but also ensured that his wife could stay home with their new baby who was born just two months before.

Despite the positive aspects, the toll showed in the pastor's youthful, but recently worry-lined face. Virginia couldn't help but notice that beneath his glasses he now sported sleep-deprived bags, and his otherwise brown hair had developed a couple of very prominent grays.

Tristan must have noticed this too because he turned to the pastor with a sympathetic smile.

"That's all right," he said. "We're just glad you could meet with us."

Normally, lateness was one of Tristan's biggest pet peeves, but she knew that he was able to overlook it for pastor Phil. The appreciation showed in Phil's smile when he turned it gratefully to Tristan.

"Thanks," he said reaching down and unlocking the door to his office. "The holidays are the busiest time of year for both of my jobs. So in case you're wondering, that's why I've been running around like a chicken with my head cut off."

Virginia and Tristan both offered sympathetic smiles as the door to the pastor's small office swung open.

Like the lobby outside, the office still had vestiges of its previous use. This room used to be a break room for the movie theater employees. But, Phil had put a desk, several chairs, and some knick knacks in there. Now it still looked like a break room, but one that had been inexpertly repurposed.

"Sit on down, you two," he said moving several cluttered papers off his desk. "Sorry, the office is a little bit of a mess. Somedays it seems like there's only so much I can do."

"How's the search for a church office assistant coming?" Virginia asked. She knew the church had been searching for a part-time office assistant who could come into the church at least two or three days a week to answer phone calls, organize the office and generally create a more cohesive system.

The sigh Phil gave them told Virginia it wasn't going well.

"We're not able to pay much more than minimum wage," he said. "There are a few retired members of the congregation who would be able to volunteer, answer phones and things like that. But they wouldn't be able to tackle everything we need to be done."

"And no one else has applied?" Tristan asked. "I mean from the college in the city or anything?"

Phil shook his head.

"It's a long commute for a little payoff." He shuffled some papers before looking up. "Don't look so worried you two," he said with a sudden slight chuckle at Virginia and Tristan's equally furrowed brows. "The church will be fine. We'll find a way to make it all work, we always do. Besides we're not here to talk about my lack of an office assistant, we're here to talk about you two." He directed his focused attention toward them and affixed his hands to the desk in front of him. "How have things been going?"

Virginia hated not having a helpful answer to his dilemma, so she couldn't deny that she was glad for the subject change. Tristan and Phil were long-time friends, so he had already begun to talk animatedly about the plans they'd made for the wedding as well as the new project he'd come upon.

"I can't deny it's been a little stressful balancing work, life, and wedding planning," Tristan admitted. "But we've managed to make it work so far, and as you can imagine, Virginia's doing all the hard stuff on the wedding."

"Only because you couldn't put a centerpiece together to save your life," Virginia joked.

"I admit I'm terrible at flower arrangements and bows," he conceded. "That's why you're the artist."

He glanced over at her with that smile. The smile that made her feel like the most beautiful, accomplished woman in the world. Virginia couldn't help but smile and blush as she averted her eyes self-consciously down at her feet.

"And I'm sure your families have helped too," Phil offered more matter of factly than questioningly. "Family is very important, not only when it comes to the wedding, but the marriage as well."

Virginia thought she saw Tristan wince ever so slightly before he quickly regained his previous composure.

"Yeah," he answered with a geniality that sounded a little forced, "Virginia's sister's been a big help."

"I'm sure she has," Phil said leaning over his desk and looking at Tristan with a much more serious expression. "But I actually wanted to see if we could talk about your family today, Tristan."

Virginia felt the air leave the room. She looked up at Tristan whose jaw was suddenly clenched. He gripped her hand much more tightly than he had before. She continued to look up at him and squeezed his hand back, hoping this would be enough support for him. He looked down at their intertwined hands and gave an appreciative half-smile before continuing.

"Well, my brother Adam will be coming in from California a couple days before the ceremony. He's ushering, so he'll be helping out."

"Great," Phil said. "What about your parents?"

"What about them?" Tristan was walking the line, trying to be nonchalant, but his discomfort could be felt in the air.

"Well, I know Virginia's uncle can't be at the ceremony but he's sent a check to help with the funds," Phil said. "Her sister, as you've said, is helping a lot. But I realized, you've never mentioned your parents."

Virginia felt Tristan's hand move away from hers and run down his jeans, gripping his knee. When she glanced up at him, his face was white as he looked down at the floor.

She'd known that this might happen if the pastor tried to bring up Tristan's parents.

Her fiancé had told her a little about his family. She knew he still kept in touch with his younger brother, Adam, the one who would be ushering for their wedding. Even so, they weren't all that close. When Tristan had refused to join his father in the family business after high school, his father had cut him off completely. Tristan's mother, never quite strong enough to go against her husband, had barely any contact with her eldest son since, choosing instead to safely glean messages and updates through her other son Adam.

It broke Virginia's heart knowing, or assuming, the pain it caused Tristan. Strangely though, the way Tristan's face looked now, it seemed as though there was even more to it than that. It had been years since he'd been essentially disowned and he usually acted like it was no big deal; something he was a little resentful of, but that hadn't affected his life overall.

"My parents won't be coming to the wedding," he said. His voice was much more terse and direct than she had ever heard it before.

"I take it you don't have the best relationship with them, then?" Phil asked.

"You could say that," Tristan responded dryly.

Virginia could tell by his tone that he wanted to put an end to the conversation. Phil leaned further over his desk, making it clear that he wasn't going to let Tristan off that easily. Tristan seemed to be able to sense that too.

After a moment's silence, he heaved another sigh and threw a cautious glance to Virginia. She ran her hand over his and gave it a squeeze hoping it was encouraging enough. Tristan's face softened a little and told her it was.

"My dad owns a contracting company in California," he said. "After I graduated from high school, he expected me to go into business with him. When I told him I wanted to start my own business, he threw me out of the house. Haven't heard from him since."

"And what about your mother?" Phil continued.

"Mom and I talked over the phone a couple times after I got to Seattle," he shrugged. "Then she stopped returning my calls. I asked Adam about it, he told me Dad had gotten to her. He forbid her to speak to me, and she doesn't like to go against my dad."

"So, have you tried to reach out to them since?" Phil probed evenly.

"There's really no point," Tristan said shortly. "If I've got something to say, I tell Adam and he'll try to talk to them about it. Even that usually doesn't work, but it's our system. My dad's stubborn. He won't listen to anyone."

"Do they know about the wedding?"

Tristan shrugged again. "Adam may have told them," he said. "I don't really know. Anyway, it doesn't matter. They're not a part of my life anymore."

"The thing is," Phil said, "I think it matters a lot more than you know. Marriage is a very complex thing, and it can be difficult at times. And believe it or not, problems with extended families have a tendency to bleed into it. A bad relationship with your family could manage to poison your marriage if you're not careful."

"That won't happen," Tristan said firmly. "I mean, if my mom or my dad reaches out to me, I'm happy to talk to them, but I'm not going to force it."

Tristan spoke with a firm finality that Virginia knew even Pastor Phil could not argue with; not at this particular moment at least. He proved this when he looked at Tristan sadly and threw up his hands in surrender.

"Ok," he said. "I've given my advice and that's about all I can do. Now, let's talk a little more about how you two are doing."

The rest of the meeting was much more pleasant. Tristan and Virginia blushingly admitted that it was becoming more and more difficult to keep their physical relationship in check. To their surprise, this shamefaced admission was met with laughter rather than scorn.

"Well, that's to be expected," Phil said with a booming chuckle. "When you're in love, as you two clearly are, it's hard not to express it. Just look for patterns that come with the temptation. Places and times of day when you find yourselves most tempted and try to avoid those as best you can. Just remember, it's only a few more weeks. After that, you have the rest of your lives to be together."

The meeting lasted about half an hour after that. They talked about the ceremony, the dress rehearsal, and what to expect on the day. When Phil ushered them out of the office with handshakes and hugs all around and a warm goodbye, Virginia checked the time and saw that it was much later than she had expected it would be.

"We're going to have to walk quickly to get to the ferry," Tristan said as he and Virginia made their way to the dock. "Ross is probably already there."

"To be fair, Ross is almost always there early. He's the only person I know who's more insane about punctuality than you are."

Tristan laughed and playfully elbowed her ribs.

"I'm not insane," he said. "I'm considerate."

"Call it what you will," she said, "but Ross has probably been there since nine this morning."

They crossed Main Street and turned toward the short road that led to the docks. Luckily, it wasn't a long walk from the church to the ferry and Virginia knew that the lunchtime ferry rarely arrived on time anyway. She was sure Tristan and Ross would make it to their destination with plenty of time to spare.

All the same, Tristan kept taking out his phone and glancing at it every minute or so, as though fretting about his tardiness would somehow make the time slow down. Virginia didn't say anything about this. She was too used to this habit now to care.

Indeed, his phone didn't catch her full attention until a vibrating ring sounded from his pocket.

"Probably Ross," he said taking it out once more. When he looked at the display, however, his face fell and went white, the same way it had when he'd gotten the "wrong number" the night before.

Quickly, he stuffed the phone back into his pocket, nervous that someone would see it.

"Who was it?" Virginia asked.

"Nothing," he said. "Telemarketers. They keep calling me. Don't know why."

Virginia couldn't help but think that this excuse was even lamer than the wrong number one he'd used the night before.

Virginia, whose spirits had been relatively high after their meeting with the pastor, despite the awkward exchange about Tristan's family, felt them fall significantly. Now there could be absolutely no doubt that Tristan was keeping something from her. Worse, judging by the look on his face when he'd seen the phone both times, it wasn't something trivial.

Her hand remained in his as they neared the dock though it was much looser than it had been before the phone call. Even when they caught sight of Ross waiting for them by the ropes where the ferry had just landed, Virginia realized she really didn't even feel like partaking in the upbeat banter she normally shared with the younger man.

"There you are!" Ross said, his boisterous, jovial tone still in place. "Thought I was going to have to go on my own. And believe me, I did not want to have to explain to the old hag why her main contractor hasn't shown."

"You know, Ross," Tristan said wearily. "If you want us to keep getting wealthy clients, it would probably be smart not to call them old hags."

"You know I don't do it to her face," Ross said in an animated defense. "Just behind her back. Hey, Virginia. How're things?"

Ross turned his happy, goofy face towards Virginia and she flashed a smile in return. Ross was average height and could have been a stocky boy if he weren't so well-toned. She often thought of him as a cross between a professional boxer and a business professional. With his wide, chiseled jaw and dirty blonde hair pushed back neatly, he was both boyish and ruggedly masculine, and his look spoke to the dedication he put in every aspect of his life. He was younger than Tristan and while his attitude could be more than a bit juvenile at times, she knew he was more ambitious than he let on.

Even now, he was going to the University of Seattle to earn a Master's in business, after which he had dreams of one day running his own architecture firm. Until that time came, however, he worked for Tristan to pay the bills and learn.

"Things are good," Virginia answered him. "Don't forget, you've both got lunch with me and Sam tomorrow."

"Looking forward to it," Ross said cheerily. "From what you've told me about your sister, she sounds like just my type."

He gave Virginia a roguish wink which made Tristan roll his eyes.

"Ross, you think every girl breathing is your type," he said.

Ross simply shrugged as Tristan turned to Virginia.

"We'd better get going," he told her. "I won't be in until late tonight so I'll see you tomorrow?"

Virginia found herself hesitating more than usual before answering him. She saw the smile fall slightly on Tristan's face.

"V?" he asked, his face concerned. "Is everything ok?"

She thought briefly about pressing the issue of the phone calls, but then she saw Ross out of the corner of her eye. His arms were crossed as he stared at the receding ferry line and he was tapping his foot with a subconscious urge to leave. Clearly, this wasn't the time or place for a long confrontation.

So instead Virginia forced a smile and turned back to Tristan.

"Yeah," Virginia said as genuinely as she could. "Yeah. Everything's fine. See you tomorrow."

She got up on her tiptoes and gave him a swift kiss.

"I love you," he said when she pulled away.

She couldn't help but smile even though she felt a slightly hesitant tug in her heart.

"I love you too," she answered.

With one last smile, Tristan moved as quickly as he could to join Ross. Virginia watched both of them board the ferry and disappear.

Once the ferry had left the dock, Virginia started on the path towards the cottage. It didn't take long for her to realize that, for the first time, the cottage was somewhere she did not want to go. She knew that between the secretive phone calls and the discussion about Tristan's family at the church, being alone with her thoughts wasn't the best idea. She knew she would start thinking in circles and stressing herself out.

What she needed was a project to keep her mind off everything. What's more, she needed a project that involved other people.

With a sudden spurt of energy, she pulled out her own phone and sent off a swift text to Amanda.

With the wheels in motion, she turned away from the forested path that led to the cottage and started back downtown along the road that would lead towards the bed and breakfast.

CHAPTER FOUR

*A*manda, a tired but cheerful looking woman with bouncy bright red hair and a smart suit met Virginia as she walked up Main Street towards the building that held Roger and Kathy's bed and breakfast.

It wasn't the standalone Victorian style home that most people associated with bed and breakfasts. Roger and Kathy's little inn held residence in a quaint slice of Main Street's shop-strewn facade. However, once a weary traveler stepped inside, he or she would find themselves in a cozy, home-like atmosphere, complete with doilies, mismatched knickknacks, and the owners' three cats.

"Thank you so much for doing this," Amanda said. "With the budget that Roger and Kathy have, I didn't know who else to call that could do the project justice."

"Don't mention it," Virginia replied as the real estate agent took her arm and began to lead her inside. "I was happy to come take a look. Though, I'm on strict orders from Tristan not to extend us too much. So in all fair warning, I'll have to talk to him before committing to anything."

"Of course," Amanda said fumbling with the key to the now-closed bed and breakfast. "I didn't expect you to say yes right away." Amanda gave Virginia a sly look. "Though I should mention, we don't have a strict timetable for this. So if it takes a little longer because of the wedding, that's perfectly fine."

Amanda swung the door open and the overpowering scent of cat hair, cat food, and even cat urine filled Virginia's nostrils. She knew the bed and breakfast had been closed for a few weeks. Apparently, in that time, Roger and Kathy's cats had been given free rein.

"Don't worry about the smell," Amanda said. "I'm hiring a professional cleaning team to come in and take care of that."

Virginia wanted to answer 'good' but thought better of it for two reasons: one, she thought that might seem a little impolite and two she was a little wary of taking her hand away from her nose as it was the only thing masking the terrible smell.

"What happened?" Virginia managed to get out through her nostril-pinched hand mask.

"I don't know how much you heard, but basically Roger and Kathy went out of town for a long weekend to visit one of their daughters in Florida. They left plenty enough food and water and had arranged for a neighborhood kid to come check on the cats, but on their trip, Kathy fell and ended up in the hospital. She did enough damage that the doctor wanted her to stay put and not travel for a while so they could monitor her. They made arrangements for the kid to continue coming over but apparently, he got busy with school and didn't really tell them. Long story short, they finally got a friend to come take the cats, but in that time, the three frisky felines had their way with the place."

Amanda shrugged, "Let's go to the rooms upstairs. The smell isn't nearly as bad there."

Virginia nodded and happily followed Amanda up the curving steps to the upstairs bedrooms. As the smell of cats began to fade, Virginia took her hand away from her nose and began to take in the building as a whole.

It had been quite a while since Virginia had stepped inside the bed and breakfast. The one time she had stayed here was when she and Tristan were still renovating the cottage. She'd lived in the city with her sister and had accidentally missed the last ferry back.

She remembered the place being quaint and comfortable, but certainly not the sort of place that modern, vacationing couples would flock to. Also definitely not the type of place where families would feel comfortable bringing their children. Unfortunately for Roger and Kathy, those were generally the two types of tourists who frequented the island.

The landing where the upstairs rooms stood was narrow and Virginia could hear the wood creaking beneath her feet. She found it strangely claustrophobic to walk alongside the railing and kept fearing that the floor might give way beneath them.

That would certainly have to be fixed.

In the rooms themselves, there was little to be done but minor physical improvements and some thorough decorating overhauls. She could envision stripping the dated floral wallpaper and adding decorative features such as crown molding and maybe even a chair rail. Her eyes scanned the room and she visualized the moods that could be created by using different color palettes, trying to get a sense of which she thought would work best.

Aside from cats, Kathy also had a fondness for dolls, and these collectibles made their way into almost every room. Virginia could imagine keeping one or two antique toys in some of the rooms with a touch of vintage flair. However, she knew from experience that it was more than a little disconcerting to have a row of glass-eyed dolls in old-fashioned dress staring at you while you were trying to sleep.

Virginia told Amanda that the linens would have to be replaced too. While she didn't doubt that they were comfortable enough, the drab patterned prints on the comforters were more than a little out of date and added no color or style to the room as a whole.

"The upstairs just needs a little updating for the most part," Amanda agreed when they had seen the last bedroom. "It's the other downstairs rooms off the front that need the most work. Don't worry though! We won't have to go back amidst the cat pee if we don't want. Roger and Kathy gave me some pictures of the rooms and we can look those over outside. Plus, I can fill you in on the major issues that I anticipate will need fixing or updating."

Virginia heaved a sigh of relief just as her stomach began to grumble. She hadn't eaten since the donuts and coffee at breakfast and that was more than a few hours before. Simple carbs, no matter how delicious they were, were not exactly long lasting sustenance.

"Do you think we could look at them over lunch?" Virginia asked. "I'm starving."

"Come to think of it, so am I," Amanda declared. "Let's talk it over at the deli down the street."

Virginia, who had absolutely no objection to this, followed Amanda down the street to the popular New York style deli in the town's central square. There she ordered an egg salad sandwich and matzah ball soup, while Amanda got an impressive looking platter of potato latkes. The food was perfect and immediately hit the spot. Virginia marveled at how she continued to be surprised by the little gems that Sweetwater Island contained.

Once they were seated, Amanda pulled the pictures of the bed and breakfast out of her purse and handed them to Virginia.

Trying her best not to get crumbs from her sandwich on the prints, Virginia looked hard at each shot. The establishment contained four rooms downstairs beside the main hall. The kitchen, a dining room, an old-fashioned type parlor complete with grand piano and the master suite where Roger and Kathy lived. Though they had since moved out.

"First thing we'd need to do is expand the hall to give it more of a lobby feel," Virginia said between bites of her sandwich.

"We'll probably have to sacrifice one of the rooms to do that," Amanda said.

"Well," Virginia said pulling out a picture of the gloomy looking parlor. "We don't really need the parlor. In fact, we could tear down the wall and make the dining room, hall and parlor into one large room. Then only the kitchen and master suite would be separated."

"That would make things a bit lighter," Amanda agreed, "and it would give us a lot more space to work with. How long do you think that would take?"

Virginia bit her lip in contemplation. She knew renovations, where walls needed to be knocked down, took longer than ones where just floors needed to be replaced, but she couldn't see how they could modernize that parlor without it.

"I don't know," she admitted. "That's Tristan's department more than mine. Do you mind if I take these pictures home with me so I can show him? That way he'll get a better idea of what we'd be in for if we agreed to this."

"Yes, of course," Amanda sang. "Remind him that there's not much of a rush on this project either. It's more important that it comes in on budget than that it's finished by any certain date."

"That's good to know," Virginia said. "Especially with the wedding and all, we have a lot going on."

"Oh, the wedding!" Amanda said her face brightening. "I've completely forgotten to ask you! How is that going?"

Virginia told her about the plans they'd made so far. It was to take place two days after Christmas in the old town church.

"It's the Episcopalian church Aunt Emily used to take us to when we were kids," Virginia said. "They've said that the pastor from our church can do the ceremony, which is really nice of them."

"I can understand why a movie theater wouldn't be the ideal place for a winter wedding," Amanda laughed in agreement, "and I'm sure you and Tristan are both incredibly stressed. After all, it's only a few weeks away."

"It is," Virginia echoed. "We went in for our last marriage consultation today. It was interesting."

Virginia grabbed the seltzer water that had come with her sandwich and took a long sip, looking out the garland framed window. Talk about the wedding suddenly brought back just why she had rushed to see the bed and breakfast in the first place. It reminded her of the phone call and Tristan's reluctance to talk about his family, and that nagging feeling that he was keeping something from her.

"Are you alright, Virginia?" Amanda asked after a long silence. Virginia glanced up at the older woman who looked slightly worried.

Virginia forced a smile. She started to gloss over it, to say she was fine, but when she saw the heartfelt concern on Amanda's face and heard the motherly intonation in her voice, Virginia realized what she needed. It wasn't to keep this thing with Tristan bottled up inside, she needed to talk it out with someone.

Her overprotective sister was out of the question. If her mother and Aunt Emily had been alive, she would have talked about it with one of them, but since they weren't here, she realized that Amanda was probably the closest thing she had to a parental figure at hand. She was an older woman who knew Virginia well. She knew Tristan, too. Maybe she would be able to shed some light on all of this.

"Amanda, can I ask you a question?" she said tentatively.

"Of course, dear," Amanda replied, cozying up to the table, letting Virginia know that she had all the time in the world for her.

Hastily, Virginia told Amanda everything she could remember about the phone calls Tristan had been receiving, how secretive he seemed to be about them and how concerned they made her feel.

"I know I'm probably being paranoid, but I feel like if I don't know for sure, I'll drive myself nuts!"

"Have you asked him about them?" Amanda questioned.

"Yes," Virginia said. "He keeps telling me they're wrong numbers or telemarketers. I know it's not true."

Amanda sat back in her seat and looked at Virginia thoughtfully.

"Well," she said slowly. "I may be a little biased. After all, my late husband had bouts of cheating when we were young. We were able to work through it, but it left me a bit wiser about trusting men implicitly."

"You don't think Tristan would-"

"No," Amanda said. "I don't think Tristan would ever do anything deliberately to hurt you. He's a good man, but even good men can do strange things when they're under stress."

"So, what do you think I should do?"

Amanda furrowed her brow in thought.

"Well," she said. "If he won't tell you, and if you feel like you absolutely must know, I would say there's no harm in checking the name on his phone the next time it happens."

Virginia bit her lip uncertainly. "You think I should check his phone?"

"Well, don't break the passcode or anything," Amanda implored. "Just glance at the name that comes up next time he gets one of those mysterious calls or texts. That way you'll have some idea of what's going on. Then you can try to talk to him about it and perhaps he might be more inclined to tell you the truth."

"I don't know," Virginia shrugged. No matter how she rationalized it, it still sounded too close to a betrayal of trust for her liking.

"Of course that's just my two cents," Amanda countered. "But if he's not going to be honest with you when you outright ask, he can't expect you to just sit there and accept that, now can he?"

Virginia had to admit she had a point there.

When they paid the bill and Virginia found herself saying goodbye to Amanda and heading down the road to the cottage, she became more and more comfortable with Amanda's plan.

After all, this secrecy was driving Virginia nuts and it wasn't healthy. Amanda was probably right, there was nothing wrong with a glance at Tristan's phone when she got the chance.

By the time she reached the cottage on the hill, she'd firmly resolved that the next time one of those mysterious calls came in, she would be near enough to Tristan to glance at the name on the caller ID.

CHAPTER FIVE

*S*eated at their favorite water-view diner not too far from the ferry dock, Virginia rolled the hot mug of tea between her palms and watched Tristan intently.

"I don't know, sweetheart," Tristan said shuffling through the pictures of the bed and breakfast Amanda had given them. "I mean, it doesn't seem like it would be more work than any of my typical projects, but with the wedding coming up-"

"I know it's a lot to take on," Virginia concurred. "That's why I asked Amanda to give us some time to think it over."

She almost told Tristan that the longer she'd thought about the old bed and breakfast, about all the things she could do with it design wise, and how much a remodel could help bring tourists back to the town, the more excited she was becoming about the project. At the same time, she also knew Tristan had a point about the wedding.

There was still a lot to do, and Tristan's current off-island project wouldn't be finished until later that week. The last thing Virginia wanted to do was push him into another project he wasn't ready for.

"Well," Tristan said still staring at the picture of the narrow stairwell. "I would like to help Roger and Kathy out if I can, and it doesn't sound like they've got a lot of other choices."

"Amanda did say they've got a fairly tight budget," Virginia admitted. "None of the other contracting companies would even agree to look at it for the price they were asking."

Tristan bit his lip and slowly looked up at Virginia.

"Last time I talked to Roger, he outlined this dream trip that Kathy and he have been wanting to take for years. He felt like the window was closing as they were getting older, and he knew that doing a trip like that would mainly lie on whether they could sell the B&B. The look of yearning in his eyes nearly broke my heart. You just want good people like that to get to live out their dreams before they die, you know?"

He flipped through the pictures again.

"What do you think?" he finally asked.

Virginia knew this narrow-eyed look very well. She'd seen it when they were discussing dates for the wedding and before that when they would talk about some new design idea for the cottage.

It meant that Tristan was completely torn and Virginia's opinion would weigh heavily on the answer. Luckily, this time, Virginia knew exactly what she thought the decision should be.

"I think we should take it," Virginia said. "Like you said, it's not too extensive, and Amanda did say multiple times that there's not a strict deadline. As long as we come in on budget, they'll be happy."

Tristan leaned back in his seat and nodded, his face relaxing.

"Okay then," he said. "I'll call Amanda and let her know."

A smile leaped across Virginia's face. Despite all the stress of the wedding planning and the million other things she and Tristan had going on at the moment, she couldn't help but feel a twinge of excitement at the prospect of interior designing again.

As much as she loved donut baking and painting, there was something about putting a home, or a bed and breakfast in this case, together that just felt right. Like it was something she was supposed to be doing. Hearing Tristan agree so easily, left her barely able to hide her excitement.

"We should probably get started as soon as we can," she said, all her thoughts of the mile-long wedding to-do list fading out of sight. "I can go over tomorrow morning and start making notes about the bedrooms."

Tristan gave her an adoring smile and a chuckle. "You never slow down, do you?"

"Nope," Virginia said happily, "and that's why you love me."

Tristan's smile grew as he reached across the table and took her hand in his.

"Yes, it is."

They looked at each other for several moments, seemingly unable to tear their eyes away. A second later, Tristan was leaning over the table, bringing his lips closer to Virginia's for a kiss. The second Virginia closed her eyes, a familiar voice caused them to fly open again.

"PDA, you guys! Not everyone needs to see how crazy you are about each other. It's not fair to the rest of us!"

Virginia turned to see her sister moving across the diner towards them, purse in hand and looking somewhat harried.

Virginia leaned back from Tristan and made room for Samantha to join them.

"Well, we may not have had time for kissing if you'd showed up when you said you were going to," she told her sister. "We've been waiting almost thirty minutes."

Sam threw up her hands as she slid into the booth next to Virginia.

"I can't control the ferry schedule," Sam said. "You know it gets delayed when there's snow."

Virginia gave her a skeptical look. Though it was true that the ferry could get delayed in snowy weather, her sister's harried look and the slightly guilty tone in Sam's voice told her that this wasn't the real reason Sam had kept them waiting.

Sam's face colored just slightly at her sister's stare, but she still gave a self-righteous huff of frustration.

"Ok," Sam relented. "You caught me. I slept later than I'd planned. It was a rough night at the gym."

"The regular guys still giving you problems?" Tristan asked. Sam had complained so much about the same group of gym rats that even Tristan had heard the stories, and, though he pretended to be offended on Sam's behalf, Virginia could tell that the stories amused him more than he'd like to admit.

"Guy singular," Sam said. "There was only one last night but, he was a doozy, as always."

"Is this Mr. Grammar Police?" Virginia asked.

"Yeah," Sam said. "This time he offered me private tutoring for my business class. Not exactly subtle."

"Maybe he was being serious," Tristan said innocently. Samantha looked at him skeptically.

"Guys that go to the gym that much aren't exactly the studious type," Sam retorted. "Besides, I've been dealing with this guy for a while. His attempts at flirting are pretty obvious."

"I don't know. Some guys who go to the gym are brighter than you'd think," he said with a shrug. "My assistant, Ross, goes to this gym in Seattle most nights during the week, and he's going to school for his MBA in business. When he finds time to sleep, I don't know."

"Is this the mysterious best man I'm supposed to meet today?" Samantha asked turning to Virginia. "I notice you're not upset with him for being late."

"I'm sure he's got a good explanation," Tristan said. "He's almost always on time. More Type-A about it than I am, actually."

"A studious gym rat who is anal about schedules?" Sam asked skeptically. "I can't believe you didn't set me up with him earlier, Virginia. He sounds like a barrel of laughs."

Virginia didn't miss the sarcasm in her sister's voice and it caused her eyes to give a hearty roll.

"I never said I was setting you up," Virginia clarified. "Besides, you shouldn't be so quick to judge. He could be-"

"Oh no," Sam said under her breath before Virginia could finish her thought. Her sister's face had fallen and the red in her cheeks had turned slightly pale.

Confused, Virginia followed her sister's gaze. When she did, she found Ross walking towards them wearing a surprised, but very pleased smile on his face.

"Well, hello blue eyes," he said, his sights clearly on Sam. "Isn't this a pleasant surprise?"

"I don't know if I'd call it pleasant," Sam said crossing her arms as Ross moved towards, her shocked expression turning to a glare as Ross slid into the booth beside Tristan.

"I take it you two already know each other?" Tristan asked glancing between the two and looking every bit as confused as Virginia felt.

"You could say that," Sam said tersely.

Ross's smile grew as he looked at Samantha, like a challenge shining in his eyes.

"Samantha works at the gym I've been going to," Ross said. "She and I have become pretty close."

"Just because you insist on butting in on my work doesn't mean we're close," Sam said, "and I've already told you I hate being called Samantha."

"You prefer 'light of my life', right?" he asked cheekily, clearly trying to push Samantha's buttons. When Virginia glanced at her sister, she could tell it was working. Sam's face grew red and she opened her mouth to utter a retort.

"We should order," Tristan said loudly, clearly hoping to avoid a confrontation. He waved their waitress over and the four of them ordered without incident.

The rest of the lunch wasn't as uneventful.

"Tell me," Sam fished, when Tristan started talking about the work he and Ross were doing, "is he as annoying on a construction site as he is at the gym?"

"If I'm so annoying," Ross shot back, "why do you keep letting me talk to you?"

"It's a customer service job," Sam said. "If I told you to get lost I might get fired. That's why I try to ignore you hoping you'll get the hint. Apparently, you're about as bright as you look."

"Well, I look like a genius so, I'll take that as a compliment," he said. "And you weren't complaining when I helped you correct that paper for your economics class."

"I didn't ask you to correct anything on that," Sam fired back. "You just started reading over my shoulder."

"Lucky I did," Ross countered. "I probably saved your grade. You're welcome."

"My grades don't need saving. Thank you very-"

"Why don't we get the check?" This time it was Virginia who spoke loudly in order to fend off a confrontation. Luckily, both Samantha and Ross seemed to take the hint and remained silent as the bill was paid. Even so, Virginia couldn't help but note the glares her sister kept shooting at Tristan's best man and the self-satisfied smirks Ross sent in response.

It was enough to make her wonder if these two would cause trouble at the wedding. It was bad enough dealing with Tristan's family drama but having the maid of honor feuding with the best man would add a level of stress she wasn't sure she was prepared for.

"Virginia, I think I'm going to wait for you outside," Sam said as they waited for the waitress to return so that Virginia could sign the credit card receipt. "I could use some air."

"I'll come with you," Ross said immediately. Sam shot him a glare as she stood from the table.

"Maybe you're the one I'm trying to get away from. Ever think about that?" Sam asked. With a superior smirk and flick of her blonde hair, she headed out the door of the diner without a backward glance.

Ross watched her leave for a second before turning back to Virginia and Tristan.

"She doesn't mean that," Ross told them, optimism never fading from his face. "In fact, she probably wants me to go and keep her company. I think that's what I'll do."

"Ross, I don't think-"

Tristan tried to call his friend back but before the words were even finished, Ross had already followed Sam out the door.

Tristan and Virginia looked at each other somewhat hopelessly across the table.

"Well, that went well," Virginia said dryly.

"I guess I should've put two and two together about the gym," Tristan reasoned, his tone slightly apologetic. "I know Ross can sometimes be an idiot with women. He has good intentions, but terrible instincts. I just didn't think-"

"Don't worry about it," Virginia brushed it off, putting up a hand to stop him. "I didn't think about it either. We'll just have to talk to them both about behaving civilly during the wedding."

"That might be easier said than done," Tristan said with a nod to the window. Virginia looked out and saw Ross trying desperately to get Sam's attention while Sam was firmly ignoring him with her arms crossed and back turned.

"You should probably go rescue Ross before he gets his face slapped," Virginia warned. "Sam's got a mean punch when she's provoked."

"I guess I should," Tristan said standing from the booth. "I'll wait for you outside."

He came around to the side of the table, leaned over and gave her the quick kiss she'd been expecting when Sam interrupted them.

The check with Virginia's card came back barely a moment after Tristan left. Virginia signed the receipt and made to get up from the table with her purse when a beeping sound from across the booth drew her attention.

That was when she realized that Tristan had left his phone. It vibrated and lit up with a text. She had a strange feeling this was one of those texts he wouldn't want her seeing.

Remembering Amanda's advice and the promise she'd made to herself, she reached across the table and took the phone in hand.

With her heart hammering in her chest, she looked down at the writing on her fiancé's phone.

Her green eyes widened when she read what was written there. It wasn't at all what she'd expected to find.

The name wasn't some unfamiliar woman's name. It wasn't even the name of a familiar woman.

Instead, Adam, the name of Tristan's brother, looked up at her above the most recent texts. She could also see dozens of missed calls from the same Adam listed for that day and the day before.

Blinking in confusion, she read the text written clearly on the phone.

"Tristan, I know you're avoiding me," Adam wrote, "but this is really important. It's about Dad. Please call me."

Virginia stared at the text for several seconds before setting it aside. She exited the diner and gave Tristan back his phone without mentioning a word about what she'd seen.

All the same, she couldn't help but feel just a little upset by it. Not only was Tristan keeping his family troubles a secret from her, he was also refusing to find out potentially important news about his father.

What was it he'd told pastor Phil? 'If Dad reaches out to me, I'll talk to him, but I'm not going to force it.'

Wasn't this Tristan's father reaching out, even if it was through his brother? Maybe something horrible had happened to his dad or even his mother. If that were the case, he would never know about it. All because he was too stubborn to return a phone call.

Well, she'd decided firmly by the end of the day, even if Tristan was too prideful to find out what was going on with his family, she wasn't.

That night, when she got back to the cottage on the hill, she pulled up Adam's number on her own phone and called him herself.

CHAPTER SIX

a week passed before Tristan could get away from his latest job to look at the bed and breakfast in person. Even after studying the pictures, he still needed to see the place in person before they began any work.

So on a cloudy Tuesday morning that promised a light dusting of snow, Virginia found herself clutching a cup of coffee and yawning widely as she walked down the street to meet Tristan at the bed and breakfast's front door.

She'd put extra concealer under her eyes this morning in an effort to detract from the circles hovering there. She'd spend half the evening talking to Adam on the phone about their dad. Then she spent the night tossing and turning about what, if anything, she should tell Tristan about the conversation she'd had with Adam.

Just as she had promised herself, she'd called Adam as soon as the opportunity arose. Judging from his voice, Adam had been surprised to hear from her. They'd never actually met in person, though they had emailed a little about wedding stuff over the past few months.

Nonetheless, he was appreciative of the contact and told Virginia what he had been hoping to tell Tristan. The news was about Tristan's dad and it wasn't good.

The elder McPherson had suffered a significant heart attack and was in the hospital. Apparently, he'd been there the past few weeks.

"Did your dad ask you to call?" Virginia had ventured. "Does he want to see Tristan?"

She knew Tristan's response to the news about his dad rested on whether this attempt to reach out came from his father directly.

On the other side of the phone, Adam let out a warm, tenor chuckle that couldn't help but remind her of Tristan. Maybe it was a family characteristic.

"Dad's just as stubborn as Tristan is, more so even," Adam admitted. "Mom thought I should call, and, truthfully, I thought maybe I could get some kind of, I don't know, reconciliation started or something."

"Well, I guess I can tell Tristan and-"

"No!" Adam cut Virginia off so suddenly that she pulled the phone away from her ear and stared at it.

"Sorry Virginia," Adam apologized, "I'd really rather it came from me. Just ask him to call me if you get the chance. You know, say you're worried about me knowing what I have to do during the wedding or something. Just don't tell him you talked to me about Dad."

"So, you want me to lie about the fact that I talked to you?" Virginia asked tentatively. She knew how disheartening it had been to realize that Tristan was keeping secrets from her, and she instinctively disliked the idea of carrying on the trend.

"No," Adam justified, "I mean, it's not so much of a lie as an omission. Trust me, if he thinks I want to talk about Dad, no matter what it is, he'll never call."

Virginia had hesitated before saying 'yes' to this arrangement, though she did agree in the end. Unfortunately, her mind hadn't been able to settle since. Thus the sleepless night and unusually heavy amount of concealer.

Luckily, Tristan didn't seem to notice her subtly dilapidated appearance when she arrived. He smiled at her as brightly as ever and kissed her good morning before they both walked inside.

"Wow. You weren't kidding about the smell," Tristan said covering his nose as they moved through the front door into the building.

"The cleaning team Amanda hired should be here later this week," Virginia filled him in. "Let's give our noses a little break and start upstairs. That narrow hallway will be the biggest project anyhow."

Tristan glanced around as they walked.

"I'll tell you right now, Ross won't like this. He's got so much going on with school right now that I think he's almost at capacity. Which is saying a lot considering what a chronic overachiever he is," Tristan said, running his hand along the old wood of the handrail.

Virginia considered the point as they climbed the stairs to the hallway and the bedrooms beyond. Ross had been talking about his finals, which sounded horribly difficult, for the past two weeks. Even Virginia had noticed that the strain had begun to show the few times she'd seen him.

When Ross met Tristan at the ferry these days, the dark circles under his eyes looked much worse than Virginia's did now, and the younger man's normally beaming smile looked weary.

"Of course," Virginia quipped as they reached the landing, "he might not be quite as tired if he didn't work out at the gym every night."

Tristan let out a chuckle. "Truthfully, I think he's doing less working out than he says. I'm starting to think he only makes the trip there to see your sister."

Virginia gave him a conspiratorial smile in return. She considered admitting her new theory that she didn't think Samantha minded the attention so much anymore. Despite all the complaining Sam had previously done about Ross, Virginia noticed that, lately, she'd started taking a different tone when she talked about him.

Instead of discussing Ross' cheesy pickup lines with a hard, annoyed edge, Sam had started smiling faintly when she mentioned them and giving a small shake of her head as though she were now more amused than annoyed. Sam had even taken some of Ross' writing advice for her final paper in English class.

"He was right about not using an Oxford comma," Sam had admitted earlier that week. "It does make it flow a little better. I just wish he didn't look so smug when I tell him he was right about something."

But Virginia knew that telling Tristan about Sam's potential interest was as forbidden as telling him about his father's condition. Sam would die of embarrassment if anyone other than Virginia discovered her apparent burgeoning crush on Ross. Virginia had kept Sam's sisterly confidence long enough to know what was supposed to remain secret between them.

Of course, as Virginia entered one of the bedrooms, she realized that thinking about keeping secrets just made her think about the one she was now sworn to keep from Tristan. She took a breath and tried to focus on a nondescript painting of a horse on the bedroom's beige wall.

"I think I might put a couple of the art pieces I'm working on in the bedrooms," she called out to Tristan, who was now measuring the banister on the landing. "Once we get the walls painted, I think the snow scene I've been working on would look really nice in here. Plus, it would keep the budget down."

"Sounds like a good plan," he agreed. She heard the measuring tape he kept on his belt snap closed. "Widening this landing shouldn't be too big a beast. There's plenty of space in the entryway that we have to work with."

"I was going to ask what you thought about the flooring in the last two bedrooms," she said. "They've still got these horrible carpets even though the rest of the place is wood. I'd really like to tear those up, but if you think it would be too much work-"

"No," Tristan cut in agreeably. "I was thinking the same thing. Hopefully, we'll find the original wood floors underneath and no significant damage. Ideally, we can sand and refinish all of the wood floors in the place."

The two of them stared at the wide-planked wood running the length of the hallway. The building had so much potential and the excitement of giving the place a second chance at life began to swirl around them.

While Tristan measured the banister, Virginia began to visualize the space and talk aloud.

"What if we refinish the floors with a little twist? Either a rich, dark espresso stain or even the total opposite direction with a whitewashed wood? There's a gray paint shade called Moonshine that I think would actually offset either perfectly."

Tristan glanced up and surveyed the hall.

"Yeah, I can see that. It would actually give it a more upscale feel."

Virginia nodded her head in agreement. As soon as he scribbled the banister measurements in his notebook, Virginia continued the tour through the rooms upstairs. As they walked, she talked through her plans for each one, becoming more and more inspired as she did.

Since she'd first considered the bed and breakfast as a potential design project, she had come up with a cohesive plan to re-design each bedroom. She wanted to evoke the same local feeling that the artwork she painted did; paying homage to the small island, as well as embracing the overall feel that the Pacific Northwest gave off. She loved how Sweetwater Island and the areas surrounding managed to have a special knack for blending a woodsy seaside feel with its own unique colorful and charming aesthetic. She often thought that there was nowhere else like this part of the country anywhere in the world.

"I'm thinking each room will be themed," she told him as they moved to the last room at the end of the hall. "But they'll all have something to do with the island. The first room will focus on the ocean and the ferry. The second one will be the forest heading into town. The third will be the winter room since it's such a magical season here. That's where I'll put my snow painting. And this one," she said, opening the door, "this one will be the Main Street room."

"So lots of seasonal cars and foot traffic?" Tristan joked.

"Ha ha." She shook her head at his lame joke, but couldn't help chuckling at his goofiness all the same. "There'll be old pictures of the shops on Main Street, mugs from the Main Street coffee shop next to the in-room coffee machine, and I'll see if I can get some vintage signs from some of the businesses to use as accents."

Virginia stared at the dull walls and horrible comforter in the room as a smile crept onto her face. She could see exactly what she wanted to happen in this room, and if she could pull it off she knew it would be perfect.

She broke out of her vision and glanced at Tristan, realizing that his eyes were fixed on her with a boyish smirk donning his face. Virginia blushed slightly and walked over to nestle under his arm.

"So," she said leaning into him. "What are your thoughts?"

"I think that this is why you are the artist," he answered as he put his other arm around her, "and I'm just the guy who builds stuff."

"Well," she said, looking up at him, "if it weren't for you, I probably wouldn't be an artist at all. At least not one whose art was hanging anywhere. Besides, building stuff is very useful."

He gave a small chuckle. "Well, I'm glad you think so."

The smell of felines gone wild reentered their nostrils as they made their way back down the stairs, which lead to a relatively quick survey and a measure of the other rooms.

"Let's brainstorm out in the fresh air," she proposed.

"I hope Amanda warned the cleaning crew," he cautioned as they walked back out to the street. "They may need Hazmat suits."

"It's not that bad," Virginia countered. "Face masks, followed by a full body delousing should be enough."

They exchanged amused looks.

"Well, it's put me off getting a cat for the foreseeable future," Tristan said taking Virginia's hand in his. "So I'm sorry if you had your heart set on that."

"Don't worry about it," Virginia said. "I'm more of a dog person anyway."

"I knew there was a reason I asked you to marry me," he said.

She took in a deep, satisfied breath, the arm of her coat brushing against his as they walked hand in hand through the crisp winter day.

She knew she would have to talk to him about his brother at some point. She promised Adam she would try and get Tristan to call him sooner rather than later, and she'd promised herself as she'd tossed and turned the night before that she wouldn't put it off.

Despite that, she wasn't sure she had the heart to ruin such a perfectly lovely day. She loved the feeling of connectedness and excitement she experienced when she and Tristan talked about design projects, and she knew from experience that mentioning Tristan's family created the exact opposite feeling in him. Even his brother, with whom he was on civil terms with seemed to deflate him a bit.

So she put it off, walking in companionable silence with Tristan until they reached the ferry.

"I know we have a lot going on," he began, "but I'm actually really looking forward to working on the B & B." He looked down at her with a satisfied look. "I'll jot down some of my thoughts and ideas and we can brainstorm over dinner tonight or maybe even tomorrow."

"That sounds perfect," she beamed back, juggling her enthusiasm for their new project with the dread of bringing up his family.

Maybe it was knowing that he would be gone for another full day, knowing that she had the week ahead booked solid with wedding plans, Christmas shopping and other projects that made her swallow her fear. She had to talk to him about it now or she might never get the chance.

"Hey Tristan," she said as the ferry pulled near. "Have you talked to your brother lately?"

Just as Virginia had predicted, she looked up and saw his face cloud over slightly. The pressure of his hand in hers loosened slightly.

"No," he said. "Why?"

"Just worrying about the wedding, I guess," she said praying that the lie wasn't present in her voice. "You haven't heard from him since he said he was coming. I just thought you might want to call and make sure he's still got his tickets and everything, maybe go over the basics. You know, prepare him for meeting and navigating Samantha." She trailed off casually, trying to lighten the mood.

"I'm sure he's all good," Tristan said. "If he needed something he would text me or email me about it."

As the ferry reached the dock, Virginia opened her mouth to press him again. Before she could, Tristan wheeled around and put both hands on her shoulders. He was wearing a fake smile that she knew he didn't feel.

"Look, honey," he said. "There's nothing to worry about. Everything's going to turn out fine. And, even if there was an issue with Adam's arrival, or anything else for that matter," forestalling Virginia's objection again. "We'll still be married and it will be absolutely perfect in its own way. Nothing can change that."

As he looked into her light sage eyes his face softened and his smile became much more genuine. Virginia couldn't help but smile back as she tried to think of some other argument that might force Tristan to reconnect with his family. In the end, she couldn't. So she nodded.

"You're right, I guess," she agreed. "I just want to make sure we're staying on top of things. I'm so used to thinking that I have to do everything myself that it's still an adjustment."

"Well, get used to it," Tristan said playfully. "You've got enough on your plate now. Let me at least take care of my end."

Virginia smiled at him again. She knew she should be trying harder to convince him, but then she thought about her old boyfriend, Jason. For years, she had essentially carried the entire relationship on her own shoulders, and she couldn't help but feel grateful for Tristan. He truly did want to share all the burdens and duties of the wedding with her, and she wanted him to enjoy this time, not burden him with the weight of his family.

His smile grew into the one that always melted her heart. He leaned down to kiss her and she closed her eyes just as a sharp voice called out to interrupt them.

"No time for lovey-dovey you two," Ross bellowed, walking towards them on the pier. Just as it had been for the last few days, his face was drawn and his cocky smile couldn't hide the toll his schedule was taking on him.

"We've got to get this job finished today if my final paper's ever going to get written."

With that, Ross half-jokingly made to grab Tristan's arm, set on pulling his boss to the waiting ferry. Laughing, Tristan moved his arm away.

"Calm down there, Superman. Work can wait an extra minute. I've got time to kiss my fiancé goodbye," he said. Turning back to Virginia, he gave her the kiss he'd been silently promising before Ross interrupted them.

"Ok, that's enough. Let's go," Ross said. This time, Tristan allowed himself to be pulled away.

"I'll see you tonight!" he called back to Virginia, a smile still on his face.

She waved goodbye to the pair as they boarded the ferry. Her smile soon faded when the beep of a text sounded from her phone and she pulled it out of her pocket to see Adam's name.

A guilty knot formed in her stomach as she scanned.

"Did you ask him to call?" the text read. Virginia bit her lip before replying.

"I did," she typed in reply. "He said no, but give me a little more time. I'll see if I can talk to him again."

As she headed back up the hill, she started to reflect on what pastor Phil had told them. Bad relationships with parents can poison a marriage. She'd brushed the idea off at the time, but now, as the weight of a secret felt heavy in her pocket and her heart, she was starting to think he might be right.

CHAPTER SEVEN

Only one week before Christmas and barely two weeks before Virginia and Tristan's wedding was proving to be much more stressful than Virginia had anticipated. Luckily, Tristan's job off the island finished up and the demanding older woman had given him a substantial check along with a heartfelt note of appreciation. The money from the job was originally supposed to be a considerable contribution toward the wedding costs but instead had quickly become earmarked for renovating the bed and breakfast.

After the cat mess had been cleaned, it became clear that there would be some substantial changes needed to the downstairs, more than they'd anticipated from their abridged walk-through. Of course, the carpets would be torn up, the landing widened, and decorative finishes redone throughout, all of which they'd counted on. However, once a closer inspection was able to be done, Ross and Tristan realized that the wall separating the kitchen and the dining room would have to come down since the wood inside the walls were starting to rot. They found the original source of the problem and could keep it from getting worse, but if they wanted to keep it from spreading to the rest of the building, it would have to go.

"That means we've got to take out the cabinets resting there too," Tristan said when he brought Virginia down to look at it. "I know we were planning to just refinish and reuse the existing cabinets, so having to replace them is going to up the cost considerably. Not to mention, it'll push the project back."

Virginia inspected the cabinets in question and bit her bottom lip.

"When we pulled the first one off to get a look at the wall, we realized that they were in pretty bad shape," Tristan continued. He showed her the back of the removed cabinet.

"Oh, yeah, that doesn't look like it really held up," Virginia noted that the backs of the cabinets were made of a cheap composite board which had completely fused to the wall over the many years. What she was looking at now was a large, tattered hole on the backside of the cabinet.

"We're lucky this thing doesn't have an end date," Ross said from his kneeling position on the ground where he was taking measurements. "It looks like it might take more than a new coat of paint to fix these other walls up too."

"Amanda said the walls should be fine," Virginia said hesitantly and, for the first time, starting to feel a little panicked by the project.

"That was before we found the wood rot," Tristan said. "We may not want to take the chance that it has spread to the others, or even that there aren't other trouble areas completely separate. A lot of times you don't know what's going on in these old buildings until you start opening things up."

"Should I call Amanda and tell her that the cost will have to go up?" Virginia asked.

Tristan turned from her and looked at the now doomed accent wall that separated the dining room from the kitchen.

"No," he answered finally with a sigh. "Just let her know it'll take longer than expected. We can eat the cost if it becomes an issue."

While Virginia appreciated Tristan's loyalty to both his original quote and his friend who owned the property, she couldn't help but wonder if this was wise. They'd tried to keep the wedding costs as minimal as possible but even a do-it-yourself wedding needed funds. She wasn't thrilled at the prospect of having those eaten up by a renovation project.

"Are you sure?" she pressed Tristan slightly. "I mean, with everything else?"

"Yeah," Tristan said, nodding his head slightly. "I think we can make it all work. The lady in Seattle overpaid us anyway. I told her not to but she refused to take a cent back. I'd like to see it go into a project I'll actually enjoy working on if we need to use it."

"I hope this means I won't have to take a pay cut," Ross said standing up from the floor. "Remember, I'm just a poor student living off ramen noodles."

Tristan shot him an amused side glance. "There aren't many 'poor students' who can boast about exclusive gym memberships," he said. "I think you'll be ok."

"Hey! You know I get a discount to that gym," Ross defended, though his smile told Virginia that he wasn't too concerned about his potential decrease in funds.

When Ross yawned widely and tried to hide it behind his hand, however, Virginia couldn't help but feel a bit sorry for him.

"Finals still keeping you up at night?" she asked.

He looked over with a weary smile. "That's the thing with grad school," he said. "You don't get Christmas holidays. I've got a thesis due as soon as the next semester begins. I've been trying to get a head start on it."

"Are you sure you're going to be okay to work on this too?" she asked.

"It's no use," Tristan answered before Ross could say anything. "I've tried letting him off the hook for this project. He insists on working on it with me."

"Well, it's not fair for you to get all the fun stuff," Ross protested. "I missed out on the Victorian cottage last summer."

"And if you had been able to work on the cottage, you might not be in my wedding," Tristan said brightly. "In fact, I might not be getting married at all."

He gave Virginia a knowing smirk.

"And I would still be dating a cheating jerk," Virginia added with a smile. "So, thanks for that Ross. You couldn't have picked a better time to get yourself hurt."

"Well, I'm glad you two are happy that I fell through the floor of an attic and broke my leg," Ross moaned with feigned sullenness. "But that's not happening this time. I'm going to tear down these walls even if I fall asleep while I do it."

"Gotta admire your spirit," Tristan said with a chuckle.

Virginia was about to offer a similar platitude when she felt her phone vibrate in her pocket. Knowing who it was, she hesitated to take it out, but she knew she would feel immediately guilty if she didn't at least check.

Over the past week, Virginia and Adam had been in almost constant communication. It seemed as though Adam had been taking on a lot since his father's illness, and, what was worse, with his brother refusing to take his calls, he had no one to talk to about it.

That was where Virginia came in. She had always been good at listening to people's problems. In fact, she considered it one of her strengths. The problems Adam was having with both his father and even his mother, who seemed to be breaking down every other day as well, were too sympathetic for her not to listen to.

It had also led to Tristan becoming suspicious of her phone activity. Statements like 'you've been getting a lot of texts lately' and 'every time I try to call, your phone seems to go to voicemail' were becoming more and more common.

As she pulled her phone out to look at the most recent text, Tristan looked over at her suspiciously.

Virginia knew her face noticeably colored when she glanced down at her phone.

"Mom wants to talk to you if you can," Adam had written. "Here's her number."

Beneath that was a phone number with a Californian area code. After her conversation with Adam the night before, Virginia had offered to talk to Tristan's mother. It had been an easy thing to say at the time, but now with Tristan's eyes on her, it felt like an even greater betrayal of trust.

"Another mysterious caller?" he asked half joking.

"Just wedding stuff," Virginia said self-consciously, typing back a quick reply to Adam.

"I guess there's bound to be a lot of that this week," Tristan said.

"Yeah," Virginia agreed, "and I've got to get it all done before Christmas, which happens to be in a few days."

When she glanced back at her fiancé with a half smile, she saw his expression turn from one of suspicion to sympathy.

"Be sure to let me know if it's too much," Tristan said. "Like I said, it doesn't have to be perfect, and you know I'm more than happy to help with anything you need."

"I know, babe," she said truthfully, "and thanks for that, but I think I've got it mostly taken care of. Besides, Sam's coming on the ferry this afternoon to help me out with the caterer."

"And then the bachelorette party, right?" Ross asked.

Virginia jumped and turned at the sound of his voice. Amidst her inner-turmoil about Tristan and Adam, she'd almost forgotten he was there.

"Which you're not invited to," she reminded him sweetly. "No boys allowed."

"It's only the groom who's not supposed to go to the bachelorette party," Ross countered. "The rules say nothing about the best man. Tristan might want me to keep an eye on you for him. Not to mention I know the bar you're going to. Some of the guys from the gym stand outside at night and take pictures of drunks coming out so that they can put them on the internet for fun. I wouldn't want to see Tristan's fiancé become a meme tomorrow morning."

"I don't think I'd trust you to keep an eye on anything in a bar," Tristan told Ross. "Unless it's a pretty, single girl."

"Besides," Virginia added. "Sam would throw a fit if you showed up. She sees enough of you as it is."

Ross gave a small smile and a slight shrug. "Suit yourself."

The rest of the morning was spent working on the upstairs portion of the bed and breakfast. The boys spent the morning tearing up the flooring in the last two bedrooms and Virginia worked on choosing the new paint colors for the bedroom walls.

It was a little before noon when they stopped for lunch. The trio sat on the floor talking about everything from design ideas to wedding reception songs, while they ate salad and pizza from the parlor on the corner, followed by Virginia's seasonal eggnog creme donuts. The plan for the rest of the day had the boys continuing to work on the renovations, while Virginia and Samantha had an appointment with the wedding caterer before they would head into the city for the bachelorette party that night.

"Are you meeting Sam at the ferry?" Tristan asked.

"Yeah. She's coming with the lunch rush," she answered. "She should be there soon."

"I'll walk you," he said.

"It's okay, I don't want to cut into your afternoon."

"You're not," Tristan answered. "I can grab a coffee at the place by the ferry. An afternoon pick-me-up."

"In that case, I might as well come along too," Ross said coming up beside them as they made their way towards the door. "It's been a while since I've seen Sam."

This time it was Virginia's turn to roll her eyes at Ross.

"According to her, she saw you at the gym two nights ago," Virginia countered.

"I know, exactly! That's a long time to go without weight lifting for me," Ross exclaimed. "This thesis has got me slacking on my exercise regime. On the plus side, I think she's starting to like me."

"I can see how she might admire your persistence, if nothing else," Tristan said glancing over at Virginia with a suppressed smile that Virginia returned.

The three of them walked towards the ferry, Virginia, and Tristan hand-in-hand, while Ross lagged a step behind them. Virginia felt yet another buzz on her phone.

Thinking that Adam was getting more than a little insistent, she reached in and took it out once again. Her heart constricted in frustration when the name she read was not Adam, but rather Jason.

"Another wedding thing?" Ross asked, seeming slightly suspicious now as well.

"No," Virginia said, angrily shoving the phone back into her pocket without reading the text. "Just a bitter ex-boyfriend who, apparently, still can't handle the fact that I'm getting married. Take note, Ross. Sometimes persistence can be annoying."

"Well, Sam's not getting married in two weeks," Ross said fairly. "So, I think I'm okay on that front."

"Jason's still texting you?" Tristan said looking down at Virginia, lines slightly creasing his brow.

"He does occasionally," Virginia said. "I already talked to him about everything months ago. I've told him there's nothing more I have to say, but he still insists that he doesn't understand. He keeps wanting to meet for drinks no matter how often I tell him 'no'."

"Maybe I should talk to him," Tristan offered. "Try and get him to back off."

"As tempting as that offer is," Virginia said smiling up at Tristan, "it's really not worth your time. I've known him for a long time and I'll be able to handle it. He's just not used to not getting his way."

"If you say so," Tristan said. "Still, you just say the word and I'll have a man-to-man discussion with him."

"He means he wants the chance to pound the guy for you," Ross said. "That's what man-to-man talk usually means."

"I do not," Tristan said with a chuckle. "Though, if Jason were to try anything at the wedding I can't promise that I won't be tempted to talk with my fists."

Virginia couldn't help but smile and moved closer to Tristan. Though she knew he was joking, she couldn't pretend that his protective side wasn't nice to see every once in awhile.

They reached the ferry just as it docked in the harbor. It wasn't long before Samantha walked towards them, makeup bags swinging from her arms.

"I am finally finished with my final paper," she said in greeting. "Thank god. Now, all I've got to worry about is making my big sister beautiful for her bachelorette party."

"You won't have to do much, she's already beautiful," Tristan said. Virginia's heart fluttered and she reached up so they could share a brief kiss.

"Did anyone ever tell you two that it's almost sickening how cute you are?" Samantha remarked.

"Could say the same thing about you, blue eyes," Ross cut in, turning towards Sam with his hands in his pockets. "It's really disturbing how adorable you are when you're all stressed and haggard like that."

Ross gave Sam that winning smile of his and, though Sam clearly tried to hide it behind an annoyed facade, Virginia clearly saw her sister blush.

"Don't you have a house to fix or something?" Sam asked with an eye roll towards Ross.

"We do, in fact," Tristan interjected before Ross could answer. "So, we'd better grab our coffees and get back to it."

Tristan and Ross said goodbye to the girls and made their way to the cafe by the harbor. As they did, Ross turned back to them.

"Have fun tonight, ladies!" he boomed. "Don't do anything I wouldn't do!"

"From what I've gathered, that leaves the night's possibilities pretty much wide open," Sam muttered as she took Virginia's arm and began to lead her towards downtown where they were meeting with the caterer.

As they walked, Virginia gave a last glance to Tristan who looked back at her and gave her a genuine, but somehow tentative smile and wave.

As soon as he did, the guilty feeling that had been all but driven out by Sam's arrival returned. It wasn't at all lost on Virginia that after being afraid of the secrets Tristan was keeping from her, she was now the one keeping things from him.

CHAPTER EIGHT

"*V*irginia, will you stop checking your texts for like two seconds?" Samantha pleaded as they arrived outside a little bar where they were supposed to meet Amanda and a few of Virginia's girlfriends.

"Sorry," she said, slightly shamefaced. "It's important."

She had called Tristan's mom in the ten minutes when she'd been able to extract herself from Samantha that afternoon. She had wanted to wait until she was alone before calling because she didn't want anyone else to know about her communication with the McPherson clan. Mostly because if she were to say anything to Sam, she knew it would lead to relaying the entire family history. It wasn't only that she was close with her sister, but Samantha wasn't one to take things at face value and would undoubtedly probe until she found out way more than Virginia intended to share. The whole thing felt too personal to tell anyone about, considering how Tristan barely even liked to talk to her about it. Plus, she wasn't eager to carry around the feeling that she'd betrayed Tristan twice over, once by contacting his family without telling him and secondly by talking about it with her sister.

Of course, when she'd finally had a window to call Mrs. McPherson, it couldn't have been at a worse time.

"Oh, Virginia!" the older woman had rushed over the phone, her voice high pitched and slightly dramatic. "It's so horrible we have to meet this way. I mean, in a manner of speaking."

"Adam told me about-"

"Oh, I know he's told you all about my husband's heart attack, but, to make things worse, there's been another complication. They're talking about taking him into surgery tomorrow. Oh my goodness, I've heard such horrible things about these types of surgeries, and with Tristan not speaking to us..."

Virginia heard the older woman's voice break over the phone and her heart immediately sunk, completely unsure of what to do.

"I'll keep talking to Tristan," she told her future mother-in-law. "If you like, I can tell him what's going on-"

"Oh, no!" Mrs. McPherson interjected emphatically. "Ward would never forgive me if I told Tristan about his condition. He's a stubborn man. He doesn't want Tristan's pity."

"But, if he could hear it from me. You said the surgery was serious," Virginia insisted. Honestly, all this secrecy was getting hard to justify. No matter what had happened between Tristan and his dad, surely he deserved to know that his father was about to undergo a potentially life-threatening surgery.

"I'll talk to Ward and see if maybe he'll let us tell Tristan," Mrs. McPherson toiled aloud. "But it would really be best if Tristan called on his own. I know Ward would talk things out if Tristan just reached out to him first."

Like father like son, Virginia couldn't help but think, remembering that Tristan had said almost the same thing regarding Mr. McPherson. 'If he reaches out to me, I'll talk to him.'

It seemed neither of them was willing to swallow their pride and take the first step. Virginia asked Mrs. McPherson to keep her updated on what the doctors were saying and how things were progressing

Since then her phone had been blowing up with texts from Tristan's mom and even Sam was getting suspicious.

"What could be more important than having a great time at your bachelorette party?" she implored, glancing over to Virginia with a raised eyebrow as they stepped outside the car.

"Look, I'm turning my phone to vibrate," Virginia said lifting the phone and showing Sam the mute button she pressed. Of course, as soon as she did, a text flew up on the screen.

"Seriously?" Samantha asked coming around to look at the text more closely. Virginia couldn't gauge her sister's sudden reaction and went to look at the phone, but Sam was too quick. She grabbed the phone out of Virginia's hand before she could stop her.

Virginia's heart sunk into her chest.

"Sam, don't! It's not-"

"Oh my gosh, is that pretty boy jerk still texting you?"

Virginia's eyes widened in surprise and she moved to look over her sister's shoulder. Sure enough, the text she'd just received was not from Mrs. McPherson, or even from Adam. Instead, Jason's name read clear across the screen.

"I need to talk to you!" the text read. "If you won't answer me, I'll come to you."

"Oh no," Virginia said taking her phone back and deleting the text.

"Please tell me that's not who you've been texting with this whole time," Samantha said warily.

"It's not," Virginia answered. "He's been texting me and trying to call me for the past couple months. It's like he doesn't want to accept that it's over. No matter how many times I tell him."

"You don't think he'd try and crash the party, do you?" Sam asked worriedly as they walked up to the bar and showed their ID's to the bouncer at the door.

"I certainly didn't tell him about it," Virginia said nervously. "He'd have to do some serious snooping to find out, and he's not really one to go above and beyond, if we're being honest."

"I don't think he's above that," Sam said as they walked into the bar and set up shop at their reserved table in the back of the bar. Virginia had to admit, it was a nice setup. The bar wasn't too noisy and she could see one of her favorite local jazz bands setting up on the stage nearby.

"He's not crazy," Virginia said. "He's just not used to being turned down."

"Well, for the record," Sam said as she set down her purse and sat down. "I still think you're way too nice to him."

"I haven't answered any of his phone calls or texts since Tristan and I got engaged," Virginia answered. "How's that being nice?"

"With the number of times he's bugged you," Sam said. "I would've threatened him with a restraining order by now. Or, at the very least, threatened to sick Tristan on him. You know Tristan's a lot stronger than Pretty Boy. The threat alone would send your self-consumed little ex-running."

Virginia couldn't help but chuckle at the image. As soon as she did, she felt her phone vibrate inside her purse. Against her better judgment, she pulled it out and glanced down at the screen. This time it wasn't from Jason. It was from Mrs. McPherson.

"Surgery tomorrow at ten in the morning. Please pray!"

Virginia bit her lip, a sinking feeling in her stomach and a telltale tug in her heart. Something about this last simple text suddenly made one thing clear to her, she couldn't keep Tristan in the dark anymore. She knew it in her gut, she needed to tell him about his father, no matter what his brother or his mother said about it. He was her fiancé, and very soon to be her husband. She couldn't keep something this big from him. It wasn't right.

"Seriously, Virginia, you promised!" Samantha boomed.

"I told you I was muting my phone," Virginia corrected. "I never promised not to look at it."

"Well, you'd better put it away now, and I'd better not see it the rest of the night, or else I'm just going to have to take it away from you."

"Yes, Mom," Virginia said with a roll of her eyes.

Sam put her hands on her hips and gave Virginia her best narrowed-eye glower.

"Ok, ok! I promise! No more phone for the rest of the night!"

As though to seal this promise, Virginia stuffed her phone back into her purse. Though Sam gave her one more eagle-eyed look, she didn't say another word about it.

The rest of the night, Virginia found it much easier than she'd expected to forget about all of the stresses from earlier, her phone, Jason, Tristan's parents and everything else. To her surprise and delight, Amanda not only came to the party but proved that she could get just as loose as the younger women when the time called for it.

"This is the first night I've been without the grandkids in over a month!" Amanda said happily sipping her third glass of red wine. "You don't know how ready I am to let loose!"

Of course, as per Virginia's instructions to Sam, 'letting loose' at this bachelorette party didn't include male strippers or even an inordinate amount of drinking. It did include swing dancing to the aforementioned live jazz band, Virginia getting funny gag gifts meant to help her with the "wedding night" and the entire party being pulled up on stage with the band to sing a slightly off-key rendition of "Get me to the Church on Time".

It wasn't until midnight when things were just starting to wind down that Virginia was starkly reminded of one of her happily forgotten problems from earlier. The reminder came in the form of a familiar face at the bar.

Jason, apparently oblivious to Virginia's presence, was sitting on a stool, nursing what looked to be his favorite drink, rum, and coke.

Virginia's head started to feel dizzy and she knew it wasn't just because of the champagne she'd had to drink. She hadn't seen her ex-boyfriend in close to a year. Now here he was, perched at the bar, deep in thought.

Quickly, Virginia looked around for Samantha, hoping that her sister would talk her out of what her champagne-addled brain was telling her to do.

Virginia wasn't exactly drunk, but it was the first time she'd had anything to drink in longer than she could remember and she couldn't pretend it hadn't gone to her head a little bit.

That said, she had a feeling that, even if she were completely sober, she'd still want to confront Jason. Sam was right, he had to understand that she wasn't going to put up with him anymore. He had to know that he couldn't keep calling and texting and harassing her. Clearly, ignoring him wasn't working, meaning it was time to take the direct approach. So before she could change her mind, she set her jaw and marched up to the bar.

"Jason, what are you doing here?" she asked.

When he turned and looked at her, Virginia had to stifle a gasp. He definitely looked worse than he had the last time she'd seen him. His black hair, usually worn slicked back was mussed, his usually neat and stylish five o'clock shadow was now growing out of control, and his hazel eyes were glassy and bloodshot.

"Heeeey, you. Wanted to pay my respects to the bride," he slurred, raising his glass towards her. It was clear that he was much drunker than she was. Possibly drunker than anyone else in the bar.

"How did you even know I'd be here?"

"Your real estate agent hasn't unfriended or blocked me on Facebook yet. S'on her page."

Virginia clenched her jaw in an attempt to keep calm. She also made a mental note to talk with Amanda about Facebook privacy settings.

"And since you won't talk to me," Jason continued, raising his voice so that people near them at the bar were now stopping their own conversations and turning to listen, "I figured I'd come to you."

"I am not going to do this with you here," Virginia whispered glancing around at the bar patrons, her face going red with embarrassment.

"Can't do it anywhere else," Jason said loudly and very dramatically. "I lost the apartment! Lost my Mercedes too! Lost everything when I lost you!" Jason's voice broke and he let his face drop into his large hand, stifling a drunken sob. "And now, you're getting married! Married?! To some chump! It should be to me and you know it."

"Jason," she whispered plaintively, trying desperately to get him to lower his voice. "We've talked about this. You know exactly why we broke up and you know that it was because of the choices *you* made. It wasn't-"

"We were together all those years," he cried over her. "We were building a life together! All the plans. And now-"

Jason swept his hand out, knocking over his highball glass with an aggressive clank.

"Ma'am, is this guy bothering you?"

Virginia turned around to see the large bouncer from the front door standing behind her. Though his words were directed at Virginia, his intimidating glare was pointed decisively at Jason. Samantha was standing behind the muscular man, her arms crossed in front of her chest.

It was instantly clear that when Sam had heard Jason's loud, drunken voice, she had called security.

Virginia looked between Jason and the bouncer unsure exactly how to answer. She knew it would serve Jason right if she had him tossed out onto the street. Yet when she looked back at her ex, now pathetically sobbing into his drink, something wouldn't let her. She thought about what might happen if he was tossed out with no way to get home. The state he was in, he might very well stumble into traffic, or worse, try to drive. She knew she couldn't live with herself if something happened to him or anyone else because she hadn't seen him safely into a taxi.

So with a reluctant sigh, she turned back to the bouncer.

"I'm ok," she said. "But if you could do me a favor and call a cab for him that would be terrific."

"Sure thing."

The bouncer made his way back to his post, pulling out his cell phone as he did. She heard him ordering the cab just as her sister stepped up to her.

"Virginia, what the heck are you doing?" Sam asked. "What did I tell you about being too nice to this jerk?"

"I know," Virginia said. "But Sam, look at him!"

Both girls turned to Jason who was now both sobbing and muttering into his drink. When they listened carefully his words sounded a lot like, "Lost the apartment, lost the car, lost the girl..." being said over and over again, like a litany.

"He could hurt himself or someone else if we just toss him into the street," Virginia said. "He's in no state to get home on his own."

Sam continued to stare at Jason for a few more seconds before heaving a sigh through her tightly pursed lips.

"Fine," she said. "Make sure he's got a ride, then you're coming right back to the party."

Luckily, the cab arrived only a few minutes later. Virginia slung Jason's arm over her shoulder and helped him walk to the curb.

"You're too nice to me," Jason muttered as he stumbled into her.

"That's what everyone says," Virginia answered dryly.

"I've been such a jerk."

"Not gonna argue with that," she agreed as they arrived at the cab. "Just get home safe."

Jason was just sober enough to remember that he now lived with a friend from work and to give them the address. Virginia paid the cab driver in advance and with that done, moved back to help Jason in.

As she stood holding the door for him, he stumbled towards her, a drunken smile on his face as his lips came dangerously close to hers.

"Kiss for ol' time's sake?"

Luckily, before Jason could follow through on the threat to kiss her, they were blinded by a flash from across the street. Virginia blinked, remembering what Ross had said. Lots of college guys take incriminating pictures of the drunks and homeless people around there. Virginia could only pray that she wouldn't end up on an internet meme the next day.

"Goodbye, Jason," she said turning her attention back to her ex. She shoved him into the back seat of the cab and before he could say another word to her she slammed the door and watched the taxi disappear down the street.

Virginia looked up to the night sky and let out a long, slow breath of relief. Closing her eyes she gave thanks for the events in her life that lead to her extricating herself from Jason. At that moment, she felt more complete than ever. Although shaken by the unexpected run-in with Jason, she knew that everything was going to be all right. The journey of finding her own strength again had led to finding the true life and love that she deserved. This encounter felt like a sign that she had come full circle and watching Jason being driven away felt like the final goodbye that she didn't know she wanted.

Letting out another breath of relief, she noticed how frigid the air had become and scampered back inside. It was time to spend a little more time with the people she cared about, celebrating her new life and the future that was just around the corner.

THE NEXT MORNING, she woke up in the cottage with a slight headache and a phone full of unchecked messages.

Blearily, she clicked her phone open to check them. She was sure that most of them would be from Mrs. McPherson giving her more details about Tristan's dad. However, when she clicked on the first message, she was horrified to see that it was not from Mrs. McPherson at all. Suddenly feeling wide awake, she sat up on her bed and stared down at the message for what felt like hours. It was a picture from the night before. A picture of her leading Jason to the cab and him leaning in for a drunken kiss. Above the picture was a message from Tristan.

'We need to talk about last night.'

CHAPTER NINE

"Tristan, I told you what happened" Virginia repeated, still feeling a mix of exasperation and anger as she sat across the table from her fiancé in the kitchen of his apartment.

After taking two aspirins and washing them down with a healthy-size cup of coffee, Virginia had gone immediately to see Tristan. She'd considered bringing donuts, but she worried that it would seem too much like an apology. Like those celebrities who cheated on their wives and bought them diamond rings, or new cars, out of guilt. Instead, she'd arrived empty-handed to find a disheveled, and clearly displeased, Tristan standing at the door. It was obvious that his sleep had been just as restless as hers. More than that, what had upset Virginia was his expression when he looked at her.

Whenever she'd shown up at his door before, even if he was exhausted or stressed from work, he was always happy to see her. This time he looked like he was in pain.

Nonetheless, he let her in and suggested they sit down. Apparently, Ross had been coming out of the gym just as Virginia was seeing Jason out to the cab. He'd understandably misunderstood what he'd seen and snapped a picture, unsure what to do about it, but ultimately decided he needed to share it with Tristan, who he considered one of his closest friends.

Virginia had told him her side of the story, which was to say, she'd told him the truth, but even now, as they continued to sit at the table sipping tea, he seemed reluctant to believe her completely.

"He followed me there because I haven't communicated with him," she repeated defensively in the face of Tristan's still unmoving expression. "I don't know what else to say. He was drunk, his life is a mess, and regardless of the fact that I would be happy to have never seen him again, he is still someone that I've known for a very long time and I was just trying to make sure he got home safe. That's it."

Tristan continued to take in her words and sit quietly, trying to discern between his innate trust in his fiancé with the late night image of Jason leaning in to kiss her that was burned into his brain. "You said he'd been calling a lot last week," he finally said after a long pause. His voice sounded relatively calm, but she couldn't help but note the hint of suspicion that still lingered in his eyes.

"Yeah," she said, "and he apparently came to the bar because I wouldn't answer them."

"You've been getting a lot of calls," Tristan said. "Ones you won't talk to me about. And I want to believe you about Jason, but when I think about him and those weird texts and phone calls, it's really hard not to think-"

"They don't have anything to do with one another," she said with conviction.

"Well, I know they're not about the wedding," he stated firmly. "I talked to the caterer and the venue and they all say that everything's set. There's nothing more to do for next week."

"There's always more to do," she asserted defensively.

"I mean, there's nothing more to do that someone would have to call you about," Tristan said equally defensive. "So, if those calls aren't from Jason, who are they from?"

Virginia bit her lip and looked down at the ground. Suddenly, despite her earlier decision to tell Tristan about his brother's calls and his father's illness, she was having a hard time getting the words out. She was having a hard time deciding whether or not she should say anything at all.

"Virginia," Tristan said more softly. "Look, I don't mean to sound jealous or defensive. It's just, I know those calls are upsetting you. I can see it when you look at them and..." He sighed and ran his fingers through his hair. "Look, just for my own peace of mind, I need to know what's going on in your life. Okay?"

He took her hand in his and when she looked up into his eyes, she could see just how serious he was about this. She couldn't put it off anymore. She would have to tell him.

"Okay," she said finally heaving a sigh. "You're right. Those calls weren't about the wedding, but, they weren't from Jason either. They were from your brother."

"Adam?" Tristan asked, his eyes wide. "Why would you be talking to Adam?"

In a rush, Virginia told him the whole story. Starting with her suspicion about his own mysterious phone calls. She told him about Amanda's advice and checking his phone at the restaurant. Then she told him about his father's illness and how she'd been in contact with both his mother and his brother.

As she spoke, Tristan let go of her hand and started pacing the room. When she'd finished, he didn't stop, he didn't speak, he just kept walking back and forth across his kitchen, his hands balled into fists at his sides.

"I wanted to tell you when Adam told me your dad was in the hospital," she said, "but he was adamant that he wanted to tell you himself. He didn't want you to hear it from someone else. Not even me."

"Idiot," he muttered under his breath. "Why wouldn't he just tell me what was going on? More to the point, why wouldn't you?"

"He asked me not to. Pleaded with me actually. He was emphatic about it."

"And you'd rather be on my brother's good side than mine?" he asked sending her a glare that made her both hurt and angry.

"Look, I asked him to let me tell you. He made me promise not to," she said. "You know that I keep my promises. I thought it was something you liked about me."

She crossed her arms over her chest and sent him a glare. She knew it was the harshest look she had ever given him and she couldn't help feeling momentarily satisfied when Tristan shrunk under her gaze.

"Besides, I know for a fact that Adam was trying to tell you about your dad, but you wouldn't answer his calls or texts about it. I don't understand how you can be angry with him for trying to talk to you about it when you were the one avoiding him."

"It has to come directly from my dad," Tristan burst without even thinking first. "He's the issue and I don't want to hear anything about him if he's not willing to talk to me himself. I don't want to know about his life or feel like I have a relationship with him when he's not the one interested in that." Tristan fumed.

"I'm sorry, Virginia," he said after taking a few moments to breathe. "I'm just so infuriated right now. I can't believe Adam dragged you into this mess."

"That's not entirely fair," Virginia reasoned aloud, discovering a sudden urge to defend her future brother-in-law. "I was the one who called him first. I asked him to tell me what was going on."

"He still didn't have any right to tell you to keep this secret from me," Tristan said, equally determined to put the blame on his brother.

"Maybe not," Virginia continued. "but I would've been dragged into this eventually one way or another. I'm going to be your wife, that means I'm going to be part of your family."

"Dad and I haven't felt like family for a long time," he said.

"See? I don't even know why that is," she said, her frustration coming back.

"I told you-"

"You told me your dad wanted you to be part of the business and you didn't want to, but I feel like there's more to it than that. I feel like there's something you're not telling me."

"Did Adam tell you to ask me about that?" Tristan questioned suspiciously.

Virginia, with another well of frustration, heaved a sigh and raised her eyes to the ceiling in order to compose herself. "Believe it or not, your brother doesn't dictate everything I do."

Though she was angry, she immediately regretted the snarky attitude that was creeping in. She thought back to their couple's counseling sessions with the pastor and remembered his words. This was not only someone she loved, but someone she genuinely liked. By choosing to be together, they were forging a lifelong partnership based on mutual respect and admiration. The pastor reminded them that they always needed to keep in mind that they were allies, even in the moments where they were frustrated and wanting to win an argument. The end goal wasn't winning, it was working together toward solutions that would make their life together better.

Taking a deep breath, she stood from her seat and walked over to him.

"Tristan, I know I should have told you about what was going on, but I don't know how to be here for you if I don't know what happened. I want to know why you and your dad are so distant. You remember what the pastor said? It's important. Remember that I'm your partner and your support system. You don't need to handle life alone anymore."

Tristan stopped pacing and pursed his lips, still looking away from her. He cast his eyes down to the ground as though he was trying to gather his thoughts. It seemed ages before he looked back up at her.

"I know you think it's important," Tristan said, sounding as though he was going to make another excuse not to talk about it. "And you're right. There's a lot more to it than that. It's just that I didn't want to have to talk about it again. I didn't think I would have to go through it all again. Not even with you."

"Tristan, you know you can talk to me about anything," she said softly. She reached out and took his hand in hers, giving it a gentle squeeze. He glanced down at her and offered a small, pained smile of acknowledgment before turning away from her to pace again.

"Did Adam say Dad wanted to talk to me?" Tristan asked suddenly.

Virginia realized that was not something either her future brother-in-law or her mother-in-law had actually stated in so many words. They'd both told Virginia that Tristan needed to talk to his father, that the two men needed to make amends. Yet, for all that, they hadn't actually said that Tristan's father wanted to talk to his eldest son.

"No," Virginia said unwilling to lie to her fiancé anymore. "They didn't exactly say he wanted to talk to you."

"And you said his surgery went fine, right?" Tristan confirmed. "He should be out of the hospital soon?"

"That's what Adam said this morning," she admitted reluctantly. She had a feeling she knew where this was going and she wasn't sure that she wanted it to.

"Then there's nothing more to do," Tristan said. "I stand by what I said. If he wants to talk to me, he knows where I am. He knows my number. He can call me."

"But what if something like this happens again? What if he has another attack and you're never able to make up?"

"That won't happen," Tristan said, though she could tell by the tone of his voice that even he didn't believe that.

"And, even if it does," he continued. "It won't be my fault that he was too stubborn to apologize."

"From what I gather, he's probably thinking the same thing about you."

"I have nothing to apologize for."

"Maybe not. But you could at least make an effort to talk to him."

Tristan stopped pacing and sat back down in the chair across from her, running one hand over his face.

"If you knew what he did, you wouldn't ask me to forgive him."

"But see, that's the problem. I don't know what he did. You won't tell me."

Tristan heaved a sigh and clenched his jaw as he glanced away from Virginia and out the kitchen window, which overlooked the pine forest. It was as if he was hoping the trees outside would give him some kind of answer.

"What if I take a couple of days to think about it? We've got two days until Christmas Eve. I'll let you know what I want to do then."

Virginia's heart was torn in two. With the wedding and the bed and breakfast renovation, she wasn't sure that she wanted to have this family drama hanging over their heads. Not now, and not like this. Still, she tried her best to understand Tristan's need to set it aside for a while. That was why she felt herself nod in acceptance.

"Ok," she said reluctantly. "We don't have to talk about it for a couple of days. We can just focus on the renovation and…"

"No, I mean I need a couple days alone to think about all of this," he said as his gaze rose up to hers quickly, and then lowered at the same pace. "Meaning we don't work together or see each other. I might not see anyone."

Virginia felt her heart sink down into her chest. It had been months since she'd gone more than one day without seeing him. She was so used to him being there when she needed to talk or wanted someone to test a new recipe out on. The idea of him not being there, especially so close to the wedding, was particularly cutting. Not to mention, she had a feeling it wasn't what he really needed. She knew from experience, after her parents died, that being alone with that grief and anger hadn't done her any good. She'd nearly wasted away before her sister pulled her out of herself.

She also knew Tristan, and he didn't do well being alone with difficult emotions. He needed someone to talk them out with. The idea of him spending days alone in his apartment, potentially wasting away, wasn't something Virginia wanted to contemplate.

"Are you sure that's a good idea? I mean, if you don't want to talk to me about this, I guess I understand, but maybe you should call pastor Phil or even your brother."

"No," Tristan said confidently and adamantly. "This is something I've got to work through on my own."

Tristan met her eyes and Virginia knew he meant exactly what he'd said. He wanted to be alone. He wanted to think and work through all this without anyone else.

Realizing suddenly she was never going to change his mind, she nodded in acceptance.

Again.

However, once she'd said goodbye and set off on the road back to the cottage again, she felt her old stubborn streak return. She wasn't going to let Tristan fold in on himself. He had to talk about his family with someone. She'd meant what she said when she told him that it didn't have to be her, but it had to be someone. If he wouldn't reach out, which he had made abundantly clear to her several times, she might have to do the reaching out for him.

When she got to the fork in the road, instead of heading back up to the cottage, she turned back down the hill and headed towards Sweetwater's Main Street. She only hoped that pastor Phil would be in his office.

CHAPTER TEN

*B*y the time Virginia reached the church, her nerves were starting to fail her. During the walk, she'd begun to think about the wisdom, or apparent lack thereof, of introducing yet another person into this family drama. Even if that person was a pastor.

Even with these doubts in mind, she made her way down the hallway determined to see her plan through. If nothing else, she had to discuss this with someone and Phil was certainly a better choice than her sister, who would, no doubt, take Virginia's side and bad-mouth Tristan. That was the last thing she needed at the moment.

Yes, she was still convinced that the pastor was her best hope.

All the same, her stomach performed a small flip when she saw the light on in his office. During her walk, half of her had started to hope that he wouldn't be there and she could leave the whole story in a cowardly message, or simply take it as a sign that she wasn't supposed to confide in him. No hope of that now.

With a shaky hand, she knocked on the door. It was only a moment before it opened and Phil's harried but smiling face was looking out at her.

"Virginia! This is a surprise. Come on in."

"Thanks," Virginia said in a voice that sounded small and wary even to her own ears.

Phil ushered her into the office that was definitely worse for wear since the last time she'd been there with Tristan two weeks before. Papers were now crumpled all along the floor near the unemptied garbage basket. Schedules and Christmas sermons, which were started and then later abandoned, littered the desk, and two boxes of Chinese take-out stood like towering sentinels in front of the pastor's chair.

"Sorry about the mess," Phil apologized, following Virginia's gaze. "It's a busy time of year, and, since I didn't have any office visits scheduled for this week, I didn't think about cleaning up."

He sheepishly ran around to the other side of his desk and hurriedly crammed several crumpled papers and the two take-out containers into the overflowing garbage next to his desk.

"No need to apologize," she said. "I should have called or something to let you know that I was coming. But, I wasn't sure if-"

"Don't worry about it," Phil said sitting down in his chair and wiping a few crumbs on the desk haphazardly to the floor.

"So, where is Tristan today? Working on that bed and breakfast?"

"You heard about that?" Virginia asked, desperate to delay the impending conversation as long as she possibly could.

"Everyone has," he said. "It's really wonderful what you two are doing for Roger and Kathy."

"Well, we'll see how wonderful it is when it gets finished," Virginia blushed self-consciously. "Regardless, Tristan's not there that I know of. He was back at his place when I just left him. We had, well, we had a fight of sorts."

She proceeded to tell the pastor everything she could remember. About being jealous and worried when Tristan kept getting calls he wouldn't tell her about. She told Phil about calling Adam and about Tristan's father's illness and surgery. Then about the night before at the bachelorette party; the misunderstanding and how the whole thing had come out into the open.

"Now he wants two days on his own," she said. "To think about things."

"Given what's happened, that doesn't sound too unreasonable to me," Phil reflected.

"But what if he changes his mind about the wedding?" Virginia suddenly exclaimed, voicing a fear she hadn't dared to put into words before, even in her mind. "What if he says he needs more time. What if he changes his mind completely and-"

"Has he said that he might change his mind?" Phil asked calmly. "Has he given you any indication that he doesn't want to marry you?"

Virginia took a breath and thought. The truth was, he hadn't. Even when they'd argued earlier that day, he hadn't said anything about calling off the wedding or thinking about not getting married. That was a fear she'd come up with all on her own.

"No," she admitted truthfully, "but it's only a week before the wedding and my fiancé isn't speaking to me. That doesn't bode well, does it?"

"Well, when you put it like that, I'll admit it's problematic," Phil laughed slightly. "Mostly because that makes it sound like he's a ten-year-old holding a grudge, but from the story you've told me, it doesn't sound like that's what's happening."

"Then what does it sound like?"

Phil looked at her intently over the papers still crumpled on his desk. He took a deep breath and let out a sigh before answering.

"It sounds like he needs to take some time to think," he said, "and that's what he told you, isn't it?"

"It is," Virginia had to agree, however reluctantly. "But what if that's not what's best for him? I know Tristan, and I know when he doesn't have someone to talk things out with he tends to brood. I'm just worried that he's going to get stuck thinking about whatever his father did to him and it's going to shut him off to his family even more."

"Do you know that's what will happen?"

"I'm afraid that's what'll happen."

"Okay," Phil said evenly. "Then what do you think you should do about it?"

"Well, I was hoping you might be able to go and talk to him," she conceded. Now that the words had been spoken out loud, she realized just how awkward they sounded.

He sat back in his chair and looked at her thoughtfully. Finally, he leaned forward. "Well, you know I don't make unannounced visits. If Tristan wants to talk I'll be here, but he'll have to come to me."

"I know. I just thought if you went over there, if you talked to him about all this, he might listen to you more than he listens to me."

"Because you think being alone isn't good for him? You think he should talk to someone?"

She wanted to protest the part of those questions that seemed like she was being overprotective and knew what was best, but as she thought about it, she could sense where he was going with it.

"Virginia, you know we've talked about this. You can't make someone do what you think is good for them. I know that's something you learned from your last relationship. You can't make someone change."

"I know. I just-"

"I know it's frustrating," Phil said cutting her off with a gentle raise of his hand. "If you want to do something productive, however, it might be better to think about something you can do on your own."

"That's just the problem, now I don't know what to do. It feels like my brain is consumed with fixing this drama before the wedding."

"Think back," Phil encouraged. "How did all of this start?"

Virginia looked down at her hands, examining the nail polish Sam had put on them the night before. Discovering the sudden urge to peel it, as well as the memory of last night off.

How had this started?

It started when she got suspicious and jealous. When she checked Tristan's phone and called his brother on his behalf, but, she argued in her mind, that might have happened anyway. Tristan hadn't even been that upset about that. What had he really been upset about? He'd been upset that she'd lied to him. He'd been upset that she hadn't just told him about what she was doing, told him about his father. She'd only done that because his brother had asked her to. Adam had asked her not to say anything because he knew he should tell his brother himself, but as it stood, Tristan wasn't willing to hear Adam out on their dad's behalf.

"I should have told Tristan what was going on once I knew," she said slowly. "At the very least it would have given him the chance to digest the information that his dad is in the hospital with a serious medical condition."

"Well, now Tristan knows what's going on," Phil filled in. "And I think he realizes he needs to take some time to process the reality of the situation, but I think perhaps the only one who can really talk to him about his family, is someone from his family."

"So there's nothing I can do except wait for it all to play out?"

The idea sat like a heavy ball of stress in her stomach.

"Well, you are involved at this point, but you likely aren't going to be able to help Tristan through things right now. It sounds like he has his own personal hurdles to overcome, and that's not something you can really help him with," Phil said. "There is something that you can do, however."

"And that would be?"

"Sit quietly and pray for a bit, and if something comes to you during that time, follow up on it. You may just need to be patient and let the situation go, or you may gain insight into your role. All you can do is take the time to stop and ask, then listen." Her kind-faced pastor gave her a reassuring smile. "If Tristan wants to talk to me, I'll be here. It's his place to seek me out. I had to learn that I can't force people to change either."

"Glad to know it's not just me," Virginia said with a half-joking laugh.

She left the pastor's office feeling more nervous, yet strangely more confident, than she had when she'd gone in. It was as if she'd been given a shot of adrenalin. Her hands were shaking and her heart was going a million miles an hour. She took the long way home, stopping at her favorite sitting rock that looked out over the water. There, bundled in her scarf and winter coat, she sat and prayed. Whether it was five minutes or twenty, she wasn't sure, but at last a calm came over her as she opened her eyes. She walked slowly the rest of the way along the path awash in peace, and when she got back to the cottage, she was one hundred percent sure of what she needed to do.

Without hesitation, she walked into her house, sat down at the kitchen table and pressed the call back button for Adam on her phone.

"Virginia," he answered almost immediately. "I'm glad you called."

"Hey, Adam," she answered. "Look, I called because I wanted to tell you that Tristan knows about your dad. He asked me about it and I couldn't keep it from him anymore. He's pretty shaken up right now, but I think he really needs to hear from you."

"Way ahead of you," he said.

Virginia blinked in surprise and opened her mouth unsure of how to answer.

"What do you mean?"

"I mean, if Tristan won't talk to me on the phone, I'm just going to have to come to him," he said. "I changed my plane ticket from December twenty-sixth to December twenty-third. I'm coming tomorrow, and Mom and Dad are coming on Christmas Eve as soon as Dad gets out of the hospital."

Still surprised at Adam's proactive attitude, Virginia promised to meet Adam at the ferry the next day. She would drive him over to Tristan's house, which he would enter on his own, and she would walk away.

As Virginia said goodbye and hung up the phone, a nervous energy re-emerged. She couldn't help but wonder how Tristan would greet his brother, let alone what Tristan would say or do when he learned that he would be seeing his father for the first time in years, and on Christmas Eve no less. She placed the phone on the table and turned to look out the snowy window. Reminding herself that she could do nothing more than ask for advice and then trust she was doing the right thing, she took in a breath of reassurance and decided to change her focus. She stood up and walked to the pantry where she could busy herself with creating a new donut recipe inspired by the winterscape outside and her trust that everything would work out as it needed to. She would call the pure, delicate donut creation Winter Solace.

CHAPTER ELEVEN

"I still can't believe you've been going through all this drama and you didn't say anything to me," Sam said with an exasperated tone.

Virginia, unable to take the stress of waiting alone in her cottage for Adam's arrival that afternoon had called Samantha to come and wait with her. Consequently, that meant that she'd had to tell Sam the whole story about Tristan's father, Adam and the whole misunderstanding with Jason at the bachelorette party. She had even convinced Sam to try her new recipe, and the two had been gossiping over the light and flaky Winter Solace donuts for over an hour. Samantha had even licked the remnants of the gentle almond-scented eggnog cream filling from her plate, which was not like her at all.

"It's because I know how terrible you are at keeping secrets," Virginia said as she locked the door to the cottage and the sisters made their way down the road towards the dock.

"That's not true," Sam objected. "I can keep a secret when I really want to."

"Tell that to the boy I liked in seventh grade," Virginia answered, giving her sister the side eye. "The day after I told you, the whole neighborhood knew about it."

"I was nine years old," Sam recounted. "You can't hold that against me. Besides, my best friend at the time had double-dared me to tell her. You don't just turn down a double-dare."

"So you can keep a secret as long as no double-dares are in play," Virginia said with a teasing smile. "Good to know."

Samantha shrugged her shoulders cutely and a comfortable silence fell between them as they walked down the hill, newly fallen snow crunching under their feet.

Once again, the snow had made driving through the streets of Sweetwater nearly impossible, which Virginia didn't mind. The walk had given her a chance to talk things out with Sam and as she'd predicted, talking things out made everything that much easier.

She only hoped that Tristan would feel the same way when his brother arrived.

"I still can't believe that jerk, Ross," Samantha said angrily as they walked. "What business did he have taking that picture totally out of context? Then, even worse, he sent it to Tristan!"

"It looked like I was about to kiss another guy," Virginia said in Ross's defense. "I mean, if that had been Tristan and his ex-girlfriend, what would you have done?"

"I would've marched across the street and asked him what the heck was going on," Sam said defiantly. "I wouldn't have acted like some shifty private investigator or something."

Virginia gave Samantha a skeptical glance but didn't say anything more. The truth was, she'd been angry with Ross for taking that photo at first, too. Then, the more she thought about it, the more it made her think of Sam. No matter what her little sister said, it sounded a lot like something Samantha would do. At the end of the day, both Samantha and Ross were fiercely loyal and protective of the people they loved.

They finished the wooded walk to the ferry with lighter banter. Virginia couldn't help but be a bit surprised when the boat pulled up exactly on time. She felt her heart began to beat quickly in her chest as she searched through the crowd for Adam.

Pictures of Tristan's brother were all she had to go on since she'd never met him in person. In fact, this would mark the first time she'd meet any member of Tristan's family. The fact that it was under less than ideal circumstances made her even more nervous.

"Virginia?"

She jumped when the male voice called to her from the side of the boat and she turned anxiously. A young man, a bit shorter than Tristan but with the same water-hued eyes and textured brown hair was standing in front of them. Unlike Tristan, his chin held no hint of a five o'clock shadow and he had a wider face than his lanky older brother, but he was undoubtedly just as cute.

"You must be Adam," Virginia said, not sure if she should hug him or hold her hand out to shake. She threw her hands out only a little awkwardly and gave him a hug. "It's nice to finally meet you in person."

"You too," he said with a genuine smile.

When he turned his attention to Sam, Virginia saw the young man blush and his eyebrows raise slightly.

"This is my sister, Sam," Virginia said with a knowing smile. She was used to most men reacting that way to Samantha. With her slim figure, blonde hair and bright blue eyes, her sister was difficult for men to ignore.

"Nice to meet you," Adam said clearing his throat. "I'm Adam."

When Virginia turned to Sam, however, she was surprised to find that her sister's cheeks had colored the same way Adam's had. What's more, her gaze was cast to the ground as she took his hand.

"Hey," she said quietly. "Good to meet you."

They smiled awkwardly at each other without saying another word. Eventually, Virginia felt as though she should step in.

"Tristan will probably be at his apartment," she said. "Should we head over?"

"Yeah," Adam said. "No point in delaying it, I guess."

There were a million questions swirling around in Virginia's mind as they headed through Sweetwater's downtown and towards Tristan's apartment. She wanted to ask Adam how he'd managed to convince his father to come visit. She wanted to know exactly what had happened in their family, how Tristan and Mr. McPherson had gotten to this point in the first place. However, Adam didn't seem keen on discussing any of that at the moment. He and Samantha had walked slightly ahead of Virginia and her sister was now animatedly giving Adam a tour of Main Street.

"And that's the old bed and breakfast," Sam said as they came to the front of the red brick building. "That's the one Tristan and Virginia are renovating."

"Really?" Adam asked turning back to Virginia as they moved further down the street. "Virginia, I didn't know you were in the contracting business. Tristan said you were a baker or something."

"I am," Virginia answered with an amused giggle, "but I do some painting and interior decorating these days, too. That's how Tristan and I met actually. Well, technically he was my contractor, but in the end, we did a lot of the project together. I'm surprised he hasn't told you."

"We don't talk much," Adam said. "Just a call every few months or so. Really, after Tristan left, the whole family kind of fell apart."

"Well, let's see if we can change that," Virginia offered hopefully.

"I don't know," Adam with reluctance. "Maybe. Hopefully."

Almost as soon as they'd reached the apartment complex, Virginia felt her phone vibrate in her pocket. She pulled it out and was more than a little surprised to see Tristan's number. Pressing the call button, she stopped behind Adam and Samantha who, realizing that she was no longer following them, stopped as well and looked back at her.

"Hello?" Virginia asked feeling more hesitant than she ever had with Tristan before.

"Virginia," he said. "I got a call from Adam saying that he's coming early."

Tristan's voice sounded strained with a kind of forced calm.

"I know," Virginia admitted, feeling relieved that Adam had told Tristan about his sudden change of plans. "In fact-"

"I want to talk to you before he gets here," Tristan said quickly, as though he couldn't wait to get the thought out of his head. "Can you come over?"

Virginia looked at Adam and Samantha both of whom were still standing motionless in the snow, looking at her expectantly. Virginia bit her lip, unsure just how much she should tell Tristan. Wondering if he would be upset when she told him she was two minutes away from his front door, with his brother in tow.

Finally, she decided that she was done lying and telling half-truths, so she took a deep breath and told him the situation.

"I'm actually on my way to your apartment now. Adam asked me to pick him up at the ferry and walk him over. Sam's with us, too."

There was a brief silence on the other end of the phone. Virginia heard shifting which she was positive was of the uncomfortable variety.

"Okay," Tristan said with another wave of forced calm. "Can you just ask him to go get a cup of coffee or something? I really need to talk to you first."

Anxieties filled Virginia's mind. They were the same ones that she'd told Phil about the day before. She imagined Tristan reluctantly telling her that the wedding was off, that he didn't want to marry her after all. Shaking her head, she set these fears aside as best she could.

"All right," she said finally. "Like I said, Sam's here. I can ask her to entertain him for a bit."

"Good. I'll see you when you get here."

Virginia hung up the phone and walked towards Samantha and Adam who were still waiting on the snowy hill, looking at her intently.

"Well? What did he say?" Adam asked.

"He said he wants to see me alone first," she told them. "Sam, would you mind showing Adam around town? Just until Tristan and I finish talking?"

Though Adam looked at Virginia hesitantly, Sam's face lit up.

"Sure!" she said and turned to Adam. "Come on, I'll take you to the coffee shop. Their coffee is amazing. So much better than anything you'll find in the city, believe it or not!"

Before Adam could respond, Samantha took his arm and started leading him back toward the main thoroughfare. As they disappeared, Adam looked back at Virginia.

"You'll text me when he wants to see me, right?"

"I will," Virginia promised.

She watched the two move out of sight before taking a deep breath and heading towards Tristan's apartment.

CHAPTER TWELVE

*V*irginia raised a shaking hand to the door and knocked. A thousand thoughts about what might or might not be said between her and Tristan flooded her mind.

That's why she was more than a little surprised when the door opened and it was pastor Phil who greeted her.

"It seems you and Tristan think alike even when you're not together," he said after inviting her into the apartment. "He called me over to talk not five hours after you left."

Virginia, still a little discombobulated, didn't answer as Phil led her to the kitchen table. There, Tristan looked up at her. His tired blue eyes rimmed with the dark circles he always had when he'd stayed up all night. Nonetheless, she was happy when he gave her a small smile in greeting. It was better, at least than the cold greeting that had met her the previous morning.

She smelled coffee brewing in the kitchen and saw two steaming cups on the table, Tristan's looked untouched. Phil offered her one and she nodded in answer.

"I thought you said you wouldn't talk to anyone," Virginia said quietly as soon as Phil had made his way out of earshot.

"I said I might not talk to anyone," he clarified, "but once I was able to clear my head a little, I realized I needed someone to talk stuff out with. Someone who wasn't so close to the situation."

"Well, I'm glad you called on Phil," she said, an encouraging smile now gracing her face.

He looked across at her and mirrored her expression. The look in his eyes made her heart turn over in her chest, the way it had always done before all of this chaos had started. Before either of them could say anything more, Phil came back with another cup of coffee.

"Now Tristan's told me that he'd rather talk to you alone, Virginia," Phil said, "and really, I should get back home to my wife. She's been alone with the baby since last night and I'm sure is ready for some relief."

"Sorry about that," Tristan muttered.

"Don't worry," Phil said with a casual wave of his hand. "She knows what the job entails and she supports me. Pastors aren't restricted to regular office hours. Plus, I checked with her first, so she gave the okay." He winked at the two of them.

"Still feel bad though," Tristan said sheepishly.

"You can make it up to me by talking things out with your fiancé," Phil said patting Tristan on the shoulder.

Tristan looked up and gave him a grateful half smile.

"Thanks for everything, Phil," Virginia said.

The young pastor looked back and gave her a tired, but genuine smile. "I'm just down the street if you need me."

With that, he headed out the door and let himself out, leaving Virginia and Tristan looking at each other awkwardly from across the table.

"Phil said you came to talk to him, too," Tristan finally began.

"Yeah," Virginia answered, a little embarrassed. "Yesterday. I wanted to see if he'd come talk to you."

"What did he say?"

"He said neither he nor I could force anything from you. It was up to you and God to work it out."

"He said something similar to me," Tristan said. "He told me that I can't force my dad to apologize to me. That it's between him and God, but that doesn't necessarily mean I should cut him out of my life forever." He ran a hand over his haggard face and Virginia could almost see the remnants of the difficult night he'd been through.

"So, have you decided to talk to him?" she asked tentatively. "Your dad, I mean."

Tristan let out a heavy, pent-up sigh and put his hand on the table.

"That's the thing, Virginia," he said. "My dad's got so much to apologize for. More even than I've told you. In fact, that's why I wanted to talk to you. I don't think it's fair to keep it from you anymore."

Virginia almost unconsciously moved forward in her seat, trying her best not to look too eager. It was hard for her to gauge where he was going with his story, and her mind was racing with every possibility. Even though she'd been waiting to learn the whole story about Tristan and his father for such a long now, she wanted to try and maintain as much patience as she could, so he could relay it how he needed to.

"You know that years ago I had a problem with drinking, right?" he asked.

Virginia nodded.

She remembered when Tristan had told her about his past. How, when he'd first come to Seattle, several years before, his drinking had gotten out of control. He'd gone through a program and talked to the pastor about his struggles, but, she knew his past still plagued him.

"The thing is," he continued, "when I was growing up, my dad had the same problem. Well, worse really. I eventually realized that my issues were a reaction to him; sort of doing the thing to such an extreme because you want to both understand it, and also because you really don't know how to cope with it. When he wasn't drinking, he was fine. But when he was, he was mean. Adam and I learned fast and were usually quick enough to stay out of his way. Our mom wasn't always so lucky."

"Did he hit her?" Virginia asked gently, her face trying not to externalize a natural urge to cringe at the thought.

"Once or twice," Tristan said. "He mostly just yelled and threw things, but he'd say horrible things. Like, he'd call her fat and lazy and he'd call us good-for-nothing mistakes. Said he wished he'd never made us. That sort of thing."

Tristan's voice started to tremble and Virginia put her hand over his.

"It became so constant that all of us just lived in a state of high alert. We never knew when he was going to come home and just turn the house into chaos. I had been working for the business but I could just see that I would never be able to get ahead or do anything really, with him being so volatile. I knew I couldn't stay and trying to get him to get help was useless. The night I told him I was leaving, he got drunk," Tristan said. "He said if I didn't help with the family business, I was no son of his. That I'd always been good for nothing and always would be. I got mad then, called him a lousy drunk. We were shouting at each other by that point. Mom was there, crying, telling us to stop. I said the last thing I wanted was to grow up and be like him. He threw a punch at me then, but my mom stepped in the way.

It hit her in the jaw and she ended up with a fractured jaw. He stepped back and just kind of looked at her and then back to me like he was shocked by what had happened, what he'd done. Then he looked at me and had the audacity to say 'look what you did' with so much disdain and denial in his eyes. Adam was helping my mom and before I knew it, I just flew at him. I put my hands around his neck and just tackled him. I don't remember what I was thinking. Maybe I wanted to kill him. Maybe I just wanted to hurt him like he'd hurt my mom. I'd never felt such anger and hurt and rage in my life. It was like everything that had happened over the years came to the surface at that moment." Tristan swallowed hard at the painful memory. "Either way, it took Adam and Mom a good few seconds to pull me off of him. He just kept yelling but didn't get up to follow me or anything. After that, I didn't say anything more. Just grabbed my bag and left."

Virginia stared at Tristan who was looking down at his hands, clearly trying as hard as he could to hide the tears that were forming in his eyes. Her hand remained limply over his as she tried to process what he'd told her.

When she looked at this man, so kind and gentle, it was hard to imagine him attempting, even briefly, to harm anyone, but she knew that before they'd met, he'd been a different man in some respects.

"Did you tell pastor Phil about all this?" Virginia asked, still quietly.

Tristan nodded.

"He said he understood why I would want my father to apologize before I spoke to him, and why I'd want him to be the one to reach out first, but he also said forgiveness isn't always about the other person, sometimes it's about you. That living with an abusive person can create baggage that manifests itself in ways that aren't always obvious. Even if you think you've moved past it, or let it go, if you don't deal with it or resolve it, it will always hold power over you. He said if I don't forgive my dad for the things he did, I might never be able to let go, and that's a lot to hold on to."

"Do you think you're ready to forgive him?" Virginia asked as gently as she could.

"Honestly, I just don't know," Tristan said. "It was like he was two different people. A normal dad, and then this horrible human who just needed to inflict hurt on the people who loved him. We tried so hard to be perfect and it just didn't matter."

"Adam told me he's stopped drinking," Virginia said after a minute of silence. "He says he's changed."

"I know," Tristan said. "He's told me the same thing. I just have a hard time believing it, I guess. He tried twelve-step programs and stuff when we were kids. None of them lasted long."

"Maybe he needs a different kind of support system," she suggested. "I mean, you've been through recovery. Maybe you could help him with his, or something."

"I don't know if I'm the best candidate for that," he said with a humorless chuckle. "My drinking was out of control for me, but it was pretty in line with what a lot of young guys do. I mean, I drank just as much as the dumb friends I hung around with, but that wasn't the type of person I wanted to be. I needed to deal with things and not use drinking as an escape. My dad; he was just on a whole other level."

Thinking a few minutes more, she had a thought. "You know, I'm obviously just hearing all of this now, so this may not be relevant at all, but when I was teaching art in the schools we did training about identifying kids who might be bullied, or maybe had issues at home. One of the things that I really took away from that training was that they said that most people who bully or abuse are basically people who have experienced some kind of trauma or pain in their own lives, and instead of dealing with it in a healthy way, they end up externalizing it by hurting others. It's like this really unfortunate way to regain a feeling of power and control over their lives."

As she thought it through she saw that Tristan was listening and thinking about it as well, so she continued. "So I don't know how much you know about your dad's past, but maybe there was something there that triggered the way he treated you guys. I don't know. That doesn't excuse it in any way, but it may be something that he'd be able to explain now that he's older, and even been faced with some serious health issues." Virginia twitched her lips, unsure whether or not she should say the final thing she was thinking. There had been something she'd been wanting to say to Tristan since this whole business with his dad had started. She hadn't brought it up because she didn't want him to think she was trying to manipulate him in some way, but now it seemed like something he might just need to hear.

"Look, Tristan," she said. "This is the last thing that I'll say. I know there are lots of things I wanted to say to my Dad before he passed. I never got a chance to. I just don't want you to miss your opportunity to make things right again because if you do miss it, you'll regret it. Trust me."

He looked up at her with pensive eyes and searched her face. Finally, he squeezed her hand which was still holding onto his.

"You really think I should do this?" he asked.

"I do," she answered.

He nodded his head ever so slightly, coming to terms with the idea, then let out a deep breath. "All right."

CHAPTER THIRTEEN

"Maybe they decided not to come after all," Tristan said, his voice shaking with more than the chill of the cold air as he, Virginia, Samantha, Adam and Ross stood on the ferry dock the afternoon of Christmas Eve.

"They would have texted or called if that was the case," Adam chimed in.

The three o'clock ferry had just arrived and about a dozen people had slowly meandered off.

On Christmas Eve, no one seemed in a great hurry. People were happily greeting friends and family members, hugging and laughing, often with packages and presents in hand.

However, there was no laughing among their group. Even Ross and Samantha, who were only tangentially connected to the history of the McPherson family, seemed to share in the tension. The nervous energy wasn't helped by Tristan's constant pacing back and forth along the dock.

"Maybe they missed the ferry, or decided to spend the night in Seattle," Tristan said.

Virginia thought he sounded half hopeful and half terrified that this might be the case.

"Babe," she said walking up to him and taking his hand. "I'm sure they'll be here. You'll talk it out and everything's gonna be fine."

Tristan looked down at her. She saw his shoulders relax and a smile crossed his face as he squeezed her hand in turn.

"You might be-"

He stopped mid-sentence and the smile instantly faded as he looked straight ahead to the arrival platform. One last couple was making their way slowly down the ferry.

An older woman with obviously dyed bright blonde hair and worry lines well worn into her forehead led a man down the ferry plank who was making his way with the help of a cane.

This man's lips were pursed in what seemed like a permanent frown. His dark hair was marked with grey. When he lifted his head and looked up at the group waiting on the dock Virginia could easily see that his eyes were the same color and shape as both of his sons, though she didn't see any of the natural warmth she was so familiar with in Tristan's bright, inviting blue eyes.

No, the older man's eyes remained hard and emotionless as they reached the small group. The woman next to him, however, brightened as soon as she reached the end of the plank. Virginia immediately saw Tristan's warm smile reflected in his mother's.

"You must be Virginia," she exclaimed as soon as they were close enough. Before Virginia could answer, she found herself enveloped in a warm, clinging hug. "Oh! I've waited so long to meet you!"

"Good to meet you too, Mrs. McPherson," Virginia returned, feeling her face grow warm in embarrassment.

"Oh, no need for that, hun," Mrs. McPherson said pulling away from her. "Call me Iris, everyone does."

"Okay. Iris, then."

"And, of course, this is my husband, Ward," she said.

"Pleasure to meet you," Virginia said warily, but with a convincing positivity. Ward did not look at her, merely nodded in her direction. His hard gaze was fixed on Tristan.

What felt like a prolonged silence fell over the group. Eventually, Virginia realized that she would have to break it.

"And, Mrs...I mean, Iris. This is my sister, Samantha."

Virginia introduced Samantha and Ross to Mr. and Mrs. McPherson and while Tristan's mother greeted both of them warmly, Tristan's father was again content merely to nod. Soon another silence fell over the group. The crisp winter air swirled around, twirling off the ocean water.

Virginia was trying to think of something to say when suddenly, to her surprise, Tristan spoke.

"I'm glad you could make it, Dad," he said. "It's been a while."

Ward looked at his son appraisingly. Finally, the corners of his eyes softened just a tad. "It's been a long day, but your mother and I are glad to be here," his dad replied.

The two men appraised each other a moment longer before Tristan spoke to his father again.

"I suppose we've got a bit to talk about, haven't we? Do you want to go get coffee or something?"

"If you think that's best," Ward answered gruffly.

A quiet agreement seemed to be made and the group shifted slightly with the idea that they should all start walking toward the parking lot and downtown.

"Well, while you boys are doing that," Iris chimed in with an upbeat attempt at normalizing the awkward reunion, "I really wouldn't mind the chance to go lie down awhile. If that's at all possible? It's been a long few days."

"We'll take you up to the cottage," Virginia interjected quickly. "I've got the guest room all ready for you."

The sleeping arrangements had been decided the day before. As Tristan's apartment only had one room, Virginia would put his family up in the three bedroom cottage.

Once Ross and Adam had helped gather Mr. and Mrs. McPherson's luggage, the five people heading up to the cottage made their way to the car, leaving Tristan and Ward still eyeing each other warily.

Samantha, Adam, and Ross moved ahead with the luggage while Iris and Virginia lagged behind. As they walked, Virginia couldn't help but notice Ross trying to insert himself between Samantha and Adam who were moving closer and closer together.

"I can't tell you how long I've waited for this," Iris said quickly as they approached the car. "I know how angry Tristan was when he left. Of course, I can't blame him. It was a different time back then, but a difficult one, for all of us, but years passed and things changed. I wish I could have told Tristan how much his father had changed. I was tempted to so many times, but I always promised Ward I would never go behind his back and talk to Tristan. No matter how stubborn he can be, he's still my husband."

"Well, Tristan can be equally stubborn," Virginia admitted.

"I swear I aged years, long before I should have," Iris continued. "Then, miraculously, life got better. We worked through so many things and so much was healed, which makes it almost harder now to see Ward's health fail. We are finally in the golden years and I want to be able to enjoy them." She gave a weak smile and glanced at Virginia. "Being here is a good start to that though."

As Virginia looked at her future mother-in-law, she could certainly see that behind the warm and energetic exterior, the older woman was under significant strain.

Thus it was no surprise when, after thanking Virginia for putting her and her husband up, she retired to her room to lay down.

Virginia, on the other hand, didn't feel a bit tired. She was filled with an anxious anticipation as she thought about how the long-awaited, and long-overdue conversation between Tristan and his father was going. That was why she didn't hesitate a second at Ross' suggestion that the four of them head down to Main Street. Sam, it seemed, was keen on the idea as well.

"Have you seen the bed and breakfast yet, Adam? It's Tristan and Virginia's new pet project."

"You say that like they're the only ones working on it," Ross jumped in with a hint of a childish pout.

"Tristan told me you've been helping him out with his jobs," Adam said to Ross amiably. "Some of them are tough to do alone, I know that much."

"I do more than help out," Ross corrected. "We're sort of partners."

"Anyway," Sam said with an exaggerated eye-roll, "We should take a look at it. I've been helping Virginia pick some of the furniture in the rooms."

"Then I'm sure they'll look extra great," Adam said with a shy smile. "I can tell you've got great taste."

To Virginia's surprise, instead of giving a witty or even flirty reply, Sam smiled at Adam just as shyly and looked down at the ground.

"Thanks," Samantha said in a quieter, more coy voice than her sister had ever used before. She glanced back up at Adam and they smiled at each other for a moment, before Ross abruptly cut in.

"Well, are we going or what?" he asked jovially, the undertone of jealousy clearly present in his voice to Virginia's ear, but well hidden all the same.

Sam shook her head in mock annoyance at him but led the way out the cottage door nonetheless.

On the walk, Adam allowed Ross to pull ahead with Sam while he and Virginia trailed behind.

"I wanted to thank you again for everything you did," Adam said to Virginia, as Samantha and Ross started a half-playful argument about something Virginia couldn't quite make out.

"No need," Virginia said. "In fact, I almost ruined it."

"You didn't," Adam said. "I'm the one that almost ruined it. I shouldn't have asked you to lie to Tristan, and I'm sorry for that. It's easy to get caught up in the whole thing. When people aren't talking to each other, you try to orchestrate everything just perfectly and walk on eggshells. I'd gotten too close to it, you know? I know if it wasn't for you, Tristan and Dad might not have talked for the rest of their lives."

Virginia, unsure what to say to that, simply gave a half-smile.

They soon made their way downtown, surrounded by the holiday glow of twinkling overhead lights and festively adorned lampposts. As the sun began to set, more and more people were seen hurrying out of closing shops, laden with last minute gifts.

"So, I guess your parents being here means that they're coming to the wedding?" Virginia asked as they got closer to the bed and breakfast.

"I think that depends on how Tristan and dad's little talk goes," Adam said truthfully. "Mom and Dad drove their car up here, and that's not only because they wouldn't let Dad fly so soon after his surgery. It was

272

so they could leave if things didn't go well. They paid for ten days worth of parking at the ferry parking lot over in Seattle, but they were assured they could always get a refund if they need to."

"Well, let's hope they don't need to," Virginia said, her heart hoping that was the case.

Finally, they reached the bed and breakfast where Ross was only too happy to show off the work he and Tristan had started doing in the rooms upstairs, the downstairs kitchen and the dining room.

The friendly banter between everyone was casual, but Virginia began to notice a slight back-and-forth cropping up between Ross's natural inclination to brag in front of Samantha, and Adam's push back to it. If you knew Ross well, you knew that he was always half joking, but it was definitely something that wasn't apparent from the get-go. It didn't help that the obvious threat of Adam was bringing out an extra weird side in Ross. Before it escalated any further, Virginia broke the pattern.

"Let's go upstairs," she said quickly with a ton of enthusiasm. "I've got one of the rooms painted up there, and I just put in one of my paintings to see how it would look."

She led the way upstairs to what she was calling the Winter Room. It was the only upstairs room that was partially done. After she'd finished her snow painting she'd been too excited to wait until Tristan had finished the upstairs flooring before she hung it. It was only in there temporarily until she removed it so they could complete the other areas, but looking at it made her happy, and also helped to inspire her shopping for the other things still needed for the room.

"Wow," Adam said when Samantha and Virginia led the way inside. "It's gorgeous. I know Mom and Dad would love to stay here. My mom can't get enough of winter views."

"I picked out the wardrobe," Sam said proudly, nodding to the antique wooden wardrobe in the corner.

"And she helped paint the walls," Virginia added.

"Like I said," Adam said turning to Samantha with a very charming smile. "Beautiful."

Sam blushed again.

"It'll look really good once we refinish the wood floors," Ross said loudly, clearly trying to turn Samantha's attention back to him, "which is luckily my specialty."

"I just hope you use the finish that I told you to," Sam said turning to him. "If you use the one you wanted it won't look nearly as good."

"You know I always take your advice," Ross said. Sam let out a disbelieving snort but smiled all the same.

Virginia walked Adam through her plans for the other rooms. The more she talked about her design plans for the bed and breakfast, the less anxious she felt. For some reason, throwing herself into this type of work gave her a sense of peace she didn't often feel, even when baking.

It seemed that even Adam noticed it.

"If you ask me, I think you're wasting your talents by baking," Adam said. "Don't get me wrong, I'm sure you're really good at that, but you're amazing at interior decorating. Not to mention your painting is incredible."

"Wouldn't that be nice," she laughed. "Though renovation jobs here on the island are few and far between. As Tristan can tell you, lots of the jobs he takes are in Seattle or on the surrounding islands. And I'm not sure I want to lug furniture that far."

"I'm sure it's better than Northern California," he said. "Jobs have been drying up there for years. In fact, I thought more than once about joining Tristan out here."

"You should," Samantha said eagerly. "It would be nice to see more of you."

"But like Virginia said," Ross put in just as quickly, "things are pretty dry here too. I mean, Tristan and I stay pretty busy, but not nearly enough to need extra help. I mean, I just do this to get more hands-on experience, so that right there is pretty telling."

Adam looked like he was about to respond, but before he could, both he and Virginia caught sight of two people exiting the local coffee shop just in front of them. Virginia's heart turned anxiously over in her chest as the figures came into view.

Tristan and his father were standing across from each other talking quietly. Even as their group continued to move closer, there were no clues on either face to say which way their conversation had gone.

Just as Virginia thought her heart just might explode from anticipation, she saw Tristan extend his hand to his father. His father stared at it for a moment then his face slightly softened and he grasped his son's hand.

She saw the father and son duo look at each other again, half-formed smiles on each of their faces.

"Tristan," Adam called out to them from across the street. It was only then that Ward and Tristan turned to the group walking towards them.

Virginia saw Tristan smile at her and was more than relieved that he looked less strained than he had in the last several days.

"I thought you guys would be at the cottage," Tristan called back, as the group made their way over to where he and his father stood.

"Your mom's still there," Virginia answered. "She's lying down though."

"I should probably join her then," Ward said. His voice sounded just as gruff as it had earlier that day but his face looked a little less tired than it had.

"My truck is parked right over here," Tristan pointed to the group. "I guess we could all pile in."

"If it's all right, could one of the others drive me back?" Ward asked his son. "I think you could use a little time with your fiancé."

He looked up at Tristan with more warmth than Virginia realized the older man was capable of.

"I'll see you tomorrow, Dad," Tristan said with a small nod.

"See you tomorrow, son," he answered.

With that, Tristan handed over the pickup truck keys and Ward along with Adam and Samantha headed back to the cottage, while Ross bid his farewell and made his way to the ferry to meet up with his family.

Tristan and Virginia watched them in silence for several moments before starting their own trek towards Tristan's apartment in the opposite direction.

"So, is it safe to say that things went well?" Virginia asked, taking Tristan's hand in hers.

"As well as they could go," he answered. "Dad's involved in a good recovery program that he's stuck to for quite a while now, so that's something. He admitted he made some mistakes. I admitted I made some too. I mean, things still aren't perfect but..."

"But they'll be at the wedding?" she asked hopefully.

Tristan turned to her with a look of contentment.

"They will," he answered.

She leaned into him and he wrapped his arms around her in a comforting embrace.

The rest of the walk along the charmingly decorated streets, Virginia told Tristan about the tour they'd given Adam of the bed and breakfast.

"I think Ross is a little jealous," she said. "Sam seems pretty taken with your brother. If we're not careful, we'll have a mini soap opera on our hands."

"That's surprising," Tristan said. "Didn't you say your sister didn't go for small-town boys? Adam's about as small town as you can get."

Virginia could do nothing but shrug. "People change I guess."

"That's true," he said quietly.

When she looked up at him, she knew that one simple sentence had brought his thoughts back to his father. Instead of saying anything more, she snuggled closer to him and just enjoyed the magic of the Christmas lights shining brightly.

They didn't speak again until they reached the front door of Tristan's apartment.

"So you'll come to the cottage tomorrow morning?" she confirmed. "Sam will be there, along with Adam and your parents."

"Wouldn't miss it," he said, "and thanks again for making this happen."

"I didn't make anything happen."

"Yes, you did, and for what it's worth, I'm sort of glad you went behind my back."

"I'm just thankful it worked out," she said, feeling a small wave of relief wash some of the remaining guilt and apprehension away.

He lifted his hand and placed it gently on her cheek. "I think it's just who you are, and I'm thankful for that."

Before she could say anything, he leaned forward and placed his lips gently on hers. She wasn't sure when the kiss ended or who pulled away first, but for the first time in well over a week, she felt like she'd been whisked back to the deliriously happy place that she and Tristan usually called home. She opened her hazy eyes to see Tristan's face looking bright and passionate again.

"I love you," he said.

"I love you too."

With another kiss and a word of good-night, Virginia headed back out into the snow feeling lighter than she had in weeks. Finally, after all the planning, secrets and misunderstandings, she knew that she and Tristan were going to have a very merry Christmas.

CHAPTER FOURTEEN

*A*fter a simple, but family-filled Christmas day with food, church, Christmas movies, and many rounds of board games, the McPherson clan, and the Ellis sisters had quickly found a comfortable rhythm with one another.

The days between Christmas and the wedding passed in a flurry of activity. Virginia and Tristan would have breakfast with his family, then head off to work on the renovation. Tristan's dad was supposed to sit tight and heal, so they were perfectly content to stay at the cottage and relax. Riding a wave of motivation, Tristan, Virginia, and Ross went to the bed and breakfast every day. They worked out a nice routine in which the men would work downstairs, while Virginia finished decorating the upstairs bedrooms. All the floors had been sanded and refinished in a gleaming high gloss stain. Stately crown molding was added along the ceiling with a handsome chair rail to match. The rooms and hallway had been painted in what Virginia considered the perfect complementary shades, which managed to be refined and elegant yet comfortable and inviting.

Both Samantha and Adam were frequent visitors to the property-in-progress as well. Samantha had volunteered to be Adam's regional tour guide, and they would often pop into together before or after one of their day trips. Virginia found Sam's change of demeanor around Adam particularly telling. She was finally able to probe Samantha about it one afternoon as her sister helped arrange the new bedding in the Main Street themed bedroom.

"So, you and Adam seem to have gotten pretty close," Virginia casually mentioned as they tucked opposite sides of the bed sheets under the mattress. Sam rolled her eyes dismissively, but could not hide the tell-tale blush which was becoming more and more common.

"You're using your matchmaking voice again," Sam said.

"Just making an observation," Virginia asserted. "I didn't think you liked men who grew up in small towns and worked with their hands."

"Well, Adam's different," Sam shrugged. "He's traveled places for his construction business. He manages the crews that his dad contracts to help on big projects. He's smart. Smarter than some of the guys I meet in college," she said and gave Virginia a sideways glance, "and don't give me that look."

"What?" Virginia asked innocently. "I'm not allowed to smile at you?"

"Not in that all-knowing big sister way," Sam asserted. "There's nothing going on between me and Adam. It's just nice to be able to talk to a guy who's not trying to hit on me or correct my homework all the time."

"I guess you get enough of that with Ross," Virginia said cheekily.

"Exactly," Sam said with another eye roll.

Though, Virginia couldn't help but notice that Ross had not been quite as overt in his attempts to woo Sam lately as he had been before. He was still clearly trying to get on her good side but in a much more subtle way. In the past week, he'd opened doors for her, complimented her writing without a hint of grammar correction, and hadn't tried a cheesy pick-up line once.

Virginia learned the reason for this as she walked Tristan back to his apartment one evening. Somehow the issue of her sister's little love triangle came up, as well as Ross's changed attitude.

"That's partly me," Tristan said. "Ever since Adam got here he's been moping about how my brother's taking all of Sam's attention. He asked me what I thought Sam saw in Adam. That's when I suggested that Ross might want to ease up on the pickup lines and homework help."

"So now you've gotten into the matchmaking game?" Virginia asked slyly.

"I never said anything about that," Tristan answered with a chuckle. "I have a feeling whatever's happening with Sam, Adam, and Ross, God'll work it out. Just like he did with us. I also have a feeling that I won't regret helping Ross be a little more mature when it comes to women. Even if it doesn't help him with Sam, it'll help him with someone."

"Either way," Virginia said as they reached Tristan's apartment. "I think it's really sweet of you to give him advice."

The kiss goodnight was longer than usual and Virginia had to fight the urge to go into the apartment with her fiancé. In the end, she headed down the path to the cottage, happy that the wedding was only two days away.

And being able to finally spend the night with her husband rather than alone wasn't the only thing she was looking forward to. Even though, as she continually told Tristan, she was perfectly happy to put her future in-laws up in her house, she couldn't pretend that the experience wasn't becoming just a tad bit draining.

Surprisingly, the issue wasn't with Tristan's father. Mr. McPherson, due to his need for rest after his surgery, was rarely out of his room. When Virginia did see him, however, he was polite and soft-spoken.

No, the issue was Mrs. McPherson.

It wasn't that Tristan's mother was rude. In fact, quite the contrary. She was more than eager to help Virginia in any way she could. She just didn't seem to realize that these constant intrusions, especially in the kitchen, could be more invasive and condescending, than helpful.

"Oh, honey," she told Virginia the morning of the wedding as Sam and Virginia were making breakfast. "If you cook the eggs like that, they'll either burn or come out all rubbery. Here, let me."

Before Virginia could protest that it really wasn't necessary, Mrs. McPherson had taken the frying pan out of her hands and pushed her gently out of the way.

"You never use high heat," Mrs. McPherson said taking the spatula out of Virginia's hand as well. "Even for scrambled eggs. Always use medium heat. That way they cook evenly."

"Iris," Mr. McPherson said from the table where he was staring at his newspaper, "I'm sure Virginia's cooked eggs in this kitchen before. Just leave her to it."

"Oh, she doesn't mind, do you, dear?" Virginia had no sooner opened her mouth to respond when Iris continued. "Besides, a bride shouldn't be cooking on the day of her wedding. When I married Ward, my bridesmaids waited on me hand and foot. Virginia, hun, you just go sit down at the table. Your sister and I will take care of everything."

Virginia wanted to tell Iris that she didn't mind cooking, or that doing something productive gave her a chance to put her excited and nervous energy to good use, but she knew the moment she opened her mouth, Iris would simply talk over her.

She looked at Sam for help; after all, Sam was never shy about voicing her opinion. This time, however, Sam was simply attempting to stifle a laugh.

"Well, you heard the lady, Virginia," she said, amusement lacing her voice, "Just sit down and let your handmaidens serve you."

With a sigh of defeat, Virginia consented to sit down and allow them to serve her breakfast. All the same, she was glad when Samantha turned down Iris' offer to help with the dress. She didn't know if she could take the older woman's fussing and suggestions about how to wear the gown or what jewelry would go best.

"Almost makes you want to get a hotel for the wedding night, doesn't it?" Sam asked. Virginia and Tristan had planned on spending the wedding night at the cottage. Of course, that was before Tristan's parents had taken up residence.

"Yeah, I wish, but that costs money that we have earmarked for more important things," Virginia said with a hint of wishfulness in her voice. "Plus, by the time we knew that Tristan's parents were coming, it was too late to find a hotel that had space at a reasonable price."

"I just hope the walls are thick," Sam said with a wink at her sister. Virginia made a shocked face and threw a pillow, nailing her sister perfectly upside the head.

Once Virginia was dressed in her wedding gown, Samantha helped her down the stairs. Amanda and the two other bridesmaids arrived at the cottage already dressed and the small group congregated in the living room. Last minute touches were put on the bouquets, makeup, and hairdos.

Finally, there was a knock at the door. Sam opened it to announce that Virginia's carriage had arrived.

She knew that Tristan had hired someone to take her to and from the wedding, but the horse-drawn carriage sitting in the snow outside filled her with giddy surprise that she wasn't prepared for.

That giddiness increased when she stepped outside and saw a large Victorian sleigh, decked out with pine garland and red bows waiting for her. Two large white horses whinnied, shaking their harness bells while the coach driver, dressed in Victorian garb, helped her into the red velvet seat.

She waved goodbye to her bridal party who would meet her down the hill at the church. She was grateful for the quiet serenity to reflect and give thanks for all the changes in her life that had lead to this moment.

After a few minutes of quiet communion, the horses began moving and Virginia opened her eyes to take in her surroundings. The enchanted, wintery ride to the old church on the edge of Main Street passed in a blissful, beautiful blur. The snow on the hill and resting on the branches of the trees seemed to glimmer more than Virginia had ever seen. Even the sound of the birds seemed sweeter as they rang out. It was as if they were joining their voices together to create the sweet soundtrack to the happiest day of her life.

When she arrived at the church, the dazzling decorations there put even the picturesque carriage ride to shame. Fully decorated Christmas trees in gold, silver, and white lined the aisle and an arch covered in pure white gardenia flowers stood behind the altar.

In what seemed like no time at all, music from the chapel's golden pipe organ accompanied Virginia's march down the tree-lined aisle. At the end of it stood Tristan.

Her heart leapt at the sight of him. When she saw his eyes cloud over and small tears appear to dampen the rims, she couldn't help but be glad they had waited for him to see her for the first time today at this exact moment. It felt as if everything was brand new, like their world was somehow re-starting at this very moment. His expression of wonder slowly transformed into her favorite smile, which she couldn't help but return as widely as her face would allow.

"You are so beautiful," he whispered to her as he took her hand at the end of the aisle.

To keep from crying, she ran a hand along his lapel and whispered back, "You clean up pretty well yourself."

She took in his nice silk tuxedo complete with a white suit jacket and white tie that somehow made his adoring blue eyes sparkle as brightly as the candles surrounding them. She tried to take in every decoration, every scent of every candle and pine tree, and every perfectly written word that was repeated.

As hard as Virginia tried, she couldn't seem to hold on to the memory of the ceremony. Even Phil's sermon, which like all his sermons, was filled with humor, heart and more than a few groan-worthy puns, passed in a blissful fog.

Before she knew it, Phil was pronouncing them husband and wife, and Virginia was making her way back down the aisle arm in arm with her new husband.

Virginia and Tristan rushed down the steps of the church amid applause and thrown grains of birdseed. While fending off the shower of grains, Virginia heard laughter rise up around her, taking a minute to register that it was coming from herself. Even though she didn't seem to know why she was laughing, she couldn't seem to stop.

When they got into the carriage and felt it pull away, she noticed that Tristan was laughing just as hard as she was. Wiping tears from her cheeks, the giggles finally subsided and the two looked at each other with wide grinning expressions.

"So, this is what it feels like to be married," he said finally.

"I guess so," Virginia said. "What do you think of it so far?"

"Not too bad," Tristan replied cheekily.

Virginia, with another chuckle, gave him a playful swat before laying her head on her husband's shoulder. "I almost wish we didn't have to go to the reception," she said. "I'd rather just ride around for a while, then head straight for the cottage."

"We do have to put in an appearance," he said, sounding equally reluctant, "but, not for a while. I think I have an idea. Do you have your overnight bag?"

"It's under the seat," Virginia said remembering where she placed her change of clothes and toiletries at Samantha's behest. "Why?"

It was only then when Virginia realized that they were headed not towards the church hall where the reception would be, but back toward downtown Sweetwater.

"Does the driver know where we're going?" Virginia asked quietly, a tad bit concerned that he'd been misdirected.

"Just enjoy the ride, Mrs. McPherson."

Her answer came sooner than she'd expected when the carriage driver pulled up in front of the bed and breakfast. Tristan stepped out and offered his hand gallantly to Virginia.

"It was agreed that, since the upstairs rooms are finished and painted, it's only fitting that you and I should be the first guests in the newly renovated bed and breakfast."

"Are you serious?" she asked, a surprised smile on her lips.

"Well, you didn't expect me to spend my wedding night in the same house as my parents, did you?" Tristan asked with a teasing grimace.

Virginia's own smile grew as Tristan turned the key, opened the door and led her inside. The entryway had been cleared of all traces of construction debris, replaced with white paper runners and fresh flowers. Garland was wound up the stairway banister complete with white twinkling lights.

"Now," he said as they reached the bottom of the landing. "You get to choose which bedroom we'll spend the night in."

"Number 2, definitely," she gushed without hesitating.

"We're keeping with the winter wonderland theme, I see," Tristan said. "Good choice."

"Now, aren't you supposed to carry me across the threshold?" Virginia asked.

"I didn't think you cared about old traditions," Tristan retorted with a mock skeptical look.

"I like some traditions."

"Well then..." His voice trailed as his eyes danced with mischief. Virginia let out a gasp as Tristan scooped her effortlessly up into his arms and carried her up the stairs, down the hall, and to the awaiting suite. They made their way through the open door and the calm cool color of winter filled her to the brim. He set her down gently on the bed and leaned down to meet her lips.

Virginia felt her heart soar in her chest. After so many years of searching, after everything they'd been through, this was what mattered. Here they were, in a home they'd built together, surrounded by her artwork and his handiwork, filled with love, respect, and joy.

And it was perfect.

~

ACKNOWLEDGMENTS

It is humbling to find myself finishing this book so long after I planned to. Another year, another child, another phase of life; things get in the way of our best intentions. I'm thankful to have had each of those new experiences, while also eventually finding myself in a place to come full circle and complete this series. I am beyond blessed for my friends and family, and the most amazing community of readers! Thank you all!

To Ani: Who would ever imagine, all these years later, still finding ways to work on projects together. From high school plays to published novels, and a million random adventures in between. May we continue to bring our unique brand of randomness into each others lives forever!

To Robert: It is always an absolute pleasure collaborating with you! Your creativity is a natural gift and I'm glad you are one of the good ones out there shaping our future generations.

To Drake: Thank you for being by my side, day in and day out, during this journey. Thank you for supporting my crazy ideas, even when you think there very well may be easier ways. And thank you for being my perfect other half, as odd and complex as I am.

WITH LOVE...AND REALITY TV

To My Dear Readers~

It has been a whirlwind since publishing the first book in this series. From a little manuscript called "The Flip" to finally publishing the third book in my intended trilogy, a lot has changed. I still remember where I was when I wrote the first line of "For Love...and Donuts". I was sitting in my car waiting on someone to run something out to me and I started writing. My awesome cousin owns her own donut shop and I must have had it on the brain as I wrote out the words "Maple-glazed Pistachio donut". I don't know if that is a flavor that ever got made, but the recesses of my brain obviously thought it was a good idea. From that day to now, a lot has happened in all of our lives, but I want you to know that being able to write for you has made my life more complete than you will ever know. Thank you for your loving kindness, your support & your time. Thank you, thank you, thank you~

CONTENTS

CHAPTER ONE

*V*irginia McPherson smiled at herself in the mirror. She was getting ready for the day, brushing the final tangles out of her hair when she caught sight of it. She smiled at the ring on her finger that was a symbol of Tristan's everlasting love. It wasn't the ring, which he had slipped on her finger during their wedding ceremony four months ago, that caused this reaction. It wasn't that she didn't adore the simple gold band. She loved it, and all the memories of that day, and all of the days since.

She was smiling now at the simple brass ring Tristan had given her months before their wedding day. He had somehow made it himself, forged from a key that she had used to lock her diary when she was a little girl. With that ring he promised his undying love to Virginia and told her that he would wait for as long as it took for her to come back to him. It was probably the single most romantic gesture anyone had ever done for her, which, if you knew Tristan, was saying a lot.

Virginia sat the brush next to the bathroom sink and softly twisted the brass band round and round on her finger. It seemed like a lifetime ago when she and Tristan were not married, and yet it had only been four months. When she thought about all of the things that had happened since the day she and Tristan first met—and she had rediscovered the key to her diary—it felt like much longer. Back then she thought that she was meeting a contractor to get her aunt's cottage ready to sell, the same cottage where she and Tristan now lived.

She had planned to sell the cottage to pay off the college loans of her boyfriend, Jason, believing that would clear the path for the two of them to get married. Of course, Jason had turned out to be a lying, cheating, self-absorbed jerk. At the time, however, Virginia thought that he was the love of her life. When Jason tried to convince her that they should get back together the month before her wedding, she had already come to the conclusion that he was little more than a minor annoyance.

Virginia wasn't the only one with baggage from her past that needed to be dealt with before the wedding. The difference was that Tristan's was much heavier, and much more difficult to unload. Virginia had been aware that her then-future husband had been estranged from his father for years, but she only learned the depth of the rift between them in the weeks leading up to the wedding.

It turned out that Tristan's own history of drinking ran in the family, and his father, Ward, had a far bigger issue with it than Tristan. Their story had a happy ending, though. Ward and Tristan's mother, Iris, had come to Sweetwater Island for the wedding, and Tristan and Ward had forged the beginnings of a truce that, to this day, had continued to grow stronger.

"But you are taking the medicine, right, Dad?" Virginia heard the subtle mix of concern and frustration in the smooth tenor tone of Tristan's voice as she went back into the bedroom. Before his heart attack last December, Ward had run his own construction firm. Since then, he had to reluctantly cede control of much of the daily business to his younger son, Adam, but old habits died hard. Ward was still up with the chickens, as Iris liked to say, and with nothing else to do, he was taking advantage of the fact that Tristan was once again a part of his life. It was only seven-thirty in the morning and they had already been on the phone for nearly a half an hour. "The doctor prescribed it for a reason," Tristan continued, sounding more than a bit vexed.

"Remember your tone," Virginia lightly reminded him with a big smile and an overly silly bat of her eyelashes. Tristan shot her a toothy smile that was so obviously fake that she laughed out loud and had to cover her mouth to muffle the sound.

"Okay, Dad, I have to go," Tristan said after a deep, centering breath. "V and I have to go and take a look at a cottage for a new job. That's right; we're kind of a team now. No, Ross still works for me, I haven't fired him. No, I don't think that you should fly out here. We have it covered. Now please, do what the doctor says and take your pills. V and I will be out to see you as soon as we can." When the call ended, he tossed the phone on the bed and raked his fingers through his messy brown hair. He had let it get a little longer than normal over the winter, but Virginia didn't think now was the best time to suggest a haircut.

"So, what?" asked Virginia playfully as she sat on the edge of the bed and pulled Tristan down next to her. "Are you saying that you don't want to work with your dad again, you know, for old time's sake?"

"God, no!" groaned Tristan.

"Hey, at least you two are talking daily now. That's a big leap from before," she said.

"And I know the wonderful woman who helped make that possible," he said and leaned in to kiss her. Before she knew it, they had fallen back into the bed. The kiss became increasingly more passionate, and it was all Virginia could do to muster the strength to push him away. Feeling his strong arms around her and looking up into that impossibly handsome face, it was the last thing she wanted to do. "We have an appointment, remember?"

"It might not hurt us to be late, just this once," Tristan said softly as he gently pushed a swooping strand of hair away from her face and caressed her cheek. Tristan hated being late, so the gesture was almost too powerful.

"Nope, come on," she said, pushing him so that he rolled over onto his back next to her. "If you're late it will put you in a foul mood all day."

"I'm pretty sure it won't," he called as she got up from the bed and headed down the stairs. She turned back at the door and gave him a sly smile.

"I promise I'll make it up to you," she said suggestively. "You know I always keep my promises."

They walked down the stairs, grabbed their jackets, and headed out to Tristan's truck. Even though the calendar said it was spring, there was still a chill in the air as it blew in from the bay. A few stubborn mounds of snow held on, even as green grass and flowers began to reclaim the island. One of the things that Virginia loved about living here was the change in seasons. While some might find the transition period between winter and spring to be boring and maybe even a little ugly as they waited for the annual rebirth to fully take hold, she found it beautiful. She and Tristan had converted the bedroom she had used as a child, when she and her sister, Sam, had come to stay in that same cabin with her Aunt Emily, into an art studio. Virginia had just finished a landscape depicting the view out of her window showing this transition.

Virginia smiled at Tristan as he held the passenger door open for her. It was little things like that, and how he always smiled when she entered a room, or complimented her hair, that reminded Virginia how truly lucky she was. Some men, she knew, only did those things early in the dating process to try and impress a woman. Tristan was different. He never tried to impress her, although he almost always did. He was kind, and sweet, and generous. Simply put, he was the most amazing man on the planet, and he was all hers.

"What?" asked Tristan with a small chuckle when he looked over and saw Virginia smiling at him.

"Nothing," she said, feeling her cheeks get a little warm. She knew it was because she was blushing, and not due to the heater in Tristan's old pickup finally fully kicking in. "I was just thinking how thrilled I am to be Mrs. Tristan McPherson."

"Really?" he asked in mock surprise. "You mean the novelty hasn't worn off after four whole months of the two us spending virtually every waking minute together?"

Shortly before their wedding, Virginia had worked with Tristan and his partner, Ross, to restore an old bed and breakfast. They did it as a favor to the owners, whom Tristan had known for years, and Amanda, the real estate agent that eventually brokered the sale. Both Virginia and Tristan viewed Amanda as a friend and were happy that they could do something to help.

That job, combined with the time they had spent working together to fix up the cottage, had shown that the two of them made a pretty good team. Tristan's carpentry skills and Virginia's interior decorating prowess proved to be the perfect match, even if they didn't always agree on every single detail.

"We survived our first fight as husband and wife," she reminded him. "I think it only brought us closer, both as a couple and as business partners."

Winter isn't normally a busy time for construction work on Sweetwater Island, or any of the neighboring islands, but Amanda had been so happy with their work that she mentioned Tristan and Virginia to a few of her real estate friends in Seattle, and because of that, they had enough work to at least pay the bills. It did mean that the two of them were, as Tristan had said, spending pretty much every minute of every day together. That type of arrangement was bound to make even the steadiest of nerves fray, and that was what had happened when the two of them were finishing up a house for a couple that planned to give it as a wedding present to their son and his new bride. The job held a sort of sentimental place for both Tristan and Virginia, but even that wasn't enough to keep tempers from rising when Tristan questioned Virginia's choice of wallpaper for the master bedroom.

"All I'm saying is that the flower print is a little frilly," he had told her with a shrug. Virginia was excited about her choice and was more than a little taken aback when Tristan didn't feel the same way. "Not every guy is as progressive and willing to put up with flowers and lace as I am."

"This from the man who insisted on bringing his own comforter because the one that *we both agreed on* was, and I quote, 'too girly'?" she retorted.

"I agreed on it because I thought you were going to sell the cottage," he pointed out. "Had I known at the time that I would be living there, I would have had a much different opinion."

"I thought you said you loved me from the moment that you first laid eyes on me?" was her pointed response.

"I did," Tristan told her, "and I still do, but that doesn't mean that I have to love every piece of furniture, or every scrap of cloth that you own."

Things escalated from there. Virginia pointed out that they had agreed that she would handle the interior decorating and he would handle the carpentry. Tristan reminded her that he had been doing this long before they had begun working together and said that none of his previous clients had ever complained about his decorating decisions. It got so bad, in fact, that poor Ross practically ran out of the house, making some feeble excuse about forgetting that he had an assignment to do for one of his college classes.

It didn't take long for the two of them to come to an agreement, though. By dinner, they were laughing about it. Even if Virginia and Tristan were able to put the incident behind them quickly, Ross continued to be affected for some time. Virginia wasn't convinced that he ever truly recovered. He seemed to jump every time she came into a room, and she could swear he was always holding his breath every time she and Tristan talked to each other.

"I wouldn't worry about it," Tristan said with a shrug when Virginia asked him about it once. "Ross has always been a little, what's the word?"

"Weird?" asked Virginia with a sly grin and an arched eyebrow.

"I was going to say 'different,'" Tristan responded with a smirk, "but yeah, 'weird' works, too. The fact is that he hasn't ever had a relationship last longer than a few weeks. He probably thinks that every disagreement is the beginning of the end."

"It's too bad he can't find someone," Virginia had said at the time. "For all of his quirks, he is actually a sweet guy."

"So, there's no chance for him and Sam to get together?" asked Tristan. His tone was strange, and Virginia couldn't tell if he was happy or sad.

"My sister is her own kind of weird," Virginia said flatly, getting a hearty chuckle from Tristan. "The truth is that both are just too busy. They both work and go to school. Ross still manages to make it to the gym where Sam works a couple times a week, but that's the extent of their contact."

"How can you be so sure?" pressed Tristan. "Maybe Sam isn't comfortable telling her big sister all the intimate details of her love life."

"That would be a first," Virginia deadpanned. The truth was that, over the years, Sam had been all too forthcoming about the men she had dated. Not that there were all that many. "Trust me, if there were something going on between Ross and Sam, I would know about it."

"You know," Tristan began a little tentatively, scratching the side of his cheek, "Adam asks about Sam every time we talk."

When Adam and Sam had first met just prior to the wedding, there was instant chemistry between the two of them. Virginia had even entertained the notion of the two of them becoming a couple, but that was before Ward, Tristan and Adam's father, had asked Adam to step in and run the business until he could recover from heart surgery. That kept Adam busy pretty much seven days a week, and that made the prospect of any sort of relationship, especially one with Sam, who was plenty busy herself, unlikely. There was also geography to consider.

"Isn't your brother running the company for your father?" asked Virginia.

"He is," Tristan confirmed.

"The company that's based in California."

"Okay, I get it," said Tristan, sounding defeated. "You don't want my brother dating your sister."

"You're awful," Virginia told him, but with a smile.

That conversation had taken place two weeks ago, and Virginia hadn't stopped thinking about it. Maybe it was that she was finally happy and wanted the whole world to feel the way she felt. Maybe it was that she had always wanted her sister to find a man who was interested in more than just her beauty. Maybe it was something else entirely, but whatever it was, the thought of getting Sam and Adam together was seeming less and less crazy.

"We're here," said Tristan, bringing Virginia's thoughts back to the present. He pulled into a driveway of small house just off Main Street. The house belonged to Harold and Mary Tate. Virginia and Tristan had met them a few times at church, and even though finishing their basement and turning it into a man cave for Harold wasn't the sort of job they normally did, with it being the slow season, they knew that they really couldn't turn it down.

"Let's see if we can get through this project without ripping each other's throats out," said Tristan as he held the passenger door open for Virginia.

"What's that supposed to mean?" she asked, feeling her brow twitch as she stared up at him.

"Nothing," he said quickly, giving her a quick, innocent smile. "I was just trying to be funny."

"Epic fail," she said squeezing his arm.

"I mean, this is a man cave, after all. That isn't exactly your specialty."

"We've discussed this," Virginia reminded him as they made their way up the driveway and towards the front door. "My job is to handle the walls. I'll decide on the paint and suggest a few things to hang."

"Right," Tristan agreed, "and I'll take care of the drywall and the floors."

"It isn't like it's a big deal anyway," she grumbled, feeling herself becoming more annoyed at Tristan's little joke. "A big-screen TV, a wet bar in the corner, and a pool table. Anyone could handle that."

"What's that supposed to mean?" asked Tristan.

"I was just trying to be funny," Virginia told him with a shrug. He looked like he wanted to respond, but before he could, the front door opened.

"Good morning!" said Harold Tate, his cherubic face beaming from ear to ear as he held the door open and beckoned Virginia and Tristan inside. "Right on time," he said, shaking Tristan's hand first and then Virginia's. "I heard that about you. Punctuality is a trait I admire." Virginia shot Tristan a satisfied smile.

"I pride myself in that," said Tristan. He and Virginia followed Harold to the kitchen. Harold was almost as tall as Tristan, and his build suggested that he had once been an athlete. He was carrying a few more pounds than he should, and the widow's peak in his short brown hair flecked here and there with gray, along with the lines beginning to make their way across his friendly face, told Virginia he was close to fifty, or maybe even a little past. She knew that both of his children had moved out.

"I just brewed a fresh pot of coffee," said Mary Tate with a smile to match her husband's. Her brilliant auburn hair was pulled back into a single ponytail, and the way the freckles highlighted her face when she smiled gave her a youthful look. She was in better shape than Harold, and Virginia thought she must be a few years younger. "Can I interest the two of you in a cup?"

"That sounds wonderful," said Virginia, accepting the cup when Mary offered. She took a seat at the simple kitchen table across from Harold.

"I'm not myself until I've had my coffee," Tristan told Mary, and she poured him a cup. Tristan sat down next to Virginia and squeezed her hand. Feeling the warmth and gentle firmness of the gesture made all the frustration Virginia had felt only moments ago disappear.

"I can't tell you how much I appreciate this," said Harold when they were all finally seated. "From what I hear, this isn't the kind of thing you normally do."

"So, you checked us out?" said Tristan.

"Not really," Mary put in. "There aren't that many contractors doing business on Sweetwater Island, but the truth is that you two are as close a thing as we have to celebrities around here."

"What are you talking about?" asked Virginia. She knew that it was a small, tight-knit community, and while she wasn't surprised to hear that people knew about their work, the term "celebrities" caught her off guard.

"The work you did on the bed and breakfast downtown is the talk of the island," Harold explained. "Everyone was impressed by your attention to detail and how you really captured the essence of the island with what you did."

"Well, thank you," Tristan said, stumbling over his words. He couldn't hide the pink in his cheeks. Virginia had to smile. She knew how much Tristan prided himself in doing quality work, and she also knew how modest and unassuming he was. "We were just trying to do a good job."

"I know that what I'm asking is a far cry from that," said Harold, "but Mary and I have lived here since we were married. I would rather have the work done by someone local, someone who cares about the island."

"How long have you lived here?" asked Virginia as she sipped her coffee.

"It will be thirty-two years in June," said Mary, beaming at Harold. "It took a little convincing to get him to agree, but he finally came around."

"I just didn't like the idea of taking the ferry boat every day," Harold explained, "but I could tell that Mary loved the place, and in all honesty, so did I. I'm glad that she was so persistent."

"He has sacrificed so much over the years to make a good life for our kids, and for me," said Mary. "He deserves something for himself now."

"I guess a man cave sounds like I'm having a mid-life crisis, and maybe I am," said Harold, "but even if that's so, I don't believe in doing anything halfway."

"That much seems clear," said Virginia, and she wasn't just referring to the house. Even in the short time they had been talking, she could tell that Harold Tate had spent a lifetime paying attention to the details of his life. She was thrilled that he felt comfortable entrusting this job to her and Tristan.

"Well, maybe we should go and take a look at that basement," Tristan suggested, and without a word, the four of them stood up. Everyone followed Harold to a narrow staircase just off the kitchen. Tristan immediately pulled out a pad and paper and began scribbling notes.

"I think maybe calling it a 'diamond in the rough' would be a little too generous," said Harold as he flipped the light switch. I hope I'm not scaring you off." Much of the basement was exactly what Virginia was expecting. It was dusty, and a little dank smelling. The walls were drab and unadorned, but that was to be expected. For most of the time that the Tates had lived there, the basement was little more than a storage space. Most of the boxes had been removed, and what remained was a wide-open, poorly lit area, but there was one thing that Virginia noticed right off, and from the smile on his face, she could tell that Tristan had already made note of it.

"You didn't mention that your basement had poured walls," he said to Harold as he walked over and ran his hand along the surface of one of those walls.

"I'm sorry," said Harold with a look of slight confusion. "I'm not much of a handyman. I don't know what that means."

"Well, most of the homes here on the island don't even have a basement at all," Tristan told him. "That's because the island is so small and the water table is so high that water leakage is a constant problem. The ones that do have a basement usually have cinder blocks. That's cheaper, but like I said, the risk of water damage is higher. Poured walls give you a foundation that's stronger than most, and one that's able to withstand most of what Mother Nature throws at it."

"So, that's a good thing, right?" asked Mary.

"That's a very good thing," Virginia confirmed as she and Tristan shared a smile.

CHAPTER TWO

dam McPherson ran his fingers through his mop of hair and bit his lip. He stared at the computer screen and tried in vain to keep his frustration at bay. This was not what he signed up for. Staring back at him were expense reports, bank statements, and daily schedules. His brain was starting to feel like that computer, multiple windows open running multiple tasks, and at risk of locking up or overheating at any minute.

McPherson Restorations and Renovations had been a respected business in their community for thirty years. What had started as a one-man operation, Adam's father, Ward, and his beat-up Chevy pickup truck had grown into a multi-site operation that employed thirty men. Ward McPherson had always maintained that the business would be family run, and when he was slow to recover from surgery, Adam felt like he had no choice but to take over for his dad.

The trouble was that while Adam was every bit the carpenter that Ward and Tristan were, he lacked the business acumen. More than that, he lacked the desire to gain this talent. Adam loved working with his hands, and while his dad and older brother shared that feeling, there was never any doubt that they would each one day run his own business. Adam, on the other hand, would have been happy to just rebuild and restore old houses.

He turned away from the computer and his eye caught a picture on the wall of him, Tristan, and their father. It was taken at Adam's high school graduation. They all looked so young and so happy. Adam loved his brother, but sometimes he hated him, too. Back when that picture had been taken, they had all just assumed that it would be Tristan who would one day run the company. Adam could never have predicted that, in less than a year after he left high school, his older brother would strike off on his own.

There were reasons, of course. There always are. Ward McPherson was not an easy man to love, and his drinking and violence had taken their toll on Tristan. That was a lifetime ago, and the fences had been mended to some extent, but Tristan had a life now out on Sweetwater Island, one that suited him. There was no chance that he would ever return and take over the family business. A ringing telephone reminded Adam that he had no time to dwell on what might have been.

"McPherson Remodeling and Renovations," Adam said as he picked up the phone, remembering to smile as he did. His mom, Iris, always told him that you could hear a smile over the phone, and you could hear a frown, too. "How can I help you?"

"Adam, it's Jessie," said the voice on the other end of the line. Jessie Davis was one of the foremen, and he was currently working on renovating a building that was being turned into a micro-brewery. For the life of him, Adam couldn't remember where. "We need the mahogany for the bar and the tables. It isn't here."

"I know," said Adam, rubbing his temples with his free hand. "I meant to call you. The delivery truck was delayed. It should be here in about an hour, and then I'll get the wood out to you."

"The owner is already barking at me," Jessie moaned. "What do you want me to tell her?"

"I want you to tell her the truth," Adam said simply. "We can't control the supply chain."

"She keeps reminding me that they open in a week, which will be hard to do without tables or a bar."

"The wood will be here today," Adam assured his foreman. "Is there anything you and the guys can do while you wait for it?"

"There's a few little things," Jessie said meekly. "There's still some trim work, and a couple of light fixtures that need to be hung. None of that will take too long, especially with a full crew. Do you want me to send some of them home?"

"No," said Adam firmly. His father never gave him special treatment when he worked a job, and that meant if you got sent home early, you didn't get paid. Ward always tried to make sure that didn't happen, and as an hourly employee, Adam appreciated it. He wasn't going to change that policy if he could help it. "Keep everyone there and do whatever you can. If the wood isn't there by the time you finish, make sure they clean the place spotless. That will take some time."

"There's no doubt about that," said Jessie with a chuckle. "But what happens if the wood isn't here when you say it will be? The owner still needs to run the lines for the kegs, and she says she can't have that done until the bar is finished. She's worried that if it isn't done today, they won't be able to get it done by the time she is supposed to open."

"The wood will be there today, I promise," said Adam. "If the truck gets delayed again, I'll take one our trucks and go get it, and then I'll finish the bar myself if need be." As much as he wanted to make his customer happy, Adam had to admit that part of him wouldn't mind having an excuse to get back out in the field and do what he loved.

"Adam, you remind me of your old man more and more every day," said Jessie. "Don't worry about the owner. I'll find a way to calm her down. You just find a way to get me that wood."

When he hung up the phone, he found himself looking at a different picture. This one, sitting on his desk, was taken at Tristan's wedding. It was of him, Tristan, Tristan's wife, Virginia, and Virginia's sister, Samantha. From the moment he laid eyes on Sam, Adam knew there was something special about her. It wasn't just her looks, which were stunning. She was smart, funny, and seemed to know exactly what to say to make him smile. Adam never felt like he had to try to impress her, and he never felt like she was trying to impress him. They just clicked.

They tried to keep in touch after the wedding, and Adam thought more than once about sneaking up to Seattle to visit her, but almost as soon as he and his parents got back to California, it became apparent that his dad wasn't ready to go back to work. Adam knew how difficult it was for him to admit as much and ask his son to take over for him, so he agreed without hesitation.

He continued to email Sam, and called her a few times, but it became increasingly obvious that he would have to devote the bulk of his attention to learning how to run the business, while simultaneously actually running it. Besides, it wasn't as though Sam was just waiting around for him to call. She was busy, too. Between going to school and working at the gym, she didn't have much more free time than he did. Still, as looked at her picture and remembered how much fun they had, and how much he really liked being with her, he couldn't help but think that maybe, just maybe...

Adam had a sudden inspiration. With all the chaos going on around him, he needed something to help him center, to help him catch his breath. Maybe Sam could be that something. He was just about to pull out his cell phone and call her when the office phone rang again. It was the loading dock telling him that the mahogany delivery had just arrived.

"Get it over to the micro-brewery as soon as you can," Adam instructed, and then immediately called Jessie to give him the good news. As much as he hated to admit it, Sam would have to wait.

CHAPTER THREE

"*O*kay, the studs are in place," Tristan called. "Now, let's fill the insulation so we can hang the drywall."

"If you needed a stud, all you had to do was ask," said Ross with a smug grin. "I'm right here."

"Gee, that joke *never* gets old," said Virginia with a healthy dose of sarcasm as she walked into the new room Tristan and Ross were creating. The three of them had been hard at work on the Tates' basement, and the first order of business was to turn the one huge room into two smaller yet still nicely sized spaces. The plan was to make one a game room, complete with a pool table and a pinball machine, and put a television and bar in the other room to watch football, hockey, or whatever sport was in season. Virginia had to admit that she was a little out her element here. Still, she was finding a way to get excited about the decorating end of the job. It was the rest of it, at least the part that included Ross, that was causing her grief.

"You should try and be more like your sister," Ross replied as he brushed past her to grab a roll of insulation for the wall frame he and

Tristan had just finished. "Sam loves my sense of humor."

"What would possibly give you that idea?" asked Virginia. Ross had always been little more than a source of aggravation for Sam. Even though her attitude had softened towards him since the wedding, most of the times that she mentioned his name it was to complain about some part of his personality.

"Because she told me as much the other night at dinner," Ross informed her.

"Wait, you had dinner with my sister?" asked Virginia, setting down the tablet she had been using to scroll through sports memorabilia on the internet.

"Why would that surprise you?" said Ross. "Sam and I are becoming quite an item."

"Uh, guys," said Tristan quietly but firmly. "Harold and Mary are right upstairs. Could we do more remodeling of their basement and less talking about Ross's love life?"

"That sounds wonderful," Virginia agreed. "In fact, I vote that we never speak of any aspect of Ross's personal life again."

"Oh, come on, Ginny," said Ross with a playful smirk as he bent close to Virginia's face. "Don't be like that. I was just going to suggest that the four of us go on a double date sometime soon."

"We have talked about you calling me 'Ginny' and decided that it was in everyone's best interest if you not do that," Virginia reminded him as calmly as she could. "As for Tristan and me double dating with you, let me get back to you on that."

"Ross, I think we're going to need that other roll of insulation," said Tristan, his eyes darting back and forth between Virginia and Ross. Virginia could hear the concern in his voice, but she noted that Ross seemed to be oblivious, as usual. "It's up in my truck. Would you mind going and getting it, please?"

"Sure, no problem," Ross said. Then, after shooting Virginia another cheesy grin, he bounded off to fulfill Tristan's request.

"So, Ross and Sam are dating," said Tristan after the other man had disappeared up the stairs. "I must admit that I'm a little surprised."

"There isn't anything to be surprised about," said Virginia, "because they aren't dating."

"Why would Ross lie about that, and especially to you?" chided Tristan.

"Oh, I have no doubt that he believes every word," Virginia responded confidently. "It's how his brain works. That 'dinner' that he mentioned was probably nothing more than Sam ordering a pizza at the gym and him stealing a piece. Those are the kind of crazy ideas he comes up with."

"Really?" said Tristan, his arms folded across his chest and the look on his face beyond skeptical. "You really think that your sister was eating a pizza? Now who's talking crazy?"

"Okay, I take your point," she grudgingly conceded. "The idea of a health nut like Sam buying a pizza is pretty far-fetched, but I was just trying to point out that Ross will twist anything to his unique point of view. Trust me, if the two of them were dating, I would be the first to know about it."

"Why are you so down on Ross anyway? You used to like him."

"That was when I only saw him occasionally," Virginia pointed out. "He's a little hard to take on a regular basis."

"Come on," said Tristan, wrapping his arm around Virginia's shoulders. "You know Ross isn't that bad. Deep down, he really is a sweet guy. He means well, it's just that he has no idea how to act around women, especially a woman he really likes. I think this thing with Sam could be good for him."

"There is no *thing* between Ross and Samantha," Virginia insisted. "I told you, if she were dating anyone, I would know about it." Before either of them could say anything else, Ross returned with the roll of insulation.

"Why don't you start installing it?" asked Tristan of Ross. "I want to go over a few things with Virginia about the other room. Once that's done, we can break for lunch."

"That sounds like a plan," said Ross and then he set to work on completing the task he had been given.

Virginia scooped up her tablet and followed Tristan to the other side of the wall. "Why don't you show me some of your ideas for the walls," he suggested.

"I have to admit, this has been a little tricky," said Virginia. She knew that Tristan was purposely changing trying to change the subject, and she appreciated it. "I don't know much about sports, and I'm surprised how much this stuff costs." She showed Tristan a website that she had been browsing. She pointed to a football jersey autographed by Tom Brady. The price listed was over two thousand dollars.

"Yeah, that's a little out of the Tates' price range," said Tristan. Harold and Mary had told them they had saved up three years' worth of income tax returns to pay for the remodel. While the amount was more than enough to cover the materials, it didn't leave much for extras, especially after you factored in the pool table and pinball machine. "It's too bad we can't use some of your artwork."

"I know what you mean," she said. "I don't really have any experience painting sports scenes. All the sports bars I've ever been in have stuff like this on the walls. I picked this guy because I've heard of him. I had no idea that he was so popular."

"Well, no offense, sweetie, but I'm guessing that an autographed anything of a player whose name you recognize will be priced about the same." Virginia saw the grin on Tristan's face and felt a little angry.

"Why would you say it like that?" she asked. "I'm doing everything I can to make this work."

"I didn't mean to imply that you weren't," said Tristan, sounding defensive. "I just meant..."

"You just meant that I'm clueless about sports and that I should let you handle this."

"That isn't what I meant at all," Tristan tried to assure her. His tone was soothing, but Virginia was already too upset to be placated.

"If you don't want my help with this project, then just say so," she said, unblinking as she glared up into his blue eyes.

"Why don't we break for lunch a little early?" he suggested. "It's been a long morning and I think we could all use some food."

"That reminds me," called Ross from the wall where he was still working on installing the insulation, "Virginia, why don't you bring donuts to these jobs anymore? I miss those."

"You know what?" said Virginia, tossing her tablet into her bag and grabbing her coat. "I think it would be better if the two of you have lunch by yourselves. I suddenly feel like being alone." Without waiting for a reply, she marched up the stairs and out the front door. It was still a little cool out, but in her current mood, Virginia barely felt it. She walked down Main Street towards home. Along the way, the events of the morning replayed in her mind.

This was the second time in as many jobs that Tristan had implied that she couldn't handle the decorating choices for their job. Even if that wasn't the way he had meant it, it was still awfully insensitive of him to make the comments he had made. Maybe she didn't know many other football players other than Tom Brady. Okay, she didn't know *any* other football players. It takes more than just knowing the names of players to make good decorating choices. You need to understand the space and the mood of the room, and that was a skill that she possessed, no matter what Tristan thought.

It would be different if this had been the only time something like this had happened. Questioning her choice of wallpaper on their last job had nothing to do with sports. Maybe, she was starting to think, the two of them working together wasn't such a good idea. Maybe they needed some time apart.

All of this was new to Virginia. Until recently, she and Tristan always seemed to be on the same page. There was some tension before the wedding, when she revealed that she had been in touch with Adam about Tristan's father. At the time, Tristan and Ward weren't speaking, and Virginia worried about how Tristan would react. It took some time, but eventually they were able to get past it. What was happening now wasn't the same. This was petty bickering, and while Virginia told herself that it didn't mean anything, she had never been in a relationship where it had happened.

The only other relationship of this type she had was with Jason, her high school sweetheart. They dated for several years after graduation, and Virginia had always thought that he would be the man that she would one day end up marrying. It took a long time for her to conclude that what they had wasn't healthy, but there was no real arguing or confrontation until the very end.

In the case of Jason, it was that over time their relationship had moved from one of mutual love and trust into first Virginia taking care of Jason, and eventually to Jason taking advantage of Virginia's nurturing and trusting nature. Had there been a lot of arguing, Virginia wanted to believe she would have ended things much sooner.

That had her mind going to places she knew it shouldn't. It wasn't that she doubted Tristan's love for her, it was just that she wanted to make sure this wasn't a symptom of a potentially larger problem.

Maybe the best fix really was for her to go back to her baking business or focusing on her art instead of working all the time with Tristan.

She really loved helping him, though. Transforming homes and offices into entirely new spaces was every bit as much a labor of love for her as it was for him, and the fact that they were able to do it as a team made it so special. That wouldn't continue to be the case, however, if incidents like today became the norm.

She knew that the sensible thing to do would be to sit down and talk to Tristan. They loved each other and that should mean that they could talk through and solve any problem that arose. But what if talking about it led to more arguing? What if she just ended up making him feel defensive? She needed advice, and there was only person she felt comfortable asking. She considered calling Sam, but her sister was incredibly loyal and protective of her, and Virginia was certain that Sam would just insist that Tristan was being an idiot and that he needed to be put in his place. Impulsively, she pulled out her cell phone and scrolled through her contacts until she found Phil Sherman's number.

"Virginia! How wonderful to hear from you," said the voice on the phone when Virginia dialed. Phil was the pastor of their church, and he had officiated at Tristan and Virginia's marriage. He had also counseled them leading up to the ceremony and helped Tristan deal with his family issues. In the short time that she had known him, Phil Sherman had become a trusted friend and sounding board on many issues, from spiritual to marital.

"Hi, Phil, I'm sorry to call you out of the blue like this, but I need some advice, and you always seem like the best one to give it."

"I'm always happy to help," Phil assured her, his voice ever jovial. "Is everything alright?"

The moment she heard the question, Virginia began to feel foolish. She and Tristan had an argument. Couples argue all the time. It's to be expected, even in a good marriage. Maybe this was a bad idea.

"Everything is fine, Phil," she said. "In fact, I think I'm overreacting. I'm sorry to have bothered you."

"It's no bother," he said in that same upbeat tone. "I must say, you don't sound fine."

"It's nothing, really," she said, not sure if she was trying to convince him or herself.

"Well, if you aren't doing anything, why don't you stop by anyway?" he suggested. "I only get to see you on Sundays after church these days. It will be nice to catch up."

"I'm actually walking down Main Street right now," Virginia admitted. "Maybe I will stop by for a quick chat."

"I'll put on a pot of coffee."

For the rest of her walk, Virginia found her thoughts drifting to what Ross had said about him and Sam. Her first thought was that the notion of the two of them dating was ridiculous. Since the moment they had met, Sam had done nothing but complain about Ross and his self-centered attitude. He seemed to soften around the time of the wedding, but that could be attributed to the fact that he was competing with Tristan's brother, Adam, for Sam's attention. Adam was considerate of and attentive to Sam's feelings, and he took a genuine interest in what she had to say. Almost immediately, Ross seemed to transform into that type of guy as well, but it was all just an act. As soon as it was clear that Adam was out of the picture, Ross reverted to his normal self.

Still, Ross was a good-looking guy. In that respect, he was certainly Sam's type. It was also true that even though Sam complained endlessly about his personality, most of the men she dated were equally obnoxious. The more she thought about it, the more Virginia could see Ross and Sam as a couple. But that was silly. Sam would have told her if she were going out with Ross, wouldn't she?

Virginia looked up and realized that she was so lost in her thoughts that she had passed the church. She turned on her heel and doubled back to the old movie theater that had been repurposed as a place of worship. She walked down the hallway that led to Phil's office and was greeted by his new receptionist.

"Oh, hello. It's Mrs. McPherson, right?" asked Clara Samuels. Clara had been on the job for less than a month. Phil had searched for what had seemed like forever to find a new church secretary. Ideally, he would have hired a college intern, but the small amount he could pay and the distance out to the island made that unrealistic.

Clara had lived on Sweetwater Island since she and her husband had retired twenty years ago. After working for as long as they both had, they were content to sit back and enjoy the island's beauty. That changed when Walter, Clara's husband, suffered a heart attack and died shortly before Virginia's wedding. Suddenly, sitting in her cottage didn't seem as appealing now that she was doing it alone. Someone mentioned the secretary job to her, and she called Phil.

For his part, Phil was happy to give Clara a shot. Anyone was better than no one at all, or at least, that was what he thought. Clara was eager enough, and always seemed to be in a good mood, but her secretarial skills were a bit lacking. She had never used a computer and was even intimidated by scheduling appointments in a book. While she did have a solid grasp of how to file, she seemed to forever be behind in her other duties. The result was that the office really didn't look much different than when it was just Phil.

"Hi, Clara," said Virginia with a warm smile. "You can call me Virginia. How have you been?"

"Oh, pretty good," Clara responded with a smile. "I'm still learning the finer points of my new job, but it's wonderful. Are you here to see Pastor Sherman?"

"Actually, I am," said Virginia. She stood smiling at Clara, who only smiled back from behind her desk. After several awkward seconds, Virginia realized that she would have to be the one to continue the conversation. "The pastor is expecting me. Is he in his office?"

"Let me check," said Clara as she stared expectantly at the phone on the desk. Virginia knew the office had an intercom, but it seemed clear that Clara had no idea how to work it.

"Maybe I could just take a peek for myself," said Virginia as she started around the desk. Just then, the door opened and Phil came out of his office.

"Virginia, it's so nice to see you," he said with a warm smile.

"Pastor Sherman, this is Mrs. McPherson," said Clara, not seeming to have heard Phil. "She says she has an appointment, but I don't see her name in my book."

"That's okay, Clara," he assured her. "She just called."

"Oh, well, I guess that will be alright," said Clara. Virginia could only smile.

"Virginia, come on in," Phil said, holding open the door to his office.

"Should I hold your calls, Pastor Sherman?" called Clara over her shoulder.

"That's a wonderful idea," Phil told her, and then closed the door and moved a box of files so that Virginia could have a seat at his desk. "Between you and me, I don't think she could transfer a call to me anyway," he said with a chuckle.

"Well, at least you haven't lost your sense of humor," Virginia observed as Phil set a cup of hot coffee on the desk in front of her, and then poured one for himself.

"She means well," he said with a wan smile as he settled into his chair on the opposite side of his desk. "It's good for her to get out of the house, and I'm happy to have another person here."

"Well, it was nice of you to do this for her," she said.

"Enough about Clara. How are you?"

"You're going to think I'm being silly," said Virginia. Then she took a small sip from her cup, let out a long sigh to steady herself, and then told Phil everything.

He listened patiently and didn't interrupt, for which Virginia was grateful. Getting everything out felt good. She didn't realize how much she needed to talk about this until she began, and once she was finished, she felt as though a huge weight had been lifted from her. Still, she knew she needed Phil's advice and was eager to hear what he was going to tell her. Phil had a way of putting people at ease, and even without saying a word, he had done just that. When Virginia was finished, he didn't respond right away. He smiled and softly patted her arm, and then asked if she needed a refill on her coffee.

"That would be great, thanks," she said, looking at the empty cup.

"Well, first of all," Phil finally began as he poured more coffee for both of them, "I don't think you're being silly."

"Are you saying you think that we really do have a problem?" she asked as her muscles suddenly tensed.

"Of course not," he said in a soothing voice. "All I meant is that you shouldn't feel guilty about your emotions. This is all new for you, and for Tristan."

"I don't understand why that should be the case," she admitted. "We love each other, and we worked together restoring our cottage, and the bed and breakfast."

"That was before you were married," Phil pointed out.

"Why should that make a difference?" asked Virginia.

"When I was a young pastor and my wife and I were still just dating, we had the opposite problem," he told her. "I was always working, either preparing sermons, holding counseling sessions, or doing something else church-related."

"That sounds pretty much like your life right now," she observed.

"Exactly, and just like with you and Tristan, before we were married, there was no issue. She would always encourage me to do whatever I had to do.

"Are you saying that things changed after you were married?"

"It wasn't a huge shift," Phil said, "but she started to grow more and more frustrated when I would tell her I was working late or that I had to reschedule plans that we had made."

"Well, like you said, that's the opposite of what's going on with Tristan and me," said Virginia. "I could understand if we were never together and he got upset. We see each other all the time, and I'm worried that it's becoming too much."

"The point I'm trying to make is that your basic routine hasn't changed," Phil told her. "What is different is that now you aren't boyfriend and girlfriend. You're husband and wife. Like it or not, you both view that relationship differently."

"What should I do?" she blurted out. It was sounding to her as if Phil was saying that marriage changes you, and not for the better.

"The first thing you need to do is accept that both of you view your relationship a little differently now," he said, his soothing baritone voice remaining calm. "Can you honestly say that you don't expect Tristan to be more attentive to you now?"

Virginia was about to say how silly that was, until she took a moment to think about it. Maybe he had a point. Being husband and wife was different than just simply dating. She couldn't say why, but she knew that was how she felt. She felt a little chagrined.

"Okay, I see what you mean," she said as she idly spun her coffee cup between her palms. "But it's normal, right? I don't need to worry about it, I just need to understand this is how we both feel."

"It isn't that simple," he said. "Realizing it is the first step. It may be normal to raise your expectations about this new phase of your relationship, but if you don't address it, then it could lead to some unpleasantness down the road."

"So, how do I address it?"

"Well, talking to me is a good first start. I'm always here for you if you need me, but there is another conversation that you need to have."

"I know I need to talk to Tristan about this," Virginia groaned. She had secretly hoped that Phil would tell her that there was something she could do all on her own, but she was at least wise enough to know that marriage didn't work that way.

"You do need to talk to your husband," Phil said with a chuckle, "but that isn't what I meant. I meant that you need to have a conversation with God. You need to pray about this. He will reveal to you how you should handle the discussion with Tristan."

"Oh," said Virginia.

"Is that a problem?" asked Phil. He seemed to sense her uneasiness, not that she tried to disguise it.

"I've never been much good at praying," she admitted. "I always feel a little awkward, like I'm doing it wrong."

"There's no wrong way to talk to God," Phil said simply. "As long as your mind and heart remain open, you will be just fine."

"You make it look easy on Sunday," she said with a roll of her eyes. "I wish prayer came as easy for me as it does for you."

"What you see on Sunday is a little different," Phil told her. "I put a great deal of time into my sermon, and that includes poring over the bible and other religious texts so that I can find the right passages, and the right prayer to connect it all together. When I pray in my personal life, it's a different process."

"Are you saying that *you* have trouble praying?" she asked, a little surprised.

"Sometimes," he admitted with a shrug.

"What do you do?"

"It depends on many things," he said. "My mood, my surroundings, the issue at hand, all of those things come into play. A lot of times, I turn to the bible. One of the many amazing things about it is that there is a passage for seemingly every emotion and circumstance."

"That's good advice," she said.

"Marriage and relationships are a pretty popular theme," he said as he pulled a leather-bound bible from his desk drawer and started flipping through it. "Here's something you might find helpful. Ephesians, chapter four, verses two and three." He turned the book towards her, and Virginia read aloud from where he indicated.

"With all humility and gentleness, with patience, bearing with one another in love, eager to maintain the unity of the Spirit in the bond of peace." She thought about the words for a moment. "So, you're saying that I need to be patient and humble when talking about this to Tristan."

"I'm not saying anything," Phil said with a firm shake of his head. "These words come from God, and he will give you proper understanding. There are plenty of other passages as well. I could jot a few of them down, if you like."

"Thank you, I would like that," she said.

Phil grabbed an index card and scribbled several more bible passages on it. He then handed it to Virginia, and she stuffed it into her purse. When Phil walked her out, she impulsively hugged him. "Thanks, I feel so much better now," she told him.

"I'm glad I could help." They walked out into the reception area and found Clara taking papers from a box and filing them in the cabinet next to her desk.

"I thought I'd start getting a handle on my filing while it's quiet," she said to Phil with a smile.

"That sounds wonderful, Clara," Phil said as he smiled back at her.

"Maybe there's hope for her yet," said Virginia as they moved towards the front door and out of earshot.

"Well," said Phil with a small sigh, "I asked her to shred the papers in that box a week ago."

CHAPTER FOUR

*V*irginia didn't see Tristan again until he got home that evening. She had thought about going back to the Tates' and apologizing, and then telling him they needed to discuss the matter further. She didn't want to talk about any of it in front of Ross, though, and she was worried that trying to work before having a conversation might be a little distracting.

Instead, she sent Tristan a text telling him that she was sorry for running out the way that she did and asking if they could discuss the matter more when he was finished for the day. To his credit, Tristan didn't press her for more information. He just said he was sorry if he made her angry and agreed to discuss the matter later. He finished by telling her that he loved her and that he would bring home dinner.

"I hope Chinese is okay," said Tristan as he walked through the front door.

"That sounds good," said Virginia. She put the book she was reading aside and moved a few things to make room on the coffee table. "How about we eat in here tonight?"

Tristan smiled and sat their dinner down. Then he went to the kitchen to grab some utensils. No matter how many times they had Chinese, he could never master chopsticks. He handed Virginia a bottle of water and settled in next to her on the couch. When he saw the book she had been reading, he gave her a crooked smile.

"You were reading the bible?" he asked, sounding a bit surprised.

"Is that okay?" asked Virginia before dipping a small chunk of chicken into the tub of sweet and sour sauce.

"Of course," he affirmed. "I guess we haven't done that a lot lately."

"I'm sorry about the way I acted today," she told him. "There are better ways for me to handle my emotions, and what I did was unprofessional."

"I'm less interested in the what than I am in the why," he said.

"When we began working together, it was agreed that I would handle the interior decorating," she began. "On the last couple of jobs, you have questioned my choices. To tell you the truth, that upsets me." Virginia had a few hours to think about how she should approach the matter, and she decided to be direct. She loved Tristan, and she knew that he loved her. Because of that, she felt that being direct was the best option.

She had read multiple bible verses that dealt with love and marriage, and they all spoke about honoring each other and cherishing the new union that had been created, and that, combined with a promise they had made to each other to always be honest, reaffirmed her decision. It was important that Tristan understand how she truly felt.

"Virginia, I've just simply tried to give you options that you may not have considered," Tristan said, looking more pained than upset. "I'm sorry if you misinterpreted that."

"You told me that flowered wallpaper isn't manly," she reminded him, "and you laughed at me for not knowing the names of football players and not realizing how expensive items with their autographs are. My response to all of this may have been unprofessional, but your attitude wasn't any better."

"This sounds more like a company meeting than a marital discussion," Tristan observed with a slight chuckle.

"Actually, it's both," Virginia explained. "We are married, and we work together. When we're on a job, we can't separate the two."

"I don't see any reason why we should," he said, now sounding a little defensive. "One of the great things about us is that we have always been totally in sync about everything, work included."

"Tristan, why do you love me?" asked Virginia suddenly. She was sure that she already knew the answer to this, but she wanted Tristan to say it so she could make her point.

"You're the most beautiful woman I know," he said. "Not just physically, but in every way. I love your intelligence, your strength, and your passion."

"Thank you," she said with a satisfied smile. "It's because of all of those things that I don't think we should work together anymore." Tristan dropped his fork and sat there, staring. "Sweetie, say something."

"I don't... I don't understand where this is coming from," he stammered. "I thought you liked us working together."

"I thought so, too," she said, reaching over and squeezing his hand. "For a while I really did, but look at what's been happening. I ran out today because I had my feelings hurt. We had a big fight because you criticized my choices. I'm afraid that all of this will start to affect our personal life, and I love you too much to let that happen."

"I can work on keeping my comments to myself," he said quickly. "I didn't realize you felt this way." Virginia could tell that she had upset him. She was starting to wonder if her decision to be blunt was a mistake.

"You should be able to be yourself at work," she said with a shake of her head. "Don't you see? If you feel like you have to watch what you say around me, that won't be any better. I don't want any more instances of us fighting at work and having it spill over into our personal life. Trust me, this will be for the best."

"Well," Tristan began, sitting back and lacing his fingers behind his head, "you've clearly given this a lot of thought. I guess that as long as you aren't asking me for a divorce, I can find a way to be okay with it."

"Not a chance," she said, sliding over and pressing up snuggly against him. She wrapped her arms around him and laid her head softly on his chest. "You will have to do a lot more than that to get rid of me."

"I'm glad to hear it," he said, and even without looking at him, Virginia could tell that he was going to be okay. "So, what will you do?"

"I can go back to my baking business," she said with a shrug. "I got an email just the other day from one of my clients begging me to start supplying them again. I think I might even be able to pick up a client or two here on the island. The extra income would be nice, too."

"I suppose you're right about that," he agreed. "Ross will be happy to find out that you're baking donuts again. You might even get him to pay for them."

"There's another reason for me to stop working with you," she said. "You pointed out today that I used to be a lot nicer to Ross. Lately I've been treating him kind of badly. Maybe now I can get back to finding him sweet and quirky."

"Well, we'll see how long that lasts if it turns out that he and Sam really are dating."

"I had totally forgotten about that," she said. It was true. Since her conversation with Phil, Virginia hadn't thought about anything other than what was happening between her and Tristan. She tried telling herself that Ross really was a sweet guy and that Sam could do—and had done—a lot worse. It didn't help. Try as she might, Virginia just couldn't picture Ross and Sam as a couple.

"Should we turn on the television?" asked Tristan. Virginia was starting to relax as she felt him softly stroke her hair and caress her shoulders.

"Actually, I have a better idea," she said, peering up at him with a knowing grin. "A couple days ago, I made a promise. Now seems like a really good time to keep it." She pulled him closer and kissed him passionately.

"I like the way you think," he whispered when their lips finally parted. "Should we move to the bedroom?"

"That's too far to walk," she said, pushing him flat to the couch and kissing him again.

CHAPTER FIVE

*S*amantha listened to the voicemail again. "Hi, Sam, this is Adam. I just wanted to say that I'm sorry I haven't done a better job of keeping in touch. Running the family business has taken more than I thought it would. I know you're probably busy, too, but I really miss talking with you. I hope that when you get a minute, you'll call me back. It would be great to hear your voice."

Adam had left that message a week ago. Sam had listened to it every single day since then. She felt guilty for not staying in touch with Adam. He was totally different from almost every guy she knew, and in the short time they had spent together, she discovered that she really liked him. They didn't live close to each other, and between him taking over for his dad, and her trying to finish her master's degree and still work enough to pay the rent, they both led incredibly busy lives. That wasn't the reason she hadn't called him back, though. The reason she hadn't called back just walked in the front door of the gym.

Sam tossed her phone back in her purse and opened her text book, trying not to look as guilty as she felt. She smiled up at the handsome, muscular man striding confidently towards her and

334

waited for him to approach. Why, she wondered, did life have to be so complicated?

"You're looking lovely tonight," said Ross as he sauntered up to the reception desk and tossed his gym membership card on the counter. Sam slid it through the reader and gave it back to him.

"I look like crap," she said. "I went to school all morning, then got maybe four hours of sleep before getting up and cleaning the condo. I barely had enough time to shower and make dinner before having to rush here. One of these days I'll have to remind myself how to apply makeup or even just brush my hair."

"I think you look amazing just the way you are," Ross told her, and there it was. There was the reason she hadn't called Adam back.

When Sam had first encountered Ross, she had found him cute, but obnoxious. He was self-centered, arrogant, and all together unpleasant in pretty much every way. Like so many of the gym rats that frequented the place, he didn't even try to hide his attraction to her. Unlike the others, however, he was totally oblivious to the fact that she continually ignored his advances and shot him down every time he asked her out.

Sam might have found his relentless pursuit of her endearing, but in between Ross's bouts of obvious flirtation, he was constantly trying to prove his superiority by correcting the grammar on her term papers, belittling her opinions, and telling her over and over the proper way to do virtually everything. The fact that he was right more often than not was all the more infuriating. When it turned out that Ross not only worked for Tristan, her sister's then-fiancé, but that he was going to be the best man and she the maid of honor at the wedding, Sam came painfully close to bailing on Virginia. That was how much Ross got under her skin.

In the end, her love for Virginia slightly outdistanced her loathing of Ross, and Sam followed through on her promise to stand up with her sister at her wedding. Meeting Adam, Tristan's brother, made that easier. His personality was everything that Ross's wasn't. Adam listened to her opinions and treated her like an equal. When he did feel the need to correct something she said, he did it in a subtle way that didn't make Sam feel like an idiot.

The thing was that when Ross saw what Adam was doing and how she reacted to it, it caused a change in his behavior. He became more attentive overnight and began treating Sam a little better. Even after the wedding, when Adam went back to California, Ross tried to maintain his new persona. He slowly began to revert to being overly critical, but he continued to compliment Sam, and the truth was that she didn't mind being kept on her toes a little, anyway.

Even though Ross hadn't been able to totally change overnight, he had given Sam a glimpse of what was possible. When she combined that with the things about him that she already liked, his confidence and his looks, it finally wore her down. The next time Ross asked her out, Sam found herself eagerly saying yes.

"So, you, Tristan, and Virginia started a new project, right?" asked Sam. "How's it going?"

"Okay, I guess," Ross responded. "We're actually almost done."

"Does Tristan have anything else lined up?"

"No," said Ross, sounding a bit dejected. "Things should pick up soon, though."

"That's good," Sam said with a smile. "I'm sure winter can be a tough time of year in your line of work." Sam hated small talk. Even though she liked Ross, she felt like her head might explode if he didn't say something interesting soon. Fortunately, he didn't disappoint.

"For a small company like ours, it's always tough," he began, and just when Sam was about to insist they change the subject, something stopped her. "I was actually thinking for awhile about finding a job with a bigger company. The jobs we do usually don't require three people, but since Virginia isn't going to be working there anymore, Tristan will need me to stay."

"What?" asked Sam, her eyes wide. He certainly had her attention now.

"I know, I was surprised, too," he said casually. It was as if he didn't have any clue how shocking this news was for Sam.

"Virginia quit?" she asked, reaching over the counter and grabbing his arm.

"Yeah," he told her with a chuckle. Sam couldn't believe he was acting so casual about this. "She's been acting weird lately. Do you think she could be pregnant?"

"Don't be an idiot," said Sam, still trying to process the information about Virginia no longer working with Tristan. "If she were pregnant she would have said something."

"She didn't tell you she quit," Ross observed. "Maybe there are other things she hasn't told you."

"I don't know, we tell each other pretty much everything."

"Have you told her that we're dating?"

"I told you, I've been waiting for the right time," Sam said, feeling a little defensive.

"Maybe she's waiting for the right time to tell you that she quit," he said, "and that she's pregnant."

"Virginia is not pregnant," Sam insisted, slapping him on the shoulder.

After that, Ross went off to begin his workout, leaving Sam to ponder what was going on with her sister. She didn't like the idea of Virginia keeping secrets from her, especially big ones like this. Okay, she had kept the fact that she had starting seeing Ross from Virginia, but that was different. They were in the beginning stages, and it was perfectly legitimate to not say anything until she was sure they really had a future.

Virginia quitting working with Tristan was different. Sam remembered how her sister had gushed about getting to help Tristan restore old homes and redecorate them. She had finally found her calling. That was what she had said. For her to just suddenly quit was huge.

Sam briefly entertained the notion that Ross had somehow gotten it wrong. That made more sense than Virginia not sharing such big news with her. It was possible that he just misunderstood something that Virginia or Tristan had said. Still, the job they were working on now wasn't very big. If Virginia suddenly wasn't there anymore, Ross would obviously notice.

The more Sam thought about it, the more she realized that Ross hadn't gotten it wrong. That just raised more questions. Why hadn't Virginia discussed this with her? Why hadn't she at least called to tell Sam that she had quit? Most importantly, what drove her to quit in the first place? If Ross was right about her quitting, could he be right about her being pregnant? That would certainly explain everything.

Sam rubbed her eyes and shook her head to clear it of all those silly thoughts. While she couldn't come up with a reason that would cause Virginia to leave a job she clearly loved without saying a word, she was sure it wasn't because she was pregnant. She checked her watch. It was after two a.m. She still had almost four hours left in her shift. It was clear that she wasn't going to get much studying done, so she busied herself with cleaning.

Ross stopped by the reception desk again before leaving so they could chat a little more. Why hadn't she told Virginia about the two of them? Was it because she was somehow embarrassed? No, that wasn't it. She had dated other men that were far more objectionable than Ross, and she had never hesitated to tell Virginia about them. Maybe it had something to do with the message on her phone that she refused to delete.

That Virginia preferred Adam to Ross was clear, and maybe Sam had, on a subconscious level, avoided telling Virginia so as not to have to hear her complain that Sam was making a huge mistake. It certainly wouldn't be the first time that her older sister had disapproved of her choice in men, and she had never been shy about letting Sam know.

Maybe there was something else. Maybe *she* felt that she had made the wrong choice. She told herself that was silly. While Adam did seem on the surface to be a much better match for her than Ross, she could never see herself with a man that worked with his hands all day. Okay, yes, that was what Ross did, too, but that was only until he got his degree. Then he would either start his own company or manage one for someone else. They had talked about it and Ross had told her that was his goal.

Adam was only running his father's company until Ward recovered or until a better solution could be found. Then, he would be back at one of the job sites getting dirty and sweaty, probably growing a beard and wearing old flannel shirts all the time. That was the way Sam always pictured those construction types.

Adam was a great guy, there was no denying it. Sam loved the way she felt when they were together. She didn't have to try too hard and could tell that he had no desire to try and impress her. While Ross still had plenty of rough edges to be smoothed out, Adam was more of a finished project. That was the issue. Adam had pretty much reached his full potential, and while that meant he was already a great guy, Ross still had a high ceiling. Even if there were times when he was still crass, rude, and self-centered, Sam felt that she could clearly see the man he might become. He just needed an incentive, and she was happy to provide it.

Sam took out her phone and pulled up Adam's message. There was really no need to keep it. He lived in California and she lived in

Washington. She was dating Ross and he was married to his work. It was silly to think that they had any future. She was about to press delete when Steve, her co-worker, came up to the desk.

"Hey, Sam, I was just informed that there are no paper towels in the women's locker room," he said, looking a little uncomfortable.

"So, go take care of it," she snapped as she stuffed her phone back in her purse. It wasn't that she minded refilling them herself, but Steve was always trying to find ways to get out of doing even the simplest of tasks.

"Come on, it's the *women's locker room*," he repeated, as if it should make a difference.

"Oh, Steve, are you shy?" she asked with a sarcastic smile.

"It's just that, in this day and age, I would hate to be accused of anything," he explained, but Sam wasn't buying it.

"You mean like being a lazy jerk?" she said under her breath.

"What was that?" he asked.

"Excuse me, I'd like to renew my membership and maybe look at setting up some sessions with a personal trainer," said a brunette in nurse's scrubs. Sam recognized the woman, who looked to be at least ten years older than Sam.

"I'd be happy to help you with all of that," said Sam with a smile, but she was smiling at Steve. "It will just take a few minutes. Steve, you will have to handle that issue on your own." He stormed off, and her smile only broadened.

Steve was finished refilling the paper towels before Sam was finished helping the customer, but the fact that the job was quick and easy didn't stop him from scowling at her every chance he got. This didn't bother Sam one little bit, and if anything, she got a small sense of satisfaction out of seeing the man upset because he actually had to work for a few minutes. He didn't speak to her for the rest of their shift, and that suited Sam just fine.

As she waited for the clock to reach six and tell her it was time to go, she tried to keep busy. This had less to do with showing up Steve than trying to keep her mind off everything else. She wasn't very successful. Sam liked working the graveyard shift at the gym because it was hardly ever busy, and that gave her time to study.

Tonight, however, she had far too much on her mind. She was worried about Virginia. Sam couldn't fathom what would make her suddenly just leave a job that she professed to love so much. What was only slightly less worrisome was that she hadn't said a word about it to Sam.

Thoughts of Adam kept popping up as well. Memories of the time they spent together before Virginia's wedding on Sweetwater Island would unexpectedly insert themselves into her train of thought, and each time they did, it would make her smile. She was surprised by how many of those memories she had. They were only together for a few days, but it seemed as if she had a year's worth of happy thoughts about Adam to fill her head.

That was how she spent the last few hours at work. She would alternate between fretting about her sister, and then reliving happy memories with Adam. It was a kind of emotional roller coaster, and by the time six a.m. rolled around, Sam was ready to be off the ride. When she finally left, she found that she was more drained than if she had spent the entire eight hours running on one of the gym's treadmills. A quick run was normally what she would do after work, but feeling the way she did, she decided it wouldn't hurt to skip it just this once.

She wanted nothing more than to go back to the condo that she and Virginia used to share and climb into bed, but she couldn't do that. She had a class at eight, which gave her just about enough time to run home and grab a quick breakfast. Since she was skipping her run, she should even have time for something a little more satisfying than instant oatmeal and a banana.

She drove home, dragged herself inside, and tossed her purse and bag with her school books on the kitchen table. She went through the ritual of pulling out the things she would need: her textbook for a little last-minute studying, a highlighter to mark the important passages, a hairbrush to make herself look at least slightly human, and her cell phone.

She started to set the phone on the table, but all the night's memories began again, playing out just as they had at the gym. She checked her watch and thought for a moment. "It might be a little early," she said out loud, even though she was the only one there. "Oh well, I've been putting this off for too long." She became more and more resolved as she dialed and heard it ring. She waited nervously for an answer and when it finally came, she knew right away that she was doing the right thing.

CHAPTER SIX

*J*ason Burnett sat at his desk, nervously drumming his fingers as he stared at the computer screen and tried to look busy. As his eyes darted to the closed door that led to his boss's office for the thirtieth time in the last minute, he thought he might just go insane. No, that wasn't possible, he told himself. It wasn't possible because it had already happened months ago.

It wasn't that long ago, about a year and a half earlier, that Jason felt his life was going smoothly. He had a good job as an ad exec for a television station in Seattle, and he was dating a wonderful woman, Virginia Ellis. No, he corrected himself, that wasn't her name. Now, she was Virginia McPherson. She was supposed to become Virginia BURNETT but he had made way too many mistakes for that.

Way back in high school when they had met, everyone considered Jason the catch. He was the stunningly handsome captain of the baseball team, the alpha jock that all the guys admired, and all the girls hoped would ask them out. Jason dropped more than a few jaws when he started dating Virginia.

Virginia was very beautiful even back then, with her rebellious art school bob and bright green eyes, but she didn't even know it. She was fiercely smart and loved art, so she really had very little contact with Jason's jocks & cheerleaders crowd. When Jason first started flirting with her, she thought he had gotten her mixed up with some other popular girl. But he kept at it and she, of course, couldn't resist his chiseled jaw and piercing hazel eyes.

What none of them knew back then was that Jason's life was a lie. There was no doubting his baseball prowess, but the rest of it, the things that everyone just assumed were part of being a star athlete, was an act. Despite his good looks and physical abilities, Jason was never especially confident. That came from being the youngest of three brothers, and the older two being chronic overachievers. His oldest brother, John Jr., or J.J., had been given a full scholarship to play baseball at Stanford, and everyone was sure he would have been drafted if he hadn't blown out his knee during his junior year.

The middle brother, Jeff, was even better. He had been drafted by the Detroit Tigers straight out of high school. He had never made it to the major leagues as a player, and after bouncing around the minors for a few years, he got into coaching. He was currently the pitching coach for Seattle's triple-A affiliate in Tacoma, and his dad, John Sr., couldn't be prouder.

Everyone assumed that the talent level would keep increasing, but even though Jason was captain of his high school team and all-city in Seattle all four years of high school, he wasn't anywhere near as good as his brothers. A few colleges and even a couple of pro scouts came to check him out, mostly as a favor to John Sr., but nothing ever came of it. Jason was never offered even a partial college scholarship.

Spending his life trying to live up to the lofty examples set by his older brothers—and always falling short—robbed Jason of much of his confidence even before high school. Still, teenage jocks are expected to have a certain persona, and Jason did his best to adopt it so he could feel like he was fitting in.

Meeting Virginia during high school was the best thing that ever happened to him. On the surface, she was like so many girls he had dated. She was beautiful and loved going out with him. The big difference was that she didn't expect him to act the same way that everyone else did.

The cheerleaders and volleyball players he dated up until he met Virginia were every bit as popular as Jason, with the lone difference being that they felt as though they were entitled to their popularity and became offended when he didn't put them on a pedestal. Virginia was the opposite—generous with her time and emotions and she didn't ask much from him in return

For a while, Jason appreciated Virginia for this. He liked not having to impress her, and the things she did for him was a welcome boost to his fragile ego. He didn't even mind the limitations she placed on their physical relationship. In a strange way, it took the pressure off and allowed him to relax. Of course, his jock friends exuded a different kind of pressure, and he found himself lying and telling them that he and Virginia were doing things that they really weren't. He eased his conscience with the knowledge that his friends were doing the same thing. He had been out with many of the girls that his friends bragged about bedding, and he found it hard to believe they were doing the things that his friends claimed. It was all part of being in high school, or at least, that's what he told himself.

When they graduated, it became easier and easier to take Virginia for granted. She was smart, determined, and driven. She had a plan for their entire life, and since Jason had no plan of his own, it was easy to just fall in line. Jason couldn't remember when he started purposely using all of this to his advantage, but he couldn't deny that it did happen.

After four years of college, which he paid for with student loans instead of a baseball scholarship while Virginia's tuition was paid for with a trust fund, he suggested that they should work "together" to pay off his college loans. After all, if they wanted to get married one day, it made sense to eliminate their debt first. He knew that she would take charge of that, as she had most other things, and accomplish it much more quickly and efficiently than he would. He got used to just leaving things on her shoulders. After all, she seemed to like being in charge and making things happen.

From then on, it became easier and easier to take advantage of her. Virginia did his laundry. She cooked his meals. She cleaned up after him. She made sure his debts were getting paid. She never even said anything about his occasional "indiscretions". Maybe she never knew, but he justified that by reminding himself that he had physical needs she refused to meet.

When he looked back now, it was obviously ridiculous for him to have expected that this sort of behavior could continue forever, and the only surprise about Virginia leaving him was that it actually took as long as it had. He wasn't sure if he would ever deserve a woman like Virginia, but he knew that she deserved a better man than who he was back then.

The funny thing was that Jason never thought Virginia would ever leave him. She was so kind and loving, and so devoted. Taking advantage of her was so easy that Jason almost didn't know he was doing it, almost. He could try to blame the jock persona that he had created for finally taking over, and it certainly led to so much of what he had done, but if he was really being honest with himself, Jason knew what he was doing the whole time.

When she finally had enough and broke things off with him, Jason was in shock. That mood lasted for months. It nearly cost him his job and drove him to the brink of depression, but in a strange way, it may have been the best thing that could have happened to him.

Losing Virginia was beyond painful, and he knew that he would never meet another woman like her, but when she was finally gone, it forced Jason to examine the reasons why. At first, of course, he blamed Virginia. How could she do this to him? If she had only stayed, blah, blah, blah. Once he got past that, however, he was finally able to truly see himself for the person he had become.

Fixing his issues was not easy, but developing the courage to actually face problems and the discipline to work hard and accomplish his goals helped him breathe a lot easier and like the person he saw in the mirror a lot more. That was what he was trying to do now and had been doing for the past couple of months. His college degree was in broadcasting, and he loved producing. When an opening came up in show development, he applied and got the job. That was mostly on the strength of his resume and his reputation, and now that he had pitched his first show idea, he was on pins and needles waiting to hear his boss's decision. When the door swung open, Jason did his best to look busy.

"Jason, could you come in here, please?" asked Bruce Murphy, the station director.

"Of course, Mr. Murphy," Jason replied, keeping his eyes glued to his computer screen. He was determined to make it look like he had been hard at work the whole time. "Just let me finish one more thing." After pretending to type something, he sprang up and bounded into Mr. Murphy's office.

"Have a seat," Mr. Murphy said, indicating a leather, wing-backed chair as he closed the office door.

"What can I do for you?" asked Jason.

"I've been reviewing this idea you have for a Sunday morning show," Mr. Murphy said, flipping through a folder as he spoke. "I have some questions."

"Ask me anything," said Jason eagerly.

"I'm not sure this type of a show is right for our market. None of the other local stations are doing anything like this. What makes you think that we can make it work?"

"Well," said Jason, clearing his throat and shifting uncomfortably in his seat, "while I do understand that no one else is running anything like this, when I was an ad exec, my sales clients used to talk about how much they loved shows like this. Plus, I checked the local ratings for similar cable shows, and they're impressive. I'm convinced that if we do a show with a local team, it would create huge excitement."

"So, you're talking about creating an all-new show, not picking up something already in syndication?"

"That's right," Jason affirmed. "Then, one day we can say that we were the first local station to do it."

"I do like the sound of that," said Mr. Murphy with a grin and a thousand-yard stare that told Jason he was seriously considering it. It was just the reaction Jason had hoped to get. "Are you sure a home improvement show will really garner that much attention?"

"It's more than a home improvement show," Jason assured him. "It would be like they do over on HGTV. We would have a couple restoring vintage homes here in Seattle and out on the islands."

"Okay, I like it," said Mr. Murphy with a smile that Jason proudly returned, "but I have one last concern. Where are we going to find the right couple?"

"Leave that to me," said Jason, his smile widening.

CHAPTER SEVEN

"$\mathcal{I}$ can't believe you and Tristan aren't working together anymore," said Sam to Virginia before taking a sip of coffee. When she called her sister after leaving work, they both agreed that given the amount of catching up that they needed to do, a phone call wouldn't suffice. It had taken a couple of days to arrange due to Sam's hectic schedule, but as soon as she was able, she took the ferry to Sweetwater Island. She arrived the night before, and this was the first chance that they had to really talk.

"It really isn't a big deal," Virginia told her with a shrug as she pulled a fresh batch of maple-glazed donuts out of the oven. Before she started baking for clients again, she thought it best that she did a couple of trial runs on people she knew. She had sent a dozen cinnamon sugar twists to work with Tristan the day before. He, Ross, and the Tates devoured all of them and Tristan reported back that they were delicious. Maple-glazed donuts were a little more involved, and kind of Virginia's signature pastry, so she wanted to try them out on a less-forgiving critic. Sam had grudgingly agreed to a cheat day on her diet to be Virginia's guinea pig.

"I just was so sure that you and Tristan were the perfect couple," Sam responded while watching Virginia slide a fresh donut in front of her. She had to admit that it smelled wonderful, but she couldn't stop herself from mentally calculating the number of calories and carbs that were sitting on that plate. Oh well, she finally decided. One or two wouldn't hurt, just this once. She could work them off later by walking around the island. The first truly springtime day, complete with sunshine, blue skies, and warm ocean breezes, made that idea even better.

"Don't say it like that!" Virginia chided. "It isn't like we're breaking up. I made this decision to keep the happiness alive. Now that we're married, working together was just too much. We were together every minute of every day. We were starting to get on each other's nerves."

"Do you even hear yourself?" asked Sam, her arms folded across her chest as she arched one eyebrow at her sister. "The two of you have only been married four months."

"We have been married almost five months," Virginia corrected, and Sam noted that her tone sounded a bit defensive.

"Whatever," Sam conceded as she crossed the kitchen to refill her coffee cup. "My point is that it hasn't been any time at all. Do you remember the way Mom and Dad used to fight?"

"Right," said Virginia, "and how they would send us to our room to play because they thought we wouldn't be able to hear them. I think you're making my point. I don't want Tristan and me to get to that point."

"*My* point," said Sam as she returned to her chair and glared lovingly across at Virginia, "is that they were happily married for their entire adult lives, and they still fought. It is just part of being in love."

"You may be right," Virginia admitted, "but Mom and Dad never worked together. Think of how much more they might have fought if that had been the case."

"It isn't a fair comparison," Sam insisted. "Dad was a bank manager and Mom stayed home to raise us. It isn't as if her passion was to be his assistant. You love redecorating old houses. Plus, you're good at it. Look at what you've done with Aunt Emily's old cottage."

"I do love that," Virginia confessed, "but I love my husband more. I've done a lot of thinking and praying about this and I'm convinced that I'm doing the right thing."

"If you say so," said Sam, shaking her head slowly from side to side. She wasn't buying it, and she wasn't sure that Virginia was buying it either. "How does Tristan feel about this?"

"He's fine with it," said Virginia. As she spoke, her eyes darted quickly from side to side and she hooked a strand of hair behind her ear. "He agrees with me that I made the right decision."

"Just stop!" said Sam, sitting up straight. This time, both eyebrows arched as she glared over. "Every time you do that thing with your hair, I know you're not being completely honest."

"I have no idea what you're talking about," Virginia argued. She looked and sounded like a child that had been caught with her hand in the cookie jar and was trying to insist that she was innocent. "How is the maple-glazed?" she asked, clearly trying to change the subject.

Sam wasn't going to push any further. She knew Virginia, and she could tell her sister wasn't about to budge.

"It's good," she responded, "but it isn't your best work. You're definitely out of practice."

"I was thinking the same thing," Virginia said, looking at the half-eaten donut on her own plate. "Let me ask you something else. Why did I have to find out that you were dating Ross from Ross?" Her gaze never left Sam as she sipped from her coffee cup. Sam couldn't help but think that this was how Virginia must have felt only moments ago when Sam was grilling her.

"I don't know," said Sam truthfully. It wasn't as if she was hiding it, but she wasn't broadcasting it to the world either. "It just sort of happened."

"I thought you found him annoying," said Virginia.

"I did," Sam admitted, "but then I spent some time getting to know him. Ross is smart, and funny, and he can be really sweet."

"Ross can be sweet?" asked Virginia, sounding as though it was the hardest thing in the world to believe.

"It's true!" Sam insisted with a grin. "Don't give me that look. I know him a lot better than you do. I admit that he's still a little rough around the edges, but since your wedding he's changed a lot."

"Well, I have to say that I certainly don't miss working with him," said Virginia.

"I don't work with him," Sam pointed out. "We see each other at the gym, and we go out about once or twice a week."

"Whatever happened with you and Adam?" asked Virginia suddenly.

"Why do you ask?" Sam suddenly felt uneasy.

"It's just that the two of you seemed to hit it off so well at my wedding," said Virginia. "I really thought that I sensed some chemistry between you both."

"I don't know," Sam replied, her uneasy feeling growing by leaps and bounds. "Adam is really nice, and cute, and wonderful."

"Yeah, I know what you mean," said Virginia dryly. "I hate guys like that."

"Very funny," said Sam. "Traditionally, guys like that don't think very much of me."

"That's not true," Virginia scolded. "When you were younger, you put more emphasis on pretty boys, and they didn't have much substance."

"I guess you would know," said Sam. "You are the expert on pretty boys." It was a reference to Virginia's ex-boyfriend, Jason. "Pretty boy" was Sam's nickname for him and wasn't meant to be endearing. As expected, Virginia got it, but she didn't seem to see the humor.

"We're not talking about him," she said curtly. "In fact, let's never talk about him again."

"Fair enough," Sam agreed. She could tell that she had touched a nerve.

"It sounded like you were trying to say that Adam is too good for you."

"I didn't mean it like that. Adam is a great guy, and I really like him, but he lives in California, and he's running his dad's business, which takes up most of his time."

"That's only temporary," Virginia reminded her. "Once Ward is fully recovered, he plans to take over."

"Right, and then Adam goes back to work," said Sam. "He goes back to hammering and sawing, and whatever else lumberjacks do."

"He's not a lumberjack, he's a contractor," said Virginia with a grin. "There's a difference."

"Not to me," Sam told her, "and anyway, I'm dating Ross now."

"Okay," Virginia said, "you said it just *happened*, but how? You and Adam were having such a great time together."

"I guess I just saw something in Ross," Sam said. "Maybe he got jealous of Adam, but all of a sudden he just started trying a little harder. I got a glimpse of the man he could be. He just needs my help."

"Yes, but Adam is already that man," Virginia told her. "You don't need to fix him."

"Where's the fun in that?" asked Sam with a knowing grin.

"It doesn't matter," said Virginia with a smile. "You're my sister. As long as you're happy, I'm happy. I just have to ask, though—are you sure about Adam?"

Sam hesitated for a long moment. She had planned all along to tell her sister about the message that she still had not deleted from her phone, but now she was rethinking that. Virginia had sounded so down on Ross, and after talking it through she felt much better about their relationship, so that she was beginning to feel like there was no point in even bringing it up. Unfortunately for her, Virginia knew her as well as Sam knew Virginia.

"I know that look," Virginia told her, her eyes narrowing and her eyebrows twitching. "There's something you're not telling me."

"I have no idea what you're talking about," said Sam, feigning innocence. It didn't work.

"Come on, spill it!" Virginia demanded.

"Alright," she said with sigh. Then she proceeded to tell Virginia about how they had tried to date, but between the distance, Adam's work schedule, and her emerging feelings for Ross, it just became difficult. "I like Adam, I really do, but how can I have anything with him when I have a great guy right here?"

"Because that guy is Ross," said Virginia.

"Virginia! Don't say things like that!"

"Fine, I'm sorry," said Virginia. "I promise I will try *really* hard not to say mean things about your boyfriend."

Boyfriend. That was the first time Sam had heard the word out loud. She wasn't sure why, but it didn't sound right. Admitting to that would mean opening up a whole new can of worms, though.

"What did Adam say when you told him about Ross?" asked Virginia suddenly.

"Well..." Sam began, but for some reason she couldn't find the words to continue.

"Unbelievable," said Virginia with a shake of her head. It was clear from the tone that she was trying to be funny, but Sam knew there was a bit of truth in her sister's next words. "After everything you said to me about Tristan, you didn't say anything to Adam. You just left him hanging."

"It isn't the same," said Sam defensively. "You and Tristan are married, and you were working together. Adam and I only went on a couple of dates."

"So, then, did you tell Ross about Adam?" asked Virginia. Sam was pretty sure her sister already knew the answer.

"What good would that do?" she demanded.

"None," Virginia admitted. "I just want you to be as uncomfortable as I was."

The truth was that even though the conversation did make her a little anxious, Sam had to admit that it felt good to talk about it, and especially with Virginia. She had always valued the closeness the two of them shared. Because of that, she made an impulsive decision.

"Okay, listen to this," she said, and played Adam's message for Virginia. "What do you think?"

"I think that there are still some unresolved feelings."

"I agree, and I do feel a little guilty," said Sam.

"I'm not talking about Adam," said Virginia. "His feelings seem clear enough. I think yours are the ones that are unresolved."

"They are not," said Sam, trying to sound convincing. "I've made my decision and I'm happy with it."

"Then why haven't you erased the message?"

355

"I can't believe I had to hear that you quit from Ross." This time it was Sam who was changing the subject.

"I can't believe I had to hear that you're dating Ross from Ross," Virginia countered.

"What I really can't believe," said Sam, narrowing her eyes at her sister, "is that you turned my room into an art studio."

"There's a futon in there," Virginia shrugged.

CHAPTER EIGHT

*J*ason felt an unexpected rush of nerves as the ferry docked at the Sweetwater Island pier. He kept scanning the crowd of people waiting to greet loved ones as if he expected to see Virginia there. While he knew that wasn't likely, he couldn't help himself. When the gates finally opened, he picked up his suitcase and followed Mr. Murphy down the pier and onto the island.

"So, where is this place?" asked Bruce Murphy over his shoulder. "I can't believe they don't have a rental car place here."

"It's a small island, Mr. Murphy," Jason explained. "It isn't far. I think they do have one or two Ubers, and I can call one if you like." While Jason still had his athlete's physique, Bruce Murphy, who was at least fifteen years older, was carrying around a pronounced paunch that didn't exactly look like it was made for walking.

"You say it isn't far? I guess we can walk," he replied. "It's a nice day and my wife is always yelling at me to exercise more. This should keep her quiet for a while."

Jason pulled out his phone and got directions to the bed and breakfast. In all the time he and Virginia dated, he never so much as set foot on the island before now. "It looks like it's about a fifteen-minute walk," he said to his boss. He motioned to the left and then led the way, closely monitoring his phone even though it quickly became clear that there was little chance of getting lost.

For Jason, selling Bruce Murphy on the idea of a home renovation show was the easy part. Now he had to sell him on the notion that Virginia and her husband were the perfect duo to star in this show. What could prove even more difficult was convincing Virginia and Tristan.

Getting over the breakup took Jason a long time. Once he saw Virginia and Tristan's marriage announcement, he finally realized that chapter of his life was over and that it was time to move on. He slowly began working on the new chapter, and part of that was finding a way to make up for the way he had treated Virginia. Sending a card or a fruit basket crossed his mind, but it didn't seem enough. He wanted to show her that he was no longer the selfish jerk that she remembered.

"So, this place where we're staying, you say the couple you like for the show fixed it up?" asked Bruce.

"That's right, and I'm told they did a wonderful job," said Jason. It took him a second to realize his boss had stopped moving. "Mr. Murphy, is everything okay?" Jason was worried that the man had already became fatigued.

"What do you mean you were *told* they did a good job? You haven't seen the place?"

"No, sir, I haven't," Jason admitted.

"But you've seen other places they've renovated, right?"

The truth is that he hadn't. He had never viewed any of the places Virginia had worked on with Tristan, but he knew people that knew people, and he was confident enough in what he had heard to pitch the idea. While he had always known that the conversation he was having was a distinct possibility, he had hoped to avoid it. He clearly wasn't going to be afforded that opportunity.

"Mr. Murphy, you have to trust me on this," said Jason quickly. "I have spoken to several people who are impressed by the work this couple does. While I haven't seen any of it myself, I trust my sources, and I actually know Virginia personally. I will vouch for her."

"Isn't Virginia the name of that brunette who used to bring donuts to the station?" asked Bruce as he rubbed his chin.

"That's right," Jason confirmed.

"She was a good baker, but that doesn't mean she knows anything about fixing up houses."

"I understand that," Jason assured him, "but I am confident in her ability, and everyone I've spoken to confirms that she, and her husband, do a great job. Plus, they have the kind of chemistry we're looking for to make a television audience fall in love with them. Besides, we came all the way out here. Shouldn't we at least have a look?"

"Well," Bruce said, "there isn't another ferry for at least a few hours, and we've already paid for the rooms, so sure, why not?" It didn't exactly sound like a ringing endorsement to Jason, but he guessed that it was the best he was going to get.

"Great," he said. "Let's go and get checked in. After we take a look at the place, we can grab some lunch." They walked the relatively short distance to the bed and breakfast, and Jason actually found himself liking the scenery. Part of the reason he had never come to the island with Virginia was because he had been raised in the city and never cared much for the thought of rural living. The quiet streets and the relaxed feel of the island started him thinking that maybe he had been too quick to dismiss it. He could never see himself living someplace like Sweetwater Island, but a vacation in a place like this might have its advantages.

When they reached their destination, Jason watched as Bruce seemed to stare at every inch of the place. The look on his face was unreadable. Jason couldn't tell if his boss loved the place or hated it, and he was a little scared to ask. Bruce just stood there in the lobby, turning one way and then the other. The suspense was killing Jason, but he couldn't bring himself to ask the question that was foremost in his mind.

"So, what do you think of our place?" asked an older gentleman as he smiled and walked over to Jason and Bruce. While he was glad that someone else had relieved him of the burden of asking the question, Jason found that he couldn't draw a normal breath as he waited for Bruce's response.

"So, are you the owner?" asked Bruce, taking the man's hand when it was offered.

"I sure am," he said. "My Name's Devin Thomas. I bought this place a few months ago from the couple that had run it for decades."

"I understand they had someone fix it up before they sold it," said Bruce.

"Yeah, Tristan and Virginia McPherson," Devin told him. "They did a nice job."

"The place certainly looks nice," said Bruce, taking another look around. Jason finally exhaled the breath he had been holding for what seemed like hours. "What did it look like before you bought it?"

"I didn't actually see it myself," Devin admitted. "I'm just going off the photos I got from Amanda, my real estate agent."

"Is there any chance I could get a look at those photos?" asked Bruce.

"That's kind of an odd request," said Devin suspiciously, but after Jason explained why he and Bruce were there, the man was more than happy to oblige.

"I have to say, this is pretty impressive," Bruce admitted after looking at pictures showing the place as it looked right before the remodel. The wallpaper was old and faded. Where there now were beautiful hardwood floors, there used to be ugly, dingy carpet. It didn't look like the same place.

"I'll tell you something else," said Devin, who had been regaling Jason and Bruce with stories about all of the compliments he had received since buying the place. "Even though I wasn't around when they were renovating the place, I've gotten to know Tristan and Virginia a little. We're a pretty tight-knit community here. I have always thought those two have even more personality that that Chip and Joanna from the cable show."

Jason was thrilled to hear that. After all, that was the show on which he was basing his idea. He knew it was also the only real frame of reference Bruce had to go on, so this positive comparison came off as a ringing endorsement. It caused Jason to show his first real smile since they boarded the ferry.

"I guess the next step is to sit down with the two of them and see if we can hammer out a deal," said Bruce, and while that was exactly what Jason was hoping to hear, he knew that the real work was about to begin. After all, he still hadn't said anything to Virginia and Tristan. "I would like to see some of their other work before committing to anything, though."

"I think I know a way we can do both," said Jason.

"Really, how?" asked Bruce.

"Well, the house where they currently live was the first place they worked on together."

"What are we waiting for?" asked Bruce. "Let's go pay them a visit."

"Don't you think that maybe we should get settled into our rooms first?" asked Jason. "I'm starving. I think lunch would be a good idea, too."

"I'll be happy to show you to your rooms," said Devin with a smile.

"Boss, why don't you go on up," said Jason. "I'll go and find us a place for lunch and meet up with you later."

Bruce didn't question that, and when Devin took him upstairs to get settled in, Jason went outside, sat down on one of the many benches that lined Main Street, and took out his phone. He scrolled until he found Virginia's number. This was a call he had been looking forward to, and yet dreading, for some time. His heart was pounding as he waited for her to answer.

"Hello, Virginia, it's been a while," he said when she answered. "Please don't hang up. I think you'll like what I have to say."

CHAPTER NINE

The same morning that Jason and Bruce arrived on the ferry, Sam was contemplating a phone call of her own. Even after her conversation with Virginia the day before, she couldn't bring herself to delete the message from Adam. When she saw Tristan later that evening, she couldn't help but think of his younger brother.

Sam watched closely how Tristan and Virginia interacted. She wanted to see if she could tell if Tristan had any resentment about Virginia's decision to quit. If he did, she couldn't detect it. Tristan seemed to hang on her every word as she described the walk the two sisters took out to the outcropping of rock where they used to go to sit and think when they were kids. Sam didn't think the subject matter was all that interesting, but Tristan appeared to be genuinely interested by the things Virginia had to say.

That was what got her thinking about Adam. That was the way he was with her back at Christmas, when they were all together for the wedding. Ross made a much better effort ever since then to at least appear to care about the things Sam said, but there were times when she could see his eyes looking like a couple of Virginia's maple-glazed donuts when she talked about a topic he had no real interest in discussing.

Talking to Virginia had been wonderful, but it had also brought back to the surface some emotions Sam thought she had long since buried. In the past, she had always said that she wouldn't stay with a man if she didn't see a future with him. She was beginning to question if that was possible with Ross. There was no doubt that he had made great strides since they had first met about a year ago. Sam also felt that he had only scratched the surface of how great of a guy he could be.

She was starting to question if she wanted to put in the work. In many ways, Ross still reminded her of the guys she used to date. Virginia's term "pretty boy" was apt for more than one reason. Yes, they were all above average in looks, and yes, for a long time that was a huge part of her criteria. Those men also tended to be self-centered and full of themselves. That, in fact, described Jason perfectly, and that was why she gave him that unflattering nickname. The more she thought about it, the more Sam had to admit that Ross met that description to a T.

He tried, she knew, and she appreciated the effort. Still, she had to admit that she wished he would do it because it was what *he* wanted, and not simply to make her feel better. The difference was subtle, but when she watched Tristan, she could see it, though. Sam had spent a great deal of time in her life, with Ross as well as with the other men she had dated, trying to coax them to their potential, or at least what she saw as their potential.

What had that gotten her? She would invest months of hard work, and in the end the guy would reach a certain level and be unwilling or unable to go any further. Worse, some had even reverted to their old ways and simply expected her to understand and accept it. That would leave her jaded, bitter, and frustrated until she met another man that seemed promising and she began the cycle again.

She wanted desperately to believe Ross would be the one to break that cycle, and times like that night at the gym, when he had complimented her out of the blue, made her feel that he really could be the one. While it would be wrong to call those moments few and far between, they certainly weren't the norm.

Virginia had told her during their walk about her own frustrations with Ross. He had become crass and clueless at work—Virginia's term—and that was what had caused her to change her own attitude about him. He had even taken to calling her "Ginny", and when she told him how much she hated that, he seemed to take delight in doing it even more just to aggravate her.

That was the Ross Sam had met in the beginning, and it was starting to look like instead of changing, he was simply doing to others the things that he used to do to Sam. That would mean that he really hadn't changed—he was just hiding who he truly was. If that was the case, then it was only a matter of time before he started acting like that again in front of Sam. It was the same old cycle.

There was something about being back here, back on the island and in Aunt Emily's old house, that allowed Sam to clear her mind and think objectively. Not that it looked much like her aunt's old house anymore. While the futon might not be quite as comfortable as her old four-poster bed, Sam was impressed by how nice the place looked. Virginia had done a great job modernizing the place while still holding onto the charm it always had. Tristan had something to do with that, too, but Sam was biased and was giving most of the credit to Virginia.

It made her sad to think that the two of them couldn't make it work as a professional team. They seemed to mesh so well in every aspect of their lives. Maybe Virginia was right and the two of them working side by side all day and then going home and sharing the same house was just too much togetherness. That was too bad, Sam thought. Virginia had a real talent for this, and she seemed like she really enjoyed it.

Sam looked at her phone. Should she call him? It wasn't as if he had done anything wrong; she had just made a different choice. But would calling him be a betrayal to Ross? Virginia had called Ross her boyfriend. That didn't sound right to Sam, but it wasn't as if she was dating anyone else. Maybe she should at least have a conversation with Ross first, one about where their relationship was headed.

That could take a while, though. The job he and Tristan had been doing was all but finished. For the past couple of days, the work had been so light that Tristan was handling it himself. He only had about half a day's work left. Ross was back in Seattle working on a term paper and his pecs.

Sam only had a couple of things to finish for her class before spring break, and she could do them online. She decided to use the personal days she had coming and spend a week reconnecting with her sister, so that meant that unless Tristan suddenly got another job, she wouldn't be seeing Ross again for at least the next several days.

This was driving her crazy, and Sam knew it was silly. If nothing else, she and Adam both needed closure. She dialed the phone and found herself feeling more excited than she thought she would. After four rings he still hadn't picked up, and Sam felt disappointed when she realized she would have to leave a voicemail. She was considering just hanging up when she heard his voice.

"Samantha, are you there?" asked Adam, sounding a bit urgent.

"Uh, yeah," she stammered. It took her a moment to realize it was actually him and not his voicemail.

"I'm sorry, I was on a call with one of my contractors. The guy seems to think the world is coming to an end because we were shipped the wrong color tile."

"If you're busy I can call back," she offered. For some reason she couldn't explain, this suddenly felt like a bad idea.

"No, I'm glad you called," he said. "It's been too long since we last spoke, and to tell you the truth, I was looking for a reason to get off that call. You may have just saved what little sanity I have remaining, at least temporarily."

"I'm sorry I didn't call you back sooner," she said. "I know I should have."

"I didn't want you to call because you felt that you had to," Adam told her. "I wanted you to call because you wanted to."

"I did. I do," she said, and immediately felt frustrated. She was sounding like a goofy school girl and that was the last thing that she wanted. "I'm sorry. I swear I know how to talk."

"You're doing fine," he said with a chuckle that made her smile and feel instantly at ease. "Trust me, I know how difficult it is to find the right words after so much time. One phone call in three months should prove that. I'm sorry I waited so long."

"I understand that you're busy," she told him. "How is it going, running your dad's company?"

"I seriously hate it," he said, but even so, Sam noted a cheery tone to his voice.

"You don't sound too stressed," she observed.

"Well, talking to you always has a way of making me feel at ease," he said, producing another smile. There were a million things she wanted to say in that moment, but she couldn't bring herself to say any of them.

"How much longer until your dad comes back to work?" was all that she could manage.

"Actually, he came back today," Adam said, but sounding much less cheery.

"That should be a good thing," Sam pointed out. "Why does it sound like the opposite?"

"Well," Adam began with a long exhale, "our day started with him criticizing that I transferred all of the company invoices to the computer."

"He's old school," said Sam. "You had to expect that would happen. He'll get used to it."

"I know," Adam said. "After ten minutes of berating me, he admitted that it would make things easier for our customers. Then he took a coffee break. That was about nine fifteen."

"What happened when he came back?"

"I'll let you know when he does."

Sam looked at her watch. It was almost ten. "Okay, I think I'm starting to understand," she said. "But it's his first day back. I'll bet that you've been doing such a good job that he just doesn't feel needed."

"Thanks," he said softly. "I needed to hear that."

"I'm sorry I didn't call you back sooner," Sam said. "My life lately has been... complicated."

"There's no need to explain that," Adam told her. "I can relate."

At that moment, Sam was struck with an impulsive notion. To her own amazement, she acted on it. "I'm staying out here on Sweetwater Island with Virginia and Tristan for the next few days. Since your dad is back to work, why don't you sneak off and hang out with us? Trust me, it is impossible to be stressed out in this place."

"Gee, Sam, that sounds great," Adam said. From the tone of his voice, Sam could tell there was a "but" coming. "I would love to, but I just can't. If today is any indication, it's still going to take Dad a couple of weeks at least to get fully back into the swing of things."

"Sure," she said, trying her best to sound casual, like it was no big deal. "It was just a crazy thought."

"It wasn't crazy," Adam said. "I would love nothing more than to come out and see my big brother and new sister-in-law, and to spend some quality time with you. The timing just doesn't work."

"I understand," she told him. She was beginning to think that bad timing was a symptom of her life. "Maybe we can try again this summer, after I graduate."

"Well, I hope that we don't have to wait that long," said Adam. "Maybe in a couple of weeks, after Dad is feeling a little more comfortable, I can come up and we can have dinner."

"Yeah, maybe," Sam said. "That would be great."

"Well, I suppose I should get back to work."

"Right, and I suppose I should do... something."

"Thanks for calling. I'm glad we got to talk," said Adam, and Sam could almost see his warm, handsome smile coming through the phone.

"I am, too," she replied. A second later the call ended, and Sam was left to try and sort out the jumble of feelings bouncing around inside her. She was trying to do that—and not having much luck—when she heard footsteps on the staircase leading up to her room. A moment later there was a knock at the door.

"Sam, is everything okay?" asked Virginia.

"Of course," said Sam with her best fake smile as she opened the door to the art studio/guest room. "Why do you ask?"

"Because it's after ten and you're still in bed," Virginia told her. "You're usually up with the sun."

"Well, I am on vacation," Sam reminded her as she returned to the futon. "Give me a second to make my bed." She lifted the back, turning the bed into a couch. When it clicked into place, she turned back to Virginia and smiled. "There we go."

Virginia returned her smirk and came over and sat on the other side of the futon. "Seriously, what has kept you up here for the entire morning?"

Sam thought about telling Virginia about the call that just ended. She truly did want to discuss it, but not just yet. She felt that she needed a chance to digest it and sort through the feelings before she could do that. She couldn't tell her sister that, though. Virginia would insist they break it down from every angle.

"I have been going on about four or five hours of sleep a night," she said instead. That much was the absolute truth. "I think that just getting to actually lie down and not having to set an alarm was exactly what I needed. Maybe the sea air had something to do with it, too."

"Okay," said Virginia, sounding as if she didn't quite buy the explanation. She didn't argue, though. "Well, Tristan just called and said he should be finished at the Tates' by noon. I'm going to meet him at the café downtown for lunch. He told me to be sure and invite you, too."

"That sounds great," Sam said. "Adam is so thoughtful."

"Yes, he is," Virginia agreed, "but *Tristan* is the one that invited you."

"Isn't that what I said?"

"No," said Virginia, looking at her like she'd lost her mind, "you said *Adam*. It isn't hard to figure out what's on your mind." Sam felt her face turn warm, but she was helpless to stop it.

"It was just a slip of the tongue," she contended.

"Right," said Virginia, "a Freudian slip."

"Are you done?" asked Sam, tossing a pillow at her incredibly annoying sister.

"For now," Virginia replied with a satisfied smile. "If you think you can be ready, we would love to treat you to lunch. You have about an hour and a half." Then she stood up and left, but not before swatting Sam with the pillow. She rushed out the door just before it came flying at her again.

As Sam showered and got dressed, she replayed her conversation with Adam over and over. She couldn't decide how she felt. It was great to talk to him, and she could tell he felt the same. His reasoning for not dropping everything and whisking off to the island made perfect sense, and in general, Sam valued practicality over impetuousness. Still, she couldn't shake the feeling that her invitation was a mistake, and that Adam was using his dad as a convenient excuse. She went downstairs to join Virginia, not having resolved a single thing.

"You really have embraced this whole 'I'm on vacation' attitude," said Virginia.

"What do you mean?"

"When I told you that you had an hour and a half to get ready, I didn't really think that you would take every single minute."

Sam checked her watch. She had refined her routine so that she could be showered, dressed, and ready to go in less than a half an hour. She was certain Virginia was exaggerating, but no. It was almost noon, which meant that she had accomplished exactly nothing, and the day was already half over.

"Wow," she said. "V, I'm really sorry. There is something going on, and I do want to talk to you about it, but not now. Would you mind if I skipped lunch? I really just think I need to go for a walk and clear my head."

Virginia took a few seconds to respond. Sam recognized the look on her sister's face. She was trying to decide if she should let Sam do as she asked or if she should be the big sister and insist on trying to fix the issue herself. Sam really hoped this wouldn't turn into a debate.

"Okay, Sam, if that's what you want," she said finally, and Sam gave an inward sigh of relief. "But you missed breakfast, and you need to eat something. I made a new batch of donuts this morning. They're over on the counter, and I think we may still have some apples in the fridge."

"A donut will be fine," said Sam. She was just relieved that Virginia wasn't going to insist on more information.

"You are eating empty carbs two day in a row?" said Virginia, looking positively shocked. "We are definitely discussing this later."

"Fine, but not until I've had a chance to think about it. I'll tell you when I'm ready to talk, okay?"

Before Virginia could say anything, her phone rang. Sam assumed that it was Tristan wondering what was keeping her, and instantly felt guilty for holding her up. The pained look on her sister's face told her that whoever was calling, it definitely wasn't Tristan.

"Well, I don't think you'll have to worry about me butting into your business right away," said Virginia as she stared at her phone. "It looks like I'm going to have to deal with some drama of my own."

"Who is it?" asked Sam. Virginia turned the phone around and showed her the name on the caller I.D. It was Jason.

"Pretty Boy returns," she said grimly.

CHAPTER TEN

*V*irginia stared at her phone for a few more seconds. There was no good reason that she should answer. The last time she saw Jason was right before her wedding. He managed to find his way to the bar where she was having her bachelorette party. He made a scene that included trying to give her an unwanted kiss. She felt that she had made it perfectly clear that she wanted him gone from her life, and the lack of contact in the months since seemed to indicate that he had gotten the message.

She couldn't fathom what he could possibly have to say that would be of any interest to her. She was about to simply put her phone back in her purse when another thought occurred to her. Jason had been an important part of her life from her formative years of high school until shortly after her Aunt Emily died. Their lives overlapped in more ways than she could count, even if she didn't want that to be true. The possibility did exist, however remote, that he could have a legitimate reason for calling. Besides, if she didn't answer, he would just leave an overly long voicemail. If she answered and it was nothing, she would have the satisfaction of hanging up on him mid-sentence.

"Just ignore it," Sam suggested. It was the most logical choice, but Virginia wasn't so sure it was the correct one.

"No, if I do that, we both know that he'll just keep calling," she groaned. "I better take it. You don't have to wait."

"Are you kidding me?" said Sam with a goofy, childish grin. "I wouldn't miss this for the world."

"What do you want, Jason?" asked Virginia tersely when she accepted the call. She just wanted to get this over with.

"Virginia, it's so good to hear your voice!" said Jason, sounding genuinely excited. That gave Virginia no comfort, but at least he wasn't drunk.

"If you're about to tell me that you've been thinking about me and that it took a long time to work up the courage to call, let's just skip the preliminaries. Get to the reason you called so I can end this as quickly as possible," she said. Tristan would be waiting for her, and she didn't want to keep him.

"I know that you don't think very highly of me," Jason told her.

"I wouldn't say that," Virginia responded. "I don't *think* of you at all. That's the way I prefer it."

"Virginia, I know that I was a jerk when we were dating, and I know that I was an even bigger jerk the last time we saw each other," he said, remaining calm even as her frustration level soared. That aggravated her to no end.

"If you're calling to apologize, then fine," she interrupted. "I accept your apology and I forgive you. Now take care and have a nice day."

"Virginia, don't hang up!" he said quickly. She didn't say anything, and just waited to see what he would say next. When he seemed to realize the call hadn't ended, he continued. "There isn't anything that I could ever do or say to make up for the things that I've done to you, I get that. It actually took me until just recently to fully understand that. If you'll just hear me out, I think I've come up with a way to at least show you that I really have changed and that I only want what's best for you."

"Jason, if this is some pathetic attempt to win me back, you can just forget it. I'm a happily married woman, and for the record, my husband could crush a silly little jock like you without even breaking a sweat."

"What's he saying?" whispered Sam eagerly as she tugged on Virginia's arm. Her goofy smile had grown even larger. "Put it on speaker so I can hear!"

Virginia mouthed the word "no" and shot her sister an angry glare. She just wanted to focus on getting Jason off the phone as quickly as possible. Sam continued to stare at her like a puppy hoping to catch a few table scraps.

"That isn't it, I swear," Jason maintained. "When I say that I want what's best for you, I know that isn't me. Even though I meant what I said about changing, I understand that Tristan makes you happier than I ever could. Even without knowing him, I know the truth of that. If it weren't for him, you'd still be teaching school in Seattle. You probably still would have dumped me, but I remember the way you looked when I tried to talk you into selling that cottage. I know that's where you belong."

Virginia could feel her defenses eroding. Jason certainly was saying all the right things, and there was a sincerity to his voice that she hadn't heard in a long time. People do change and grow. There was no reason to believe that Jason couldn't do that, too. Virginia decided to hear him out.

"Well, that's very mature of you to say," she conceded. "I'm glad to hear that you've changed. I always believed that you were a good person. I want only the best for you, too."

"I'm glad to hear you say that," he told her. "I have a business proposition that I'd like to discuss with you and Tristan." All at once, her defenses returned to full strength.

"Jason, if you think for one second that you can butter me up with a few well-chosen words and then convince Tristan and me to invest in some crazy money-making scheme of yours..."

"Virginia, that isn't what I meant," he said, interrupting her this time.

"This is killing me!" said Sam. "Please let me hear!" Virginia didn't say anything; she just stomped her foot and shook an angry finger at Sam before turning her back when Jason started speaking again.

"I swear I'm not asking you for any money," he claimed. "If you and Tristan will just give me and my boss fifteen minutes, I promise you'll be impressed. If I'm wrong, not only will I vow to never contact you again for any reason, but I'll just stand there and let Tristan beat me to a pulp."

"He would never do that," Virginia admitted. "I only said it because I thought you were about to hit on me. So, what is this 'business proposal' that you claim is so great?"

"I think it would be best if I discussed it with both you and Tristan," he said. "It involves both of you."

"Fine," she said, feeling worn down. "You have to come to the island, though. We're very busy and can't take the time to go all the way to Seattle right now." That was a small lie, but Virginia knew she didn't want to go back to the city just to see Jason, and she was certain Tristan wouldn't be too keen on the idea.

"I'm actually already here," he told her.

"What? Where are you?" asked Virginia, looking around as if she expected him to jump out from behind a tree.

"I'm staying at the bed and breakfast that you and Tristan remodeled back in December. You did a wonderful job."

"Thank you," she said. "Okay, I was actually just leaving to meet Tristan for lunch at the café on the corner."

"Yeah, I think I see it," he said.

"Tristan is probably already there waiting for me," she told him. "DO NOT go in until I get there. If he sees you, there is a good chance he really might try and do something we would all regret."

"Okay, I promise to wait right here in front of the bed and breakfast."

"I'll be there in about fifteen minutes." Virginia hung up her phone, shook her head to try and unscramble everything that she had just taken in, and then, remembering her sister, wheeled on Sam.

"What did you think you were doing?" she demanded. Sam looked nonplussed.

"I was trying to eavesdrop," she admitted freely. "You weren't making it easy."

"Sometimes you can be so infuriating."

"Well, I learned that from my big sister."

"Look, I can't believe I'm saying this, but I've got to go and meet with Jason and Tristan. If you want to know what's going on, you're welcome to come. Having another person to act as a buffer between those two would be a good idea."

"What makes you think I wouldn't help Tristan rip him to shreds?" asked Sam, her omnipresent grin not fading even a bit.

"Come on, Sam," said Virginia. "You know you wouldn't want to see Jason actually get hurt, or at the very least, you don't want to see Tristan get into any trouble."

"Well, as entertaining as all this sounds, I really do need to do some thinking by myself," Sam said. "I guess if I really believed that Pretty Boy had anything intelligent to say, or better yet, that Tristan actually might take a swing at him, then that would be different. But, since I figure this will just be one great big tease, I'll let you handle it."

"Well, okay then," said Virginia. "I need to get down to the café before Jason does something stupid."

"Well, then you'd better hurry," said Sam. The two of them hugged, and then went off in their separate directions. Sam headed down the path that would take her to the island point and their favorite thinking spot. Virginia wished her luck, but knew she had her own problems right then. Not wanting to waste any more time, she jumped in her car and drove toward Main Street. While she had no idea what to expect, she was sure of one thing. She and Sam would have a great deal to talk about.

CHAPTER ELEVEN

*I*t didn't take Sam long to put the nonsense with Virginia and Jason out of her head. In all of the time that idiot had been dating her sister, and that included the year while they were in high school and he was at least semi-tolerable, Sam couldn't remember him having even one worthwhile thing to say. While the thought of the chance to get in a few more insults for old time's sake was inviting, Sam had two other, more important men on her mind.

It wasn't as if she felt like she was trying to choose between Ross and Adam. Well, not exactly. What she wanted to do was sort out what feelings she had, and how that would impact her relationship with both men. She wasn't sure if she would be able to do that in a single afternoon, or in a single week, for that matter, but she was at least grateful to have this time away from both of them to do that.

She started with Ross. That made the most sense, as she had known him longer. She thought again about the changes she had seen in him. They had been enough to convince her to give him a chance, and that he still had potential. That was the key word, potential. Ross was far from a finished project.

She knew that she had feelings for Ross. He wasn't perfect, but was there a chance that he could be perfect for her? On the positive side, he was handsome, smart, and had made tons of progress in putting her emotional needs ahead of his own. He was also close and there was no doubting his feelings for her. On the negative side, his humor often had a hard time finding its way out of sarcasm, which was great for witty, snippy repartee, but could get tiresome. Despite the progress he had made, there were also still times when he quickly became bored with listening to her and preferred talking about himself. It wasn't that Sam was looking for a man that would fawn all over her, but the truth of the matter was that she was still the one making most of the compromises. She let him pick the restaurants where they would eat and the movies they would watch. He usually made good choices, and that was to his credit, but it would be nice to get a say in the matter from time to time.

Sam had to admit that she enjoyed molding Ross into quality boyfriend material, and there was a part of her that believed that he would one day get there. She just couldn't help but wonder that if she held out for however long that might take, she might actually miss the guy that was already perfect for her.

That was where Adam came in. His positives were that he was handsome and kind, and he had a great sense of humor. He seemed to always be able to put her at ease and never asked anything in return. In fact, he was always willing to put everyone's needs above his own, but was that really a positive? Sam had to admit that she would like him to be a little more forceful at least some of the time. It was also true that his selflessness was making him unhappy.

It was clear that running the family business for his dad wasn't Adam's long-term goal, and it was equally clear that he had no intention of saying anything about it. As much as she admired a man who was willing to give of himself, Sam also appreciated the importance of standing up for yourself and setting limits.

It was also a negative that he lived in California. Sam had been born and raised in Seattle. She had spent all her life there and loved it. The Emerald City was her home and she knew she could be happy there for the rest of her life. Even if his dad did eventually begin running the business again, it was perfectly plausible to assume that Adam would one day take it over permanently. He might not want that, but Sam knew that his father wanted to keep it a family business. Since Tristan was firmly entrenched in his life here on Sweetwater Island, that left Adam. He had already proven that it was unlikely he would disappoint his dad, even if it meant sacrificing his own dreams.

Sam reached the rocks and climbed up to her favorite spot and stared out at the ocean. She closed her eyes and let the sound of the crashing waves engulf her. She could feel the mist on her face and the sweet, salty smell of the water in her nose. After a moment, she felt her mind start to drift. She found that she liked how that felt and didn't try to fight it.

"What am I going to do?" she asked out loud, as if the answer would come rolling in with the waves. After several minutes, she opened her eyes. She watched the waves, and slowly her mind came back to the issues that were confronting her. The only conclusion that she was able to find was that she had no idea what she wanted.

She was looking for a man who was happy to do what she wanted, but was still willing to stand up for himself. She wanted someone who shared her dreams but had some of his own. The thought occurred to her that what she was actually hoping for was some strange amalgam of Adam's self-effacing sweetness and Ross's self-assured stubbornness.

"Maybe I'll just date them both," she said to the ocean, and then chuckled at her own lame joke. Then a thought came to her. She read somewhere that if you flip a coin, it will tell you what your real choice is, because you'll either be excited or disappointed by the outcome. While she thought that it was a silly thing to do, she also felt like she had nothing to lose. As she reached into her pocket to find a quarter, a seagull perched on a rock a few feet away and eyed her.

"So, what do you think?" she called over to the bird. "Should Ross be heads, or should it be Adam?" The gull only flapped its wings and squawked at her. Sam got the distinct impression it was annoyed. "You're right. It doesn't matter. Heads is Ross and tails is Adam." She tossed the quarter into the air and caught it with her left hand. She slapped it onto the back of her right, and before she pulled her left hand away, the seagull gave another squawk and flew off.

"Oh, come on!" she called after the bird. "Don't you want to see how it turns out?" She watched the bird until it flew out of sight, and then she looked at her hands. She closed her eyes and pulled her left hand away. When she opened them, the coin was showing heads. Sam smiled for a moment before stuffing the coin back in her pocket.

CHAPTER TWELVE

*V*irginia's breath caught in her throat as she parked her car on Main Street. She purposely drove so that she could park across from the bed and breakfast and the café. Tristan's truck was parked in front of the café, but she already knew he was inside before she saw it. The missed phone call and text message told her as much. At first, she was worried that Jason had ignored her plea and went into the café before she arrived. Then she saw him.

Seated on a park bench with his back to the road, she almost missed him until he turned. There was an older man sitting next to him, and they appeared to be having a conversation. Virginia guessed that was the boss he mentioned.

There was no mistaking Jason. He had the same thick, dark hair, the same chiseled jawline, and the same athletic build. Why, she wondered, couldn't he have a beer gut and at least a few gray hairs?

It wasn't that Virginia was still attracted to Jason. Nothing could be further from the truth. Almost from the moment she met Tristan, all other men paled by comparison. It was just that she was hoping for the satisfaction of seeing him adversely affected because of being dumped by her. Oh well, she told herself. You can't have everything. As she composed herself and got out of the car, her phone rang. It was Tristan.

"Hey, sweetie," she said, trying to sound upbeat. "I'm just parking now. Sorry it took so long."

"Let me guess," he said. Virginia could already hear the sarcasm in his voice. "You and Sam were doing each other's hair and nails."

"Aren't you funny?" she replied. "Actually, Sam isn't coming. She had something else to do."

"So, I guess it will just be the two of us."

"Not exactly."

"I don't understand," said Tristan, and it was clear from his tone that he didn't.

"I know," she said quickly. "I'll be there in a minute and I'll explain." She hung up and crossed the street. When Jason finally saw her approach, he jumped to his feet and smiled.

"Virginia!" he gushed with a huge smile. "It's so good to see you!" Before she knew what had happened, Jason had her in a huge bear hug. Not knowing what to do, she lightly patted him on the back and waited for it to end.

"Hello, Jason," she responded. "Okay, that's enough." She pulled away and he released his hold, but his smile never faded.

"I can't believe how good you look," he said, looking her up and down. Virginia felt like a show horse at the county fair. "You've lost some weight."

"Is this your boss?" asked Virginia, ignoring all of Jason's gushing.

"Oh, right," he said, as if he had forgotten all about the other man. "Virginia McPherson, this is Bruce Murphy."

"Pleased to meet you," the older man said, extending a polite hand. Virginia felt much more comfortable with this than she did with Jason's hug.

"I'm sorry, but I don't remember you," Virginia confessed. "I've been to the station a number of times, but I just can't place your face."

"Maybe that's because we stole your friend here from the marketing department," Mr. Murphy said with a grin.

"Bruce is in charge of new programing at the station," Jason explained. "I work for him now, and I just pitched him an idea for a new show. That's what we're here to discuss."

Virginia was totally confused. On the drive over, the only thing that she could come up with was that Jason was going to try and get Tristan to advertise on the TV station. She didn't think it was a bad idea, but she knew that Tristan would never go for it. Clearly, a commercial wasn't what Jason had in mind, though. Virginia had no idea what was happening.

"I don't understand," she said. "If the two of you aren't here to talk about us advertising with you, then what could you possibly want with Tristan and me?"

"I think we should wait until your partner is present to discuss all that," said Mr. Murphy.

"My partner?" said Virginia. "Do you mean Tristan, my husband?"

"Of course," Mr. Murphy answered, still smiling.

"I think we should head over to the café," Jason suggested. He took each of them by an arm and started down the road. Virginia's head was swimming far too much to object. Before she knew it, they were inside the tiny eatery. Tristan smiled and waved when he saw Virginia, but that smile quickly faded when he realized who she was with.

"Hi, honey, sorry to keep you waiting," Virginia said to Tristan, quickly grabbing him and planting a kiss on his lips.

"Would someone please explain exactly what is going on?" he asked with a look that was part surprise, part anger, and part something Virginia couldn't identify. It was somewhere between confusion and total insanity.

"I would love to," she said, gently guiding Tristan back to his chair, "but I can't. Sweetie, this is Jason."

"Oh, I recognize him," said Tristan firmly, a wary gaze settling on the man smiling and extending his hand.

"Hi, Tristan," Jason said. "We've never been formally introduced."

"There's a good reason for that," Tristan said as he grabbed Jason's hand and shook it firmly. Virginia noted a slight wince from Jason, but he still managed to keep smiling.

"This is Bruce Murphy," Virginia said, directing Tristan's attention to the other man. "He's in charge of creating new programs for the TV station in Seattle where Jason works. Apparently, they have some sort of business proposition for us."

"What does that mean, exactly?" asked Tristan. Everyone settled in around the table, and then all eyes turned to Jason.

"I guess I'll just get right to it," said Jason. "We want to make the two of you the next Chip and Joanna Gaines."

"You want to do what now?" asked Virginia.

"Chip and Joanna Gaines," Jason repeated. "From HGTV. Surely you've heard of them."

"I know who they are, Jason," said Virginia succinctly.

"Everyone knows who they are," Tristan added. "I think what Virginia means is..." he paused for a moment as if trying to find the right words. Virginia wanted to chime in, but she was as lost as him.

"I think what she means is that we have no idea what you're talking about."

"What Jason is trying to say is that we are developing a home improvement show along the lines of the Gaines's show, and we're considering the two of you as the stars," Mr. Murphy explained.

Virginia could only stare at Tristan, and he seemed to be able to do nothing but stare back at her. Had she really heard the man correctly? Were they seriously considering putting her and Tristan on television? This was apparently Jason's idea. He said he had pitched the show to his boss, and Mr. Murphy certainly wouldn't have any idea who they were before this meeting.

"I must say that they are an attractive couple," said Mr. Murphy. "They do look right for the part, especially him." Virginia glanced over to see him point at Tristan. She had heard them right. They actually were talking about her and Tristan starring in a television show. That wasn't the strangest part. What was really weird was that Virginia didn't hate the idea.

"Guys, I'm not sure what could have possibly made you think this was a good idea," said Tristan, "but I'm a contractor, not an actor."

"That's the beauty of a show like this," said Jason. "You don't have to act. You just have to be yourselves. There wouldn't be any script. You would just have to explain what you're doing, and because you would be working together, you wouldn't even have to look at the camera all that much. You could just talk to each other the way you probably already do. I mean, come on, you're husband and wife and you work together. You must have great chemistry."

"Even if I did think this was a good idea," said Tristan, "you should know that Virginia and I aren't working together anymore."

"What do you mean?" asked Jason, his smile fading for the first time since he first saw Virginia on the street.

"What he means is that we aren't working together right now, because we just finished a job and haven't lined up another one yet," Virginia put in quickly. "Isn't that right, honey?"

"Uh, right," said Tristan, staring at Virginia with a dumbfounded look.

"Actually, I was hoping you'd say that," said Jason, his smile returning. "The idea actually came to me when a neighbor of mine mentioned that his parents just gave him a cottage that he wants to use as a vacation place and it needs some renovations. Does that sound familiar?"

Virginia knew Jason was referring to the cottage where she and Tristan lived. She had to hand it to him, he was smooth. What better way to get them fired up than to recreate the situation that brought them together in the first place? What she also had to admit was that, despite her normally dim view of pretty much everything that Jason said or did, she found this idea fascinating.

"The best part," Jason continued enthusiastically, "is that the cottage is right here on Sweetwater Island." He pulled out a piece of paper from his wallet. "The address is two twenty Sandpiper Lane."

"That's Mike and Susan Weston's place," said Tristan.

"You mean that cute little two-story with the wraparound deck and the gazebo out back?" asked Virginia.

"That's the one," Tristan confirmed.

"Don't they own the flower shop up the road?"

"They used to," Tristan corrected, shaking his head. "Don't you remember? Amanda said she sold it for them a few weeks ago."

"That's right," said Virginia. "Something about Mike's asthma getting to be too much. They're retiring to Lake Havasu City in Arizona."

"Yeah," Tristan agreed. "Susan has complained about the winters here for the last couple of years."

"I've never been inside the place, but the outside needs some work," said Virginia. "The paint is peeling, and that gazebo has at least a few boards hanging."

"Just from what I've seen driving by, the roof looks like it might need to be replaced. If the inside is in similar shape, it could be a big job."

"True, but it would be a lot of fun," Virginia added.

"Don't worry about the cost of materials or anything else," said Jason. Virginia had gotten so into her conversation with Tristan that she had almost forgotten about the other two men at the table. "This job would be like a trial run, or a pilot episode, if you will. The station will cover all of your operating costs."

"Well, within reason," Mr. Murphy added.

"This is all a bit overwhelming," said Tristan, raking his hand through his hair and cracking a smile that was either nervous or forced. Virginia wasn't sure which.

"You don't have to decide right away," Jason assured them. "I know that I sprang this on the two of you, but I didn't want to do it over the phone or through an email."

"We do have a lot to discuss," said Virginia. Tristan still looked overwhelmed. Virginia couldn't imagine what must be going through his mind. Only a few days ago, she told him they shouldn't work together anymore. Now she seemed to be reversing that decision.

"I tell you what," said Jason. "Why don't we leave you two alone? When you decide what you want to do, you can reach us at the bed and breakfast."

"But we haven't ordered yet," Mr. Murphy grumbled. "I'm starving."

"I saw a Chinese place a couple of blocks away," Jason told him.

"I do love Chinese," Mr. Murphy confessed. "But that means more walking."

"Come on," said Jason. "Your wife will be thrilled with all the exercise you're getting."

"That's true," the older man decided. "I have to use the restroom first, though. I'll meet you out front."

"Sweetie, I'm going to walk Jason out," Virginia told Tristan. "There's something I need to say to him." Tristan just nodded. If he was at all upset about Virginia wanting to talk alone with her ex-boyfriend, he didn't let on.

Virginia doubted that would be the case. Tristan wasn't the jealous type and he knew that Virginia loved him more than anything. She also figured that his brain so overloaded with thoughts and emotions at the moment that he couldn't really take the time to be upset. She directed Mr. Murphy to the men's room and then ushered Jason out the front door.

"Okay, I need you to look me in the eye and swear that this isn't some bizarre scheme you've cooked up to embarrass us, or worse, to win me back," she told him.

"Virginia, how would that even work?" asked Jason.

"I don't know," she admitted, "but I do know you. This is potentially a big opportunity for Tristan. It isn't like you to do things for other people."

"What will it take to convince you that I've changed?" he asked, looking suddenly serious. "This *is* a big opportunity for both of you. I owe it to you. For years, I used you and took you for granted. I strung you along and acted like your feelings didn't matter. This is the least I could do to try and say I'm sorry."

Virginia was still skeptical. She had come to believe that if something seemed too good to be true, then it probably was. The thought of her ex-boyfriend showing up out of nowhere with an offer to put the man she loved on television, and that she could actually share in that success, definitely felt too perfect to believe. Apparently, Jason saw the look of apprehension on her face.

"Look, if it makes you feel any better, I do get something out of this," he confessed. "If the show is a success, I will become a producer, and if it ever goes national, then I'll get a share of the royalties. But with all of that on the line for me, I still thought of you first. Not only that, but there is no backup plan. I'm putting all of my faith in you."

"Jason, that's the sweetest thing you've said to me in years," she said with a soft smile.

"You've never let me down," he said with a shrug. "I don't think for a second that you will this time, either."

"Okay, where is this Chinese place?" asked Mr. Murphy, appearing next to Jason.

"It's across the street and two blocks up," said Virginia, pointing the way and smiling. "It was nice meeting you, Mr. Murphy. My partner and I will have an answer for you shortly."

"Well, hello, Pretty Boy!" Virginia and the two men turned to see Sam strutting towards them. Apparently, whatever issue was on her mind had been worked out. "I'm a little disappointed to see you didn't drink yourself to death."

"Jason, do you know this woman?" asked Mr. Murphy.

"This is my sister, Samantha," Virginia explained. "She's always making jokes like that."

"I must say that I don't get it," he said.

"I didn't say they were good jokes," Virginia told him. She grabbed her sister by the arm and turned her in the other direction before anyone could say another word.

"I can't believe I missed everything," said Sam. "What did he have to say?"

"You're never going to believe it," Virginia told her, still not sure if she believed it.

CHAPTER THIRTEEN

"You're right, I don't believe it," said Sam. "Explain it to me again."

"I've explained it to you four times," Virginia reminded her. "I don't know how else to say it." After leaving Jason and Bruce Murphy, Virginia took Sam back inside the café. Over lunch, she and Tristan tried their best to make sense of the offer that Jason had presented them. Along the way, they tried to catch Sam up.

"Ladies, I don't mean to be rude," said Tristan, "and Sam, you know I love you, but this kind of feels like something my wife and I should be discussing alone."

"She knows all about me quitting and why," Virginia told him. "Besides, where is she going to go?"

"Yeah," said Sam. "What do expect me to do, go out and just walk around?"

"Isn't that what you did earlier?" asked Tristan with a grin. Sam just smirked back at him. "Fine, stay. Maybe having another, more rational opinion might even help."

"I think 'rational' is a bit of a stretch, but okay," said Virginia.

"We need to stop joking and discuss this seriously," Tristan said to the both of them. "The first question I want to ask is if we really think this is a legitimate offer or if Jason is just trying to play us."

"He swears it's a real offer," said Virginia, shaking her head. "I had a hard time believing him, too, but I doubt he would have dragged his boss all the way out here just to try and mess with us."

"That's a good point," said Tristan. "That poor guy looked positively miserable. He wouldn't have come unless he believed it was serious."

"I called Amanda," Virginia said. "She told me that Mike and Susan did say that they were giving the cottage to their son. She was pretty disappointed that she wouldn't get to sell it for them just like she did with the flower shop."

"So, let's say for the time being that the offer is genuine," Tristan said. "What in the world makes anyone—Jason, Bruce Murphy, or us— think that we can pull off a television show?"

"Oh, I can answer that," said Sam. "The two of you are so cute that it's almost disgusting." Tristan and Virginia just stared at her. "What, you don't believe me? Tristan, you have the rugged good looks that television producers love. You're probably better looking than most of the guys on those cable shows."

"I never knew you felt that way," Tristan said as his face turned from pink to red.

"Don't let it go to your head," she said with a dismissive wave of her hand. "You Paul Bunyan-types don't do a thing for me. I just call 'em as I see 'em."

"Well, it's still a good point," said Virginia.

"As for you," Sam continued, pointing at her sister, "with that whole adorable look of yours and those big green eyes, the camera will absolutely love you. Besides, if I may be so bold, since you quit baking donuts and started doing something more physical, you've gone from being pleasantly plump to downright hot."

Virginia knew that was no idle statement. Sam viewed her own body as the proverbial temple, and she was forever counting carbs, calories, and steps in an effort stay firm and fit. While she never shamed or even made fun of Virginia about her weight, this was the first time Virginia could ever remember her sister complimenting her figure, much less calling her hot.

"Sam, that's so sweet," she said. "Thank you."

"That's not even the best part." She was on a roll and didn't seem willing to stop. Virginia was more than willing to let her keep going. "When the two of you are together, you positively glow. People don't need to hear you say that you love each other. It's totally obvious by the way you look and act when you're together. Sis, that's why I thought you were nuts to quit in the first place. You're never happier than when you're near Tristan. That's never going to change, no matter how much time you spend together."

"I never knew you felt that way," said Virginia quietly.

"*Everybody* feels that way!" she exclaimed, raising her arms and letting them drop as if to say that it should be obvious. "I wouldn't be surprised if the two of you were the hottest couple on TV in less than a year."

"I have to ask," said Virginia, "when did you become such an expert on television and home improvement shows?"

"Ross watches those shows all the time," she said. "He even records them."

"So, did Ross have anything to do with why you couldn't join us for lunch?" asked Tristan.

"We're not talking about me, we're talking about you," Sam insisted, "and we haven't resolved this issue yet. So, bottom line, V, are you serious about wanting to work with Tristan again?"

"That was smooth," said Tristan with a chuckle, "but since she asked, I wouldn't mind hearing the answer."

"I told you the reason I left," said Virginia with a shrug. She knew that this would have to be discussed. She had just hoped it wouldn't be so soon. "I was worried that we were spending too much time together and that would put a strain on our relationship."

"Because I questioned your choice of wallpaper and your knowledge of NFL quarterbacks," Tristan pointed out.

"Okay, you're right, there is more," said Virginia. She had spent a great deal of effort on convincing herself that was the only reason for her decision, but she always knew there was more to it. Admitting it, even to herself, was the problem.

"V, what is it?" asked Tristan.

"It's silly," she said with a wave of her hand and a shake of her head.

"We are trying to make a huge decision that could change our lives," he reminded her. "I think it's important that we put all of our cards on the table."

"Okay," she said, and then took a deep, centering breath. "Since the day I graduated high school, I had a clear picture of how my life was going to be. I would teach art and bake my donuts on the side. I was going to marry Jason and have a nice, quiet life."

"If by 'nice and quiet' you mean boring and miserable, then okay," said Sam.

"The point is that until I met you," she said as she looked lovingly at Tristan, "I never even considered the possibility that my life could go any other way. My life was planned out based on Jason's needs. Then

I met you, and all of that changed. You asked my opinion about things and you encouraged my to expand my horizons."

"Now it makes perfect sense why you want to spend less time with him," Sam interjected.

"Are you going to let me finish?" snapped Virginia. When she was satisfied that her sister would keep quiet, she continued. "At first, things were going great. We seemed like we were in perfect sync. Then, you questioned a couple of my decisions, and I started to get scared. I was worried that I was actually in over my head. I thought that if I kept working with you that you would start to feel like I was a liability."

"V, first of all, second-guessing decisions is part of the job. I'm constantly asking Ross if he's sure about something he thinks is a great idea."

"That's true," said Sam. "He tells me about it all of the time."

"I even second-guess myself," Tristan admitted. "I can't tell you how many times I've hung a door, or kitchen cabinets, just to realize they didn't look right."

"For me, it was a new feeling," Virginia said, "and it wasn't a pleasant one. I began to feel like I should just stick to what I know."

"I wish you would have just told me this in the first place," said Tristan, then he leaned in and kissed her. It felt good not just physically, but it was also the emotional lift she needed.

"I know," she said when their lips parted. "I didn't mean to keep the truth from you, but I was having a difficult time admitting it to myself. I'm sorry."

"This is a really sweet moment," said Sam, "but the original question was whether you are ready to work with Tristan again. I'm not hearing an answer."

Virginia knew she was right and, by the way he was looking expectantly at her, Tristan knew Sam was right, too. Virginia had to be honest. Like Tristan said, this decision could change their lives.

"Tristan, I don't want you to miss this opportunity," she said. "You work so hard, and you're so good at what you do. You deserve to have not just all of Seattle see that, but the whole country, the whole world. Jason made it pretty clear this is a package deal. He wants both of us."

"V, none of that matters to me," he told her as he held both of her hands. "I never wanted to be on TV. I'm happy just doing what I do and most importantly, I want us to be good."

"Yes, but with this, you wouldn't have to worry about the next job," she pointed out. "You would have steady work that is fun and interesting. You wouldn't have to do man caves during the off-season to make ends meet."

"I like doing man caves," he told her with a chuckle. "I like repairing old decks. I even like building the occasional tree house. Do you know why I like those things? Because they make people happy. If we take this TV job, I wouldn't be able to do that."

"I love how selfless you are," she said, brushing her hand against the side of his face.

"It's the way I was raised," he said. "My parents taught me that not only is helping people the right thing to do, but it feels good, too. That was the way they always have been. I guess it runs in the family."

"I know," said Virginia, "but I also know that if you had your choice, you would spend most of your time renovating old homes and hotels. I see the way your eyes sparkle when you're working on a job like that, and there was none of that sparkle when you were redoing the Tates' basement. I saw how excited you were today when you realized he was talking about the Westons' place. You know you want to do this."

"Okay, I admit that I would love to get my hands on that beautiful old house," Tristan told her. I saw the look on your face, too. You were every bit as excited as I was."

"Maybe I am," she admitted reluctantly.

"I can't promise I'll always agree with every decision that you make," he confided with a small smile. "What I can promise is that I will always trust and love you. You are an amazing partner and I could never do what we did, alone." Virginia didn't say a word. She just leaned in and kissed him passionately.

"So, does that mean that you're doing this?" asked Sam impatiently.

"The truth is that our unity and love is more important than anything else. Quitting was just me taking the easy way out. I didn't really want to face my own insecurities or deal with our communication challenges. But the easy way out never worked for us, did it?" Virginia asked, looking deeply into Tristan's gorgeous eyes.

"No," Tristan smiled back at her, "we face things together."

"So, what do you think?" Virginia asked Tristan. "Are you ready to become TV's newest heartthrob?"

"Well, when you put it like that, how can I say no?"

CHAPTER FOURTEEN

"So, what was going on with you today?" asked Tristan of Sam. The inquiry came out of nowhere. Virginia had just gotten off the phone with Jason to tell him they would take the job, and they were deciding where to have their celebratory dinner when he just blurted it out. Sam didn't have to ask what he meant. That didn't mean that she was eager to answer.

"Yeah," said Virginia. "You stayed in your room all morning and then you cryptically announced that you have some thinking to do, and you disappeared down to the point."

"How do you know that's where I went?" asked Sam.

"Where else would you go?" asked Virginia.

"Fine, I went to the point," Sam conceded. "There, are you happy?"

"Not really," said Tristan. "We still don't know why you went there."

"I just had some thinking to do," she said, shrugging her shoulders and trying to sound casual.

"It had to be something pretty important," Virginia observed. "You and I solved some of our biggest childhood issues down there."

"It wasn't anything like that," she said dismissively.

"Then you shouldn't have a problem telling us," said Tristan with a grin.

"I have no problem telling *her*," Sam said, pointing to her sister. "I'm just not comfortable telling *you*."

"Oh, come on," said Tristan, sounding hurt. Sam was pretty sure it was an act. If that was the best he could do, he wasn't going to last long on television. "We just included you in our biggest conversation since our wedding. You owe us."

"Okay," she said finally, "but it involves your brother and your best friend, so you have to promise to remain neutral."

"I give you my word," said Tristan, raising his right hand for effect.

"Virginia knows that Adam called me a couple of weeks ago," she began. "What she doesn't know is that I called him back this morning."

"Does Ross know that you're calling other men?" asked Tristan with a grin that said he was trying to be funny. Sam wasn't amused.

"Well, for starters, Ross and I are not exclusive, so he can't tell me who I can and can't call, and I thought you were staying neutral."

"I was just asking a question," he said with a shrug.

"What did the two of you talk about?" asked Virginia.

"Not much, really," she said. "He had to get back to work."

"It has to be hard for him, running the business all by himself," said Tristan.

"He said that your dad came back to work today," Sam mentioned.

"I guess that explains why he didn't call," Tristan deadpanned.

"Well, that's wonderful," said Virginia. "Maybe now the two of you can spend a little more time together."

"I don't think that's going to happen," said Sam. "He says that it looks like it's going to take some time for Ward to fully get back into the swing of things. He sounded like he plans to be pretty busy for a while."

"Sam, are you okay?" asked Virginia with a look of sisterly concern.

"Of course I am," said Sam, trying to sound like she really meant it. "Why do you ask?"

"Because in your entire life, you've never spent any serious time thinking about any one guy, let alone two. So, what gives? Why have these two men suddenly have you skipping lunch and walking out to the point to think?"

"The truth?" asked Sam.

"That seems to be the theme of the night," Virginia pointed out.

"After seeing you two together these past few months, I've started to feel like there's something missing in my life. I want what you have."

"And you think you can get that with Ross or Adam?" asked Tristan, producing a sour look from both women. "What? I wasn't taking sides. That was a neutral question."

"Ignore him," said Virginia, turning her attention back to Sam. "Did you talk to Adam about this?"

"Of course not!" Sam told her. "How would that conversation go? 'Hey, Adam, I know we haven't seen each other or even talked in weeks, but I'm thinking about getting serious with a guy and was wondering if you would like to throw your hat in the ring.' That would have gone over great."

"Okay. I don't think I would have worded it exactly like that," Virginia told her, "but how is he going to know that you have feelings for him if you don't tell him?"

"That was part of the reason for the call," Sam admitted. "I was trying to decide if I really do have feelings for him."

"Did you decide anything?" asked Tristan, this time sounding sincere.

"Tristan, your brother is a great guy," Sam said, sounding almost apologetic. "But let's face it. He and I want different things. When your dad does fully get back to work, he's going to go back to ripping out walls and putting them back together, or whatever it is that you do. Besides, he won't ever leave California. I love it in Seattle."

"That seems awfully final," said Virginia. Sam knew that she had been rooting for Adam.

"What was I even basing the possibility on, anyway?" she asked. "We spent a few days together and had a couple of casual dates. He is incredibly sweet and really cute, but I think I was basing everything on some kind of fantasy."

"Sometimes fantasies can become real," said Virginia, smiling at Tristan.

"Don't get me wrong," Sam said, "I truly believe Adam is an amazing guy. I owe him a lot. Without him paying attention to me the way the he did, I never would have gotten to see the real Ross."

"Are we saying that's a good thing?" asked Virginia.

"Look," said Sam, "I know that you have some problems with Ross."

"I'm not the only one," Virginia reminded her, arching an eyebrow.

"Okay, sure, I've had my issues with him in the past, too," Sam conceded, "but once I took the time to get to know him, I realized that there is so much more to him than the guy that corrects my grammar and makes lame jokes. He has so much potential, and I can see him getting so much better."

"It sounds to me like you're saying that you are hoping that he becomes more like Adam," Virginia observed.

"I'm saying they have similar qualities," Sam amended. "Ross has some great qualities of his own, too. He's confident and focused. Plus, he loves Seattle as much as I do. As much as I hate it when he corrects my term papers, he's rarely wrong. He pushes me to be better, too. I like that."

"Yes, but Ross can be standing in the middle of a room with other people and not hear a word they say," said Virginia. "It isn't because he doesn't hear them, it's because he doesn't listen."

"Like I said, he's focused," Sam said.

"What you call focused, I call self-centered," Virginia argued. "It's more than that, though. The lame jokes you mentioned are almost always at the expense of someone else. I agree that he's smart, and driven, and okay, he's cute, but I'll just say it. Sometimes he can be a jerk."

"I think you're being a little hard on Ross." This time, it was Tristan coming to his defense. "I agree that he can be a little clueless, but he's just about the most loyal friend that I've got. He doesn't always sense what you need, and maybe that's why people say he's self-centered, but if you need something, all you have to do is ask and he'll be there for you, no questions asked. As for Adam, Sam has a point about him never leaving California or the family business. That's a lot to put on anyone, especially a confirmed city girl like Sam."

"Are you really singing Ross's praises over your own *brother*?" asked Virginia, sounding absolutely flabbergasted.

"Hey, I think Sam is an amazing woman," Tristan said. "Adam would be lucky to have a woman like her in his life. I just want her to be happy, that's all."

"I do, too," said Virginia. "I mean, she is my sister. Maybe you're right about Ross being loyal, but what good is it if Sam has to tell him what she needs all the time?"

"I'm not saying Ross is perfect, but neither is my brother," Tristan said calmly. "You make some good points about both of them, but trust me, Ross has come a long way."

"That's something you say about a toddler," said Virginia. "Ross is a grown man. Can we really expect him to change all that much at this point?"

"Anyone is capable of change," Tristan shrugged. "We saw an example of that today."

Virginia was confused. "What are you talking about?"

"I'm talking about Jason," he replied. "I would have never believed that the man you described when we first began dating would one day come and do something as nice as he did for us. If this TV show really does turn into something big, it will be all because of him. He didn't have to come out here and offer it to us. Admit it, you were shocked, too."

"Fine, I admit it," Virginia said, if a bit reluctantly. "But that is just one example. Just because he changed doesn't mean that Ross can, too."

"You need to give him a chance," Tristan said firmly.

"You guys know I'm still here, right?" asked Sam, feeling a bit ignored.

"I'm sorry, Sam," said Virginia. "I'm making this about me. Tristan and I agree about one thing at least. We both want you to be happy."

"Thank you," said Sam softly. "Ross makes me happy."

"Well, then, I guess it's settled," said Virginia. Sam wished her sister sounded more convincing. That way, maybe she would have convinced Sam.

CHAPTER FIFTEEN

$\mathcal{J}$ason called Virginia early the next morning to tell her that it would be a couple of days before they could begin on the Weston house. He had to get a film crew out there first, and none were available. Virginia and Tristan were a little frustrated, but Jason did his best to soothe their emotions.

"Everything is going to be fine," he insisted. "The two of you are going to be amazing."

What upset Tristan more was that he had to turn down two other jobs while they waited. The Weston house wasn't going anywhere, he reasoned. The jobs he turned down, turning a home office into a nursery for expecting parents and tearing out a wall to expand a living room, would have been quick and easy jobs. They would have brought in some extra money and made a couple of people really happy, but he couldn't do either of them because he was waiting on the film crew.

"You'll be paid for the episode," Jason assured him. While the money would be welcome, and was more than they would have likely made for the smaller jobs, Virginia knew that wasn't the only thing concerning Tristan.

"I know that you wanted to do those smaller jobs to help out our neighbors," Virginia told him as they lay in bed the night before they were finally going to begin the television show.

"I built my reputation not just on doing good work for a reasonable price, but on being the guy people can turn to," he grumbled. She was lying with her back against his chest and his arm wrapped around her. She could feel him propping himself up on his other elbow as he spoke. "Now I'm going to look like a spoiled TV star that's too good for everyone else."

"No one that really knows you is going to think that," said Virginia, patting his arm softly.

"I wouldn't be so sure," he contended. "People tend to believe what they see." Virginia understood what he was saying, and she had no good response. Instead, she just snuggled closer and pulled his arm tighter to her.

"We don't have to do this," she offered after a moment. "We haven't signed a contract yet." Jason had been ready to sign the contract for an entire first season of the show, but Bruce Murphy was a little more cautious.

"Let's see what kind of response we get from the pilot," he told them. Jason, in his continuing show of being the exact opposite of the man Virginia had dated, remained ever-optimistic.

"When people are as thrilled about the show as I know they'll be," he said, "you can demand even more money."

"No," Tristan told her. "We made a commitment. Jason brought out a camera crew and everything. I'm sure this is all just nerves. It will be fun."

Virginia rolled over to face him and wrapped her arms around his neck. "I love you," she whispered, as if it was a sacred secret between the two of them. Even in the near total darkness of their bedroom, she could see his smile.

"I love you, too," he whispered back, and then they shared a kiss.

The next morning found their little cottage more alive than Virginia could ever remember. She and Tristan were both up early because Jason had asked them to be at the Westons' place no later than eight. They were doing fine except for the fact that Sam was awake and trying to get ready, too.

"I want to be there to support the two of you on your first day," she responded when Virginia tried to suggest that Sam didn't need to be there as early as them.

"I understand, and I love you for that," Virginia told her, "but, to be blunt, no one cares when you show up. It would be really bad for Tristan and me to be late on the first day. Tristan is nervous enough about this. If we aren't at least ten minutes early, I firmly believe he will have some sort of breakdown." After Sam agreed to make coffee while they finished getting ready, things went much smoother.

Virginia and Tristan were out the door by seven-thirty with Sam pledging to be right behind them. Virginia smiled and said that would be great, but her mind was already on what was coming next. It took less than ten minutes to get out to the house, and the camera crew was already setting up.

"Holy cow," said Tristan, raking his fingers through his hair as they got out of his truck. "This is way more than I expected."

"What were you expecting?" asked Virginia.

"One, maybe two cameras, a couple of microphones, and a couple of lights," he replied, never taking his eyes off what was on display as they walked up the driveway. There were four cameras, three boom microphones, and Virginia counted at least seven lights placed around the outside of the house.

She wasn't as intimidated by all of it as Tristan. When he first started at the TV station, Jason liked to show off, so he would occasionally bring her on the set for the evening news broadcasts. Once, he even got her backstage for the talk show they did every morning. He may have only been in sales back then, but that still afforded him a certain amount of access.

This was about what she had expected, and she mentally chastised herself for not preparing Tristan. She knew he was already nervous and even dreading what was to come. She should have realized that actually seeing what goes into producing a television show would be a bit overwhelming for him.

"Don't worry about it," she told him. "Once we start, you won't even notice the cameras."

"I wouldn't bet on that," he replied grimly. Just then, they saw Mike and Susan Weston coming down from the house to greet them. They both were smiling from ear to ear.

"Isn't this exciting?" asked Susan, grabbing Virginia's hand and squeezing excitedly.

"That's one word for it," said Tristan as he shook Mike's hand.

"Everyone is waiting for you," Mike said.

"What do you mean *everyone*?" asked Tristan, wrinkling his brow in confusion.

"Besides Jason, the sound crew will want to see us to set the levels on our microphones," Virginia explained. "The camera crew may want to do a few test shots, too."

"That sounds lovely," Tristan said with a smile that only Virginia could tell was fake.

"Your assistant has been asking for you, too," said Mike.

"Your assistant?" asked Virginia, looking at Tristan questioningly.

"The two of us can't handle a job like this alone," Tristan told her. "I called Ross yesterday. Is that going to be a problem?"

"I guess we'll find out," she said with a crooked smile. As if on cue, Ross appeared from the house and headed straight for them. He didn't look all that thrilled at becoming a TV star.

"For the record, I hate all of this," he groused when he met them.

"Mike and Susan Weston," said Virginia with her own painted-on smile, "this is Ross. He works with Tristan."

"I'm actually his right-hand man," Ross corrected, "but I don't know if I can work like this."

Great, thought Virginia. They hadn't even gotten started and he was already being a diva. She knew this wasn't what she wanted, and she didn't think it was what Tristan needed. She could only hope that he didn't turn around and get right back in his truck. To her surprise, Tristan looked perfectly calm.

"Ross, what's the problem?" he asked evenly.

"People are asking me all kinds of questions," he said, pointing a thumb back at the house.

"What kinds of questions?" Tristan wanted to know.

"Things like 'who are you?' and 'why are you here?' It's really annoying," he said.

"Ross, this is a big deal for Tristan, and for me," said Virginia through gritted teeth. She didn't have the time or the patience for Ross being Ross right then.

"Calm down, V," said Tristan, sporting the first real smile she'd seen from him all morning. "He's joking." Virginia looked over at Ross and found him grinning like the Cheshire cat from Alice in Wonderland.

"Since you weren't here yet, I told them where we would probably start," said Ross to Tristan. He was suddenly all business. "That Jason guy says he wants to get a shot of you and Ginny talking with them," he explained, pointing at Mike and Susan.

"Ross, if you call me Ginny one more time, Tristan will be doing this show alone," Virginia warned him.

"What do you mean?" he asked her.

"I mean that I'll be in jail and you'll be dead!"

"Maybe we should just meet you down at the house," said Susan, casting a wary eye at Ross as she and Mike slowly walked away.

"Okay, I think we need some ground rules," said Tristan, who seemed to be enjoying this way too much to suit Virginia. "Rule number one is that Ross and I have to be able to be ourselves. V, you know that we joke around while we're working sometimes. If I'm going to do this, I have to do it my way, and that means I need Ross."

"Okay," she said after taking a breath. She would do anything to make this work for Tristan. "As long as Jason and Mr. Murphy are okay with it, so am I."

"Well, they had some reservations at first," Ross admitted. "I had to promise not to get in the way."

"And you were okay with that?" asked Virginia skeptically.

"I don't need to be a star," he said with a shrug. "I just want to show up, do my job, and get paid."

"Well, okay, then," said Virginia, mostly because she couldn't think of anything else to say.

"They said I might be on camera some, but the focus will be on the two of you," Ross added.

"That brings me to rule number two," said Tristan. "The name 'Ginny' must never leave your lips again."

"Okay, if you insist," said Ross.

"Then I think we should get this party started," Tristan told them both.

"Well, look who's here!" said Ross, rushing past them both. Virginia turned to see Sam looking more than a little surprised.

"Ross, what are you doing here?" asked Sam as the man lifted her in a huge bear hug.

"You didn't really think these two could do something like this without me, did you?" he responded.

Virginia saw a look on Sam's face she wasn't expecting. She figured Sam would be surprised at seeing Ross. If she had been expecting him, Virginia figured Sam would have mentioned it. What threw Virginia was the look of discomfort on Sam's face. After their conversation a couple of days ago, she would have thought her sister would be at least a little happy to see him.

They never got a chance to discuss it, though. She and Tristan left the two of them standing there and headed down to the house. Jason quickly ran through a schedule for the day, and although he questioned a couple of things and asked for a few changes, Tristan was by and large compliant.

They began, as Ross said they would, with the Westons taking Tristan and Virginia on a tour of the house. They both tried to act natural and ignore the cameras as Jason had told them to, but it was more difficult than Virginia had imagined. What was even harder was when the director, a man named Bruce Keller, would stop and ask them to do a particular sequence again because it didn't look natural.

"How do you expect me to make it look more natural if we do it again?" asked Tristan in frustration. Finally, around noon, Bruce announced they were breaking for lunch. Virginia didn't feel like they had accomplished much, and she could tell from the look on Tristan's face that he shared her sentiment.

"I have to admit," said Mike Weston to the two of them as they sat around the kitchen table, "that with all of this starting, stopping, and starting again, I'm a little confused by what we're doing."

"That makes two of us," said Tristan.

"I think we all feel that way," Virginia had to admit. Without warning, she felt a tap on her shoulder. She looked up to see Sam standing there with an urgent look on her face.

"Virginia, can I talk to you for a minute?"

"Sure, Sam," she said, and found herself being pulled from the kitchen. "Where's Ross?"

"There's a table full of food outside," Sam told her. "He said he's starved. What is he doing here in the first place?"

"Tristan called him," Virginia explained. "He needs Ross's help. I thought you'd be happy to see him."

"I am," Sam said quickly, but then backtracked. "I mean, I'm not *unhappy*. I just wasn't expecting him."

"Neither was I," said Virginia, looking towards the door to make sure he didn't suddenly appear. "But if Tristan needs him, I'm not going to complain."

"Hey, V, I don't mean to interrupt, but can I see you for a second?" asked Tristan, poking his head around the corner. Virginia looked at Sam to see if she had anything else she needed to say. It still worried her that Sam wasn't more thrilled to have Ross there.

"I'm good," Sam assured her. "Go do what you have to do."

Virginia followed Tristan back into the kitchen. "What's up?" she asked.

"I don't know how this is going to sit with Jason or that guy Bruce, but while they're getting some lunch, I thought the two of us could take a couple of minutes and tell the Westons what we really think about their house. Then, maybe when they come back and ask us to do it one more time, it'll go a little better."

"It's worth a shot," she said, and then all four of them wandered into the living room. One of the camera men, a younger guy with red hair and freckles, was just putting away his equipment. Tristan paid him no mind.

"Like I was trying to say before," Tristan began, "the hardwood floors are in good shape, but they need to be sanded and refinished." He got down on his knees and ran his hand over a section of the floor.

"Tristan, what do you think about pulling up this wallpaper and going with the original wood paneling?" asked Virginia.

"It's a little unconventional," he said, scratching his jaw. "The wood paneling is awfully seventies."

"I know," said Virginia, "but I was thinking we give the place a more rustic look. We could get rid of this furniture and go with an antique sofa and table. After all, this is going to be an oceanside vacation home."

"So, you want to make it look older instead of newer?" asked Susan.

"Yes and no," said Virginia. "It would be wood panels and antique furniture, but everything would be spruced up and refinished to look new."

"I think it could work," Tristan said finally.

"I trust them," said Mike, looking at his wife.

"It sounds good to me," said Susan.

WITH LOVE...AND REALITY TV

Tristan then led them through the rest of the main floor, telling them about the overall condition of the place, and going over what needed to be changed and what he felt was okay to keep as is. Virginia threw out suggestion after suggestion about furniture, window treatments, and wall decorations. The Westons loved everything they heard.

"Okay, about that gazebo out back," Tristan said, leading them all out the back door. The food table Sam had mentioned was set up a few feet away from the gazebo, but again, Tristan ignored everyone else and focused on the object of his attention. "I don't think you're going to like what I have to say."

"I was wondering when you were going to get to that," Virginia said.

"What's wrong?" asked Mike. Tristan was standing close to the structure, looking at it intently.

"Just as I thought," he said, shaking his head. "The salty ocean air has done a number on this. Apparently, the wood wasn't treated properly."

"This was kind of a do-it-yourself project," Mike admitted. "Susan wanted a gazebo, and I didn't want to pay someone else to build one. I bought this online and had it shipped. I never thought to ask if the wood had been treated."

"Honestly, if it were almost anyplace else it would probably be fine," Tristan admitted. "The salt in the air out here can be pretty unforgiving. This thing is going to have to come down."

"That's fine," Susan said. "I don't think our son really cares for it much. This is going to be his place now."

"I have an idea about replacing it," said Virginia.

"Are you thinking what I'm thinking?" asked Tristan.

"This would be a perfect spot for a firepit," she said.

"Now, you see, that's why I love you," he said, and they both chuckled.

"Hey, what's going on?" asked Ross, walking over with a sandwich in one hand and a cup of soda in the other.

"I'll fill you in later," Tristan told him.

Ross pointed behind all of them. "I just didn't realize you started filming again."

Tristan and Virginia turned to see the same freckle-faced kid from before, but he had a small camera in his hand, and it was pointed directly at them. "Have you been filming this whole time?" asked Virginia.

"Yeah," the kid said. "It was a little hard to keep my distance inside, but I didn't want to interrupt what you were doing."

"I don't understand," said Tristan, looking totally confused.

"Neither do I," said Bruce Keller, sounding a bit perturbed. "I told you to break for lunch. The union will have my head if they find out you're working off the clock."

"I know," the kid said, "and I'm sorry, but you really need to see this." He handed his camera to the director, and Bruce plugged it into a nearby monitor. Some of what the kid had recorded was rough, because he was clearly trying not to let anyone know what he was doing, and that was no easy feat inside the cottage, but after watching it, Bruce turned to the kid and smiled.

"I don't care what the union says. You did good, Taylor."

"Thanks, Mr. Keller," Taylor replied.

"Are you saying you liked that?" asked Tristan.

"It was exactly what I wanted," he said. "I mean, it may take a little creative editing here and there, but I finally see the chemistry I was told exists between you two. It's really impressive. From now on, we'll shoot the stationary shots with unmanned cameras, and when you're moving, we'll use Taylor on the hand-held camera. Apparently, you're more relaxed when there isn't anyone around."

"You'll get no argument from me," said Tristan with a smile of relief.

The afternoon went much better than the morning, but Virginia felt there was still one area that needed improvement. While Tristan set about removing wallpaper from the walls in the living room, Virginia and Ross began sanding the floor. It didn't take long for him to start criticizing everything from the type of sandpaper she used to the technique she employed while doing the sanding. She thought that she had done a good job of not sniping back at him, but, as the saying goes, the camera does not lie. There were plenty of times when she responded heatedly to his comments, and two instances that could only be described as blatant arguing.

"Maybe they can edit that out," she grimaced at one point while watching the replay.

"I hope not," said Sam with a chuckle. "Watching the two of you fight is hilarious." Ross, who was seated next to Sam with his arm around her, didn't seem to have any opinion on the matter.

"I agree," said Jason. "While I think the main focus needs to be on you and Tristan, bringing Ross in for a bit of comic relief changes things up nicely."

"So, you're saying you want me to fight with him," said Virginia flatly. "I can do that."

Later that night, Sam and Ross went for a walk on what turned out to be the warmest night of the year, leaving Tristan and Virginia alone to reflect on their first day in front of the camera. With all of the ups and downs, and with all of the stress that she felt initially, Virginia concluded that it was a good day.

"I agree," said Tristan as they sat on the couch listening to music and sipping wine. Virginia had her head resting against Tristan's chest and her arms draped around him. Tristan lightly stroked her hair while they talked.

"So, does that mean that your opinion has changed?" she asked, not bothering to look up and risk having him stop. She loved the tingle she felt along her spine every time his fingers would brush against her cheek or her ear.

"It has only been one day," he reminded her, "but it isn't looking quite as horrible as I had feared."

Their quiet bliss was interrupted a few minutes later when Sam and Ross returned. Sam looked much more comfortable than she had when she first discovered Ross was on the island. Virginia figured that a quiet walk in the warm island breeze at sunset may have had something to do with that. It still seemed strange to her that Sam reacted the way she had in the first place.

"I'll see you guys tomorrow," Ross said, avoiding everyone's glances, as he left back out the door.

"Good night," Tristan and Virginia said in a hurried, confused response. Both turned to Sam with raised eyebrows.

"*Well!* I told him!" she answered their looks defensively. "It's your fault! With all your 'let's be honest' nonsense... I guess it got to me and I *was honest.*"

"Oh boy!" said Virginia as she pulled up a chair for Sam to sit next to the couch where they were. "Okay, spill."

Sam retold the conversation they had on the beach as best she could. She had told Ross that she had some misgivings about their relationship and she wasn't sure of her own feelings. She explained that perhaps they wanted different things in the future and she was questioning where to go from here. To Ross's credit and everyone else's surprise, he responded relatively well. He wasn't happy about it and was a bit shocked since he thought they were having a good time. He suggested just having fun and seeing where it led, but after some more discussion, he did end on a rather sweet note, insinuating that Sam may have been "too good for him anyway".

"So, what made you change your mind?" asked Tristan. "You were pretty set on giving Ross a chance when we last talked."

"It's silly but I think more than anything, it's a gut feeling," answered Sam.

Tristan and Virginia's questioning glances made her explain.

"I did that silly coin toss... you know how they say that no matter what the coin says, you'll know the truth because you'll either be disappointed or excited by the result?"

Virginia nodded.

"Well, the coin landed on Ross and I was instantly disappointed," Sam continued. "I didn't mean to be. I didn't expect to be, but I was. I dismissed it, of course, because it was silly. But today, when he surprised me at the filming site, it was a bit of the same gut feeling. And then I watched the two of you work so hard to be honest with one another and I thought I should give that a try."

"That could not have been easy," said Tristan, "for either of you. I'm sorry."

Virginia agreed. To her surprise, she had a sudden pang of sadness for Ross. Even though he was generally annoying, Virginia did care about him. In truth, she had been a lot less harsh on Ross before he started dating her sister, and she knew that he actually did possess a lot of the good traits that Sam saw in him.

Before anyone could say another word, there was a knock at the door.

"Who could that be at this time of night?" asked Tristan, checking his watch.

"It's probably Jason wanting to tell us again how wonderful we are," said Virginia as she stood up and walked over to the door.

"I'm glad he's changed, and I'm thrilled that we like him now," said Tristan, "but we might have to set some boundaries."

They chuckled as Virginia opened the door. She couldn't suppress a gasp when she saw that it wasn't Jason after all.

"Hi, Virginia, I know it's late and I'm sorry to show up unannounced," said the man at the door. "Can I come in?"

Virginia was so stunned that she couldn't get a single word out, so she just looked at Tristan for help. He got up and instantly had a big smile on his face as he looked at the door.

CHAPTER SIXTEEN

"Adam!" Tristan exclaimed as he hugged his brother.

"Adam, what... what are you doing here?" stammered Sam. All eyes were on the new visitor as they waited to see what he had to say.

"Don't you remember?" he asked. "You invited me."

"You did?" asked Virginia with a quizzical smile at her sister.

"What they mean to say is 'We're so glad you're here!'" Tristan said quickly with an admonishing stare all around.

"Yes, of course," Sam enthused. "But I thought you said you couldn't make it," she reminded him. Her heart was pounding so hard she thought that everyone in the room could hear it. There was a lump in her throat that would not go away no matter how many times she tried to swallow.

"Dad and I have been at each other's throats for the past couple of days," Adam said. Sam could hear the distress in his voice. "Today, when he told me to get out for what felt like the millionth time, I just did. I got in my car and drove all the way to Seattle. When I realized I was going to miss the last ferry, I just kept driving until I got here. That bridge is quite an adventure."

"Yeah," said Tristan, "tell me about it. Well, we're glad you're here. I know how tough Dad can be sometimes."

"Come in, come in," said Virginia as she stepped behind Adam, ushering him inside. She darted a glance at her sister, who responded with raised shoulders and a look of innocence.

Virginia took out some snacks and sandwich makings and offered everyone something to eat while they peppered Adam with questions and caught him up on their exciting new TV show adventure. Sam tried her best to act nonchalant, convincing herself that Adam was just here to visit family and that it had very little, if anything, to do with her. She had forgotten how handsome he was and every time he smiled at her while making his sandwich, she couldn't help but smile back. They all ate and talked for a while but everyone was exhausted and soon headed to bed. Adam was relegated to the living room couch, which he didn't mind one bit. After having to deal with the business and his dad for so long, it felt so peaceful to be away from all that, even just for a night. He finally closed his eyes and slept better than he had in a long time.

The next morning, Sam was up at the crack of dawn making everyone a healthy breakfast and coffee. Tristan and Virginia hurried to get to the Westons' house a bit early to try and get some quiet, off-camera moments. They needed to visualize their plan and catch any snags they may have overlooked. Unfortunately, when they got there, film crew members were already setting up. Tristan knew the minute they got out of the car they would be peppered with questions and directions, so he grabbed Virginia's hand and said, "Let's just stay here and stare at the place for a few minutes."

Virginia smiled, took a sip of her coffee, and said, "Okay, my love, what do you see?"

This had become their favorite tradition as they started a project. They would dream a little and listen to each other's vision of what the building could be, which was always a great mixture of what it once was and the many possibilities of what it could become.

The rest of the morning flew by in a flurry of people, questions, scene set-ups, and the little bit of actual work they were able to get done. Every once in a while, Tristan and Virginia would find each other's eyes across the room and smile. In the middle of the chaos, they could mentally go back to those few quiet moments of dreaming together from this morning. It was their little secret and it kept them focused on the bigger picture and on each other.

Ross showed up on time and was uncharacteristically quiet while doing some of the demo. Virginia found herself being nicer to him than usual and it was all a bit awkward and too polite. Both felt bad about what happened with Sam and they were both trying desperately to be nice. After lunch, Tristan and Ross were deciding how to handle some structural wooden beams and Virginia had the idea to refinish them and leave them exposed as a nod to both the age and the farmhouse style of the house. Without even thinking, Ross scoffed loudly at her suggestion and replied sarcastically under his breath, "I want to see *you* climb up there to refinish that beam."

"Excuse me?" shot back Virginia.

"You come up with these harebrained ideas and then I have to do all the work," Ross said.

"That's ridiculous! You're so full of yourself I don't even need a ladder to get up to the beam, I can just climb up on your ego!" said Virginia.

"I can't help it if you need me so desperately." Ross came back with one of his flashy smiles.

"Oh my goodness!" exclaimed Virginia, finally looking around.

All eyes and cameras were on them and the crew were muffling their giggles. Somehow their bickering had become the comic relief of the show and the crew. Tristan was even watching with a smirk. To Virginia's surprise, she even felt a little relieved to be out of that awkward, polite, trying-to-be-nice phase and back to their normal selves. Since everyone else was finding this funny, Virginia lightened up a bit, too, and continued, "If you can take a break from your 'Ross is great' diatribe, maybe you can get a ladder so we can take a look."

CHAPTER SEVENTEEN

*B*ack at the house, Sam finished cleaning up breakfast after Tristan and Virginia left. Adam naturally started to help and they chatted comfortably as they worked.

"So, I didn't know you were such a wiz at breakfast. I mean, that was delicious and I didn't feel at all guilty eating anything on my plate," Adam complimented her sincerely.

"Well, I've been working toward starting my own health and wellness coaching business and I really wanted to develop some excellent recipes that my future clients would love. I mean, my sister bakes a mean maple-glazed donut and everyone jumps to get one. It's much harder to get people excited about oatmeal or veggies," said Sam.

"I would certainly jump at the chance to have this breakfast again, so I think you succeeded. I'm lucky to grab coffee in the morning before the craziness starts," Adam said and he suddenly felt heavy again. He instantly remembered all the responsibilities he had back in California and how difficult it had been to work with his father again these last few days. He felt helpless and stuck.

"Hey, where did you go?" asked Sam, bringing him back from his thoughts.

"Oh, just family and business stuff. I guess it's weighing on me more than I thought."

"Tell me about it," Sam said as she handed him a cup of coffee.

So Adam did. They walked out in the backyard and talked and talked and talked. Neither of them realized how much time had passed and both found a strange comfort in just openly sharing their struggles. While their families were amazing blessings to both of them, it felt so much easier talking to someone with no agenda, no vested interest in their future choices. When talking to Virginia, Sam always felt that Virginia wanted to push her in a certain direction, for her own good, of course. When talking to Tristan, Adam always felt like he was somehow making his brother feel guilty for not being in California more. But when talking to each other, Sam and Adam could just be honest and at ease. It made them both feel lighter. The next time Sam looked at her phone, it was 5 p.m. She gasped in surprise.

"Oh my goodness! The day is almost gone and I was gonna show you all these cool places on the island."

"Honestly, I really didn't feel much like sightseeing today. All my worries were weighing on me more than I realized. But... weirdly, I feel like I can breathe a lot easier now," said Adam with a smile that surprised him.

"I know exactly how you feel," Sam said without even thinking. "It felt good to have you really listen to the endless wonky thoughts in my head."

They both looked at each other for a long moment.

Sam suddenly and awkwardly interrupted. "I have to go," she stammered.

"Are you okay? Did I do something?" Adam asked in surprise.

She turned back to him, breathed in a long breath, and said, "You were perfect! I cannot wait to walk and talk and drink coffee again soon. But right now, I have to go. Understand?"

"Not at all," Adam said patiently with a slightly amused smirk.

"You will," she smiled and slowly turned and headed inside.

CHAPTER EIGHTEEN

a few moments later, she was out the door and headed toward the docks. She knew exactly where Ross would be. Whenever Ross wasn't quite at ease, he would go watch the sunset, with a beer, on his friend's boat. As expected, she found him lounging on the front deck of the catamaran sailboat. Without a word, she sat next to him, picked up the beer, and took a sip. Ross chuckled and continued watching the sun go down. Looking at him in the warm dusk light, Sam knew that for all of their ups and downs, she truly adored Ross. There were so many things that made them alike. They were both fiery but loyal, opinionated but kind-hearted. For all of Ross's personality quirks, she knew that she could always call him no matter where she was or what hour of the night it was, and he would be there for her.

After a long while of sitting in silence together, Sam crossed her legs and kindly asked, "Can we talk?"

Ross nodded with a resigned acceptance.

Sam laid out everything that was in her heart. She and Ross could've made a go of it, they both knew. But the same fire and spark that made their relationship so adrenalized and electric was the same thing that made it more difficult than it needed to be. She wanted them both to be with people who made them feel at ease, rather than the two flint rocks that she and Ross were together, always striking against one another, working together to create a warm fire, but causing a lot of sparks and bruising in between. Sam reckoned that maybe they both deserved to try out what life could be like with a little less resistance.

As they sat on the deck watching the amber sky filter down to molten red, Ross draped his arm around Sam and gave her a squeeze. He had been thinking some of the same things since the other night. Things had gotten a little too complicated, with Tristan and Virginia watching and judging his every move with Sam. Sam was wonderful, but they had just started dating and it was already so hard. He would miss having her as the person he got to talk to every morning on his drive or walk to work and every evening when his work day was done. He thought for a moment, and then realized, not unhappily, how intertwined their lives would inevitably have to remain. He smiled as she rested her head on his shoulder and he gave it a little nudge.

"Are you going to be all right?" she asked.

"You know me, I'm always all right," he joked, rustling her shoulder a little. "Are you going to be all right?" he countered.

"Probably," she smirked. "I hope so."

"You're going to be fine, Samantha Ellis. If there's one thing about the two of us, we're both survivors, right? We are. We're fighters and we are survivors. But in our own way, we're also family."

Sam looked up at the guy whose shoulder she still rested on. His words lifted a little of the weight and burden from her heart. She didn't feel the need to articulate it, but she appreciated it more than he would ever know.

Ross went on. "I'm not going anywhere, you know that, right? I'm still gonna be here for you, still going to push your buttons."

Sam let out a laugh at that. "I don't think I could handle a life without that at this point."

"From the moment I saw you at the gym, I knew you were someone special, Sam. I knew you were someone who could handle someone like me, and that's a pretty sexy trait, if I do say so."

She blushed, adoring him and all they'd been through all the more. This was the side of Ross that nobody knew, and she was glad she was one of the few who did. He was getting more jovial, but was still sincere, as he went on one of his Ross-like diatribes.

"We're young, headstrong, we both have a lot we want to do. With the show taking off, who knows what our future looks like? I mean, my heart's going to be a little bit broken because you're my girl, but I just got to trust that it's all gonna be all right," he reassured her. "Plus, I'm pretty sure I just heard women around the world sigh in relief that I'm not *completely* off the market yet."

Sam would have spit out her drink had she been sipping one. Good old Ross. She knew him well enough by now to know that all his bravado and confidence belied a fragile heart. But the way he balanced the two always made her laugh with his rash approach.

As the sun set, the two friends leaned on each other for what they both knew would not be the last time. The sound of water lapped against the hull as the boat bobbed gently homeward. Maybe their romance was over, but Samantha Ellis got the sense that Ross would be a person in her life for years to come. Almost like the annoying twin brother she never had... the one she never knew she wanted, but now wouldn't quite want to live without.

EPILOGUE

As filming progressed, Virginia and Tristan had fallen into a more natural rhythm. Initially, Tristan had developed a deer-in-the-headlights reaction to seeing the red filming light on the camera and Virginia had found that her nervous reaction to hearing them shout out "rolling" was to smile really big in the direction of the camera. Bruce, following his camera man's smart example, set up unmanned cameras everywhere, which made a huge difference. Virginia noticed right off that Tristan was getting back to his old self and Bruce had much more footage to choose from on any given day. He was satisfied, and the newly ever-optimistic Jason was already predicting big things for the show. Sam had taken it into her own hands to make sure her sister and brother-in-law developed some health and wellness routines to help them focus and look good on camera. She started making them delicious energy drinks in the mornings and she even had them starting the day with a bit of exercise to give them an endorphin kick. Virginia fought it at first but then quickly saw the benefits and started enjoying the time with Tristan and her sister before the filming craziness began each morning. Bruce heard about his stars' new health routine and asked Sam to coach him as well, if nothing else, to get his wife off his back.

He was surprised when he started enjoying himself. Sam's generally fun, upbeat attitude combined with the beauty of the island certainly didn't hurt.

ONE DAY ON SET, when Sam came to get Bruce for his exercise routine, she noticed Alison, one of the production staff, lingering by Ross. Alison's body language was cute and coy and Sam could see that the pretty strawberry blonde was obviously flirting with him. Ross wasn't doing much in response, but as Sam looked on and thought about it more, she could see how the two of them would be a good fit. From the few conversations she'd had with Alison, Sam could see how Ross would be her type. *Whatever type Ross was*, Sam chuckled inwardly. It felt good to still have Ross around and she wanted him to be happy.

THE FEW DAYS that Adam had visited had allowed him and Sam to spend a lot of time together. The ease which they felt that afternoon at the house translated into how they acted around each other the rest of the time. She did get to show him a bit of the island, after all. They went kayaking, jet skiing, and got to take some late-night strolls along the harbor. They had even taken a day to go hike Mt. Rainier, which prompted them to try and make plans to go hiking again as soon as possible. There was something so peaceful about getting lost on a trail, away from the world. On those long walks, they had talked through so many of Adam's issues with his family, shared a lot of their dreams and the visions of what each of them wanted in their lives. Sam had proven to not only be a good listening ear, but she offered some really helpful advice. Adam felt that having her as a sounding board provided a stabilizing force for him that made everything more manageable. When conversations with his father were especially difficult, he found that speaking to Sam or spending time with her would significantly improve his stress level and help him think clearly. Similarly, Adam pushed Sam to talk about the things she was truly passionate about. He saw things in her that other people often overlooked. Watching her spunky spirit and her ability to inspire people, like she was doing with her sister and even Bruce, he began to encourage her to officially start her own health and wellness coaching business.

Their phone calls became an almost daily occurrence and Adam snuck away a couple of more times to come see Sam and his brother. One day, when Sam and Adam were at the top of a hike and had just set up a little mountaintop picnic, Adam turned to her and told her everything he felt. From the first time he met her and with their months of intermittent communication, he had routinely felt a pull toward her. These last few months, spending some quality time together and seeing how natural of a fit they were, even when they were spending time with Virginia and Tristan, he felt more sure than ever that there was a reason he was compelled to call her. He wasn't sure how to make it work, but he knew if he was more sure than not, then they needed to try. Between Adam running the family business and Samantha finishing school and developing her new health and wellness business, they figured that they would spend as much time together as they could and reevaluate their next steps in a few months.

Atop the mountain, Adam gave Sam a silver necklace with a beautifully etched locket attached.

"I chose this because I want you to have something to remind you of me when we're apart. And so that you know that I'm thinking about you. But it also reminded me of you and how much I believe in you and want you to tap into your dreams. I like that it opens, and the lady at the shop said that you are supposed to keep inside a little paper with whatever your next goal or dream is on it. Hopefully it will help you to remember and help it come true," Adam said.

"I love this, Adam," she told him sincerely. "Us ladies get all the cool stuff. I really can't tell you how much it means to me that you believe in me. I feel like, in some strange way, you see a part of me that most people don't." Her eyes flickered up to his and then back down to the locket. "That was something that I didn't know if I'd ever find in another person. At least not in someone who wasn't related to me like my sister," she smiled.

Samantha picked up a small, smooth stone lying nearby. It had a narrow one-inch hole tunneled through it. She brushed her thumb back and forth over the smooth rock, then she turned to fish in her bag until she found what she was looking for. Out came a little note pad that she carried with her and two pens. She handed one to Adam along with a small piece of paper torn from the notebook.

"Okay, you turn that way and I'll turn this way and let's both write down our dreams, or the goals that we hope we achieve within the next year or two."

Adam took the piece of paper and thought about it for a minute. "Okay, I'm game."

"Take as long as you need," Sam said.

"And write super tiny," Adam followed.

Back to back they sat, each staring out at the incredible panoramic vista that surrounded them. When they were done, they turned back to face each other. Sam rolled hers into a teeny-tiny scroll and placed it inside the locket, then she rolled Adam's up and slipped it into the perfectly tunneled-out stone. Adam helped clasp the locket around Sam's neck.

"Yours is admittedly a little clunkier than mine, but it will do the trick," she quipped as she handed him the smooth, gray rock.

As his hand lingered around hers, he said, "I don't know what you're talking about. I can keep this in my bag, my pocket, almost too many places. It's uniquely versatile." He smiled. "It's perfect."

They agreed to meet up one year from the day, hike the same trail, and open up their mountaintop wishes. Neither knew where life would lead them during that time, but their futures both suddenly felt as epic and endless as the view in front of them.

~

AS THE SEASON 1 project wrapped up, Virginia and Tristan had some decisions to make. At the weekly production meeting, the two sat around with Jason and Bruce to discuss the future.

"All right, I admit that I've enjoyed the process way more than I thought I would," Tristan admitted to the group. "But I'm just not sure how many more shows we could realistically do at this point. I mean, I have a couple clients that want us to do a little project here or a little one there, but Sweetwater Island is only so big. I've really enjoyed working with you guys, but I just don't know how much more V and I have to offer." Tristan shrugged. "I don't want you guys investing more time and energy into us, only to find out that we ran out of material for you to shoot."

Bruce gave Jason a glance before turning his attention to Tristan and Virginia.

"As you guys know, we've been teasing out behind-the-scenes footage and other fun stuff on the website while we've been shooting. We have a little bit more info to run by you at this point." Bruce leaned in and continued. "There's no doubt that Sweetwater Island is a backdrop that people love, and the two of you are absolutely in your element here. We don't want to lose that angle. But..." he paused for dramatic effect, "we've been receiving insane amounts of calls and emails from people across the country who have special restoration projects and who feel like the two of you have the proper heart and soul—"

"And know-how," Jason chimed in.

"And know-how," Bruce echoed, "to give their properties a second chance."

When nobody spoke, Bruce went on. "Now, before you ask, we would work alongside local construction crews to help with the tight turnaround needed so that you guys wouldn't have to be away from home for too long. And these projects are being sent in by good people, all right up your alley. We're talking real folks with historic homes and properties, not developers or cookie-cutter anything."

Jason jumped in now. "So, what would you guys think about, for Season 2, you sifting through all of the pleas and offers and choose one that really speaks to you?"

Virginia and Tristan both looked slightly taken aback. As the news from Bruce and Jason sunk in, they turned to one another, trying to gauge the other's reaction.

A smile suddenly crept onto Virginia surprised face. "I don't know, Trist, that sounds kind of... exciting, actually."

His face began to mirror hers and he slowly nodded. "Yeah, actually, I have to admit, that does sound pretty interesting. Restoration renovations all around the country, of places that need a second chance. I can definitely wrap my head around that."

"One thing, though," Tristan turned back to the guys. "I really don't want our community here to think that we've abandoned them completely. Is there any way that we could do a small renovation on Sweetwater Island done and paid for, pro bono style, between the bigger projects? Something like that?"

Bruce looked pensive for a moment, then began to nod his head in agreement. "You know what, I think that could be a great twist on things. We will have our main A story showing the major renovation in the new town or city, and then the B story could be the charity or pro bono project done back around here."

Jason excitedly added in, "Wait, I think that's how we should begin and end each episode. We'll start with you guys in Sweetwater, then travel to the new location, bust out the new renovation of the restoration project, and then at the end, we wrap up with you guys back in Sweetwater finishing up that project and giving the final reveal of how that one turned out!"

Bruce slapped the table enthusiastically and pointed a finger at Jason. "Yes! I can totally see it. That way if you tune in at the beginning, you are going to want to watch the show the whole way through because you need the satisfying conclusion of seeing what the community Sweetwater project ended up looking like."

"Eureka!" enthused Jason.

Tristan and Virginia looked at each other and silently chuckled. By this point, they were used to the way Jason and Bruce operated. The two TV guys had been very willing to work with them on their various ideas, but at the end of the day, the execs were always trying to figure out how to get more ratings. However, if that meant that Virginia and Tristan could help people in the community, like restoring old Mrs. Henley's backyard gazebo to its former glory, which they both knew would mean the world to her, they were grateful for the opportunity.

Before the meeting wrapped up, Jason handed Virginia a binder containing all of the different offers that had been sent into the show asking for Virginia and Tristan's help.

"The production coordinator put this together so that you can easily go through and see all of the details at a glance."

Virginia flipped through the red plastic binder. Each page had a header with a title like "Texas music hall monstrosity" or "New England Silo in need of some love". Underneath was a main image, followed by facts about the job from the initial email sent in, the history of the property, why the person wanted to renovate it, the location, size, and other goodies. On the second page was a gallery of images showing more of the tentative project. Page after page, Virginia saw one neat-looking project after another. "Tristan, this is unbelievable. Every one of these projects looks incredible."

Tristan glanced over her shoulder, one of his eyebrows arching in impressed agreement. "Wow, you aren't kidding."

Jason grabbed his bag and headed toward the door. "I gotta jet to catch the ferry back to the mainland, but you guys take this in over the next couple days and sort through it. Pick your top 8 favorites, then we'll discuss going out and scouting a couple of them to see what they actually look like in real life. If all goes according to plan, we very well may be breathing some new life into a whole lot of these old places pretty soon. I'm working out how many episodes the network wants to order as we speak. I'll check in with you both Monday. And good job, by the way." With a departing finger gun shot toward them, Jason disappeared and they were alone.

Virginia tucked the binder into her bag, then turned to face her adorably handsome husband.

"It's been a little bit of a whirlwind, hasn't it? It doesn't feel like that long ago when I walked onto the cottage property and saw this surprisingly hot guy scoping out my decrepit, falling-apart back porch," Virginia reminisced.

"Yep, I think we've packed in quite a bit since that day," Tristan agreed. "And actually, I had been wanting to take some of the money we made from the show and take you on a proper vacation. In a weird way, it feels like things may be falling into place better than I could have ever imagined."

"I've heard rumors that there's a bigger plan at play. So, who knows, people may be onto something," Virginia winked and smiled. "I, for one, am keen to find out."

"Well," Tristan reached down and took hold of his wife's hand, lacing their fingers together. "I think this calls for a little celebration and brainstorming. What do you think? You want to be taken out to dinner by a small-time TV star, or—"

Virginia cut him off. "Or grab a white pizza from Pete's Za's and bring it back to the cottage?" she finished, looking into his sparkling blue eyes. "Maybe spread these all out on the coffee table in the living room, put on comfy pants, and dream a little about each one?"

"I think you are reading my mind, Mrs. McPherson," Tristan smirked.

They made their way outside, hand in hand, as the crisp ocean air swirled up around them, a bright red binder of brand-new adventures slung over Virginia's shoulder, just waiting to be unbound.

I hope you have enjoyed traveling along on Virginia and Tristan's adventures in love and life with me!
If you would like to read more heart-filled stories, hop from Sweetwater Island over to the East Coast and visit quaint, colorful Magnolia Harbor!

Sophie Mays' Magnolia Harbor series

♥ *"If you love Hallmark Movies, breezy beach reads, or a heartwarming series like Debbie Macomber's Cedar Cove, you will love these books!"*

Enjoy 'Magnolia Harbor' Now!
ON SALE NOW!
(Limited Time)

READ & REVIEW

If you enjoyed these stories, please consider leaving a Review online or telling a friend!

Every single review makes a tremendous difference. I cannot express how much I appreciate that you took the time to read this book.

From the bottom of my heart, thank you.
~ Sophie

ANYTIME ESCAPES

Anytime Escapes: A Sweet Collection of Feel-Good Stories

Get Swept Away~ Any Time of Day

Prepare to be entertained with eight full-length stories full of laughter, mystery, and romance! Best selling authors, fantastic books!

♥ *"Perfect stories for an afternoon at the beach. I loved them all!"*

♥ *"Fun, feel-good books to take you away from it all."*

♥ *"Delightful stories from the heart about family, friendship, and new beginnings."*

♥ *"Sit back and let the pages fly by!"*

Enjoy 'Anytime Escapes' Now!

BOOKS BY SOPHIE MAYS

Enjoy all of Sophie Mays' wonderful books!

Magnolia Harbor series

Hope's Bakery

When Hearts Collide

From New York, With Love

Unexpected Events

The Vacation Cottages

Sweetwater Island Ferry series

For Love...and Donuts (Book 1)

To Love...and Renovate (Book 2)

With Love...and Reality TV (Book 3)

Holiday Books

Christmas Wishes & Heartwarming Kisses: A Sweet Holiday Romance
Collection

A Girl's Guide to Creating Christmas

A Whole Latte Christmas

Key West Christmas

Scottish Holiday

Santa Baby, Maybe

ABOUT SOPHIE MAYS

Sophie Mays is a bestselling contemporary romance author who focuses on inspirational and heartwarming stories with a little bit of humor and a lot of heart.

She lives in the coastal South, where she feels lucky to get the best of both worlds: the sound of rolling waves, salty air, and Southern charm. Aside from writing, Sophie is addicted to audio books, DIY projects, inspirational podcasts, and scours the globe (aka recipe websites) in search of the perfect "healthy" dessert to bring to parties.

Believing that we are all put on this Earth with a purpose, no matter how big or small it seems, Sophie knows that without a doubt, each and every one of our contributions is essential to making the world go round. After many years of writing, she found that her contribution was the thing that was obvious to all...she was through and through, devoted to bringing hope, happiness and motivating inspiration to everyone around her. Whether through her books or her personal relationships, Sophie has always been known for her dogged dedication to making people believe that anything is possible if you truly believe.

To find out about new books visit:
www.LoveLightFaith.com
Sophie@LoveLightFaith.com

f

Made in the USA
Middletown, DE
13 November 2020